OFFICE SPACE

OFFICE SPACE

BEA REY

Books & Things Publishing, LLC

Books & Things Publishing, LLC
4410 Brookfield Corporate Dr. #220149 Chantilly, VA 20153

Office Space
Text copyright © 2024 Bea Rey
Cover design by Butter Bird Books
Design and format by Books & Things Publishing, LLC
First Edition: September 2024
ISBN 978-1-962140-05-8
Library of Congress Control Number: 2024914183

For more information on author events and bulk orders, please visit www.booksandthingspublishing.com.
Help support the author and publisher by leaving reviews on all platforms.

To my family, friends and co-workers going through stupidity with me. For the customer service representatives, I see you!

Unintentional Target

My hands give the steering wheel a tight squeeze and twist. *It gets easier.* I grab my black leather gloves from my passenger seat and quickly examine them. Every time I pick up these gloves, they are cold to the touch. It's strange, but they seem to transform my hands to something other than my own. As if someone else's hands are in them. I shouldn't, but I'm starting to embrace the changes in my personality, as scary as that has become.

I reach around to grab the blue crossbody bag from the floor behind the driver's seat, thrust it over my head and exit the car. I park a few miles away from my target's neighborhood so I start running at warp speed to get to his house. Within seconds, I am at the beginning of the cul-de-sac. My target's home is located at the end. The house I am standing next to is having a party, so the noise will be a big help. I sit outside this house and watch my target's home while dancing to the music inside.

About an hour later, my target finally turns off the light on the second floor. The dark green house to the left is pitch black. The beige house to the right has lights on but I can't wait any longer. I will have to come down from the left to avoid being seen. I decide to get to the target's house by the roof. I need to jump on 10 roofs to get there. The houses have a decent amount of space between them, so I have some hurdles coming.

You are going to need to increase your speed. Be light on your feet, Elle.

I climb up the side of the party house. I take a few steps back to the edge and balance myself on the balls of my feet and take off.

Fail!

I am dangling from the edge of the next house. My right hand is gripping the edge. I am pissed because that shouldn't happen. This should be second nature at this point but I never intended to be here. My doubt has me making mistakes I would never make. Focus, Elle. I will not misjudge again. I pull myself up and try again. I balance again, clearing my mind to everything but the task at hand. I need to be fast and light. Faster and lighter. I tighten my cross-body bag and take off. I jump from house to house. Within seconds, I land on the top of the target's house.

I stop to listen around me. I make sure nothing has changed. The house party is still going and there is no movement at my target's house.

"All clear," I whisper to myself. I climb down the house to the security box outside. I know it is bold, but the front door is the easiest entrance. I play smarter, not harder -- sometimes. The house to the right still has their light on but I am not worried about them. The windows with the lights on face the opposite direction. I find the security box and disconnect all the wires to cut the power to the alarm. I will connect them back on the way out. I peek around the corner to make sure the street is still quiet. Silence.

"All clear."

I go to the front door and admire it for a few seconds. It is dark blue with a beautiful window in the middle. The butterflies in the window give the illusion they are actively flying in an S-shaped curve. I trace the design with my gloves for a minute or two. It isn't too late for me to turn back.

Keep going, Elle.

I snap out of my trance and focus on the lock. I look at the street one more time for any movement or a car coming, but nothing. I grab my tools from my bag and pick the lock. I listen for that sweet sound of the bolt giving way to engage the staple or link -- whichever the locksmith decided to use. I hear the click and the front door is open. Once I step across, there is no turning back.

I take a deep breath and I walk into the foyer, close the door behind me and lock it. "No forced entry" achieved. The stairs are right in front of me. There is a hallway to the kitchen, and the dining room is on the left. The living room is to the right. The living room is just as the two-year-old left it three days ago. She left with her mom to visit family. He did not bother to clean it up. The toys are scattered on the floor, and there are bits of crackers in the fibers of the carpet and on the table.

Let's go!

I walk up the stairs quickly to avoid making noise. I take off my bag to get my knife. It has a four-inch-thick, curved blade. It resembles a sickle, and that is why I bought it. I took a little inspiration from one of my favorite books. The handle has knuckle holes for my fingers. It grips nicely with the gloves on, too. To be honest, there is a less invasive way to do this. A snipe from the roof is easy but it won't give me the personal touch. The knife does. Plus, police really do think a death by stabbing is a "crime of passion." That theory should keep the police busy.

As I approach the door, I feel strangely excited. I'm not exactly sure why. I am still fighting with myself about doing this. Maybe because he isn't supposed to be a target at all. Feeling excitement is weird. I should be feeling doubt, fear, or guilt but I don't. I peek through the small opening in the bedroom door. He is sound asleep and snoring. I steady my breathing and slow down my heart rate.

The moon is shining through the small openings in the blinds and curtains. It gives the room a bit of light, but not too much. The floor of the room is covered by clothes, and the comforter is hanging off the side of the bed. I am not sure how he got that to happen. This is a king-size bed. I have a full bed and that doesn't happen to me and I sleep wild. My covers never touch the ground. He is sound asleep, snoring so loud that made it way too easy to come in and not be heard. I walk over to the right side of the bed to get a better look. He looks peaceful but suddenly the snoring stops. I pause. He rolls over and starts snoring again.

The small amount of light seems to blend right into his milky white skin. There are wrinkles in his face and his hands have a few dark spots on them. Davidson looks the same when he is awake, too. He has a peaceful and cheerful look that is welcoming. He always says "hi" to everyone in the office. I want to reach out to him and let him know I have no other choice. He already had two interviews with the police. I can't risk what will be said if a third one comes up.

There is no other way.

I let out a quiet sigh and give my knife a spin around my index finger.

"Here we go," I whisper and stab him through the hand. Before he can scream, I quickly cover his mouth and wrap myself around his back. He tries to stand up, but I am too heavy for him. He thrashes about trying to shake me loose, but I'm stronger. He may have been stronger than me in the past, but not now. The more he struggles to shake me, the more he struggles against the knife through his hands. I appreciate the effort but not the mess the blood is making.

"I am going to take the knife out. You are making a mess," I whisper in his ear. He thrashes harder once he hears my voice. A combination of the fear and releasing I'm a girl gives him the assumption that he can beat me. "You won't be able to shake me." He is not listening. I get it. He has a stranger on his back and a knife in his hand. I would thrash too.

I could just end it here, but the nerve is not quite there. This is only body number two and the first was an accident. Throwing a few punches and burning some tires is nothing compared to this.

"Seriously, you are just going to get tired," I tell him. He struggles more. "I can wait. Please…make it easy for me."

After a few seconds, I can feel his body relax. I loosen my grip and unwrap my legs. He is breathing heavily, and he grunts loud enough to make an echo. Someone may have heard that. Hopefully, the music is still loud enough down the street. I yank the knife out. As soon as I pull the knife out, he screams out in pain. He uses his little bit of adrenaline to try and attack me but it won't work. I give him an "A" for effort. I push him off me. He lands on his back with the bottom half of his body off the bed. That was a stupid move and I HATE stupidity. I wipe the knife on the sheets and take another deep sigh. The taste of copper sits on my tongue when the smell of blood passes through my nose.

"Who the fuck are you?" He coughs in between the words.

"Oh, language sir," I reply. I pull him back up onto the bed.

"Who the fuck are you?" His voice is louder now but he is surprisingly calm -- enough to grab a sheet and wrap his hand.

I let him adjust himself a bit before I crawl near him. He jumps back but the headboard stops him.

"I am not sure if I should tell you," I say. "We have crossed paths, though."

"What do you want? Money? The car?"

"Nah. I'm here for another reason."

He cannot see me fully in the dark, so I crawl a little closer. He keeps pushing against the headboard, but there is nowhere to go.

"So, what do you want?" He is trying to appeal to me because his tone changes. He is hoping for another spike of adrenaline and a small ounce of bravery to fight me off. I can hear his heart racing as fast as his thoughts. He is looking for an opening. There is none.

"To be honest," I begin, "you know too much, Davidson." I slash his chest and cover his mouth before he screams. "It's the only way. You are a liability. A loose end." I remove my hand.

"Please let me go," he pleads. "Please! I haven't seen your face. It's dark! I can't identify you!"

"This is true, but you know that isn't going to happen." I put my face in the moonlight. His eyes get big. He recognizes my face, but I know it's my eye he notices.

"Wait…wha…what? Elle is that you?" he stutters. "What are you?"

"Freaky, I know. Try being in my shoes. I freaked out the first time I saw it too." I turn away from the light. "So, you should understand why I am here now."

"I don't know what you are talking about!" he yells. Maybe he didn't see anything in the office that day. The green house is stirring. I can hear them.

Time to go, Elle.

"So, you don't remember," I ask.

"Please, I beg you!" His eyes fill with tears, and I soften. I assumed that Davidson saw me fully. We were in his office, and it isn't a big one. I was wrong but it's too late now. A secret between two people is kept when one of the two is dead. It damn sure wasn't gonna be me.

It is one human man. You cannot turn back now.

Davidson makes one last attempt to escape. He lunges in my direction, but no luck. I dodge his attack. As soon as he lands on his face, I put my knee to his back and grab the thinning white hair left on his head. My knife to his throat.

"Please don't! Please!" he cries.

"Nothing personal," I whisper to him. It was quick, from left to right. No massive blood splatter to the walls, just onto the sheets. The blood almost spills on me.

Do not become careless. The longer you wait, the more humans we will have to deal with. Though I welcome the challenge.

I can hear the faint cries of the police cars in the distance. I would rather avoid that challenge right now. I grab the sheets off the bed and leave out of the window. It is a pity because he is, or was, one of the better managers in the office. But a loose end must be dealt with. I can hear the sirens getting closer. Their response time is different depending on the neighborhood. That is a soapbox for another time. I am getting out of here. Once the red and blue lights merge into an annoying, invasive purple light, the whole neighborhood will be outside. I take everything off except my shoes, bra, and panties. I wrap it all inside the sheets. I have blood on my gloves, so I wrap them in the sheets too. I do not have the time to reconnect the wires. I take off.

The world blends into colors of light as I enter warp speed to get back to my car. I know I wouldn't get caught in the house, but I want to be as far away as possible. I stop and wait for the world to catch up -- when everything comes into focus. I open the trunk to put everything on the plastic liner I put in before I left home. I became a meticulous control freak during my planning. I will always keep a plastic liner in my trunk. I toss my shoes in the trunk before hopping in the front seat.

I stopped listening to music in the car a few years ago. I take the quiet time to reflect and to unwind. I sometimes can't believe the things I hear at work and this time alone either helps me come to terms with my day or become angrier. Lately, I have been angry enough that the quiet time is used for plotting. I never liked the silence before because my thoughts always felt complicated, contradictory, and chaotic -- the three Cs. I used the radio or my favorite anime radio station to drown out my thoughts. Not anymore. I let the streetlights highlight the path of my car. My thoughts fill the silent air. I do not feel bad for what I did. Any doubt I had is completely gone.

I have no interest in reflecting on anything that just happened. It's done. Maybe the guilt will come later. I hope it does so that I know I'm still human. Right now, I'm in desperate need of a shower and food. Unpacking my thoughts is not a priority right now. I may be going insane, but I am self-aware. It was my first body – well, my first intentional body. I may have had some hesitation. Deep dive into my thoughts over.

You did hesitate more than I expected.

I finally see my driveway and let out a sigh of relief. My isolated XL tiny home is sitting peacefully in the dark. Having neighbors means witnesses and I know what I need to do with witnesses. I found a place to avoid that issue. I pull up to the front of the house and sit in park for a few minutes. I have to clean up before I can relax. I need five more minutes in the car to find the energy to get this shit done.

I feel the headache coming as I step out onto the driveway. I'm dragging my feet to the trunk to get my evidence to burn. I am tired. Even though I train and train, I can still get dead tired. I grab the entire plastic liner and my crossbody bag and begin walking to the back of the house.

Woof! Woof!

Inu realizes I'm back. He barks at the front door and then goes to the back of the house and barks at the back door. I open the back door and let him out to the yard and head over to my fire pit. I can still see some fragments of wood and fabric from my last burn. I want to get rid of everything so this fire will need to be continuously going for a few days. Good thing we all work from home now.

I toss everything in the pit, including the bra and panties I drove in, and set them ablaze. I make the fire stronger to make sure everything burns to ash. I will smash my knife up later and throw it in the fire, too. Inu is trotting around happily and stops occasionally to bark at the fire. His black fur shimmers in the light of the fire. My dog is so pretty. He runs around a bit more, sniffing around, checking the perimeter, and peeing on the same tree twice. Once he marks his territory, he bumps my hand with his massive head. That is my signal to get my naked ass inside before I get a mosquito bite in a place I don't want.

I love walking into my home. It's quiet, except for Inu barking at his empty food bowl. My things are where I left them, and I'm in my own world here. I grab two cups of food and put them in Inu's bowl before bee-lining for the shower.

The hot water burns at first, but my body adapts quickly. I'm not sure if this level of hot water is okay for the skin, but it feels fantastic. My muscles relax and any bumps and bruises are washed away. I unbraid my hair to wash it, too. I stay in the shower until the water runs cold and then stay in for another five minutes.

Once I step out of the shower, I'm met with nothing but steam. I grab my coconut oil to moisturize. I love my coconut oil, but I made sure to have good paint on my walls because I hate having oil stains on my wall. I wrap myself up in my robe and wipe down my bathroom mirror. I rub some oil through my wet hair and head into my bedroom. I want to flop onto my bed, but I need the oil to dry. So, I begin to pace back and forth.

What troubles you so?

"I thought I would feel bad or guilty by now."

No need to dwell on this, Elle. It is for the best.

"Yeah, I guess. But why don't I feel anything? This can't be good."

You want to feel something? Interesting.

"I hate it when you say that" I said. Then I call out, "Inu!" I can hear his paws happily tapping on my floor.

Oh, the dog.

Once Inu enters the room, he barks at me. He can sense something is off. I relax and take a few deep breaths. I open my eyes to see Inu wag his tail at me. I just cannot resist his face. The little smile from ear to ear is a drug that works. Inu is one of my calm spaces. I scratch him on his favorite spot and get ready for bed. I'm too tired to worry about my hair, so I let it air dry. I turn off all the lights in the house, turn on a TV show I have seen more than a thousand times and within minutes I am fast asleep. Tomorrow, I have more work to do.

Before

How It All Started

The one thing "they" never told me during the commencement speeches was that I might fucking hate my job. That was the speech I needed to hear. I was optimistic when I was close to graduation. I went to class after class being taught what corporate America would be like. All lies! I was excited to have a damn cubicle once. I thought the possibilities would be endless and an office with a view would happen within a few years. My degree is in Business Administration so I could start anywhere and learn anything. The degree did not matter. I was and am proud of being a part of the multitude of Black women going to college, succeeding, and graduating in record numbers. However, the rat race called life quickly chipped away at all that optimism and left behind resentment, frustration, and anger.

I worked hard, partied a little harder and gained weight. Through all that, I thought those work scenarios in class would be my life. The lectures taught me about nepotism and that it happened elsewhere, but it was the same here in America. We call that shit "networking." It wasn't what you know, but who you know. I didn't know anyone, and kissing ass was not my thing. The lecturers told me that an education was especially important when finding a job. What they left out: experience was better. Even the entry-level jobs that paid decently required experience. How was I supposed to get experience when even the entry-level positions were unattainable?

My last two months of college were hazy. I was in a panic trying to find a job so I could avoid going home. I was receiving rejection after rejection from jobs. They were good entry-level positions, but apparently I wasn't "experienced" enough. I think it's stupid now, but I felt like I failed if I didn't get a job right out of college. I felt everyone was bragging here and there about their internships that turned into offers and the connections they made, and I was on the verge of going back home to stare at my mom. It was the last thing I wanted, and I knew it was the last thing she wanted.

About two weeks before graduation, I got the call that changed my life and my mental state forever. A job came through! A salary-based job with benefits. I was about to enter the next stage of life. I was going to work hard, get those benefits, contribute to retirement, find a spouse, have kids, and repeat the cycle. I dove headfirst into "adulting." I wasted no time signing that offer. I found an apartment and was excited to go furniture shopping. I got a new car because mine did not have air conditioning. I had enough money now to get a car that wouldn't try and kill me during a southern summer. I was truly about to be on my own and I was so happy about it.

I was set to start work after the Christmas holiday. Graduation was the week before Christmas, so I had a good break. I decided to move into my apartment on January 3 and then the following Monday would be my first day at the new job. I should have cherished those two and a half weeks. I would never get that extended amount of time for free again.

During the break, my family and I went to look at furniture. My mom tried to keep me in the cheapest options, but I didn't listen. I could afford it right; wrong. I loved my new couch and bedroom furniture that I couldn't afford. I wanted a big television, but I spent too much on the furniture, so I had to go smaller. I had my furniture delivered the day I moved into my apartment. I had a fully furnished apartment and absolute quiet for the first time in probably my whole life. No sisters, no roommates, and no parents. It was me and myself. I was ready to start my first day at work and become an adult.

Before I knew it, Monday rolled around. It was my first day on the job. I woke up early in my new bed, ironed my clothes and packed my lunch. I made sure I had a full tank of gas the night before to be ready for my drive. I hoped traffic was lighter in the morning than what I experienced in the evenings. I had my radio on my favorite morning radio show. This show had been on air since I was a kid. I was in a wonderful mood. I was eager, nervous, and determined.

The parking lot was busy with all the employees arriving. My job was located on the 14th floor of the building. I entered the building open-minded for my training. The first day was orientation. The newbies were quiet at first and learning the work environment. We toured the building, got logged into the system, set up direct deposits and benefit elections and learned about the employee guidelines. Day one was easy.

Every day after that I looked forward to training. I even made some great acquaintances with my new co-workers. We were loud, we vented about our trainers and some of them already had connections with the gossip going around the office. Training was fun. I guess the feeling that it was okay to make mistakes at this stage helped. I learned my job quickly and wanted to be the last person the training staff needed to worry about. I never had to take a test twice. I was able to help others in class that were unsure. I was ready for my own cubicle and space.

That feeling did not last long.

I thought a new job and more responsibility would enhance my life. A little savings here, a trip with my friends there and finally a credit card. I remembered as a kid always saying, "I can't wait to grow up." I was wrong! So wrong! America runs as a business, and we were brainwashed into becoming drones for that business. The school system told of a history of income inequality but did not mention it was still a thing. The curriculum didn't teach me the things I truly needed to survive out there. The cost of living went up, but wages stayed the same. The recruiters at the job fairs did not say, "We are going to overwork you, give you 'some' benefits and pay you just enough to get to the next month." The jobs did not offer sick days anymore; I must use my PTO for that. That is actual bullshit! I caught the damn flu from a co-worker who had a child with the flu that they got from the daycare. I never had the flu before. The parents did not have enough sick leave or PTO to keep them both at home. They came to work contagious.

Slowly, the cracks formed. Small and unnoticeable from a distance but with every passing day, they grew larger and wider. I didn't notice the cracks forming either. I told myself that the people I spoke to daily at work were fed the same lies as I was. Hell, if I didn't have this job, I wouldn't know about half the things I did. My job educated me. I read every important piece of paper, saved documents in multiple places, read all policies, and minded my money better. The cracks numbed me most days at work or had me lash out at people I cared for dearly. The ill-designed, five-day work week was turning me into a loner. Not an introvert -- a loner.

I tried to approach client interaction with sympathy and understanding. Their stupidity and willful illiteracy whittled that sympathy to absolute zero on the Kelvin scale. The first four years dragged on. Every interaction made less sense than the one before. The company I worked for did a little of everything. Finance, IT, sales, insurance -- you name it, we did it. No matter what topic I handled for a client, most of those requests could have been solved within minutes if they had just read the instructions. I concluded that people can't read or refuse to.

During my "can-do" stage, I wanted to learn everything at work. I found that if my employer trusted me enough and I proved myself, I would get a raise and they would leave me the fuck alone. They didn't leave me alone. I was given more work because "I was more than capable." Worst compliment from an employer ever. It was a trap! I didn't want this to be a career anymore. I needed to pay the bills and eat. They only paid me enough to do that anyway. Every performance evaluation I wrote down some bullshit answers, saved it on my computer so I could copy and paste it the next time. The company and managers got complaints all the time, but the work environment never changed.

Each repetitive, stupid thing that came across my desk added a new crack. The dumber it got, the wider those cracks. My stress levels hit highs and lows and my mood fluctuated during the day, almost every hour. Eight hours a day I spent on the 14th floor. I got one hour to myself to eat, sleep, or take a walk. The eight hours dragged on and on. That one free hour was over as soon as I decided I needed to drive somewhere. I felt like I was wasting my time if I decided to do absolutely nothing on Saturday but order pizza, watch anime, and grab some extra hours of sleep.

I didn't feel productive at work and couldn't be more productive outside of the office. I felt so burnt out. I couldn't leave the job at the job. It haunted my dreams – well, nightmares. At home, I heard my work phone ringing and my anxiety increased. My group chat was filled with the crazy dates my friends had, our crazy family and me venting about my job. We laughed about it and some of my friends went through the same issues at their job. They could ignore it, but I couldn't. A co-worker, manager, or customer really affected my mood for the day. I told myself to never let someone else have control over how I felt. I was beaten over the head constantly by the true reality of things. I was a drone in corporate America. I no longer had control.

I did all I could to fight for my sanity and peace of mind. Work came home with me and gave me nightmares. I walked into my hell Monday through Friday and going home at night and the weekends ceased becoming a break. I didn't have an escape anymore. I needed an outlet.

I got advice from everyone in my circle. Most of the time I would respond with the "that is a good idea" or "I'll think about it. I need to do something" excuses. In the end, I suffered in silence. I was used to it. I am the oldest of three girls. I was the child that my parents didn't have to worry about. I never said it out loud, but I wanted to be the rock my family could lean on. Someone my sisters knew had their backs. I wasn't supposed to break down. Nothing should get to me. I didn't have the luxury to stay down for long. I had shit to do. I handle my friendships in the same way. I wanted all my friends to know I had their back. I knew they would do the same for me, but I didn't want them to worry. I began to develop this crazy idea that if I broke down, the whole system would. The thought of it drove me insane. I have been mentally, verbally and emotionally abused by work and at work. Holding it all in was hard. I pretend daily that I really don't care but I do.

Eventually, I ran out of excuses with my family and friends.

My mother understood me more than anyone. She was the baby of the family but the most responsible. She still handled shit for my dad, and they can't be in the same room for long. I realized that she probably felt exactly as I did. I am my mother's child. My mom's outlet was the same advice she gave to me.

"You've been in church since before you were born," she said. "Prayer is power," she assured. It wasn't like I didn't believe that. God has always been my refuge. He listens. He provides, but now humans were so loud I couldn't hear Him. My mom said she would pray for me, too. The one thing a Black southern mother will do is pray for you. She understood why I felt this way and always said, "No one said this would be easy." Good thing she said that over the phone because my eye roll would have gotten me in trouble.

"It's all in God's time," my mom said. She told me she loved me and would call me later. I loved being able to call her, but the conversations always ended with her saying that. I knew what she meant, and I have faith, but I was unable to breathe. I attended church on Sunday but didn't fully get involved like my mom wanted. Church, bible study and prayer became a chore instead of a joy. I would stop going but, the Christian guilt is strong in my family.

Instead, I decided to bury myself in a "hobby" as my sister Te suggested. My hobbies were reading and watching new anime. It was nice to dive into the Shonen and Isekai-themed anime worlds. They were action packed, mysterious, and supernatural -- plus I was learning Japanese at the same time. I would always talk to my baby sister, Crys, about a new anime I found, but Te did not understand. Anime wasn't her thing.

Eventually, anime became overwhelming and frustrating. Production hell was a normal stage in anime development. I waited years for the second season of my favorite one. There were thousands of anime to choose from. The thought of that was great once, but now I rewatched the same two anime because they were familiar. I joined a few online groups to talk about anime to keep my interest but it didn't last. I went to a few comic and anime conventions, too. I would buy costumes, take pictures, go to the different panels, and regret the body paint. I spent way too much money and I wasn't enjoying it anymore.

My books transported me to different worlds, too. Stories of Black women fighting nightmares, discovering magic, fighting aliens, and becoming gods in a new world. I read, read, and read some more. Then I was stuck. I wasn't getting excited from the stories I read. Trilogies were still being written. I waited for the release of the third one. Even the enjoyment of a re-read to find clues I missed the first time stopped being fun.

Nothing was sticking. Church became a tradition and habit. The need was there but I didn't know how to ask for it. Anime and books were a wonderful distraction for a while. Now they were a chore to keep up with. Everything was a chore to keep up with. I was running out of ideas for an outlet to my stress.

Vice #1 Eating and Drinking

My sister Crys suggested the bottles of wine. Elise and Lucas encouraged it as the workday wind down. In the end, I blamed them all for the high tolerance and weight gain. I appreciated the bad influence they had over me. Elise and I had our "fat days" where we would go to each other's apartment, grab cookies, cupcakes, or pizza on the way, and watch bad television. Finding solace in food didn't take much convincing. I love food. Too bad my metabolism and laziness plotted against me. I gained the "freshman 15" and kept going. I played sports throughout grade school, stopped the minute I got to college, and boom…weight gain.

My friends and I liked trying new restaurants, new foods, and culture. I poured my curiosity into baking and following new recipes. That love caused love handles and jelly rolls on my back. Plus, food is expensive. Although eating sent me on adventures in different countries and states, that pleasure didn't last long. Especially when I look in the mirror.

The drinking slowly started in college. I wasn't drinking until the last few semesters before graduation. Initially I was reluctant to drink alcohol. I saw what overconsumption could do to a person throughout my childhood. Anger, laughter, confusion, boisterous egos, immobility, and sober thoughts all came out when someone drank. I encountered all those things in my family. There were so many cookouts. Let me tell it, we had a damn cookout every weekend. That's what happened when both sides of the family are 45 minutes apart. Whether at our house, or a relative's, alcohol was on my "nah I'm good" list. Those memories were funny, terrifying, and a warning. I saw how an overindulgence changed people and environment within seconds.

Plus, alcohol tasted horrible. I never grew a tolerance for the taste. Still gross. I made sure to always have a chaser. The taste of alcohol made my whole-body shake. I was expecting communion wine I had at church but once I drank, I realized the church gave us juice.

At the beginning, as the parties rolled into the late hours of the night, my virgin liver had me ready for bed by midnight. The clubs don't close until 2 am, my feet started hurting at 10 pm, and I was hungry the entire time, but I was a trooper. I liked the effects alcohol gave me. I was dumb under the influence. I felt lighter. My brain was suspended in midair. I was floating. Then the next morning, my brain was at 100 again. Staying in a constant state of drunkenness was never a thought for me. I did begin to understand that this is how alcoholism starts. The one thing that I craved was to stop thinking about work, stupid questions, and disappointment. Alcohol gave me that for a few hours. As I looked back, I realized how easily these vices can affect someone.

I could hang but I knew I couldn't remain there. Eventually, my liver fortified itself. My tolerance became high over night. Now, I needed the party size wine bottle to feel anything.

Vice #2 Love, Sex and Drugs

After my fourth year at this job, the stress had physical consequences. I woke up gasping for air, violently choking or crying. My emotions were in a whirlpool. I developed anxiety because I jumped at the sound of my work phone ringing inside my house. I wasn't working from home; it was the noises on the TV or outside that mimicked my phone ringing. I was haunted because my job worked its way into my dreams. It changed my routine because I couldn't sleep in and relax on the weekend. My body decided 30 minutes before my 8:30 alarm to be awake.

One day Lucas came over to hang out and watch anime. Lucas is light skinned, has a head full of hair in tight coils, 6 feet tall, and has a great smile. I'd known him since high school. I told him what was happening to me. How work was so infuriating that I was getting phantom calls when I was nowhere near my office.

"I'm serious," I said as Lucas laughed at me. "If I hear anything that remotely sounds like my office phone, I jump." I grabbed a doughnut from the two dozen Lucas bought and stomped my feet as I walked to heat it up in the microwave like my honeybuns. Lucas gave me a slap on the butt and laughed as I groaned.

"I know what will make you feel better," Lucas teased. I knew exactly what he was going to say. He'd been saying it throughout the 10 years we had known each other.

"Lucas, I already know," I interrupted. We both laughed. Lucas was always trying to make me laugh. Whenever I cried to him, he would say, "Will my penis help?" I would laugh through the tears, roll my eyes, and pull myself together. He never invalidated my feelings. He even empathized with me. He dealt with dumbass people, too. I wasn't sure which one of us had it worse. Lucas has his own daily habit that helped. He didn't have to convince me much that day.

He rarely had to convince me after all these years. He is my best friend. We talked about any and everything. It wasn't only sex between us. I didn't wear my "don't give a fuck" mask. I saw him like my family and friends saw me. I could tell when he was holding things in. I would do the same. On those days, we don't do anything but lay around and eat like fat kids.

We used to see each other nearly every other day. We would take a week off and then go back at it. Then it went to maybe twice a week to once a week, then to a phone call to schedule it. We had our own lives. He got into relationships and so did I. We respected each other's relationships. I was always single again before him but once we were both single, we reconnected like no time had passed. Every time, we had to deal with the questions from our families and friends. The "are you guys together together" or "why haven't y'all gotten serious" questions buzzed around our relationship constantly.

It is not like we hadn't talked about it. We have! And more than once. But I can barely keep myself together. I fight with myself in my head when my emotions conflicted. I have no space to consider someone else's feelings, wants and needs. Too many people take the work of a relationship lightly. I didn't and I blame it on my job too.

I would probably have stars in my eyes about love and life if I didn't have this job. In some strange way, it's one of the very few things I give my job credit for. I learned very quickly that those beautiful wedding gowns, cute pics on social media and the anniversaries were for show. They don't mean any of that shit because they never talk to each other. I received countless files and calls of spouses not talking to each other. An unfamiliar charge on the account, or online issues turned into a phone call with me and not the other person on the account first. These people called to raise hell but when I asked them if they spoke to the joint account holder, they stuttered.

I never expected Lucas and I to be one of the people I encountered at work. I knew not all relationships were like the ones I encountered but I did know over 50% were. That's the statistic. I considered all of this and concluded that I wasn't ready right now. Lucas had a more simple explanation. "I gotta get my bread up," he said. He didn't want a traditional marriage in the sense of a stay-at-home wife and mom type thing. We both were on the "hell nah" train for kids. "I want to be more than comfortable in my money. Plus, I want my wife to have the option if she wants to work," he said. We love each other but it's the "love conquers all" people that are calling my phone. Love wasn't enough and we knew that. We agreed to continue our open communication, baked some cookies and had sex.

I never hid from Lucas but I couldn't tell him sex was getting boring. I either outgrew what I used to like or lost any real connection. Even a casual fling or one night stand did not keep sex exciting. Hell, it made things more complicated. Even with him.

Weed was to help with the anxiety and sex was to release all the frustrations. I smoked weed before (that was another reason why I gained weight and blame Lucas) and it slows everything down for me, but not enough. Even if it was a daily habit now, it wouldn't be enough. Lucas knew that, too. He knew weed and sex were pacifiers, not solutions. We tested that theory often. We would feel fantastic for about an hour, then real life set back in.

Weed was great at first. I was calmer, hungrier, and slept longer. However, I eventually got used to it, so I looked for a stronger high. That's where the white nonsense kicked in. Lucas never knew I went that far. No one did.

There were some drugs I absolutely would not do. Heroine, crack, meth, and PCP were out of the question. I still wanted control at the end of the day. Those drugs were way too hard for me to even consider trying. I started with mushrooms. This one was hard because I hate to eat regular mushrooms. I had to force them down every time and keep them down. The first two attempts, I vomited. Once I was able to keep one down, I was not prepared for the trip.

I was in the rainforest the first time I was able to digest mushrooms. The mist was cool to my skin and the air smelled sweet. I climbed the trees with the monkeys. I did not know I could do that, but it was fun. Eating fresh fruit from the trees and being able to enjoy nature, I just laid in the grass and enjoyed it.

When I woke up, I realized that the rainforest was just the sound of the fan. The grass was my rugs and swinging through the trees meant knocking over my countertop chairs and my ottoman. The fruit was some limes I had in the fridge. I was on a whole ass adventure in my living room. I tried mushrooms a couple of times and each time was a new hallucination. Once, I ended up in the backseat of my car with just one sock and a traffic cone. Still can't figure that one out.

After the mushrooms, I moved to something harder: cocaine. I did cocaine once. I didn't like the increased heart rate and my hyper-ness. I was jittery and way more paranoid than when I smoked weed. I didn't like snorting anything up my nose so that didn't stick.

The last thing I tried was ecstasy. I tried this with Lucas. We talked about it before, mostly as a joke. When I brought up the idea, Lucas didn't shy away from it. We contacted the same dealer that got me the cocaine. I didn't tell Lucas that part. We only got one pill and decided to cut it in half. We locked ourselves in Lucas' apartment, with all the provisions, and anything dangerous was locked away. We only remembered bits and pieces from that night. I knew the sex was amazing and that our sense of touch was heightened. We decided that one time was enough for that, too.

In the end, I tried all that for nothing. The stress always returned, and I could not stay high all day. I had things to do and bills to pay. Just like an alcoholic, I understood more why someone got hooked on drugs, but I stayed away.

Vice #3 Vacation

"Where is a place you can go to relax?" my dad asked. I rarely talked to my dad about my issues. He wasn't the biggest help, but I was taking any help. My dad laughed and usually said nothing helpful. He probably would have suggested alcohol, but I convinced him I didn't drink a long time ago. I planned to keep it that way. Asking me to find a place for relaxation and peace was a good question and unexpected from him. I wanted my apartment to be that space. I should be able to come home and be at peace. However, thanks to my job, I could barely do that. Every day seemed to bring about a new pet peeve, a new frustration.

"You need to find a place to relax. If it isn't your home, then think of somewhere else." I thought about this for a few seconds. His chewing filled the silence on the phone.

"The beach," I concluded.

"Really? The beach?" he asked.

"Yeah! The ocean horizon just makes everything else, including my problems, seem so small. The ocean is mysterious but calming. The sound of the waves and birds, the breeze, and the smell of the ocean, block out everything else around me." I went a little deeper than anticipated.

"Well, that is really beautiful, darling. Go to the beach next weekend. I'm headed out now. I will talk to you later," he said.

"Alright dad, I'll talk to you later," I replied.

"Love you." He hung up right when I said it back. He was right.

At the beach, the water showed an edge that was unattainable. The waves varied in size but always met my feet at the same spot. No matter how deep I dug my feet into the sand, the waves always made me a little shorter each time. The water never changed; only I did. I adapted to the cold or warmth of the water. The salt levels within my own body changed.

My density changed. The water was powerful. The laws of gravity could not hold me down.

I loved the ocean. I was weightless there. I balanced with the rhythm of the waves. The sun set high in the sky, but it wasn't too hot. I brought plenty of sunscreen but enjoyed the warmth on my skin. I would love a weekend at the beach. The only problem with going to the beach or traveling was money. This was an expensive stress reliever. I had to plan out travel at least four to six months in advance. I would be lucky to get two vacations in a year. Leave it to my dad to suggest the most expensive habit and not offer to send me any money.

I was putting a Band-aid on a bullet wound. This shit wasn't working.

Building Frustration

"Yes, ma'am. That is correct." I had been explaining this for the past 20 minutes.

"So, liability coverage will not cover my car at all?" This was the fifth time she asked me that.

"No, ma'am. Liability coverage is the minimum you need when you own your car. It is the cheaper option, but it only covers damage caused to another vehicle or property by the insured vehicle."

"What am I supposed to do now?"

"Da fuck if I know," was what I wanted to say. I took a silent deep breath and tried to find some kind of empathy. I couldn't find it, but I did sound like I had. I extended a little advice for the next car and told her I am happy no one was injured again. Although, from this damn conversation, she had obviously bumped her head somewhere. I ended the call, made my notes, and pictured jumping out of the window to see if I could fly.

The office was buzzing like usual. It was about 11 am and everyone had settled into their daily routine. It was a slow day, so I pretended I was working. We have a team meeting at 3 pm. I dreaded team meetings because most of the time it was just going over what we received in an email. I dread them as much as the phones because I didn't want to interact with anyone anymore. I caught up on the group chat during team meetings. I was taking notes if anyone asked why I was on my phone.

Some employees used social media as a release. Some of them climbed up and down the stairs to wake back up. Some were addicted to caffeine and others went out and smoked to escape their desks. Until the meeting, I stared outside the window by my desk and dreamed of being anywhere else but this cubicle. "That man is out there again," I thought to myself. The one guy was always outside when I looked. That man was a chain smoker. He had a problem, but this job creates problems. Lucky him. I hadn't found a release that had longevity like his.

Eventually, my mind went blank. I thought about absolutely nothing. I did absolutely nothing, too.

"Hey," Wes began. I did not hear him the first time.

"Hey?" I did not hear him the second time.

"Yo!" It was like I snapped out of a trance. My current location came into focus. I fell from the sky, passed a few clouds on the way down and found myself back in my work chair. Wes was standing at the edge of my cube. His brows wrinkled as he tried to figure out if I was good.

"Oh, hey," I reply. I blink a few times like I am readjusting my sight to the light. How long did I space out?

"Girl, you were out of it. Your phone was ringing, too," he said as he pointed to the flashing red light on my work phone.

"Well, shit! It's been so slow, I just tuned it out." I wanted to appear like I worked even though I had zero interest in this job. I had bills to pay, and I wanted the managers to leave me alone. Maintaining my paycheck and avoiding being micromanaged means that I need to answer my phone.

"Why do you think I am up walking around?" Wes was one of the bright spots of my job. He came in the training class right after me, so he wasn't part of the "squad." We were all scattered about the floors of the office building, so we used the company instant messenger group chat. The instant messenger chat was still not safe for work, but it always made me laugh during the day. Wes was on a different team a few cubicles down.

I would sometimes walk to his desk when I needed to get away and vice versa. He was always fresh, even at work. He was a fashionista -- enough for the both of us. He wouldn't be caught dead without his hair cut properly and the proper accessories. He was goofy, ambitious, God fearing, and someone I called a friend outside of work. He was one of the few people on this floor that had all the gossip, too.

"You better be careful. Charla might see you walking around," I cautioned. Charla was his manager. A petite, light-skinned Black woman that had no problem bopping around the office, but she better not catch her team doing it. Oh, and she snitched to anyone's manager, too. She was just…. ugh. That was the nicest way to put it.

"Girl! I have been ducking around these damn cubicles trying to avoid her," Wes said. "You know she is barely able to see over them." We both laughed because she would sneak up on people. They never saw her coming because she was so short.

"I need it to be 5:30 already," I said. "I am ready to go." Wes nodded in agreement. We vented to each other about the things we wanted to do -- a career that we wanted and ways to get away with setting the building on fire. Wes was so sure of his plans and what he was destined to do. I never had a solid idea. I wanted to be out and about. I wanted to travel nonstop but that required money, too.

"Girl you better use those titties to get a sugar daddy," was always Wes' advice. The idea was always tempting but I had to force myself to interact. I wasn't in the interacting mood.

"I got this team meeting at 3:30 and then I better be able to go home," I said.

"Girl, I hope so. No point coming back to the desks. Let me get back before Charla finds me." Wes gave me a quick wave and went back to his desk.

It was a Wednesday like any other. My alarm went off and I hit the snooze three times before reluctantly getting out of bed. I threw together some business casual outfit and my trusty black flats. I grabbed a frozen meal and protein shake from the kitchen and headed out the door. I sat in my car for a few seconds, trying to think of some excuse to call out. I felt like this wasn't my day. I started doing the math in my head because I needed vacations. I was very strategic with my PTO. "Shit," I relented. I had to go to work.

My day started off as normally as possible. A little gossip at the ice machine and coffee station, random phone conversations and paper shuffling. The normal office morning buzz. Slowly, the next eight hours ticked away. Tick tock. Tick tock. Tick tock. Tick tock.

The phone rang.

"Hello! Thank you for calling…" I began.

"Can you explain to me why my balance is so low?"

This man didn't even give me a minute to pull up his account from the phone number he used to call in. The first question was out of Mr. Rudolph's mouth before I could finish my greeting. This was one part of my job that shocked me when I started. I thought the easiest part during my training was financial because who isn't aware of what they are doing with their own money? Our clients did not pay attention to their own money. Mr. Rudolph was proof of this. He wanted to prove this at the end of the damn day. Last time I answer the phone with 10 minutes left.

"Well, Mr. Rudolph," I began, "do you want me to go through the most recent transactions on your account?"

"Yes, please do!" He already had that tone where I knew math wasn't his best subject in school.

I read all his recent transactions from the last deposit made on his account. About $10,000 had been deposited in his account. In two weeks, he spent a couple hundred at the auto supply store, groceries, restaurants, stores, and maybe a bill or two were paid. He made a big transfer to another bank account and moved a bit into his savings account. Bottom line: he spent the money. Mr. Rudolph wouldn't believe it.

"How is that possible? There was over $10,000 in there. Where did my money go?" His tone was angry and confused at the same time. I knew this was going to be like talking to a wall. I tried to get him to understand that more than half of that was sent to another institution that I did not have access to. He put another $1500 in his savings. Again, things added up. I wanted to just say, "Sir, you spent it," but I had to code switch and "smile" through it.

I explained his transactions to him for more than an hour. AN HOUR! He still didn't get it. Fuck the code switching. I stopped on the third round of explanations. I went straight into "family" mode. I talked to him like I talked to my dad sometimes and got the same results. I couldn't keep going. His brain wasn't computing.

"Mr. Rudolph, there is nothing more I can tell you," I said. "You are going to have to get your statements and read your transactions since you can't follow along. It's best to just go through it yourself and make sure you have a calculator with you. Also, check your other account because you keep forgetting that half your money was sent elsewhere." Get off my fucking phone, Mr. Rudolph.

"So, you saying I spent dat money? I ain't got nothing in my house," he replied. Most of the stuff he bought, he ate, or it went to his car. He wasn't going to see the new furniture or appliances because that's not what he bought.

"Mr. Rudolph, I went through everything. Nothing was fraudulent, according to you, and the little things add up," I explained again. "There is nothing more to tell you."

"So, you can't help me?"

"Help you how?" He needed to go back to school to learn how to add and subtract. That was the help! I knew he heard me slam my hand on the desk because I didn't know what else to say. I may get in trouble for my attitude, but he needed the real me because "corporate" me would be on this phone for hours. I did the best I could to get him off the damn phone. I couldn't take it anymore.

"Mr. Rudolph, would you like me to transfer you to a manager?" I asked. "Maybe I am not explaining this clearly." I needed this man off my phone. The best way to handle this type of customer is to push them off on someone else. It usually works. Not for Mr. Rudolph.

"I don't want no manager. I want you to help me." He was killing me!

I remained silent but something snapped. My hearing was muffled. I began to lose focus on the office space around me. The lights began to dim, and soon I was in this dark room. I could not even see my hand in front of my face. I held my hands out to feel or try to "see" with them. The only sound was the wind whistling through blackness. Soon, I heard the rush of water. The cracks finally opened, and the flood waters were coming.

I felt cold water on my feet. It rose slowly at first, then I was knocked off my feet by a rush of waves. I swung my hands to try and swim or grab on to something. I needed to find something to hold on to or I was going under. I felt the pressure of the water. I was being pulled under. It became harder and harder to breathe. I tried to keep my head above water with all my strength, but I couldn't.

I went under. Cold. Dark.

I barely noticed that he was yelling.

"Hello! Hello!!"

There I was, back at my desk. Everything the same – except Mr. Rudolph was yelling in my ear.

"Is there anything else I can help you with?" My voice was unusually soft. I hardly heard myself speak.

"You can't help me. You weren't even listening. You don't give a damn," he complained. He wasn't wrong. "I'm gonna close my account and go somewhere else. Y'all are stealing from me."

I had only one reply, "Have a nice day." I hung up the phone. I stared at my computer screen, gently tapping my fingers on the desk. Mr. Rudolph's profile was still up. I grabbed the pink post-it notes to my left and started writing down everything. His address, his car information, even who sent his direct deposit. I took down all his information and tucked the post-it in the pocket of my navy-blue polka dotted pants.

I waited in the parking garage until all the cars were gone. I usually do this anyway, but tonight was different. I yelled out inside my car. Tears were warm against my cheek as I punched the steering wheel. I gritted my teeth and shook the shit out of the steering wheel. I gave myself whiplash from whipping my neck back and forth. I let out one more scream then I leaned my chair all the way back and laid there.

I woke up in the parking garage two hours later. I had screamed my way into a nap. I wiped the drool from my mouth, sat up straight, and drove home. It was like I snapped out of a trance when I got to my apartment. My head was down, my legs felt heavy, and my head hurt. I dragged myself to my room and face-planted on my bed.

I woke up to the sound of someone knocking on my door. I wasn't expecting anyone or anything. "Probably a Jehovah's witness," I said to myself. I froze in my bed like they had x-ray vision and could hear movement. Then another knock. I waited again. Then my phone rang.

"Open the door! I lost my key," Elise yelled.
I opened the door to Elise holding four large bottles of wine. She found this great sweet, red wine that tastes like juice, and we drank it as juice. My head hurt way too much to finish a whole bottle by myself this time. I damn sure would try, though.

"You look tired," Elise opened with. She was right. Elise is one of my best friends. She is tall, with a head full of hair with a few random gray hairs. I was jealous. My hair was thin, fine and a mess to deal with. She is tall and her whole family is. Her skin was an even light brown and her eyes were mischievous. She was the instigator but in a funny way. In a passive aggressive way especially when she is in the passenger seat of a car.

"My head is killing me," I replied. I closed and locked the door as she walked in. She put the wine on the counter in the kitchen.

"So, is it a bad time to drink and order pizza?" she replied.

"I didn't say that," I said. "Same place? Same order as last time?"

"Yes," she started looking for the glasses, "and add another brownie cookie thing."

"So, one for me and one for you," I smiled.

"Girl, yes! It has been a day, let me tell you." She poured the wine and got comfortable on the couch.

"You too, huh?" I changed into a hoodie and leggings and grabbed my overflowing glass of wine.

Elise caught me up on her job. She was having similar struggles but more with management and co-workers. She didn't have to speak to the public but that didn't mean she avoided stupidity. Her stupidity signed her checks while mine gave me a reason to get a check. She was the smart one. She had a therapist. That was a good idea. I would look into that because I needed to do something. A lie I continue to tell myself.

We went to the couch with our wine and turned on the TV. I wanted to put on anime, but we decided to catch up on some stupid dating shows. The food was coming, so we got comfortable and watched mayhem unfold. I told her about my last call of the day. It was funny now, but not when I was losing brain cells explaining the shit to Mr. Rudolph. We laughed at the fact that people had calculators on their $1000 phones and a chance to look up information on the internet from wherever, but they needed to call me and ask for shit without reading.

The rest of the night was fun. Elise was her same goofy self. We kept eating and drinking and watching mind-numbing TV. I was a little wobbly on my feet and she kept falling on my ottoman. I loved nights like this. We even ordered another pizza because I was eating everything. Large this time.

"We are going to be so sick tomorrow," Elise laughed.

"Oh, well," I replied as I drank some more. "Want some pjs?"

"Hell ya! I needs to get out of des leggins," she said. "Oh shit, I gotta go to work tomorrow."

"Oh, shit it is only Wednesday!" I went into the bedroom and threw nearly everything out of my drawer and tossed some blue starry pjs to Elise and grabbed my gray owl pjs and fuzzy green socks and went back to the couch. Elise went into the bathroom and changed clothes. We wrapped ourselves in blankets and continued to watch television. We set our alarms super early because we were gonna be sick in the morning but refused to call out. I tried to work through that logic all the time. I hated my job, but I didn't want to be an inconvenience in calling out.

The alarms we set scared the shit out of us. Who wakes up at 6 am voluntarily? My headache was gone but now my neck hurt from the weird position I'd been lying in. Elise groaned and buried her head in the couch cushion. Her head was already hurting. The TV was still on. We had somehow gone down the rabbit hole of animated movies because there was some weird kid's movie on. I swear I watched normal cartoons and regular 2D animated movies as a kid. These shows were weirder or the blinders we had on as kids were thick.

I rolled myself off my couch because one of my arms was numb. My apartment came with these awesome thick, wooden, magnetic blinds that helped keep the room dark. "Thank you, darkness, my old friend," I whispered.

Elise was snoring on the couch like a grown ass man. She went back to sleep that fast. I refused to turn on any lights. I stumbled to my bed and waited to doze off again. I wanted that deep sleep that Elise was having. Then the backup alarms go off.

I laid in silence at first. My face was in the pillow and my arms spread out. I couldn't breathe that way, so I rolled onto my back. I took slow breaths and tried to drift off, but it didn't work. It was too quiet, and the third alarm was going to go off soon. I got up from the bed to find my phone. I quietly walked back into the living room to look. My phone was on the floor. I grabbed it and went back to my room. I looked at the time and realized we needed to get moving. Elise didn't live far up the road, but she needed to move faster than me.

"Elise, wake up," I shouted.

"Whose idea was this?" she groaned.

Elise started waking up. I rushed back to the bedroom and rummaged for an outfit for work.

"Where is the Tylenol?" Elise asked from the bathroom.

"Should be right on the counter. I need them, too, so they should be right there."

"Ohhhhhhhhh, I see them," she replied. "Can I take ten of these?"

I knew what she meant but I told her no and laughed. Elise shuffled back out of the bathroom and into the kitchen for some water. She gagged at the food still sitting out. To be honest, I was hungry, but I had had enough. I considered going to the gym later in the afternoon. I ate so much last night. A 30-minute workout wouldn't kill me.

I joined Elise in the living room after I changed clothes. She was chugging water like that was the cure for a hangover. We knew there was no real cure but rest, and maybe throwing up. I felt so much better once I threw up. My poor liver.

As Elise sluggishly put on her clothes from last night, she decided to get serious.

"You know, Elle," she began, "I think you need to find your therapist."

"I hear you! I hear ya!" I wasn't really surprised she suggested it. I was surprised she mentioned this now. Everyone has suggested therapy.

"You know I worry about you," she replied. I felt the tears welling up. I tried to keep them inside. "I know you are the suffer-in-silence type, but it wouldn't hurt to talk to a stranger about your life." She laughed.

"Ugh, the invasion," I shuddered.

She was probably right.

"I will look for one," I reassured her.

A Bad Day Too Many

The movies weren't lying when they said "only one bad day" was all it could take to drive a person insane. I was surprised I held on this long. I was coming up to my fifth year at this job. How was it possible to work in hell for decades? I went to work so someone would pay me just enough to endure this psychological torture. It was diabolical. Capitalism grabbed some greedy man by the nuts and fucked everyone over.

Eight hours a day, five days a week I chained myself to my cubicle in the back and lost brain cells. How was that an equal trade for the salary they gave me? It was enough to keep me above water but only to chin level.

My job trained me to spring into action at every call and beg at the end for a survey. I had monthly quotas to keep up with. I graduated years ago but I was tested daily and still receiving a fucking grade. Criticize me on something I wanted to do. I gave managers the same excuses I gave my friends and family. I was gonna skate by on giving about 75% of effort. A good C- grade of work. But that wasn't what I was giving.

I did my job and did it well. Corporate America distracted me with shiny dangling keys while chipping away at my empathy, faith, freedom and my sanity. As a customer service representative, no matter what level I was promoted, I walk a narrow tight rope suspended 14 floors in the air. "It's only a job", "I won't be here forever", "this is not my career" were my mantras as I walked across this rope. It was cruel how they played on the weakness that everyone had: security. A job secures my way of life, no matter how simple, rich, poor or lavish that life could be. America created a work environment where a loss of a job could shatter your life.

To my co-workers, family or friends, I wanted it to appear like I didn't care. But the truth was in every review, evaluation, survey, quota and training. I met every expectation in the hope to be left alone about my work and solidify my security. I did fucking care because if I didn't I could be replaced.

Too bad my mediocre was still better than half my coworkers. I wanted to be like some of the other employees here. They did the bare minimum and still had a job. It seemed that no one bothered them about anything. I forget to note something and I get a message. They forgot to disclose information that is against federal regulation and those bitches get bonuses and first dibs on the holiday PTO.

Why was I being plagued with frustration and stupidity? It flowed from these walls and windows. I noticed the stupidity when people shopped, ate, and raised children, walked, dressed. Nothing stayed in the office anymore.

I didn't have a work life balance. I was convinced it was a corporate myth. A way my employer "appeared" concerned about my mental wellbeing. I ain't falling for that shit. If they cared, they would stop the pressure of meeting quotas. "Make me feel secure" that my last paycheck could be my last. They probably posted the open position before calling me into the office for a meeting. If they cared, a five-day work week wouldn't be a thing. Fuck Henry Ford!

I was a master at hiding my frustrations and anger at work. Lately, I couldn't hide it. I felt people I never interacted with knew I was cracking. Wes knew because we vented to each other. A mere whisper turned into my loud voice cussing into the white noise. All my suffering-in-silence, martyr complex caused my body to implode. I swallowed stupidity, willful ignorance, and audacity and the anger was the acid reflux.

"Hi, I am so glad I got an actual person," she said on the phone.

"How can I help you today?" I forced a smile to sound pleasant, but I was beginning to think it was affecting my teeth.

"Umm yes, I received an email from my finance company about purchasing my new car. I just had some questions about the email."

"Sure. Let me get you verified and pull everything up," I answered. I ran through the necessary verification and then pulled up all the correspondence associated with her finance company and her account. We didn't give her the loan but we assisted the finance company to maintain their records and call volume. Side note, this company approves everyone and robs them blind. No one ever reads the fine print. I have suffered daily because of terms and conditions.

"What question did you have?" I asked. I read everything as she spoke.

"I am not sure what to do next. I went to the dealership, got the car, and then I see this email about a title and registration, but I don't know what to do." She seemed flustered and nervous. What made me mad…the damn email gave instruction on her next steps. She did not read that shit. She saw the line "increase in interest rate" and freaked out. I get several of these a month and it was getting on my damn nerves. Much more recently than before.

"Ma'am, did you receive the email dated on the 10th of February?"

"Yes, that is the one I am calling about," she assured.

I wanted to ask, "Well, bitch, did you read it?" But that was unprofessional. "Ma'am, that email lists the instructions on your next steps. It details the process after you signed the documents to purchase the car."

"It does?" she asked. Again, I want to say, "Yes, dumbass ,did you read it?" But again, unprofessional.

"Yes, ma'am." I forced a smile so hard that I felt my teeth grinding against each other. Another side effect to having this damn job. "The email states, the dealership will add your lien to the title and send it to the DMV to be recorded. However, if you receive the title personally and your finance company is not listed as lienholder, that you have to fill out the da…form attached and mail the title and form to your finance company to process the title." I almost cussed there.

"Oh, well yeah, I received the title in the mail," she confirmed.

Ninja!!! Please get off my phone!

"And you guys aren't listed as the lienholder. What should I do?"

I took a silent sigh because I sat here and read the damn email word for word, bar for bar and she still can't absorb it. I let go of the smile and hung my head. "Fill out the form and mail them both to the address listed on the email."

"That's all I have to do?" she asked.

"Yes," I replied.

"I can't just keep the title?" Ok, at this point the stupidity she showed turned to scammer mode quick.

"No."

"Well, okay, I will get that done. How should I send the title?"

"Regular mail, overnight, certified. You can use whichever is best for you. I would recommend a tracking number though." Please, let that be the last question. I lost 50 brain cells already. I refused to lose more on this call.

"Oh okay. Well, thank you for your help."

"Not a problem. Is there anything else I can assist with?" I hated asking that question because another question always popped up.

"No, thank you," she answered.

"Well, thank you for calling. Please be advised you may receive a survey from our interaction today." I gagged every time the dry begging came from my mouth. These people determined my raise and fucking vote.

The day went by without a hitch but nothing good lasts forever.

An hour before I clocked out, something changed. The straw was bending under the weight.

"Yes, finally a person," he said. I get that an automated system can be tedious and wrong sometimes, but I don't want to hear that shit when I picked up the phone.

"How can I help you?" I asked.

"I have been trying to verify the address to send my documents to, but couldn't get anyone," he huffed.

"What are the documents for so I can get the correct address?"

"Attorney documents for a claim. I have been rerouted so much. I am hoping you can help me."

"Alright I have the address right here. It's…"

"Hold on. Let me get a pen," he interrupted. My head dropped onto my desk. He called in huffing and puffing but was unprepared to get the information.

"Let me know when you are ready," I said.

"Ma'am, there is no need to be rude," he answered.

"I am not trying to be rude. Let me know when you are ready," I repeated.

"I just need an address," he said.

"And I am ready to give it to you when you are," I replied. What the hell just happened? I say this thousands of times but apparently it was "rude." Ugghhh.

"Let me find a pen," he said again. Instead of finding something to complain about, find a damn pen. I should be able to say that, but see, that would be rude. The straw was bending more.

"Ok, I'm ready," he said. I gave him the address but didn't ask if I could help him further. We sat in awkward silence until he said, "I will get that in the mail."

"Thanks so much and have a great day," I said.

"Rude bitch," he whispered.

"Excuse me?!" I said. I had the same tone my mother had when we were kids and saying shit under our breath.

"Oh nothing," he replied. Apparently, that tone worked on adults too.

"Mmhmm." That's what I thought.

After I hung up the phone, I had to get out of the building. I didn't leave quietly either. I was ready for battle. At this point, I could win a war single handedly. I punched my keyboard, cut my knuckle, and put a dent in the gray cubicle wall. I fucking hated the color gray. Before anyone could ask, I leapt out of my cubicle and went straight to the elevator. I ignored the stares and open mouths. I flipped my twists behind me aggressively. I had to pace the lobby to wait for the elevator. The 14th floor felt like the 200th because the elevator took forever to arrive and decided to descend leisurely. I could feel the tears swelling. The elevator doors opened to the ground floor, and I rushed out. The office saw my anger, but I'd be damned if they see my tears. I ran across the street to the grassy hill and collapsed.

"Why is this happening to me? I hate it here. Why am I still dealing with this shit?" I cried. I laid back in the grass and covered my eyes with my forearm. The tears flowed as I cried out. I didn't care about grass stains on my work clothes, the joggers nearby, or the chance someone was at work watching from the windows. I needed the sunlight to warm my skin because I felt lifeless. I needed silence because my ears kept hearing my work phone ring. I needed space because that cubicle folded me into a small space full of negativity.

The crying stopped, but the text message alerts were racking up. More than likely, Anderson and Wes were checking in on me. Anderson was my manager. He was this tall, hipster white guy. I say that because of his hair and the work clothes. I never had problems with Anderson. He went to bat for his team. Anderson tried to make the load lighter for all of us. He showed me early on that he doesn't baby anyone that calls in. I appreciated that about him. I lucked out. I could have Wes's manager.

I gave myself a few more minutes to soak in the sunlight and feel the breeze. Nature's so beautiful, complex, flawless, unforgiving, and simple all at once. I couldn't make sense of humans and I was one. I could lay out all day and feel better, but the rent will be due soon. I had to go back to work and pretend like I didn't leave angry.

"Don't know how to explain this one," I stretched. "Why can't I shake this, God?"

Another tear rolled onto my cheek and off the side of my face. I waited to hear from Him, but the humans were louder. The text messages kept coming. I pulled myself together. I sat up, cleaned my face, dusted off dead grass, and answered the text from Anderson but my group chat was the one blowing up. I texted Lucas to call the plug and bring tacos this evening. I walked into the building like nothing had happened.

It was just one of those bad days.

The next few weeks came and went as normal as possible. I hung out with my friends and had my weekly sister three-way call. I put my anger to good use and joined the gun club up the street. Lucas suggested the gun range and it kinda works. I wanted to think violence wasn't the answer. "Use your words." The parental answer to getting in physical fights with family or strangers. I was ready to choose violence. And I was a damn good shot, too. Lucas and I added another vice to the list. Too bad guns are more expensive than a vacation.

I was finding some sense of balance, but at the end of the night I was back in my apartment, alone, terrified that I would hear my work phone ring. I called it the "pho-haunting". It meant that I spent more time in that damn cubicle than I spent awake in my apartment. They didn't give me enough time to make my apartment a safe space or a fortress against anything.

Once I thought I could breathe and accept my existence in the corporate machine, one call reminded me why that wouldn't happen. At 5:15, after five years at Newa Solutions, I should know better than to answer a call at the end of the day. I didn't learn my lesson from the last time. The "why is there a call in the queue? The day isn't over until 5:30 pm" messages and mentions at staff meetings were the last thing I wanted to hear. I did my normal robotic greeting.

"Thank you for calling NEWA Solutions Inc. This is Elle in Customer Relations. How can I help you?" I silently gagged.

"I would like to talk to someone about my mortgage," he said.

"Make sure you give her the loan number," a lady whispered.

"Sure," I replied. Worst idea ever!

This couple kept me on the phone for over an hour. They had a problem with their mortgage payment and my explanations weren't good enough. I baby-stepped them to get them to understand, but nothing. They were talking to just respond. They weren't listening. Interruption after interruption put me back at the starting line. They knew this, but they hoped complaining would change things.

"Sir, Sir," I signaled.

He went on and on about how "no one said this would happen when I closed." "It's not fair" --this. "Bad business practice" -- that. At 6:30 pm, I snapped.

"Next time you get a loan, a contract, a credit card, or anything that needs to be signed, read the documents first!"

"Excuse me?" They were shocked and so was I. I unloaded the clip. "You were sent home with a copy of everything you signed. Did you read it?"

"I…we…"

"So, obviously, that's a no," I mocked. "I bet neither you nor your wife knows where those papers are."

"You are being so rude. This is entirely unprofessional. I want to speak with…"

"…my manager," I interrupted. "Be my guest. But please make sure you mention to him that you failed to read and understand the terms of your mortgage. Instead, you attached yourself to a half million-dollar debt without reading the fine print. Oh, and just in case, make sure you let them know that you deserve special treatment when everyone else understands how to be bound to a contract they willingly signed." I was out of breath but kept going. "What kinda phone do you have? Hugh," I asked. "Is it a basic flip phone, landline, or smartphone?"

"A smart phone, but that doesn't matter. Get me to your manager," he shouted.

"Oh, of course. Make sure you mention that you have a phone that is a computer in your hand but instead of using it to search for basic answers, you use it as the world's most expensive paper weight."

"How dare you," the wife said. I giggled because her accent went British for a second. "We want a manager now."

"Sorry, all the managers left at 5:30 pm. Around the same time I had to explain that property taxes change for the fifth time. They will be here from 8:30 to 5:30 Monday through Friday. Call back." I hung up the phone and felt relieved. I had wanted to say that so many times and finally I had the chance. I rocked myself in my computer chair as the panic crept in. The panic grabbed hold of my lungs. I couldn't breathe and my mouth was dry. My right hand shook uncontrollably. I ran from my cubicle to the stairwell. I didn't realize I was being followed.

I gasped for air in the empty stairwell and cried over the railing. The door opened and I jumped. I tried to wipe my face quickly. "Hey," Carmen said. "You ok?"

"Ummm, yeah," I replied. I patted my pockets like I was looking for something. I was wearing leggings. "I just…umm I just needed a minute."

"It's gonna be ok," she said. Carmen was one of the floor "moms." She had worked for the company for so long but still wasn't a manager. She was super sweet and had butterscotch candies on her desk. She was here before anyone and left after everyone. When I asked her why, she said traffic. I laughed so hard that day. She wasn't wrong.

"Yeah," I nodded, "Anderson is gonna be hot when he hears this tomorrow."

"And," she huffed. "I have said much worse for a lesser headache than that call you had."

"You heard," I asked.

"Mmhmm," she replied.

"How have you done this for so long?" I asked as we walked back.

"Had to get some time away from the kids and husband. All of them follow me around for something. I needed the break," she laughed.

"As good a reason as any," I laughed.

"Go home and get some rest. Try not to shout so loud; not everyone goes home right away." She threw her gray curly hair towards Charla's desk. She gave my hand a little tap of love and went back to her desk.

I went to my car, cried some more, kicked the gas pedal, and jammed my toe. Fucking business casual flats. As I left the parking lot in more pain, I decided to eat my feelings and tell the group chat what happened.

Me: Y'all won't believe what I did at work

Joy: Wat happened

Marie: Girl, work don got me 2 today

Elise: Y r u leaving so late

Me: Dats wht happened

Me: I told a customer they were stupid 4 signing a contract w/o reading it

Joy: OUT LOUD

Me: Yaaaaaaaaaasssssssss bitch out loud

Marie: LOL

Elise: Gurl no!!

Me: Yup

Marie: Well shit, had a good day den

Elise: Wat happened next

Me: Dey wanna speak with my manager

Joy: Did u send them to 'em

**Me: Nope. I said they left an hour ago while I was
explainin 2 u that property taxes fucking change**
Me: I actually didn't say fuck but I wanted 2
Marie: Oh shit! I gotta remember dat
**Me: I told em to call back 2morrow when they get n
da office and hung up**
Joy: I hope U don get n trouble
Elise: But kinda worth it tho
Me: LOL
Marie: :)
Me: Marie wht happened @ work w/ u

My group chat helped me a bit but Joy was right to be concerned. I was concerned but I couldn't let them know. I didn't need them to worry until I said "worry." I drove to the store and every time a piece of that phone call jumped in my mind, I grabbed a different junk food. The real reason I couldn't lose weight, I blamed on work because ain't no way I would make it without these snack cakes and party size wine bottles.

My apartment greeted me with silence. Everything was where I left it. I could see some colorful wall lights across the parking lot. I meant to get some for my room. I dropped my bookbag by the door, turned the oven on, and changed to some comfy pjs. Fuzzy socks, wine, snack cakes, and waited for the tacos from Lucas. By the time Lucas arrived, I was wasted. He didn't say much, even when I ate one of his tacos. He was a silent presence I needed. No lecture and no coddling. I drank so much so I could sleep. I knew that phone call would haunt me in my sleep.

Surprisingly, I slept like a baby. I didn't wake up in the middle of the night choking or crying. I wasn't up in the middle of the night to pee. My sleep felt light. I was suspended in the air or floating in the middle of the ocean. I felt the warm sun, flowed with the waves, and took refreshingly deep breaths. I floated along. Not one thought crossed my mind.

The next day, I got up early and made sure I went to work on time.

I wanted to appear like the model employee because I knew what was waiting for me. And it was. The email had the red "urgent" exclamation point on it. That made me nervous. The only one listed in the meeting with me was Anderson. I took that as a good sign. Usually, there are at least three people when someone is getting fired. My breathing slowed down and I tried to remain positive and calm. Besides the bathroom and getting water, I stayed glued to my desk but secretly ignored most phone calls that morning. I was too nervous for the 11 am meeting. I made sure I packed up everything. I hadn't gone through these drawers since I got here. I hoarded documents at work because I learned quickly at this job to always keep paperwork. Technology is the queen on the chessboard, but paper copies are the king.

Anderson was always a cool manager about most things. He always backed the team and spoke up for us when needed. I doubted that this would be one of those times. I cussed out a customer in a business casual way. I didn't know how to explain it either. Poor Anderson, I didn't mean to make things hard for you. The meeting was first thing that morning at 9:00am.

"Anderson," I whispered as I knocked on the office door.

"Oh Elle, come on in." He waved me in. He was still positive and smiling. That wasn't the face for firing someone. He was crueler than I thought if he was actually cheerful when firing.

I smile back. "Too much," I thought. I relaxed my smile a little bit. I walked around to face Anderson. I wanted to make eye contact like I was taught, but I kept my eyes on my hands. I only glanced up a few times.

"So, let's talk," he began.

"Sure," I replied. I tried to pretend I had no idea what he was talking about.

"You've been having some outbursts lately. That is very unlike you."

"Yeah, I've noticed that, too," I replied. My shoulders lowered with every last bit of hope left.

"Everything alright at home?" he asked.

"Yeah." I would have lied anyway. That was none of his business.

"Family doing ok?"

"Yeah."

"Do you have friends outside of work?"

"Yeah! Why?" I wasn't sure where this was going and I was getting defensive.

"I'm here if you need to talk about anything. Everyone knows that our clients and their customers can be a bit much. Our company has babied the customers and it can get annoying as hell, but you can't call them stupid," he chuckled. I heard it! He tried to cover his laugh with a cough but he laughed. My shoulders dropped again, but from relief. I took a deep breath and waited.

Silence.

"Anderson, I am so sorry. I couldn't help it," I giggled, then I waited. He giggled. My shoulders relaxed more.

"Just remember, we may have been in the same boat as this customer if we didn't have this job," Anderson said.

"True," I replied. He wasn't wrong. "But he wouldn't listen."

"Oh, believe me, I know. He was insufferable." I looked up. "I had to call him to smooth things over, but I noticed that he refused to take any accountability." We laughed in agreement. I even gave the examples from the call. I got comfortable really quick. "But no matter how good it would feel to let the customers know what we really think, we can't call them stupid."

"I know. I should call and apologize myself," I sighed. Being humble around stupidity leaves a bad taste in my mouth.

"Oh, you definitely have to. That's part of your punishment. Eat some crow and plea for forgiveness. I did the heavy lifting for ya," Anderson winked.

"Is that all?" I asked. I expected immediate termination.

"That's it," Anderson answered.

I opened my mouth to say something but stopped. I wasn't pushing my luck at all. I was expecting a written warning that I had to sign at least. I sat silently for a few seconds in case Anderson was messing with me. "Can I…" I whispered.

"Oh, yeah, we are all done," Anderson said.

I headed for the door as fast as I could without hinting at the happiness I felt. The praise for the Lord in my feet had to wait. I may hate this job, but I still need money.

As I reached for the door handle to get away from this "conduct hearing," Anderson stopped me.

"Oh, and Elle," he said. I turned around to face him. "I know you. I know you do great work. I also know you are very hard on yourself and will rack your brain trying to figure this out."

He wasn't wrong.

"Don't worry, the call was a transfer. Once the transfer is completed to you the recording stopped. I expect you to keep that our secret."

My lips were sealed. Well, after I tell Wes and my friends, my lips were sealed.

I decided to show my gratitude for Anderson looking out for me by going above and beyond at work. My daily tasks were done before lunch. I answered all my phone calls with a forced smile. My pet peeves were tucked away while on the 14th floor. Once I was safe in my car, I would scream and release frustrations I hid in the office. I clocked in on time with all my screens up and a full water bottle. No morning chats. I went to my desk and stayed there. I was the ideal employee.

For all of three damn days! I couldn't be happy at my job for longer than 72 hours.

The phones were annoying again. The smell of cologne and perfume mixed with disinfectant irritated my eyes. The office cold made its rounds and people still refused to cover their mouths. Or worse, they'd cover their mouth with the palm of their hand and then touch something. Eww. I could only hold on for three days. I planned on paying Anderson back for at least a month. Unfortunately, stupidity didn't respect my new-found "purpose" at work.

My forced smile made my teeth grind and my jaw sore. What made everything worse was that we had some beautiful weather this week and I was stuck inside. In between the calls, I stared out the window. One day I was gonna break out this window, jump down, land gracefully, and run off. I kept repeating that to myself like a morning affirmation.

Friday was the worst. Everything changed that day. With every email, my shoulders dropped under the weight. Every call made my body ache all over. I was throwing a silent fit as it took a customer way too long to ask his questions. I had to hear a full back story first. By the time they asked the question, they had to repeat things because I stopped listening long before.

I answered the phone late that afternoon. I knew it was stupid. If I couldn't smile any more, I could at least answer the phone. I was a glutton for torture apparently. "Let's just get this shit over with," I said as I picked up the phone.

I did my mundane phone greeting while the customer's information loaded onto my computer screen, but Mr. Patel did not want to hear it. He started complaining immediately. He had amazing breath control because he left no space for me to jump into the conversation. It was like playing double dutch trying to find an "in". He kept going and I stopped listening. I looked outside at all the cars leaving the parking lot. "That should be me," I thought to myself. I'd rather be in traffic than listening to the rabble of Mr. Patel.

I picked up the phone at random moments to see if he was still going. He was. There were some moments that were interesting though. My job has us wearing many hats and Mr. Patel tried to add more. This man needed a therapist, priest, a friend, a personal trainer, new accounts, and a new lawyer. He needed Jesus!

I got comfortable in my chair, kicked up my feet, and listened to the soap opera playing out on my phone. I threw in an "I understand" or "mmhmm" but I stayed silent most of the time. When I was silent for too long, Mr. Patel would say, "Hello, are you there?"

"Yes, sir. I am still here," I replied. Then he would go back to his rant. He hadn't asked a question yet. I got comfortable in my chair and waited.

"Are you listening to me?" he shouted. I didn't realize that I had dozed off. I hit my shin on the bar under my desk as I rushed to put my feet down. At some point, I put the phone on the desk and turned up the volume. I juggled the phone as I tried to get myself together.

"Yes," I cleared my throat, "I'm here." I glanced at the clock and realized this man had been ranting and raving about something for the past 45 minutes. What the hell happened to this man? "Did you have a question?"

"Excuse me?" he said. I really didn't need that attitude.

"Sir, is there anything I can help you with?"

"Yes, I want to know how all this will affect my account."

"...affect your account?"

"I don't know why I even tried to explain this to a woman anyway. You are all the same," he scoffed. Whatever happened to him, he deserved it. I've been called worse, but it was the disdain in his voice that didn't sit right. I couldn't shake this feeling.

"If you have a question, I can help. Do you have one?"

"Nothing you can say to me would be correct. I prefer to speak with a man. And make it a manager please. I am a V.I.P client and have been with this organization for many years. I will take my business elsewhere."

"Well sir, it's after 6 pm. You will have to wait until Monday to speak with the manager. Please, call on Monday for a man to ignore you, too." I shouldn't have said that, but that bent straw was hanging by a thread. I wasn't wasting any more of my time.

"You do not get to say that to me," he exclaimed.

"But you can say whatever comes out of your mouth," I rebutted.

"You are not speaking with me any further. I want a male manager now!"

The straw broke.

Suddenly, I only saw black. I squinted my eyes to try and see in the dark, but nothing. I reached my hand out to feel for a wall, something solid, but all I touched was air. I felt fear crawl up my spine. The chill gave me goosebumps. I let out a scream for help but there was no sound. I kept screaming but silence echoed around me. The tears fell immediately. I began to panic, but I couldn't move.

A crack in the distance broke the silence that surrounded me. It echoed in a circle. The sound was like an invisible boomerang. Then there was another crack and another. I didn't know where the sound was coming from. I still couldn't move. It's like my fear had my feet glued. My breathing became labored and there was a tight feeling in my chest. "Let me out," I screamed.

I blinked and I was back in the office alone. The dial tone was ringing in my ear. Mr. Patel was gone. I wasn't sure when the call disconnected. I quietly put the phone down and looked around. It was dark outside. I could barely make out the five cars still in the parking lot. The lighting in the office was dimmed. They did that when no one was moving around. On a busy workday, the lights dimmed often because everyone was stuck at their desk.

I stood up slowly and didn't see anyone. No phone calls and no keyboard clicks. The lights flickered on as I walked around looking for anyone. I didn't see anyone. I glanced into the breakroom and the bathrooms and didn't hear anyone. As I walked back to my desk, it dawned on me to check the time. I was out of sorts. I looked at my watch and saw that a little more than two hours had passed. "How is that possible?" I thought. I checked any clocks available to make sure the time was right.

"It is nearly 8:30," I said in disbelief. I signed out of my computer, hung up the phone, and walked to my car. The building was eerie when empty. I kept shaking my head, trying to knock a memory loose, but nothing. I thought about the call with Mr. Patel the entire drive home. I remembered him being a fucking dick and then "waking" up at my desk. Everything in between was a blank.

Once I got home, I threw my stuff down and stood by the door with my hands on my hips. "What the hell just happened?" I asked myself. I opened cabinets, the fridge, and closet doors with no purpose. I was looking for something that wasn't inside my home. I was looking for something and had no idea what that "something" was. After looking for "nothing" underneath my bed, I gave up and took a shower. Water, whether at the beach or in my shower, was relaxing to me. I let the hot water run until it turned ice cold. Once I stepped outside of the shower, I decided to forget about today and enjoy my weekend.

My brain didn't get the message because I tossed and turned all night. It seemed like every time I closed my eyes, I was in that empty, dark space. I screamed my head off but without sound. I finally gave up on sleeping and got out of bed. It was 5:30 am. "This is gonna be a long ass weekend," I said to myself. I looked up at the popcorn ceiling, "And not in a good way."

I barely talked to anyone that weekend. I baked some cookies, watched anime, and slept. Not one protein or vegetable to be had. I lived off cookies and water all weekend.

Monday morning was routine. I was already awake and dressed by the time my alarm went off. I grabbed my things from where I tossed them Friday and walked out the door. I had time to go and get a hot breakfast. Usually, the drive thru line was packed, but not at this time. I was early and it was nice. As I ate and drove to work, the thoughts of that call would be a snapshot in my mind. Each time that happened, I shook my head to clear it. I didn't want to waste any more of my energy on it.

I arrived at work with every intention of going back to the model employee. That lasted all of 10 minutes because Anderson met me at my cubicle. He was just standing there waiting for me to arrive. This wasn't good but he looked worried, not angry. Either way, I knew what Anderson wanted to talk about. I tried but didn't succeed. I had to accept what would happen next. Anderson's grace could only take me so far.

"Can I speak with you?" he asked.

"Yeah, sure," I answered. I put my stuff down on my desk and followed Anderson's lead. We walked in silence but the prayer in my head was loud. Anderson chose a conference room that appeared empty. The office buzzed with everyone coming in and getting settled for the day. I was glad that everyone was busy with their own morning, that they didn't notice Anderson and me.

The light turned on as we walked into the room. I made the decision to act oblivious to what Anderson wanted to talk about. Maybe that would help.

"Have a seat," he said. He pulled out my chair for me and then sat right next to me. Weird.

I turned to him and forced a smile and tried to keep my fear and tears in check. My throat went dry. I just couldn't keep my cool. Three days was all I could give. Now I was about to lose my job. My brain raced to find solutions and plan for when they fired me.

"So, we, well I, am really concerned about you, Elle," Anderson began.

"What do you mean?" I cleared my throat after I squeaked out that sentence.

"Friday, at the end of the day, you received a call from a Mr. Patel."

"Oh." I had no reply other than "oh."

"I listened to the call. That man can ramble on and on. He was also way out of line." At least Anderson realized that much. He understood but he still had a job to do.

"Your response," he continued, "was again, unprofessional."

I nodded my head in agreement and looked at my feet.

"That isn't the issue. My concern came when the call ended. After he demanded a manager again, you went silent. Mr. Patel kept saying hello but no response. I checked to see if you transferred him or simply disconnected the call but you didn't. Mr. Patel cussed and yelled, demanding a man to speak to, but you didn't say anything. Eventually, Mr. Patel hung up."

"Oh," I said again. I didn't interrupt because Anderson gave me my memories back piece by piece.

"My concern was that you never disconnected the call. You went silent. So, I took an additional step and requested the camera footage."

"How early did you get here?" The question came out of nowhere but it was a legit question. Sir, how did you have all this time to do this? It's Monday morning, people are still clocking in. Anderson laughed. Naturally, I assumed from that laugh, I was off the hook again.

"I do get to work really early," he said. He laughed a bit more and continued. "Now, our cameras are placed at certain angles, like the elevators, entrances, and exits. I pulled the camera closest to our team that may show something. It wasn't the best angle but I could see you, well at least the top of your head." I looked up at him, on the edge of my seat. It was like he was summarizing a movie. "For two hours, Elle, you didn't move. The top of your head stayed put."

"What?" I couldn't fight back the tears. I was scared.

"I assumed I was wrong or that the camera glitched or froze but that wasn't the case."

"Anderson, that doesn't make sense. I didn't move at all?" I cried.

"I rewound the video and checked multiple times. Elle, you didn't move." Anderson grabbed my hand and gave it a gentle squeeze. I looked up and wiped away my tears. "Elle, I am concerned about your mental health. I know how stressful this job is. When you joined my team, I was fresh off the phone. I know. I also know you are a great employee. You learn quick and remember so much that even senior employees come to ask you questions." He gave me a smile to calm me down. The recognition felt good to hear.

"It isn't what we have to do at work that stresses me out," I said.

"It's the customers and clients," Anderson interjected. "You have a bright future here, but you need to get a handle on this stress and the physical and emotional reactions you are having."

"I know. I know." I got the same lecture from my family and friends. I was convinced all three of my circles -- family, friends, and work -- have been talking about me behind my back. "So, what happens now?"

"I've put in a short-term leave of absence for you. It's just for six months to give you a chance to breathe and find healthy ways to deal with your stress."

"Really! I'm not fired? There isn't a van parked outside to take me to a mental hospital?" I joked, but I was serious too.

"No," Anderson laughed. "No involuntary commitment yet."

"Anderson, I…I don't know what to say."

"Now, Mr. Patel did file a complaint and I couldn't keep this between us because I asked for the short-term leave. His complaint was filled with exaggeration. He also said you cussed him out and called him names."

"That's a lie!"

"Oh yeah, the recorded call shows he lied but because I requested the leave, I couldn't keep this between us."

"Now I am on their radar," I answered.

"Exactly," he confirmed. "This leave is your final chance because the higher-ups know."

"I understand." I need this leave.

"Now, the leave cannot be approved fully until you meet certain requirements. You will need a therapist's recommendation after four sessions."

"Really?"

"Yes. Until you get those sessions in and get the recommendation, your leave decision will stay pending for the next three months. Then they will automatically deny it and you can't apply again for another year. You have to get this done and this requirement is the hard part. Most therapists can be out of network and won't see new patients quickly."

"I understand." I kept the joyful thought of short-term leave to myself. I sorta thought "leaves of absence" were just a corporate myth to disguise wrongful terminations. Whatever it was, I didn't care. A paid half-year out of work. I will take it.

Anderson took the next 10 minutes to tell me about the leave, how my pay would work and he kept driving home that a therapist's recommendation is key. "Don't worry, I sent you an email with everything we discussed here."

"Oh, good, because I may not remember everything."

We left the conference room and went about the day. I read and reread Anderson's email. He took me off the phone and my assigned files were reduced so I wouldn't have any pending for when my leave is approved. I met most of the requirements. Meeting those stupid ass quotas worked in my favor. I was a good employee that excelled at the job I hated. Anderson seemed sure that if I could get a therapist on board, they would approve me.

Once I got fully settled back at my desk, I texted my sisters about my meeting with Anderson. I made them swear not to tell Mom. I knew they wouldn't anyway, but I asked because they seemed worried when I told them what happened. I had to strip away the "I'm the oldest" mentality and be vulnerable with them. They rewarded my vulnerability with jokes and prayer. My family couldn't stay serious for long. I had their full support as always.

I texted Elise and told her everything, too. She called me immediately. I had to whisper inside my cubicle. She was all over the place. She was scared and worried. I tried to keep her calm but her fear for me made me cry. I walked into the empty stairwell and cried with her. My sisters cracked jokes and Elise cried. I knew if I told my mom, things would be crazy. I made Elise promise not to tell my mom either. I decided to talk to Lucas after work just in case his worry made me cry.

"Take my therapist's information. She is great! Her name is Dr. Lynn Jones. I will text it to you."

"Okay," I replied.

"You still have to stay at work today?"

"Yeah, I work like normal until I meet the requirements. I have three months but that doesn't feel like enough time. I have to get moving."

"Call Dr. Lynn's office asap," she ordered.

"I will," I answered. This time I actually meant it.

Trials, Trauma, And Assault

My family and friends have been telling me to find a therapist for a while now. I didn't listen. I was only looking for one now because there was a financial consequence if I didn't. The more I thought about how I had to jump through hoops to keep a paycheck, the more my hatred of Corporate America grows. I hated this job and should be able to walk out and find my actual dream job. But nooo! The bills didn't stop once I stopped working. College and living away from home made sure I was going to have a hard time walking away from a job.

Work felt different, with this small glimmer of hope at the end. I decided to play the long game.

I came to work every day with a sad look. I was playing for the cameras, although they really couldn't see me at my cubicle. I always greeted Anderson and kept him updated. I told Wes about the leave and he was jealous and a bad influence. He was the one who told me to play it up. I think he didn't complain about going on leave because he knew I needed it. Wes took the job to his car but the minute he stepped through his front door, he had more important things to do. I could see his escape from this office. I couldn't see it for me.

I messaged Wes all day, shackled to my desk. I still did my files at my usual full speed. Which meant I was done with my work about an hour before lunch. The rest of my time, I looked up therapists in-network and explored the rest of the floors in my building. I wrote down five therapists that were available to see me within the next two weeks and I called Dr. Lynn. She was the last appointment.

My plan was to find a tolerable therapist for a quick four sessions. I wanted my leave asap. I wanted to catch up on some sleep, read a few new books, eat, and look for a new job in peace. Six months was more than enough time to find a new job. "Wait a minute. Is this their way of 'creative firing'? Are they hoping I find something else before my leave is up?" I thought to myself. It wasn't a bad plan. Gotta give the people what they want. Then the other, evil side of me wanted to make it the six months and come back and cause chaos. "You thought bitch," I would say. Then imme-diately get fired.

My first appointment was next Monday. I was able to schedule all five within two and a half weeks. Dr. Lynn was the last appointment, but I should find someone before then. The idea of sharing a therapist with Elise feels like a conflict of interest. Weird. Although, the fact that I was able to schedule this therapist so quickly made me question my decision making. They must be fresh out of graduate school. I hoped.

I called Elise every day once I made it home: her rule. Even if she doesn't answer, I needed to call. Elise was my helicopter mom until I chose a therapist to see. She was probably gonna make sure I kept going after my leave was approved. There are some days where we would go over to each other's house and eat and talk. I never asked her about her therapy or why she was even in therapy. I let things be private unless someone was willing to share. I had intrusive thoughts but I also minded my business. There are some things that did not need to be shared but my best friend knew I had her back. I knew she had mine.

Monday

The first therapist appointment was at 10 am downtown. I had to use one of my half days for this. I hated using my PTO for actual things. I wanted to lie, say I was sick, as Lucas and I board the plane to Vegas or the beach. There was not one person in the history of calling out that didn't lie about why they were calling out.

I was running a little late because of traffic. Well, traffic and forgetting to set my alarm. I asked Elise what I should expect from these sessions. She said, "It is kinda like the movies. There's a couch, a bunch of books, a window facing other office buildings, and the therapists all wear glasses." I laughed. I assumed she exaggerated for me so that I would relax. I did, but it didn't last long.

Picturing my first therapy session was like a movie. I was cool, calm, reading the therapist before they could read me. I wasn't saying much but I gave them enough to know I needed the recommendation for my leave. It was all a "cat and mouse" genre movie in my head. But as I parked my car and sat there, I was frozen. I was supposed to check in 12 minutes ago, but I was frozen. This was not how I pictured it.

I didn't want someone poking around in my head. How the hell was I gonna do four sessions -- convincing sessions? I knew I couldn't stay out here. I had to go inside and make this work. "Remember, you want this break. You need this break!" I gave myself a pep talk, prayed for mental protection from the Holy Spirit, and walked to the doctor's office. I hoped I wouldn't have to do this every time.

As I walked to the office, every step felt like I weighed 400 pounds. I was short of breath, had sweat on my forehead, and all my joints ached. The elevator felt cramped and the air thinned the higher I went. The 5th floor dinged in the elevator and I slowly stepped out. The doctor's office door was down the hall on my right. That ten second walk felt longer. I poked my head into the door to see what was around.

"Hi, how can I help you?" the receptionist greeted me. I didn't even see her.

"Umm," I took a deep breath, and fully walked through the door. "I have a 10:30 appointment with Dr. Douglas."

"You are a little late, sweetheart," she said with a smile. "What is your name and date of birth?"

"Umm, Elizabeth Imani Martin. April 5th, 1989."

"Thank you." She clicked a few times on the computer screen. "Did you bring your insurance card?"

"Oh, yeah," I said. I went into my blue crossbody bag and handed my insurance to the receptionist.

"Please complete the new patient form. The doctor will collect it from you. She will be with you in a few minutes."

This was starting to feel like a regular medical appointment. I began to relax and filled out the form. After the regular name and date lines, I realized this new patient form was nothing like my medical appointments. There were 10 questions about myself and why I sought out therapy. These were essay questions. I tried to answer in one sentence.

Q6: Do you feel you are a danger to yourself or others?

"Ms. Martin," the receptionist called.

I grabbed my bag and the clipboard and walked through the door.

"I didn't finish the form," I said meekly.

"That's fine. You will go through that with Dr. Douglas," she replied. She opened the door to the private office and whispered, "Good luck." I walked through the open door and realized I had made a mistake. The office had a big open space decorated with pillows and a bongo drum, hiding this petite white woman behind it.

"Umm, am I in the right place? I am looking for Dr. Douglas," I slowly backed up to the door.

"You sure are. Elizabeth Martin, right?"

"I prefer Elle." I couldn't find the doorknob behind my back. It shouldn't be that hard to find but it eluded me. I couldn't escape.

"Please have a seat, Elle," Dr. Douglas waved on.

"O…k…" I find the pillow the furthest away from the drum. "This is not what I expected."

"Yeah, nothing like the movies. Many people have that general impression of a therapist."

Dr. Douglas came fully around from the drum and found a comfy pillow facing me. She was no taller than 5 foot 2, with the white version of locs and earth toned clothes. She belonged at Woodstock. "So, what brought you in today/"

"Well, I am looking for a therapist. The stress of work and life can be overwhelming sometimes," I wanted to give a small bit of the truth. I damn sure knew this wasn't going to be my therapist. My butt started going numb and if every session was going to be on the floor, I refused.

"Well, let's look at the questionnaire as a starting point. First, we need to get your body and mind in a relaxed state. So, take a deep breath in."

This lady took me through a thousand and one breathing exercises to get me into a "relaxed" state. I admit, I was fighting back. I couldn't relax. I tensed up. We never got to the questions. The whole hour was breathe, let go, and relax. She kept saying that my aura was the color brown. Whatever the fuck that meant.

"Aww, there's the bell," Dr. Douglas said.

My eyes sprung up and I rushed to grab my things and get to my car.

"Make sure you stop by the front desk on the way out to make your follow-up appointment. We need to turn that aura to a cool blue," Dr. Douglas explained.

Once I heard the office door shut, I let out a deep breath and a giggle. I pulled out my phone and started texting everyone about my session.

"Will you be scheduling another appointment?" the receptionist asked.

"Umm, I don't think this is the right thing for me," I replied.

"I understand," she smiled. "Make sure you read the sign outside the door. It will explain everything."

"Ok…" I replied.

"Have a good day."

When I left to go to the hallway, I looked for the sign. Right by the door it said, "Dr. Douglas Holistic and Meditation Therapy." I was wrapped up in finding a therapist so quickly that I didn't filter the results of my search.

Every single person I told about this laughed right along with me. I made a comic error but instead of searching for a therapist the right way, my sisters Crys and Elise told me to keep the other appointments and see what happens.

I agreed. Why not have some fun with the nonsense.

Tuesday and Wednesday

I went to work during the day. Played up my stress on my floor and explored the other floors of the building. I kept finishing all my work so I needed something to do the rest of the time. Reading manga or one of my books was not an option. Leaning back and listening to music or a true crime podcast with my feet kicked up seemed rude. I took walks during the day and then in the evening I went to the next therapy sessions.

My next two appointments were damn hypnotist therapy. It all seemed normal until the pocket watch or chime came out. I heard that hypnosis only works when someone was open to it. I wasn't. The Tuesday session ended funny because the doctor thought I was under deep hypnosis but I had actually fallen asleep. His couch was the most comfortable. I could choose this therapist and catch up on some sleep, but I don't wanna pay for that. I also doubt a hypnotist would give me my leave approval.

The one on Wednesday evening gave me so much joy. I pretended with him. I gave him a show that made him feel good. He seemed surprised that his "hypnosis" worked. The amount of times this man said "and we are going to go deeper" within an hour put Lucas to shame. After each session, I texted my sisters, the group chat, and Lucas. The therapy worked. Well, that depends on how you looked at it. For three days, I laughed my ass off with my favorite people. I should do first-time visits all the time.

Next Thursday

Dr. Scott had a normal office. This was what I pictured. He was a tall white man with hair EVERYWHERE but the top of his head. His bald spot was super shiny under the fluorescent lights. His glasses hung around his neck and he had sweat stains under his arms. When I entered the office, he shook my hand and waved me towards the maroon leather couch. His chair was already placed across from the maroon ottoman. After I sat down, Dr. Scott crossed his legs and swayed side to side in his chair. He was one cat away from being a super villain.

"Ms. Martin," he began, "How are you doing this evening/"

"Umm, good. A little nervous," I answered. "How are you?"

"Well, I'm fine. Thank you," he answered.

The few seconds of silence between us told me all I needed to know. I knew some bullshit was coming my way. The other appointments had blinking warning signs, but Dr. Scott warning was well hidden.

He started out normal. He asked me about my family and friends. He asked about life growing up, and what my daily life was like now. He wanted a brief synopsis to get an idea of future things to explore.

"So, what was today like for you at work?" he asked.

"Well," I began, "my job has been the same since I left training. I get to the office about 15 minutes before I have to clock in. I get my water, chat a bit, and then I'm glued to my desk trying to keep up with a quota at work."

"What makes it stressful now?" he asked.

"I thought adults knew more about…things…life. These people don't know anything about what it means to own a car or a home. They want convenience but are surprised when convenience costs more. They can't read at all. I was so happy to start my adult life and to work. I thought the first stupid question was a one-off."

"It wasn't, I assume," he said.

"Hell nah!!! We are taught to be aware and take accountability as kids. Those same kids become adults and forget the lessons. I hate will-

70

ful ignorance and stupidity. It was a minor annoyance in school, or when meeting new people. It has grown into something that I cannot control any more. People don't read and they've forgotten the word "troubleshoot." I unloaded the clip. I didn't expect or plan to. Dr. Scott was slick.

I sat back in the chair and took a deep breath. He wrote in his notebook. He was silent. I didn't hear him say "I see" like in the movies. The silence remained longer than I expected.

"Well?" I asked. I hate delays. Spit it out!

"Ms. Martin," He removed his glasses and cleared his throat. "People have had your job before you and people will have your job after you. Your outburst is not because of your job." I sat up when he said this.

"What are they for?"

"I believe you are lashing out from unresolved trauma."

I sat back. "Trauma?"

"Yes, more than likely you have repressed the memory, but the emotions from that memory are coming out."

I scanned my entire memory within seconds to try and find the "trauma" he was talking about. How did he come to that conclusion so soon? We were only half through the hour on a first appointment. "I'm confused," I said. I already knew my face started to resemble my mom's when she is skeptical or on the verge of mistrust and anger.

"Well, let me explain. And we will be able to explore it more in future sessions. I have seen this a lot with a few of my patients who are African American females."

If my eyes could shoot lasers, his head would have exploded. Fucking medical bias. I wasn't naïve. There were some deep-rooted issues within the Black community that continually contribute to generational curses. If I lined up a hundred Black women from different parts of the country, I guarantee more than half would have a similar story about their upbringing and the trauma. But the fact that Dr. Scott assumes that as a Black woman, that was my story sucks! Black people experienced pain the same as other races. When we seek outside help, we should be heard on the individual, rather than monolithic, level. I represented every Black woman when I stepped outside my circle. Dr. Scott was no different. He should have been, but no.

"Let me stop you right there. I'm not repressing anything."

"See, but you are. The reason you are saying no is because you cannot see it. We will work to bring those memories back so you can deal with them."

"We aren't doing anything. There is nothing to bring up," I said. This wasn't someone denying actual trauma they buried deep down. I was being "diagnosed" based off a bias.

"See, your reaction. The more you deny it, the harder it will be to deal with. I am thinking this probably involved a close friend or family member," he said. He put the notebook down and leaned towards me with his hands interlocked. I was within arm's reach. I was itching to hit him. Now, my trauma was coming up. If I hit him, I could keep going and remember the stupid things and people at work with every hit. That's my trauma.

"What the fuck is your problem? How many other Black women have you assumed had unresolved trauma?" I stood up and grabbed my bag. I didn't have a white picket fence life growing up. I saw poverty. I saw how substances changed people. I got hit on by creepy old men at the store. The difference was, I didn't repress a damn thing. My family and friends openly talk about the good, the bad, and the ugly. Open door policy.

Dr. Scott remained seated and I walked around the ottoman towards him. He didn't flinch. This man did something I hate when dealing with stupidity. He was making me second guess myself like I didn't know what I was talking about. A customer would say something stupid, explain themselves, and then second guess the answer I gave them. I knew I answered the question, but to hear the customer repeat it sounded stupid.

He was so sure of himself. He had the degrees and the office; what would a customer service representative know? I knew this conversation was over, but not without a nice "fuck you" doc.

"Get this through your judgmental bald head. I never experienced the trauma you are suggesting. You are trying to label the adults in my life to something lower than dirt. Not my family. You got a lot of nerve." I started to walk out of his office as I talked. This was the moment to be cool, calm, and read the therapist who misread me. "Don't ever put false trauma on my family or my friends. You assume that my story is the same as others. Or probably the same as your upbringing. You studied all those hours to try and figure out why a human would be a certain way. Now, well into your profession, you still haven't figured out why that person caused you trauma. I am guessing a close friend or family member. It was nice to see medical bias in action. I can't wait to tell that horrible family of mine all about this bullshit." I walked up right behind him and whispered near his disgusting ear hair, "If security weren't downstairs, I would have caused trauma to you yet again but I wouldn't want to cause more of the trauma that I hope you went through. I'm a nice person."

I backed up and grabbed my bag. I chuckled at the intrusive thought of "accidentally" swinging my bag too wide. I hoped my breath was more than unpleasant.

"Ms. Martin, this repression will not help you," he shouted behind me. Oh, so he was definitely like the customers at my job. Didn't fucking listen!

"You didn't hear a damn word I said. You twisted my stress at work to fit your narrative. A Black woman must have past trauma. That's bullshit! The beautiful thing about being Black is the shared culture. We have similar traditions, rules, and upbringings. We shine bright and radiant when we are all together and having a good time. But it is a double-edge sword that you use to your advantage. If we share the wonderful things about our culture, we must also share the stereotypes of the bad. We don't get the luxury of being judged on the individual basis. I have your ancestors to thank for that."

"But you are right. I do have trauma. I continuously get beaten over the head with the realization that I am living in a world where adults are stupid, selfish, weak, interesting, curious, illiterate, and smart all at the same time. I refuse to accept that as life. I can't deal with it much longer. I won't deal with it much longer. So, fuck you and your trauma," I replied. I made sure the door slammed behind me.

This anger felt familiar. I was in the elevator losing sight around me. I needed to get out of here fast. That man wasn't a therapist. He was my catalyst. My last connected thread. I tried to focus so I could get to my car. I was cussing under my breath and walked fast to the exit in the lobby. I unjustly said "fuck off" to the security officer wishing me a pleasant day. I quickly stopped and turned around. "You didn't deserve that. Have a good night." I lowered my head and went right back to cussing. I was wobbly on my feet as I walked towards the parking garage.

My evil eyes warned people walking towards me to get the hell out of my way. I felt closed in, it was hard to breathe, and everything faded to black. The sounds of the busy area went mute. I was in a dark place again. I didn't hear any cracks. I heard water being poured. I screamed out, but I was met with silence again.

"Move out of the way," he said. Suddenly, the world came back. I stumbled back and hit a brick wall. I knew that voice. I looked left and right and saw him, Mr. Patel. At that moment, I decided I won't take it anymore. I followed him. He was headed in the same direction as the parking garage. I sped up to Mr. Patel. I saw the opening and took it. He made a right turn to the sidewalk behind the office building. I pulled my shirt up to cover my face, took off my bag and swung a little too wide, the second we were out of sight of the main sidewalk. He stumbled and I hit him again. He was still standing, so I kicked him as hard as I could. Once he fell, I kicked him again and again and again. He was crying and using his arms to block me. I paused so he would think it was over. I had to catch my breath. Then I kicked him more.

He nearly screamed for help but I shoved my shoe into his mouth. I leaned in with my weight to keep him down. I had a good 50 pounds on him anyway. I smiled at the thought that the bottom of my shoe could have gum, spit, or shit on the bottom.

"Stop moving and remain quiet and I will remove my foot," I whispered. The darkness outside help to hide my face and the muffled whisper hid my voice.

He nodded in agreement. I took my foot out of his mouth and stepped back to hide my face more.

"You can go home now. Tell anyone and I will find you," I warned. I wanted to brag that a "worthless" woman who he lied on kicked his ass. That would reveal too much about who I might be. I walked away in the opposite direction. I would take the long way around and then come back to my car. I left Mr. Patel bleeding, bruised, and short of breath. "I shoulda snagged his wallet," I thought to myself. I laughed. I laughed so hard that I had to move out of the way of the other people on the sidewalk. I ducked into a dark alley and laughed more.

Dr. Lynn

I stood in that alley until about 1 am. The time flew by as I waited for the laughing to stop, then the crying to stop and the police sirens to start. The laughter stopped, the crying stopped, and the sirens never came.

The sidewalk was empty. The building's lights were dim. I could hear music from the bars and clubs down the block. I peeked out from the alley to see if anyone was coming. "All clear," I sighed. I walked to my car in the parking garage. It was the only car left. My little two-door hatch-back looked like home for me. I sat in my car for a bit while I looked at the missed calls and text threads. Then my phone felt like it weighed 50 pounds. I dropped it into the passenger seat and drove home slouched over the steering wheel. It took all my strength to make it to the door. I collapsed on the floor and fell asleep.

I woke up in a pool of drool. I struggled to stand and maintain balance. The alarm got louder and louder by the minute while I looked for my phone. It's been a while since I heard my alarm. I had been so restless that any other day I'd wake up before the alarm. My twists were all over the place instead of neatly in my bonnet. I moved as quickly as possible, but my body was floating. I felt tired and energized all at the same time. When I turned my head, there was a delay in my brain. I was starving, but the idea of eating was too tedious. I tingled all over, not sure how to feel. I rode the wave. I felt higher than before.

I took a shower and watched the blood wash down the drain. I didn't notice the dried blood on my hands. Other people would be alarmed at what they did. Not me. I shrugged it off. I thought I only kicked Mr. Patel but I guess not. The hot water soothed my skin, and my brain was shut off. I stared at the water in a trance. An actual thought popped up but was forgotten almost immediately. It was nice not to worry. Snapshots of Mr. Patel made me laugh. It gave my brain the shot of the dopamine I needed. I assaulted someone and I was happy about it.

I had a chill drive to work without a thought in my head.

I woke up an hour before my alarm again. I blinked and it was Tuesday. I don't remember Friday until now. I looked around and noticed my bedroom was no longer a redwood forest. The shots of dopamine weren't as powerful. I felt the ground beneath my feet again. I was back to where I started. The frustration came back, and fear set in. It wasn't the fear of hurting someone else. It was a fear of losing that feeling again. I really needed to find a therapist quickly.

My next appointment was tomorrow with Dr. Lynn. I didn't even check if she was in-network. When Anderson came around to ask about my therapist hunt, I had to show that I was actively trying. I went to work and still played the role of someone who was mentally exhausted. I didn't have to pretend much. I didn't have to force a smile or be pleasant anymore. My days felt longer and longer. I worried that this therapist wouldn't work either. Dr. Scott left a bad taste in my mouth. I hoped this appointment would be different.

Session 1

I was nervous. I bit my acrylic nails and played with my hair every five seconds. Her office had a huge, comfy, red velvet couch. She kept the ambiance of the office in a "chilling in a lounge" type feel. The music was faint, but I knew it was on an RnB station. The music calmed my nerves a little, but my shaking leg screamed "uncomfortable!"

"Miss Martin," the receptionist called. I stood up slowly to get steady on my legs. I was so nervous. The receptionist reassured me that everything would be okay. Was she a shrink, too? I must have worn the dread on my face. I gave a half smile and took a deep breath.

The room had soft lighting and felt like a day party at someone's home. African artwork and literature decorated her walls and bookshelves. She had the normal academic journals but kept them behind her desk on a low bookshelf. The doctor wasn't in her office though.

"Please have a seat. Dr. Lynn will be in soon," she said. I sat down on another red velvet couch, but I couldn't get comfortable. I stood up and then sat back down about five times. I needed something to take my mind off where I was. While I waited for my appointment to begin, I browsed through her collection of books and art. I pulled out different books and journals. I just flipped through the pages and put them back in place. There was a knock on the door, and I jumped back to the couch. "Come in," I said unsurely. "What the hell, Elle," I thought to myself. This wasn't my office.

Dr. Lynn Torii Jones was fabulous, knowledgeable, and quick. She was 5 ft 8 in heels. I was immediately impressed with her shoe game. She was about my skin tone -- a nice brown glow and a laid wig. She was an interesting character that may be too old for those long-ass lashes.

Her wealth was in her ability to interpret my word vomit into concrete thoughts. She was also quick when breaking down my sarcastic wall. To quote her, "You use sarcasm to avoid emotional intimacy. You want to be vulnerable, but it appears your work has hardened you. You must break through that."

Our first session was like two friends talking shit about life. I regret not listening to Elise earlier. I kept some things to myself like I planned, but I unloaded during this session. I told her how I really felt about people.

"They suck," I repeated. She laughed at me. I liked her.

"I feel like we can really unpack some things," she said. She thought I was interesting. She had this fascinating curiosity like me. A good experiment always fascinated me. Hell, this was an experiment. Dr. Lynn and I were going to study each other.

"Okay, your next session will be next Wednesday," she said.

"Alright. The same time?"

"Yes ma'am," she replied.

When I left that appointment, I hoped that Dr. Lynn would see what Anderson saw. I needed this leave. If I had to act with her too, I would.

Session 2

"How was your week?" she asked.

"It was a typical week. My manager takes me off the phone in the afternoon when there is a slow day."

"Is it helpful?"

"Hell no!" I explained to her if it wasn't the phone, it was the modules that had to be completed and co-workers who had questions. But it wasn't the people I work with mostly. My frustration comes from the stupidity and willful ignorance of people I encountered daily.

"Well," she sighed. "Let's figure out what your triggers are. Do you journal?"

"I don't," I replied. "Aren't the stupid questions and illiteracy enough for triggers?"

"They can be part of the problem. There is more to it. Without a positive outlet this can affect your interactions with others outside of work," she explained. She was too late. My human-to-human interaction was limited, and I planned to keep it that way. Dr. Lynn leaned in, pen in hand, ready to unpack whatever block I had with human-to-human interaction. The stupidity at work had taken its toll. She was convinced there was more to it, but nope. I lost my desire to interact with anyone new. My friends aren't like that. My family had their moments, but a new person got on my nerves easily.

Dr. Lynn didn't want my experience at work to shape my reality of how the world operates. "What concerns me is that you won't be able to come back from this feeling if you continue to internalize your interactions at work," she explained. Again, she was too late. I internalized more and more until I snapped at Dr. Scott's office. What surprised me was that I got away with it. I kept all that to myself.

"I just want my stress, anxiety, hatred, and doubt to go away. Not just in the moment, but permanently. Nothing is working," I told her.

"Do you think this short-term leave will help you?" she asked.

"I hope so."

"Mmhmm," she answered.

Dr. Lynn gave me homework. She wanted me to go out more and spend time with people outside of work. She wanted me to spend time with strangers more than my inner circle. She also wanted me to start a journal and find a relaxation technique. I stood up and stretched.

"Just try the journal, Elle," she said.

"Yeah, yeah," I said as I browsed her book collection. One book caught my eye. I was scanning the bookshelf and touching the spines of the books. It had a nice, calming effect. I traced the book's spine and loved the textures on the book's cover.

"Well, that's the hour," she said.

"Oh. Ok, cool." I didn't realize the time. How long did she let my mind drift off into her book collection?

"I'm joking," she laughed.

"Yooooo, I really thought you let me stand there for nearly 30 minutes without saying anything," I laughed, too.

"Let's talk a little bit more about this leave. Why did your manager suggest this option?"

"Anderson could not cover me for long. After I…" I trailed off. I was about to mention the blackout at work. If Dr. Lynn was anything like me, that blackout was fascinating, scary, and a hint. A hint I'd rather keep to myself for now. "After I fussed and cussed with a few of the customers, he really couldn't ignore what was happening."

"What is happening in your opinion?" she asked.

"I really think he is overreacting."

"Is he?" She peeked at me from the top of her glasses.

"Yeah," I stuttered.

"Not many managers would be that understanding," she said.

"I'll have to send him flowers or something," I laughed.

"I feel like you are holding back on me," she said. I was.

"I don't share my frustrations or feelings. It just isn't me," I replied.

"Why not? It isn't good to keep them bottled up," she said. "There could be an explosion of emotions one day. We want to prevent that."

She wasn't wrong. It happened once, and I secretly hoped for it again.

"I guess it comes from being the oldest in my family. I am supposed to be the safe space for my sisters. I make sure we keep our mom from worrying too much. I am the child you shouldn't have to worry about," I said.

"Have you always felt that way?"

"Pretty much. I love the job and I still rely on my family. They know I am stressed but I keep the details to a minimum. My mom doesn't know about this," I replied. "My sisters know but we are keeping the parents in the dark. Just what I need is another prayer circle with the mothers at my mom's church."

"No," Dr. Lynn laughed. "Well, religion can be a good option."

"I know, but eventually it became a chore, or tradition. It wasn't the same as when I grew up. I think age made me see people differently. I can't even escape the stupidity of others at church. Nothing about the teachings but the day that I found out Hallelujah had a silent 'j,' I knew I needed a minute. This job is just making me notice stupid from 1000 feet away or within the first second."

I surprised Dr. Lynn by saying this much. "Can we explore that a little more? How do you notice it so quickly or assume?

"I think the hour is up," I replied. I was right.

"Oh wow, it is. Well, we will pick this up next week then."

"I look forward to it, doc," I laughed.

"I really want you to start journaling," she said as I opened the door.

"Heard," I waved.

Work went on as usual.

"I swear people don't hear me when I'm talking," I told Wes. I walked over to his desk to take a break. I had to be mindful of his busy-bee manager, Charla. That lady could pop her short ass out of anywhere. It amazed me how she never minded her own business or her own team's business.

"Sometimes these customers refuse to listen. The customer is not always right. In fact, based on our calls, they are never right," Wes laughed.

"I thought when you became an adult, you knew what the fuck you were doing. This job slapped me in the face with reality," I laughed. "It's frustrating!" I got a little loud there.

"How is the therapy going?"

"It's cool. I've got two more appointments to go. I don't know if she will give the recommendation because I'm not sharing much. "

"The same way you are playing up here, you have to do it there. Cuz if this works, I'm taking my mental health leave next," he said.

"Only if…"

"If I can get past," he looked around, "get past Charla."

"If we say her name again, she will pop up like Beetlejuice." We laughed. "Time for me to 'play it up.'"

I left Wes's desk and took my sweet time going back to mine. I stopped at the break room and pretended to watch the weather channel. I took a lap around the office floor. I tried to look exhausted, stressed out, and lost. My favorite thing was exploring the rest of the floors in this building. The minute I hit the stairwell; my act ended. I started humming a song that has been stuck in my head and decided to try a lower floor.

Our company had most of the top floors. I'd explored them already. I danced and pranced on the way down to another floor. The cameras are only fixed on the doors to show who was going in and out. I chilled out when I passed the door, but when I was out of sight, I was playing air guitar or practicing my aim.

I stopped at the third floor. I was in my own world, and I didn't notice I went down that far. I opened the stairwell door as quietly as possible. Of course, the door squeaked and squawked every inch I pulled open. I had no idea who or what was on this floor. The noisy door was an announcement that I was coming. I peeked my head into the hallway to see if anyone was around. The hallway was empty. "Is this floor empty?" I asked myself. I stepped into the hallway. I used my butt to make sure the door didn't slam shut.

I explored the empty floor. Some of the doors to old offices and conference rooms were locked. My footsteps echoed as I walked around. The carpet didn't cushion my steps. The ceiling had exposed wires and there was a random ladder in the middle of the floor. The floor layout kinda looked like my floor. Where the cubicles would go is a large, dirty open space. I twirled around, let out a good scream and used my arm to muffle the sound. I went through random office supplies and kicked random file cabinets. I opened any door that wasn't locked. I got a little carried away because I was there for 20 minutes. I rushed to the stairs. I still had to work. Anderson wasn't that understanding.

I caught my breath once I got into the hallway. I wasn't thinking straight because I took the stairs for 11 flights. I was dead tired. My sunken shoulders weren't an act this time. I needed to catch my breath. I flopped in my computer chair to rest. "That was my exercise for the month," I whispered to myself.

Session 3

"What are your hobbies outside of work?" Dr. Lynn asked.

"I love reading, watching anime, baking. You know stuff like that. My sister Te doesn't think those count."

"Are they a good escape for you when you are stressed?"

"They were," I answered.

"What changed?"

"It started to feel like a chore. Something I had to do, not wanted to do. Plus, two of my favorite series are taking forever to release."

"Do you think you got too used to that as an escape?" she asked.

"It was like eating at the same restaurant. The first ten times were fine, but I know the menu by heart now. I still love all those things, but they may need a break from me, too."

A hobby outside of work helped like everything else I tried. It worked until it didn't and then I was on to the next. I fight the desire to chase that high from assaulting Mr. Patel. Especially since I got away with it. I smiled as I replayed that night in my mind.

"Why are you smiling like that?" Dr. Lynn asked. She looked at me with a twinkle in her eye. I knew that look. I needed to change the subject. I didn't realize I was smiling.

"Oh, it's nothing." I couldn't think of another reason on the spot.

"I don't believe that," she said.

"It was nothing. At least nothing to do with what we are talking about."

"An intrusive thought," she replied. I knew I liked her.

"Exactly! Is it weird that a random word can trigger something that has nothing to do with the subject?"

"No, I don't find it weird," she replied.

"Well, is it weird trying to reverse the thought back to its source?" I asked.

"No. Nice pivot work," she winked. In my mind that meant my pivot worked. "We will stop here for the day. I will remind you again to…"

"Journal! I know," I groaned.

"You need to do it and think about your safe spaces. We will talk about it next," she said.

"Heard."

For Thursday and Friday, 5pm seemed to take longer and longer to arrive. My weekend flew by. Monday and Tuesday never seemed to end. My last session was this coming Wednesday evening. I printed the therapist recommendation form three times in the morning. The clock at work was especially slow. I thought once Anderson took me off the phones in the afternoon my day would be less stupid. Wrong! I was now dealing with customer stupidity in the morning and coworker stupidity in the afternoon. A new pet peeve was our instant messenger at work. The work group chat was fine. It was the messages from other people that pissed me off. It wasn't bad at first, but the mole hill became a mountain real quick.

I hated it when someone used the instant message to ask a question. Well, not asking a question, but the buildup to get to the question was annoying. I let it rock and let go one time too many. I would have let this "hey" instant message rock, too. I hate when you are typing me to ask a question and there are seconds to fucking minutes between to ask one question.

Sasha typed "hey" and that was it. I ignored it. I wrapped up some files from the day and waited for the clock to say 5:30. Sasha typed "how are you." That shit was annoying. I never spoke to Sasha before this message. "Get on with your question, Sasha," I whispered to myself. I waited. After 30 seconds she still didn't say anything. When I have a question it's all typed in one damn bubble. "Hey, good morning, I have a question…" say it all at once.

I ignored it again.

Two minutes later, "I have a question."
I threw a silent fit in my cubicle. I rocked back and forth, punched the air, and bounced in frustration. "What is the fucking question, Sasha?" I grit-

ted my teeth so that no one would hear me. I could have cracked my teeth. I stared at the messenger waiting for the "Sasha is typing" bar at the bottom. She started, then she stopped. That question she had better be worth the aggravation. An aggravation that was increasing by the second. I had 15 minutes left, and it was taking Sasha 16 minutes to ask a question. After a few minutes, I go back to wrapping up my desk for the day. I walked to the break room to fill up my water bottle.

When I got back, I had five unread messages from Sasha. "This was a long ass question," I thought to myself. I opened the message, and everything went black for a second. Sasha had all the nerve to get an attitude with me. "Are you there?" "Why aren't you answering me?!" "You are wasting my time." "This is unprofessional." "Thanks for nothing."

I reread those messages as everyone else was shuffling about to follow the herd to the elevators. I focused on these messages. The sound around me disappeared. The air was thin. I felt myself slipping into that dark space again. I felt it happening. It felt like I was casually walking away from the light behind me. I shook myself back to the office but that didn't make me less angry.

I pulled up Sasha's work profile. She had her hair in cute, short curls with honey blond highlights. She had a round face like mine and a scar on her left cheek. She worked the 9 to 6 shift of the routing center on the 10th floor. The routing center takes the calls initially and then transfers the client or customer to the right department. They were wrong 80% of the time. They had a new training class every month. No one stayed on the 10th floor for long. That job didn't even have a career path due to the high turnover. I expected one of them to go off before I did.

I couldn't ignore it. I should have left and gone to my car. Instead, I wanted to find Sasha in a dark alley, too. I couldn't get that lucky twice. And since I still need a paycheck, violence may not be the smartest option. I looked at the clock and it was 5:40. Then the idea hit me. I was ready to be petty. I printed the messages and headed to the 10th floor. Every time I read the messages my anger increased, but I needed to remain calm. This would only work if I stayed calm. I rehearsed what I was going to say over and over. I kept my tone in code switch mode and I would always smile.

At first I wandered around but their cubicle maze was a bit different than ours upstairs. The search for Sasha was gasoline for the fire. When I decided to ask someone, they either didn't know or pointed in the wrong direction. I made it to the last two rows and found Sasha. Good timing, too, because she was getting packed up to leave.

"It was my pleasure! Is there anything else I can help you with?" She nodded her head and said bye. I waited for her to put the phone and headset down. Her hands typed the notes and I was here to ruin her evening.

"Hi, excuse me," I said softly.

"Yes," she answered softly.

"You are Sasha, right?" I glanced at the cubicle for a name plate. I didn't see one. Based on the turnaround numbers, there was no point.

"Yes," she replied. Her eyebrows started to scrunch together as she waited for me to say the next thing.

"Great. I need to speak to you for a second. I know we are all packing up to leave, but it won't take long."

"Umm, sure," she turned her chair to face me.

Stay calm, Elle.

"What makes you think this was appropriate to say?" I asked softly. I put the screenshots on her desk. Her skepticism turned to defense. She read the messages again.

"Well, I messaged you a few times and you didn't answer," she answered. Her real voice came out. I could tell her walls were going up. I could meet that attitude with mine but I had a plan.

"And this was the correct response? You didn't think I was away from my desk or working on something else? This is very unprofessional."

"I mean," she shrugged.

I leaned in and said, "I bet you do this all time, but no one ever called you out. They aren't me."

I stood back up and said politely, "Can you tell me where your manager sits?"

"We don't need my manager. I hear you," she replied.

"Umm, yeah we do. Just like you, I am trying my best to remain cool."

"You need to back up," Sasha commanded. She didn't raise her voice either.

"No problem. I am wasting time talking to you about this. I will back up right to your manager's desk. If you don't want to tell me where they are, fine. Someone else on your team will," I replied. She picked up on my hint. If I had to ask someone else, I was telling them all the details. I was taunting her. She was ready to fight me. I craved that idea, but this wasn't the right place.

"We can take this outside. I ain't got a problem. You do," Sasha said. She was getting louder.

"Eww, and you have bad grammar. I have to find them now." I laughed as I walked towards the other cubicles. "Excuse me, who and where is your team's manager?"

"Ummm, her desk in the center. Her name is Allie." I thanked Sasha's team member and walked to the manager's desk. Sasha was right on my heels.

"Excuse me," I said meekly. Allie was packing up as well.

"Yes," she said.

"Are you Sasha's manager?"

"I am and you are…?" she trailed off.

"Oh sorry. I'm Elle. I work on the 14th floor," I said.

"How can I help you?" She gestured for me to sit.

"Allie, wait," Sasha said behind me.

"Hey, Sasha. I'll be with you in a minute."

"But I…" she stopped.

"Well, Allie…" I started.

"Allie, please," Sasha interrupted.

"Sasha, are you alright? I am speaking with someone," Allie said.

"I can answer that. These are the messages that Sasha sent to me today. I find them very unprofessional. Rude even," I said. I laid this shit on thick! I would ignore fellow employees most of the time. I don't snitch but I make a mental note. This wasn't one of those times. I was heated and felt petty today. I sat quietly while Allie read the messages.

"I don't believe that Sasha considered the fact that I could be away from my desk or busy," I expressed. Allie nodded in agreement.

"I agree." Allie looked up. "Sasha, this is really inappropriate. You never asked a question. There are minutes before you typed the next thing, and it was never a question." Allie gets it. I bet she hated that shit, too. Ask the question! "Elle, thank you for bringing this to my attention."

"Thank you for your help. I want to be able to work as a team. Receiving messages like this can impact our cooperation with each other." Oh, I didn't believe any of the shit I was saying. This was as close to violence as I could get. This job was frustrating already. I shouldn't have coworkers that make my day more difficult.

I walked past Sasha and went back upstairs to get my things. What Allie and Sasha discussed after that, I didn't care. They could talk shit about me "overreacting," but I didn't care. I got my things and headed to my car. I had to see Dr. Lynn but I didn't feel like talking. I thought of 1000 different things I'd rather do than talk to my therapist, but it's the last session to meet the requirements for leave approval.

I sat in my car gripping the steering wheel. I was debating with my-self. One by three, I watched people leave the parking garage. Our parking garage always had traffic jams until maybe an hour after work was over. After working here for over four years, I waited in my car until the traffic died down. I learned that from Carmen. So, I waited. I leaned my chair back and tried to think of an excuse that Dr. Lynn would believe. "I don't feel good" doesn't have much weight to it. It worked for calling out at work, but she wouldn't believe that for a second. Even if I were truthful and said

I had a bad day, she would want to see me more. I closed my eyes and gave up on avoiding the inevitable.

I lifted my seat back up and got ready to leave. That was when I saw Sasha walking to her car. I should be satisfied by what I did earlier, but I wasn't. My anger was still there, and I started to see black again, walking willingly towards it. I couldn't stop myself. I didn't want to stop myself. I assumed that Sasha didn't get in trouble. Anderson would dust off a coworker complaint for me. I betcha Allie did the same.

I watched Sasha walk to her car and get situated. She started her car and began leaving the parking garage. As she pulled out towards the exit, I couldn't stop myself. I jumped in front of her car. She slammed on the brakes. I smiled, gave her a wave, and walked to the driver's side window. She stared straight ahead. She pretended like she didn't see me tapping on her window. I thought she would jump out the car and back up her "we can do this outside" threat but she didn't. I tapped again.

"Lawd, let me be calm because I need this job," she said. At that moment, I wanted to pull back. She dealt with shit at work because of the need for a paycheck too. She was me. I should just apologize and keep it moving. She rolled down the window, just a small crack. "What the fuck do you want?" she asked me.

I deserved that. "I want you to know..." I wanted to say it was nothing personal, or sorry that I was going through a lot. but that is not what came out.

Session 4

Dr. Lynn was absolutely fascinated when I told her about Sasha. She reminded me of how I felt when I figured out a math formula or the connection in a science class. I would be super excited and wanted to learn more. She kept asking for more but there was not much I could give her. I wished she could hide that Cheshire cat grin better. I would have the same grin if it were someone else other than me. She gestured for me to continue as she took notes.

"So, what did you tell her?" she asked.

"Nothing," I answered. That was a lie. "I walked away."

"What did you learn from this situation? About yourself?" She had her pen ready.

"I learned that I work with stupid, too."

"Maybe you should take this opportunity to learn how to manage your emotions and learn patience. Your brain seems to move faster than someone can get their thoughts out."

"And it's annoying as shit. They called or messaged me for a specific purpose but somehow that reason is forgotten the minute the phone rings." I hated receiving calls where people place unnecessary pauses or filler words into a sentence. The, "Hi Elle, my name is such and such" followed by a pause made me mad. Thinking about it made me mad. I stood up and walked to the bookshelf again.

"You seem to do that a lot," Dr. Lynn said.

"Do what?"

"You get up and walk around at least once during our session. Does it help?" she asked.

"I can't sit still when talking about myself. I'd rather focus on anything other than myself."

"I see," she said. She wrote things down, but I really didn't care. I traced the spines of the books again. It's been four weeks and I think I touched every book on her shelf. This time was different. As I walked the bookshelf, I found the book with an interesting spine, so I pulled it out. I wasn't going to hop around this bookshelf today. The front and back covers were blank. The outside was brown and gold. It looked like one of those big old bibles in my grandmother's house. There wasn't a title or author on the front. Nothing written on the back. Just a few swirls and twirls of the colors. I opened the book to find the entire thing blank. That was a letdown. The whole mysterious unknown cover and completely blank on the inside. The pages were this yellowish-brown color and felt like old parchment paper. I took the book and sat back down.

"Do people realize when their psyche breaks?" I asked her. I flipped through the pages again and again.

"Rarely are people aware. Most never know," she replied. She wrote constantly in our sessions now.

"Am I going crazy?"

"You are not crazy, Elle. We are going to explore this together. You need a way to cope in a healthy way."

"It's taking forever," I grunted.

"Elle, I know you want to keep everything on the surface. I know this is scary, but you need to let me in," Dr. Lynn explained.

"How do I get over the fear though?" I asked. I kept my eyes on the book.I would burst into tears if I looked at her. Talking to a person about this causes me to lose control of my emotions. Hell, even looking in the mirror made me lose control.

"I want you to really start analyzing your day. I will beat this dead horse. Have you started to journal?"

"Of course not," I answered.

"I'm gonna need you to start doing that. With your leave, we can meet more. When you feel your emotions get out of control, write until all the emotions are on the page. From there we can unpack that together. Get those feelings of frustration and anger out. It can help," she said.

"Or make it worse," I replied.

"It's possible, but I need you to try. Can you do that, Elle?" Dr. Lynn asked.

"Dr. Lynn, this one is all blank," I said.

"I'd rather not change the subject but yeah, that one is blank. Has been for decades."

"What does that mean? Wasn't it always blank?"

"Not if you believe the myth."

"Okay, I'll bite. What myth?"

"I got that book from my favorite professor during my master's program," she explained. "Dr. Afi Yeboah said that this book is incredibly special. It only reveals its contents to certain people."

"What kind of people?"

"Oh… what did he say," she paused. "I think he said the lost and unsure vessels. Then he said, 'the hidden magic within.' He was always so mysterious. I found it the same way you did, among a bunch of books. He said the book called to me, so it was my turn to have it."

"Were you lost or magical?"

"Huh," she giggled.

"Were you?"

"I was worried about my school load and wondering if I made the right decision. I may have been lost at some point."

"Well, did it reveal itself to you?" I was flipping through the blank pages and did not see anything. She hadn't written in the book either.

"Nothing," she answered. She sounded disappointed.

"Rumors and myths are fun to learn about, but that would be some real magic," I said.

"Very true." Dr. Lynn took a glance at her watch and was surprised at the time. "We only have a little time left. Did you have something for me to sign?"

"Oh yeah, my leave recommendation." I swiftly went to my bag and unfolded the recommendation. She walked over to her desk, took out a file, filled out the form, and then put it on her scanner. "I really appreciate your help, Dr. Lynn."

"You want to show your appreciation?"

"I will journal, Mom. Geez!!"

"It is not just that. During this leave from work, I want to see you twice a week, no call-outs unless it's an emergency. I want you to also go on vacation. Remember I asked you about your safe places."

"Oh yeah, we never discussed that."

"Well, what are some of your safe spaces? Where can you go and enjoy, relax, and escape reality?"

"When I am around water. The beach is my favorite. The ocean is the biggest mysterious place on Earth. God created something magical, scary, and important to nature more than pieces or land. My problems seem so small in comparison to that ocean horizon.'

"Wow, that is an interesting way to think about it."

"I prefer nature over humans."

"Why?" Dr. Lynn was still scanning documents while I talked.

"Nature is perfect. A complete circle. Humans are flawed and there are so many people who don't acknowledge their own."

The scanning stopped. She handed me the form back and confirmed she sent her reports and email. She came back and sat down. She looked me straight in the eyes and said, "This is what we are going to do. Once your leave starts, take the first two weeks to yourself. Go to the beach. I know it may cost some money, but this is doctor's orders. Go to the beach and unplug. You can still read your books and watch your anime but don't mention work. Any time work pops into your mind or you feel the need to react to something, write it down. After the two weeks, we will meet Tuesdays and Wednesdays."

"Two days a week," I repeated.

"Yup," she grinned. "The point of the trip to the beach and your short-term leave is for you to recenter yourself, but we won't succeed if you refuse to do the work. We don't have to work through everything during your leave, but we can get you back. Less chaos in that head of yours," she pointed.

"I will do my best." I would agree to damn near anything to get six months off work paid, bitch. She knew that.

I went to put the book back and Dr. Lynn stopped me.

"That is yours now," she said.

"What? Why?"

"Same rules; it looks like that book called to you. It is your turn to have it."

"I know magic isn't real."

"You never know. You are the first patient to notice this book. I have been practicing for 20 years," she shrugged.

"Really?" She looked much younger than that, and people aren't observant at all. "No one noticed the book in 20 years?"

"Not one," she said. "It's blank. Use it as a journal. Maybe it can be magical for you. Get it?" she laughed.

I laughed in embarrassment. "A magical journal, huh." I shrugged to myself and put the book into my bag and left the office with a green light to my short-term leave and homework. I needed a drink and a long nap. I was going to bed early.

On the ride home, I was happy. Not because of the deal I made with Dr. Lynn. I finished the last step to get my approval. Anderson will get the full report tomorrow. The higher-ups in HR would review it and boom, I'm out. I hoped they would approve my leave before I was covered in darkness again.

The Book

The beach was peaceful. I went to a smaller beach area to avoid the many families near the boardwalk enjoying some time off. My leave should be approved soon. I wanted a quick pre-vacation and knew I wouldn't be able to relax with people around. God blessed me with the perfect weather to lay out on the beach all day. The right warmth of the sun, the breeze came right when I needed it and plenty of empty space around. A perfect day. I didn't need an umbrella on the beach, but I did need three extra hands. I packed too much shit for a solo trip. I should have bought a cooler with an extended handle to get all my stuff in one trip. I had my books, downloaded music and anime episodes, food, drinks, extra clothes and these two big towels. I was four shots in and an edible chaser down by the time I got to a good spot.

I spent time watching the waves, praying, crying, and digging my feet into the sand. The water was cold at first but warmed up as the day progressed. I needed this. It was supposed to be the two weeks Dr. Lynn prescribed, but I used all my PTO. So, only a weekend will have to do. I could rest into this relaxation the ocean brings me. I wouldn't need another vacation to unplug from this vacation before I had to go back to work because my leave was right around the corner.

I frolicked, tried to build sandcastles, drank, and drank, and drank some more. This was the day I was going to go out further than I had ever been in the ocean. I needed liquid courage. I wasn't drunk because that's stupid. I needed to relax and not forget how to swim. Good idea or bad idea, I was going out there. As a contingency plan, I put on water wings. My heart raced and my breath was rapid. That made the trip harder because salt water was getting into my eyes, nose, and mouth. I kept walking but told myself to relax and float. The minute I didn't feel sand under my feet, I swam a little past the "land approaching waves" and went to where the water was calm. I lifted my body up and laid on the water. I closed my eyes and floated.

For the first time, I was floating in the ocean. Liquid courage worked. The waves were gentle under my back, the birds sang above me, the sun kissed my skin. I listened for God and He gave me rest. "I should have done this years ago," I thought to myself.

Suddenly, I felt a sharp pain on my left arm. My trance was broken, and I immediately began to sink under the water. I waved my arms around to pull myself back up to the surface. I popped up like a damn dolphin and took a deep breath of air. "Swim lesson and muscle memory, help me," I prayed. I started to swim back to shore with the help of the waves pushing me forward. The minute I could stand, I walked the rest of the way. I wanted to open my eyes more, but the saltwater burned. Through my squinting, I walked in the direction of my stuff. The soft sand was a new enemy because I had to use more energy to get my feet one in front of the other. I used all my strength with that damn swim. My body was already hurting.

"Ma'am! Ma'am!" I heard someone shouting but I still couldn't open my eyes fully. I turned to see who was talking. "Yes?" I called. Maybe they weren't talking to me.

"You're bleeding," they shouted.

"Huh." I looked around myself and noticed the blood dripping in the sand. I felt a stinging pain through my body but I thought it was because I was out of shape. That was not an easy swim.

"Oh God! Thank you," I replied. I picked up the pace to my bag. I had an extra shirt and towel I could use. I dropped onto my towel to search through my bag. "Oww! Shit," I yelled. I pulled out the journal with my left hand by accident. I forgot I had a cut that was literally getting salt rubbed in it. I tossed the journal down and kept digging with my right hand. How was it that the one thing I needed was at the fucking bottom? "Damn," I said to myself. "It shouldn't be this hard!"

I wrapped my shirt around my arm and used my hair tie to keep it secure. I packed everything up after I had a fight with a damn seagull for my bag of chips. I won that one! I was tired, achy, in pain, and might need stitches. I needed to get my arm looked at, so I called it a day.

I woke up around 4 am to go to the bathroom. My arm still hurt a bit and it made it hard to go back to sleep. Luckily, I wasn't cut too deep. I needed two stitches because the base of my cut was deeper then further up my forearm. I called my mom; she freaked out a bit and then told me to get some rest. I was a wild sleeper sometimes but with this cut, I had to stay as still as possible so I didn't roll on my arm.

What made finding a nice still spot to sleep worse was that I needed to pee. I tried to ignore it but that only gave me five more minutes. I couldn't ignore it any longer. I shuffled to the bathroom, feeling around for the wall because I refused to turn on a light. Why would I want to make my life easier? I nearly missed the toilet as I sat down, but I got myself together. As I shuffled back to my bed, I started hearing drums. The sound was off in the distance, so I assumed that someone was blasting music in the hotel, or it was the restaurant in the hotel.

I tried to go back to sleep but the drums were getting louder. I tossed and turned, but I could not drown out the noise. I jumped up and looked out my window like that would help. I didn't see anything. I got up from my bed and stepped out into the hallway. I didn't hear the drumming anymore. I walked back into my room and the drumming began again.

"What the hell is going on?" I looked – well, listened -- around my room but didn't find the source.

I stepped out onto my balcony and the drumming stopped again. Was this coming from inside my hotel room? I stepped back inside, and the drumming got louder. My phone was on the charger. The TV went to sleep. My laptop was closed. Where the hell was the drumming coming from? This would be the point where I got in my car and drove my ass back home. Instead, I went hunting for the drums. It was like a game. I was getting "warmer" to the drums as they got louder. I stopped right in front of my beach bag and couldn't believe it. The drums were coming from there. "Maybe I left my speaker on," I whispered. It hit me immediately that the book Dr. Lynn gave me was in there.

I dug into the bag and the drumming stopped. "No fucking way." I carefully felt for the journal's unique design. "Got it." I took out the book and stared at the front cover. "Don't open it. Don't open it. You are Black. We don't do foolishness in scary movies," I thought to myself. I wasn't in a movie. This was real life. Right? "Oh my God, it's finally happened. I have lost my damn mind. I knew it was only a matter of time."

I flopped on the small couch holding the book. The drumming stopped, but was it real? After fighting with myself for what felt like hours, I opened the book. I let out a sigh of relief. The pages were still blank. I flipped through the pages a few times and didn't see anything. I accidentally got some blood on the pages from earlier at the beach. Other than that the pages were blank. As I flipped through one last time, words appeared on the pages. I tossed the book.

"What the hell!" I shouted. I stood up and kicked the book with my foot. The book was blank. Dr. Lynn said it was blank. I saw that it was blank. How did words appear? I backed away from the book. I felt the hair on my arms stand up straight. Goosebumps tightened on my skin. My skin was cold, but my face felt hot. I backed myself up to the wall. I blinked rapidly and then slowly. The book didn't disappear. It wouldn't go away. "I must be dreaming," I thought.

I took a few deep breaths and slapped myself in the face. "Wake up, Elle! Come on, wake up!" I opened my eyes and the book was still there. I let go of the wall and approached the book slowly. It had some type of gravitational pull; that was what I told myself. I lightly kicked the book. No drums and nothing jumped out. I waited a few seconds then I kicked it one more time. Nothing. I used my toes to try and open the book. As it opened, writing slowly appeared on the page. "Nope!" I closed it again. I dropped to the floor and stared at the book like it was about to grow feet and walk away.

"No way!" I was seriously yelling at a book. I lost it; this was the moment. The book didn't grow legs, but it was teasing me. My curiosity and fear got my adrenaline pumping. Should I pick it up or leave it? I rubbed my forehead as I debated with myself. *Pick it up!*

I grabbed the book and walked over to the desk in the hotel room. I turned on the desk light. I walked backwards to the micro-fridge to keep my eye on the book. I blindly felt around for alcohol and soda. I stared at the book for a long time as I took a few shots. Then I started to pace back and forth.

This had to be a dream. Magic wasn't real. "Don't open. Totally open it. Don't you dare. But this is cool though. Should I flip a coin?" All those thoughts ran through my head. The argument kept on inside of me for a few more minutes. "I'm gonna open it," I decided. As soon as I opened the cover, the words appeared again.

> *I flow without a voice and but loudly,*
> *I have life-giving grace. I find my place*
> *transparent but vital even within the smallest*
> *space. I am in every form and hue. Mysterious*
> *and dark I can mimic the space that swallows*
> *the stars and moons. I crash, clash, fall and fill all.*
> *Deprive you of the one thing you need but I*
> *cannot exist without it.*

The words stopped right there. I laid the book down. It wasn't what I expected. Actually, I didn't know what I expected but a riddle wasn't a top contender so I read those words again.

I kept opening and closing the book and the words remained. I flipped through the other pages and the same words continued to appear. "No fucking way," I whispered. I didn't believe it but I wanted to. Magic doesn't exist but this book said otherwise.

I convinced myself I was dreaming and left the book on the desk and went back to bed. I really did not have to convince myself too much to leave the book alone. Surprisingly, I fell right to sleep once I laid down.

"Human, keep it hidden! He cannot have it. Do you understand!" I jumped up in a cold sweat.

"Who was that?"

"Your leave has been approved," Anderson said. He confirmed it first thing Monday morning.

"Oh well, I'll head home then," I said.

"Not now," Anderson laughed. "They approved you to start your leave in two weeks."

"Two weeks!?"

"Yeah, end of tax season, you know this is a busy time."

"Anderson, all seasons are busy seasons. The summer had too many adults with free time. The fall had parents letting a gaming console babysit their children. The winter was Christmas and debt, and the Spring had taxes. All seasons are busy." I walked around him and sat my bag in my chair.

"I guess you are right, but the two weeks will fly by."

"I never want your optimism because two weeks stopped flying by on year two here," I smirked. Anderson laughed and gave me a light pat on the back.

"Can I stay off the phone at least?" I shouted at Anderson. He gave me a thumbs up and kept walking. I should buy him some flowers for real.

I was great at my job. So great, I cleared all my work before I went to the beach. I told myself to look busy so I used my free time to search for anything about the book. I looked up mythologies, stories, forgotten books in the Bible and alternative views and conspiracies about humans on Earth. The closest I got were a few of my favorite fictional books. In the end, I found nothing. "How do I start searching for this?" I asked myself. I stared at the web page and typed and retyped searches. I was unsure how to "word" what I was looking for. I decided to search the same way I search for the name of a song. I used the lyrics or, in this case, the story Dr. Lynn told me. A few inspirational quotes popped up, self-help books and quotes from fictional stories that weren't exactly what I typed.

I clicked on links for about an hour. I probably gave my computer a virus from some of those websites. Getting through that search took two hours. I gave up on that and took a picture of the book for a reverse image search. "This should get me somewhere," I thought. I uploaded the image and waited to see if I got a hit.

Nothing.

I clicked on a few more links and read some more folklore. Again, nothing about a mysterious book that reveals itself to certain people. The only object that did that was, "absolutely nothing," I grunted. There were things like Excalibur that could be pulled from the stone if someone was worthy, but a damn magical book was too much to ask for. I was mad that there wasn't much on African folklore and mythology.

I couldn't remember the name of the professor that Dr. Lynn mentioned. I felt bad because I didn't remember where she got her degrees from either. So that was a dead end, too. I could ask her, but I decided to save that as a last resort. I had no idea how I would bring any of this up to her.

I decided to go down to the third floor to take a closer look at the journal. I made that place my little clubhouse. I moved some things around and made the empty space my own. I wanted to open the book without people around. I wasn't sure what this book was. I didn't want any questions about it.

I got comfortable in the area I made for myself and opened the book.

I didn't know how to feel. A piece of me is terrified and worried that I've lost my mind. Another piece of me is curious and adventurous but the majority of me hoped this was a villain arc in my life like my anime. I took all those emotions one by one. Each time, I came to the same conclusion; I'll stop the minute I felt I was losing control. Crazy or not, I couldn't go past the edge in my mind.

I stared at the riddle for a few minutes. "This is just like one of my favorite books," I whispered to myself. I read the riddle again. I clicked my pen a couple of times while I thought of the answer. Click, click, click.

"Got it! Water!" I clicked my pen and wrote in purple ink "water." The pages flipped uncontrollably after I wrote the answer. I threw the book quickly. I didn't know what was happening. I crawled away as the pages continued to flip.

Then it suddenly stopped.

I stood up slowly and watched the book. I thought it would grow legs and walk away. My legs felt heavy every time I took a step. I slowly approached the book and looked down. The words were blurry. I picked up the book like it was a hot potato. I flipped through the pages and they were all the same. "What the hell is this," I said. I closed the book and headed back upstairs. I needed to go back to a reality I knew. I went back upstairs and pretended to work for the rest of the day.

At the end of the day, I packed up and went to my car. I waited for the foot traffic and regular traffic to calm down as I usually did. However, I resisted opening my bag and looking at the book. I felt like it was staring at me, burning a hole through my mind. I looked around to see if anyone was around. They were, but they weren't paying attention. I reached to open it and I stopped. I couldn't. I knew I had to wait until I got home. So, I sped home.

I was supposed to stop for dinner but it will be a random shit kind of dinner tonight. I pulled into the first parking spot I saw by my building and ran inside my apartment. I locked the door and opened my bag. The book was still there. I caught my breath. I walked into the kitchen and grabbed my gummi worms from the cabinet. I turned on the light above my stove and stared at the book for a long time. This had to be a dream. I opened it back up. As soon as I opened the cover, new words appeared.

> *Across the infinite timeline, I search for life*
> *and light. Another chance, an endless loop to*
> *find the truth of life. You can remember my past but*
> *cannot see the future. A quest of rotation where*
> *appearance and purposes change. I am a tale,*
> *fantasy, truth, or divine to an individual or great*
> *nation. I trace the cosmos with past ties in a*
> *cycle unseen.*

The words stopped right there. I laid the book down and ate two gummy worms and read those words again.

Knock. Knock.

"Oh shit," I whispered. I wasn't expecting anyone. I set the book on the counter quietly and tiptoed towards the door. I took a look in the peephole and it was Elise. This girl kept losing her spare key. What was the point of giving her one? I opened the door.

"Hey girl, hey!!" Elise walks right in with food.

"You didn't tell me you were coming," I said.

"I just realized I had nothing to do tonight, and I wanted to eat bad," Elise said as she unpacked.

"So, I take it the boyfriend is an idiot and you need a minute," I inferred.

"Oh hush," Elise giggled.

I knew my friend. She was ready to unload about her boyfriend. She met him about four months ago and now that they were exclusive, the stupidity came out. Another reason why I kept Lucas at arm's reach. I didn't have time for relationship nonsense. I loved hearing about her nonsense though. The guy was cool when I met him but I ain't sleeping with him, so I didn't have to deal with the stupid parts.

Elise brought chicken biscuits, sweet biscuits, biscuits and gravy, some fries and jelly. I was glad I didn't stop and get food. She read my mind. It was a beautiful carb-filled night. I shut the door behind Elise as she took the food to the kitchen.

"What's this?" Elise asked as she picked up the book. The record scratched in my head. I forgot about that thing. I hesitated. I had no plans to tell Elise or Lucas about the book right now or at all really. This was a little test.

"I, umm, got that from Dr. Lynn's office." I watched her attentively. I didn't notice that I was moving closer to her.

"Are you okay?" she asked.

I had to play it off. "I was grabbing some water from the fridge," I said.

"Why did she give it to you?" Elise asked. She was feeling the detailed designs on the cover, but she hadn't opened it yet.

"Dr. Lynn said the book was given to her when she was younger, and she gave it to me. I thought it looked interesting," I explained. Elise looked at the front and back of the book. I kept watching. I wanted to see if she could see the words too.

She opened the book and flipped through the pages. I leaned in, hovering over her. I was still pretending to get water out of the fridge. I tried to see what the book looked like to her. She flipped through it backwards and said, "All I see is the word 'water.'"

"That's it!" I didn't mean to say that out loud.

"Yeah, was that in there when you got it?"

"Yeah." I took a deep breath, "I thought it was neat and ancient looking."

She examined the front, the back, and side and didn't see anything more. "It is neat," she said. "I see why you gravitated to it. You should use it for a journal." Elise sounded like Dr. Lynn.

Was I going crazy? Did I imagine all those words? Elise grabbed some food and headed to the couch. I grabbed the book and flipped through it quietly. The words were there. I flipped through the pages and the words were the same on every page except for the page I wrote "water" on. I closed the book to think. I wanted to show Elise but decided against it. I took the book into my room, put it under my mattress, and went back to have a normal night.

We ate and watched a new anime. During the long opening scenes, Elise filled me in on her boyfriend Charles. "Charlie," as she called him, was an interesting character. I thought my family was loud, but the random ass noises this dude made were on a whole different level. We laughed at his complaints about his roommates. I laughed at the stupid arguments they had. I guess when you spend a lot of time with a person, the little things were either tolerated or annoying. They picked annoying. I picked entertainment. I could tell they really loved each other though. He was a bit taller than her, brown skinned and chunky but it worked with his height. They have been dating for a few months now and it was getting serious.

I was happy to be with my bestie. Before I knew it, the clock said

11:14 pm. Elise was getting tired and decided to go home instead of spending the night. I understood the need to be in your own place, in your own bed. I would love for her to stay as a welcomed distraction, but I was ready to call it a night, too. I knew she worried about me and used the boyfriend as a convenient excuse to check on me. After the blackout, throughout the day, she checked to see how I felt, and if I had gone back to therapy. I lied about how I felt most days, but I told her I was still meeting with Dr. Lynn. Elise laughed at my concern that Dr. Lynn looked at me as a guinea pig. "I swear her eyes got so big when I talked about my blackouts and what could be the cause." I laughed.

I walked Elise to the door and gave her a hug. "We need an all-girls night," I said.

"I already messaged the group chat," she replied.

The minute I locked my door, I ran to my room and grabbed the book. Without any hesitation, I opened it back up. I flipped through the pages and the words appeared again. I started to convince myself that what Dr. Lynn said was true. The book only reveals itself to certain people. I needed to know more. I hadn't reached my edge yet.

I still couldn't find anything online about this type of magical book. There are myths with similar things but not exactly. The info I did find was about another fictional book that had a magic book. I did add a bunch of books to my reading list.

"Maybe I should try the library," I thought. I hadn't been to the library in years. Damn internet. I doubted I would find anything at the library, but I was trying to exhaust all options. I wrapped up my internet search for the day and planned to hit the library after work. I popped out to see if there was any foot traffic and everyone seemed settled in. I grabbed the book and my water bottle and headed to my private floor.

*Across the infinite timeline, I search for life
and light. Another chance, an endless loop to*

I knew this one by heart, I read it so much. I couldn't figure it out. I stared at the page for over 15 minutes. I had to do something else. I walked around the floor to think. My mind was blank. I started to rearrange the random pieces of office furniture to make a maze to the center, where I sit. "Across the infinite timeline" kept popping up in my mind. This was frustrating. I gathered my things and headed back upstairs for a bit. I had homework to finish before I had my appointment with Dr. Lynn tomorrow. A few journal entries. I doubted that she would believe these fake entries. I had to sprinkle a little truth in there. These two weeks were passing by slowly.

I loved the library when I was younger. I played terribly pixelated computer games for the hour they allowed. Then I would pull at least five books to check out. On occasion, my mom let my sisters and me check out movies from the library, too. She stopped that quickly because we were terrible at returning the movies on time. I bet I still owe something.

The library was a barren wasteland. The library was so busy when I was a kid. Granted that was the good old days of dial up and one computer designated for the entire family to use. Now, five-year-olds have their own tablets and cellphones. I was tempted to see if they had a kid's section. Even as a teenager, I went back to the kid's section for fun books and these two kid's computer games I have yet to beat.

I decided to search in an old school way. I brought a three-subject notebook and several pencils and two green pens and the book. I couldn't wait to dive back into the Dewey decimal system. Even if I didn't find anything, I was excited to be back in one of my favorite places. I wrote that piece of truth in my journal. "A safe space for me has always been the library. I neglected it, took it for granted. I was too eager to replace the library with technology. Damn you convenience :)," is what I would write. Be poetic with it.

I decided to start with a broad search and then narrow it down from there. I stood at the library's computer catalogue trying to figure out the easiest place to start. I typed in "mythological objects," "fables and folklore," "magic book that reveals itself." Simple enough. Once I hit enter, I got over 3,000 results. I picked a few titles that stood out to me and wrote down their locations. Just like college, I skipped between the search pages to get a bit of variety.

Most of the tables outlining the bookshelves were empty. A few people were around as I looked for a table in a nice corner. The librarian was moving around with a squeaky cart, putting the books back. I was sad to see bare shelves around the library. The shelves used to overflow with books. Damned internet.

Unfortunately, the library had become a haven for the homeless. It was a warm place to escape the cold, and a cool place to get away from the heat. There was a working bathroom and access to the internet when it was needed. Hell, I would read when I didn't have anything to do. There was this one guy I thought was dead. I watched him for a good minute when I got upstairs. Most people would quickly glance as someone passed by or when a little noise was made but not this guy. His head was down like he was sleeping but I swear I never saw his chest or back inflate to show breathing. Nothing phased him. He was at the table closest to the elevator and the ping didn't disturb him.

He had three layers of jackets on, and his pants were a bit torn, discolored, and dirty. His shoes were rough, too. I was happy he was able to find the time to rest. I shrugged it off and walked to an empty table in the back. After I set my table, I started searching for the books on my list. I was happy to be in the stacks. There were so many books in various conditions. The smell of new and old paper brought a pleasant meeting. I explored the shelves like I did at Dr. Lynn's office.

I could tell that some of the books I pulled were older because the laminated place card had that yellow tint to it. The cover of an African folklore book was green with some tears on the binding, exposing the cardboard and the thread. The pages had a yellow tint and as I thumbed through the pages, I prayed the brownish-green dried spots on some of them were not dried boogers. I pulled about four books to start with and went back to my table.

As I sat down, I pulled out my headphones to play some music to drown out the silence, my snacks, and my hand sanitizer. I laid out all four books in front of me and put my notebook in the center. I opened the book to the table of contents. I was excited to see a story I read as a child. It was about two daughters, one kind and one mean, who were introduced to a prince to marry. There were other stories about Anansi the Spider, Oya, and parables about life lessons. Nothing about a magical book.

I put that book aside and looked through the mythical objects and mythical creatures book. It was like a glossary. A big ass glossary. I continued to flip through the pages, waiting for something to stand out to me. This was going to take me forever. This book listed all objects and creatures across all mythology. I readjusted myself in my seat and started skimming through. I skimmed until something jumped out at me. But the only things that did had nothing to do with the damn book.

I put four books back and grabbed four more. I learned about a bunch of new things in folklore and mythology but found nothing about a magical book. I was at a dead end but that wasn't a surprise. I assumed I would leave empty handed. I put all the books back on their spot on the shelf and headed to the exit.

"I guess I gotta ask Dr. Lynn," I conceded. I hoped to avoid bringing this up, but any information would help. The book was a mystery that only I could see. I had to find a way to ease the book into the conversation.

I needed the right moment. One moment where she wouldn't ask questions.

An Open Door

My appointment started normally. The usual "how are you," "how was work," and "have you journaled" questions were asked. She should be able to predict my answers to those questions by now. They were always the same. "I'm good." "Work fucking sucks." She was surprised when I showed her a few journal entries.

"So, are you ready for your leave?" Dr. Lynn asked.

"Duh," I replied.

"Through your journaling, have you identified any more of your triggers?"

"No, ma'am. I guess it helped that I finished all my work a while ago. No phones and no emails. I still dealt with stupidity but it's tolerable for now."

"Have you felt like you were headed into darkness again? Like with Sasha or the blackout that started all this," she asked.

"Nope. Apparently, the less work I have the better I feel. So, there is my trigger. That last gray cubicle on the left."

"Well, if you don't do the work, like actually journal in real time, that trigger will remain when you get back in six months."

"So, I need to carry around my notebook at all times?"

"You can write notes in your cell phone," she giggled. I had to concede there. I got up and walked to the bookshelf like normal. I hoped it would help change the subject so I could mention the book. Nothing came to mind.

"I hope the rest of this week and next week go by fast," I said.

"It will. But the more you anticipate the start date, the longer it will feel."

"Yeah, and the six months will fly by," I replied. That was how each weekend and holiday felt. It was here for two hours. I blinked and it was Monday morning.

"Besides a nice, long trip to the beach, did you make any other plans?"

"I wanted to catch up on some reading. I may need another book from your shelf." I hoped she would respond in a way that gave me an in.

"Of course," she replied. Didn't give me much but I worked it out in my head.

"Oh, that reminds me." I shuffled through my bag. I didn't use it as a journal." I handed her the book.

"Keep it. It is your book now. I take it nothing was revealed to you either," she joked.

"Of course not," I laughed. "Did your teacher tell you anything else about the book? It is mysterious." I kept telling myself to ease into the conversation. I couldn't seem too eager or let on that I saw something written in the book.

"He didn't say much. He was told about the book when he found it."

"Where did he find it?"

"I can't remember. It was so long ago. He said the book had a seductive drumming when he found it. He liked to embellish his stories a bit," she said.

"He heard drumming?" He heard it, too. I couldn't believe it. I didn't imagine it. I pushed a little more. "Did the book reveal itself to him?"

I leaned in.

"No," she said. "Nothing was written inside the book. Dr. Yeboah was disappointed."

"Did he tell you anything else about the book?"

"Not that I can remember. You seem interested in the book."

That was my signal to back off. "I like a good mystery. This is a good mystery."

"It appears so," Dr. Lynn said. She then wrote down some notes. I didn't like that. I wanted to know if I gave something away to her. She was one of the smartest people I was around. Did I seem too eager?

We went about our session as usual. In the end, I was left with more questions than answers.

Reincarnation! I wrote it down immediately. The purple pen bled on the page as the pages started to flip rapidly. Two days on that one! I didn't freak out this time. I held the book tight as the pages flipped. I watched the book closely, but it was so fast I couldn't keep up. Once the book was still all I saw was what I wrote. I set a timer on my phone to see how long it took for new words, if any, to appear. I closed the book but kept the timer going and took the stairs to give me more time. "Alright book, don't make me walk all 11 floors," I asked. I stopped to check the book on the stairs to avoid the door cameras. It was the eighth floor and two deaths later that new words showed on the other pages. The "water" and "reincarnation" pages remained blank.

I closed the book and left the stairwell to take the elevator the rest of the way. I went back to my desk, made sure no one needed me and read the book.

> *Reason's veil torn, a fractured state, a puzzle*
> *of illusions, a relentless debate. A precarious*
> *line in this realm, I'm what you find. In a*
> *twisted maze, I dance to a chaotic rhythm,*

a wild trance. A turbulent sea of strange
sensation. I lurk in the shadows with a
distorted grin. An unraveling world within.
I whisper madness without ceasing.

I read it a few more times and shut the book. The timer had seven minutes between the correct answer and the next words were written. I grabbed a few new files from my team to work on while I thought of an answer. I couldn't sit and do nothing. I was in the back but that doesn't mean I was not being watched. By the end of the day, I almost cleared another co-worker's files, but still no answer. The next few days were going to suck. It is already dragging.

I was on a roll with the riddles, and they kept me busy for the past few days. I didn't realize it was my last day in this fucking office!! Insanity had me stuck. I went to bed frustrated about that riddle. In the middle of the night, I jumped up with the answer. I rushed out of bed, stumbled over my twisted socks, and grabbed the book tucked under my mattress. I wrote down Insanity. Once I got that one, I was on a roll.

By the gentle swish of the wind, I travel from
one ear to the next. A lamp and a coin will bring
you closer, but the odds can be spun, transformed
or cruel. With my invisible hand I can change
your direction. You will try and flee but never
will outrun me.

Destiny! Bam!

My presence is a reminder that no one is free.
I am spilled for very little and required for a
conqueror. Anger, Greed, and Hatred try to follow
me under the name of sacrifice. I stain the gras,

and air with a crimson river. Conflict, strife, and
dread feed me. What makes this interesting? I am
the cost for "freedom."

Bloodshed! Hell yes!

Silent in the corner and in dark spaces, I am stealth
and graceful. My home is both wide and thin and
inconvenient to those who cross my path. I have silent
feet and many. Of silk I spin and in the sun I glow.
I scheme and crawl towards my purpose. Thin but
unbreakable, I trap my prey with lethal precision.
I am a hunter and patiently I wait for you.

Spider! Boom!

The one I was stuck on was the hardest one. Nothing was happening at my desk, so I wandered to say my temporary goodbyes. I wasn't sure who would still be here when or if I came back. After talking to Wes for a few minutes, I went downstairs to my floor. I finished the maze of leftover office desks and cabinets. I got good at picking the locks of the office doors. There were so many how-to videos online for some things that shouldn't be taught, like picking a lock. But there was one office that refused to open. I had to conquer that door before the end of the day.

I got comfortable in the center of my maze and focused on this riddle. I found myself enticed by these riddles. No matter how many days it took, I refused to pull out my phone and search. It didn't seem fair or fun. I wanted to enjoy the ride I was on. Then again, this shit could all be in my head and my job finally broke me.

I stand tall but never walk. You see me every day,
but I never talk. A barrier that keeps secrets, big
and small. I stand before you and behind you.

"With me every day," I thought. This one was tricky. I tried to envision all those things happening at once, but nothing fit. I tucked the pen behind my ear, pulled my twists back in a scrunchie, grabbed my book, and took a walk. I always kept the book with me now. I had it in my crossbody bag and never took it off. Wes asked why I was walking around with my bag all day. I hadn't thought about an explanation when someone asked. "Oh, I forgot I still had it on," I said. When anyone asked, that was all I said.

I paced the floor twice and couldn't solve the riddle. I laid the book down and tried to clear my head. I walked my maze, danced like a ballerina, screamed into my forearm. I cleared my mind as much as I could. "Focus, Elle," I said. The "stay focus" pep talk wasn't working. I decided to focus on the other mystery on this floor: that locked office. I grabbed the book and the lock tools tucked into a cabinet here and headed to the door.

I watched another video about picking locks. This wasn't as easy as they made it look. I also hoped this search wasn't putting me on a watch list. While pieces were getting bent under my frustration, I recited the riddle from memory.

"I am in front of you and behind you."

"Literal and metaphorical. Shit!" I broke a piece. I used my phone light to see if a piece broke off in the lock. "Oh good," I sighed. I went back to picking and reciting. I heard the click of the lock and as I opened the door it hit me. I grabbed the book and wrote down my answer: An open door!

The Gate

"Owww, shit," I grunted.

I hit my chest on the floor. I lifted myself up slowly rubbing my chest on the way up. Once I got to my feet, I tried to dust myself off. "How did I fall through that door?" I wondered. I looked around and realized I wasn't in the office. I was standing on an onyx marble floor. My surroundings glowed purple and red from the fire that made up the walls. I looked around and that was all in this big ass room. I didn't see the door, the ugly carpet, the windows, nothing of the office.

My breathing became rapid and short. The fear shot through my body and tears came to my eyes. I didn't know where I was or how I got here. I ran in circles. There was no way out. I dropped to the floor, scared and out of breath. I pulled my knees to my chest and buried my face. "Where am I?" I cried.

Suddenly, I heard footsteps as a hallway appeared to my right. I had no idea where I was, what this was, or where to hide. I retreated to the corner beside the hallway. I hoped whatever was coming would see nothing in front of them and leave. I hid my face behind my knees and tried to make myself as small as possible facing the corner.

"What is this?" the first voice asked. The footsteps were getting closer.

"A visitor after all these years?" the second voice asked. There were two people. I did not realize there was more than one set of footsteps.

"How did she get here?" the second voice asked. The voice was louder. They were already in the room. "Please don't see me," I prayed.

They never touched me, but I knew they were looking at me. They didn't say anything. I was trembling. My body was going numb trying to stay still. After a few seconds of silence, the first voice spoke.

"Can you hear me, child?" I had a quick decision to make. Should I answer or keep quiet? I waited in silence. So did they.

"Where am I?" I whispered. My voice was shaky, and fear rushed through my veins. I spoke. Why the fuck did I do that? The voices speaking to me could be Lucifer, or Peter or one of the other apostles. How would I know? I sealed my fate with three words.

"Oh," voice one began, "you do not know."

"Do you know how you got here?" voice two asked.

"No," I said. I did not dare raise my head or get up. I still did not know who I was talking to, and I was scared to look. It was too late to regret my decision to talk.

"Well human, I applaud you," voice two said. "Coming to this place is not easy. There aren't many keys out there."

"Keys?" I asked. I started to move slightly. Mostly because my butt was numb.

"You are at the gates into the Mythos," voice one informed me.

I had no idea what the Mythos was but I refused to open my eyes. I squeezed my eyes closed tightly the minute they started talking to me. It was starting to hurt but I had to endure until they left.

"Human?"

I could tell the difference now between the voices. Voice one was a raspy voice and a tenor. Voice two was high-pitched, but smoother.

"My dear, you shall faint if you constrict your body any tighter," voice one said.

My eyes sprung open without a second thought. How did they know? I didn't lift my head. If I didn't see their faces then I couldn't identify them and then there was no reason to kill me. Right? I heard them start walking away so I began to relax. I did not look in their direction.

"When you find that the floor is no longer comfortable, please follow us," they said together.

I waited until I felt they were far enough away before I moved. I released my tight hold on myself. I looked around as sneaky as possible on my left and my right side. This place was beautiful. The onyx floor glowed against the colorful flames. The edges of the wall and floor were gold and shiny. The ceiling shimmered with the light reflecting from the floor. I could see my reflection in the ceiling, but I looked like a brown wavy smudge. I lifted myself up, and man, I was holding myself too tight. I had tension just to bring my knees down.

"Has she moved yet?" I could hear the two voices in the distance.

"She has; however, she seems to be struggling a bit," voice one replied. I looked to either side and as far in front of me as I could, but I didn't see them. How did he know I was struggling?

"Hello?" I covered my mouth. Why the hell did I call out? Although, if they wanted to hurt me, they would have had the perfect opportunity earlier.

"Follow us, human," voice one said.

I stood still for a little while. The same pull I felt to find the book was happening now. Not one person in my inner circle would believe this. I barely believed it. I wasn't going to tell them anyway, but this was amazing.

I took one more look around before I headed toward the voices. Again, if this were a movie, I would be yelling "don't go down there," but logic was not a priority. I started walking down the hall. I wanted to reach out to the flames on the wall because they were so beautiful and enticing. I wasn't too far from the flames while walking but I couldn't feel the heat. I knew the flames were hot, but I couldn't tell by walking next to them. I slowed my pace just enough to take in where I was. I looked closer and saw that the embers danced. They flowed like a stream around jagged rock. I was not on Earth anymore. This place was magical. I was in another realm or something.

The onyx floor had gold lining that swirled where my feet landed as I walked. It was beautiful and hypnotizing. The patterns changed every time I stepped. I noticed the air was colorful, too. Dull and faint near the fire walls but vibrant and full towards the center of the hallway. I danced through that hallway, and I could stay there forever. I took my time. I would catch up to the voices eventually. I would have taken longer if I knew what was waiting for me at the end.

"You finally made it," voice two greeted. I was too busy watching my feet and the flower pattern that unraveled until I put my other foot down. It made me feel magical and powerful. The real Black girl magic. Right at my feet, I had the manifestation of the magic that Black girls and women pour out every single day. I took a few more steps because I knew this moment could not be taken from me.

I was stopped by voice one clearing his throat. "It's like magic. It's like magic. It's like magic," I kept repeating. I put one foot in front of the other, finding joy in every step. I even slipped into a light "waltz" if you wanted to call it that. I forgot that I was following something or someone I didn't know.

"Are you quite finished?" voice two asked. I stopped but kept my back to where the voices were. The joy was replaced by fear again. If I didn't focus, I could die in a magical place or realize I was hallucinating. "Don't do it, Elle," I whispered to myself. "Don't you fucking do it!"

I shouldn't turn around, but I did. "You fucking did it," I yelled to myself. I went from pretty patterns of gold in a daydream to a walking nightmare. I froze. My mouth flew open, and my body tightened up again.

"She is going to scream, brother," voice two warned. Voice one put up his hand to keep me from screaming but it didn't work. I let it all out. I only screamed like that one other time in my life. That was when I walked in on my parents. One of the worst memories I had was replaced with what I saw now.

I cried and slowly started to back away. I tried to grab something, but the hallway was empty. I was even grabbing at the fire, hoping something would help me fight this thing off. I felt like I was about to be eaten. Not being eaten was my priority.

"Remain calm, human," voice one whispered. Voice two was smiling awkwardly and that didn't help. The thing had fangs as teeth. Fucking daggers to eat me with! "We aren't going to hurt you. We are just taking you to the gate."

"You...have...two..."

"Faces," voice one said, completing my sentence. I could not help but point and then rub my eyes and then point some more.

"What are you?" I took more small steps backwards. I was preparing to run because I stood before something with two faces. I was so shocked about that, I barely noticed that this thing was well over 10 feet tall.

"We are the gatekeepers. Do not fear," voice one began. He sensed that I was ready to flee. I did not calm down even though he seemed genuine. "I, well we, are Janus." Voice two gave a little twirl of his wrist and extended it to me. "We guard the entrance to the Mythos." I gave him a quizzical look. Then he continued.

"The Mythos is home to all gods, goddesses, magical objects, and creatures. Long ago a part of reality, and now a part of myth and legend of fantasy," voice two said.

I put my left foot flat on the floor. I heard that name before. Janus was a god of gates and doorways. It was where the month of January came from. I was still freaked out because now I was taking everything in. A 10-foot-tall, blue, shifty eyes, dual-faced god was standing right before me. Something that I read about in mythology books was extending his hand to me.

I took it. "You fucking did it again," I yelled to myself. What the hell was I thinking?

My hand felt like an infant's hand inside their mother's hand. It was the same feeling I would get when I went to the beach to get away. I was so small when you considered the size of the ocean and what is unknown about it. I felt that way when I took Janus's hand.

"So, you are Janus? The god?" I allowed them to lead me. I tried to focus on the pattern of the floor as I followed Janus. My heart was racing, and I was trying to calm down. I noticed that they did not have any patterns under their feet. My heart started to race again. I wanted to scream but I had so many questions. I felt my mind was in a hurricane of thoughts. I was scared, fascinated, inquisitive, reluctant, defensive, and open all at the same time. I wasn't sure what would win -- my fear or my curiosity.

"We are the gatekeeper for the Mythos, as we were on Earth," voice one answers. He continued, "We guard the gate from anyone getting out or in. Except unicorns and the occasional magical item. Nothing else ever goes in or comes out. We rarely see a human at the gate. How long has it been?"

"Nearly 500 years, I believe," voice two answered.

I had so many questions that I did not know where to start. I was never shy about asking anything to anyone, but nothing came out of my mouth. It did not even register that Janus said "unicorns." My head was on the verge of exploding.

"How did you get here, human?" Voice one was looking at me attentively while voice two looked ahead.

"Ummmm......could you call me Elle?" I interjected. The way they said "human" felt weird. I'd rather they call me by my name. Both faces nodded.

"Elle," voice one said. "Such a strange name."

"Well, a two-faced god named Janus is a strange thing," I laughed nervously. They did not laugh with me. "But to answer your question, I was given this old book."

"You found a key?" voice two asked.

"I was given a book by my therapist, but it was blank," I began.

"This book was bare from all writing when you received it?" voice two asked.

"Yes. It was," I replied. "Well, it started that way. You see…"

"Elle," voice one interrupted, "please do not tell us further. We need you to listen carefully. Apparently, one of us failed on his duties." Voice one's eyes looked over at voice two.

"I told her. She didn't listen," voice two answered.

"Human, think back, did you get a strange premonition with the key? Did you hear something?"

I looked down to think. "Yeah, I heard 'keep it safe' or 'keep it secret'," I replied.

"See, I told you I told her," Voice two teased.

"Well, Elle, remember that. We are not sure who you will meet beyond the gate. Do not let them know about the key's form."

"Form," I asked.

"The key was a book. There is more than one key on Earth but only this one has been found. Beyond that gate, all know about keys on Earth, but none know that the keys come in different forms."

"Do you know?" I asked.

"Only on this one."

"Did you send the same message to the other human 500 years ago," I asked.

"Exactly," voice two replied. "Keep the key form a secret."

"Okay," I replied. They were scaring me more. "What would happen if someone knew?" I asked.

"A god walking among men again," voice one answered. "Not the best idea."

I had to give him that. The key would give anything beyond the gate an, "…open door," I said.

"Exactly," voice one said.

"Can I stay out here? When can I go home? Can I go home?"

"You are human, the Mythos will expel you. You do not belong here," voice two said.

"If you stay out here, we cannot say for sure what will happen. The last human knew about the key and how it worked. We are to recreate that path for your sake."

"How do you know he didn't just die in there?" I yelled.

"That is a risk we have to take," voice one said. They swiftly picked me up. I started kicking and screaming at the top of my lungs but no one heard me. I didn't come here on purpose like the last person. Janus was unphased by my protest, fear, and punching.

When we got to the gate, I was in awe. The shine off the gate caused me to shield my eyes. It was a jewel-covered gate with precious metals I probably never heard of.

"A gate meant to keep everyone in and everyone out," voice two said. I jumped when he started talking.

"Please! Put me down!" They chose to ignore me. As Janus walked closer to the gate, I could tell it was ice cold. It was like the temperature around it did not exist. I could see my breath when I exhaled. It was a beautiful gate, designed to keep everyone in and everyone out.

"If I enter," I began as I touched the larger-than-life diamonds, "I may not leave?"

"The Mythos was made for us, not humans. You won't be able to stay here as your existence doesn't rely on magic and devotion. That is all we will say. We are just the gatekeeper. We will not open the gate a second time," voice one stated. Their words did not put me at ease. I was crying as the gate opened.

The turn of the lock was very loud and echoed throughout the hall. The vibration even caused the floor to make patterns as if someone was walking on the floor. I heard Janus whispering something, but I couldn't make it out. It was definitely in Latin, and my 10 years of Spanish did not help. Maybe it was Greek.

At first, the light was too bright. I peeked through by opening my eyes little by little. Janus put me down and closed the gate behind me. Once my eyes adjusted to the light, I could see that the air was filled with colors and soft music. It was like being in a psychedelic elevator. I wasn't exactly sure what I was going to find. If Janus was any indication, then a lot of mythological, magical, fantasy gods, goddesses, and objects were going to cross my path. I was both scared and excited at the thought.

I looked back and saw Janus mouth the same thing. It was freaky seeing two faces do this at once. "Keep it safe." Their eyes glowed intensely. Both faces gave me a nod and shut the gate behind me. It sent a chill up my spine but reminded me to keep the book under wraps.

The Spider

There was nothing around the front of the gate. I was twirling around with the wisps of colors in the air. I guess this area was like a lobby. It was a big open space but there was no one around. I just kept walking and twirling. I felt light and my mind felt blank. It was a calming atmosphere. If my time was to be spent here, at least I know there is nothing around.

I jumped up because I realized that "nothing" also meant the gate. "It's gone," I said. The fear rushed back. I started looking around me. The room had to have a door. It had to be somewhere. I was in an endless loop. I couldn't tell where I started or where I stopped. "Shit, this isn't working."

I took off one of my shoes as a starting line. Felt up the wall again and nothing. I put my shoe back on and tried to think. Maybe I wasn't meant to go any further. This wasn't where I was meant to be. I will go home soon. I walked to the center of the room to sit. I'd rather not hug the wall while I slip into madness. "Owww, shit!" I yelled. I grabbed my left foot. "There is something here," I said. I slowly kicked my foot out and hit something solid. I slowly kicked out my right foot and nothing.

I slid to my left slowly tapping along to see where it ended. It took two taps. I bent down to the base and walked my hands up. I placed my hand on the top of the long rectangle. It was up to my waist. I tried to push it like a lever, and it would move. I pulled and nothing. I smacked the flat top with the palm of my hand. No buttons.

"Maybe there are more," I thought. I took off my shoe and placed my sock on the top of that one. I tapped and slid to the left. I hit the wall and didn't feel anything along the way. I went back to where my sock was and went right. I hit the wall. I walked back to my floating sock. "Okay, I went parallel. Let's try perpendicular," I said. I turned and went to the left. Wall. I jogged back to my sock and went right.

"Got it!" I found another post. I pushed, pulled, and tapped but nothing. I took off my other sock and put it on top. "This has to be in the shape of a 'T'." I walked to the center to go the other way when my foot pushed down below the floor. I jumped back and a door opened to my left. "Stay put Elle," I tell myself, "turn back". I didn't. I grabbed my shoes and ran through the door.

The hallway was exactly like the one I landed in. I felt relief to see something familiar, although it was magic. I walked cautiously as I went around corners. I swung first and was happy when I hit air. No invisible poles. The hallway was long. I wondered when the hallway would end, but I was not prepared for it to end. What would I meet on the other side?

I staggered to keep my balance as I walked and put my shoes one. I walked and walked until something told me to stop. Maybe it was the terrible shape I was in. I was out of breath. I looked around and realized there wasn't a hallway behind me.. "Where…is…the…hallway?" I huffed. Once I got my breathing under control, from a combination of fear and tiredness, I walked forward with my hands out. I was damn sure not walking backwards to the unknown that used to be a hallway. I felt the floors and the walls. I stopped when my hand reached the end of the wall. Slowly, a light turned on. It was dim and off in the distance at first but got bigger and brighter. I realized that I was standing at the top of three large stairs. Huge, giant stairs. Maybe something normal to a god like Janus. Beyond the stairs was this beautiful forest of lavender and lilac.

I had to plan my way down. I felt like an ant trying to climb the stairs of my apartment building. I took a few deep breaths and crawled to the edge. I turned around backwards to lower myself down. I tried to hold myself up by my arms for as long as I could, but I needed to hit the gym because I flopped onto the hard marble floor. I checked my body for broken bones or bruises, but I wasn't hurt. I was able to pop up. I walked to the edge of the next stair, ready to try again.

The ground beneath me had fallen buds. They were soft like the grass in the forest but more gentle because of the buds. The buds flew around my feet as the wind blew through. The wisteria trees were bright from the roots to the tops. The trees had wide trunks, big roots, and the tops could not be seen from the ground. There were small trees too but there were so many of them I couldn't see past the few trees in front of me. I walked around one tree, feeling the bark and breathing its air. I felt like I did when I needed to unplug from everything. When I couldn't get to the ocean, I found a forest or park to sit in. There was the sound of the wind swaying the trees, the squirrels running around, and silence was a big help. I took a deep breath in. The wisteria trees were bright. I kept my hand over my eyes to shield them. I was surrounded by fallen wisteria buds and still in awe of the purple glow of the air.

I walked around but had that feeling again. Something or someone was watching me. The trees were a good cover. I put my guard up. It had been way too easy for me to let my guard down here. I knew someone was watching me, but I didn't feel threatened. But that didn't mean I needed to be an idiot. I kept walking but watching too.

"I have been watching you."

"Who said that?" My voice was shivering and deep. I remained still but nearly turned my head 360 degrees to see who was talking to me. The voice had an accent that was bold and seductive. I didn't see anything immediately around me.

"Where are you?" I did not hear any brush of the buds on the ground, a crack of a branch or bark, and no gust of wind. Suddenly, I felt something hovering over me. A few feet behind me it looked brighter. It was the same to my sides and in front of me. However, it was above me that was dark. "You are above me, aren't you?" My voice began to shake. The pressure I felt was terrifying. I thought it was just my imagination at first.

"It is a curious thing to see one of you here. The last time was half a millennium ago." The shadow moved slightly but I refused to look up.

"Janus mentioned another person 500 years ago." I wanted the voice to keep talking so I could know where he was. I started to move with the shadow. Soon we were walking through the forest side by side. The only thing that could help me escape was the cover of these trees. "Who are you?" I asked.

"How did you get here, human?" I was called human by Janus too, but the way it said "human" felt ultra degrading – offensive, too. He might as well call me "nigger" with a hard "er" at this point.

"Could you call me Elle?" I asked. I got zero confirmation.

"Elle, that is a unique name," the voice said. The accent was African, but I couldn't figure out anything else.

"What is your name?" I asked.

"You do not know," he said. The pressure shifted more to my right side. "You did not intend on being here?"

"You first. You haven't answered my question," I replied.

"You are a smart one, too. I will give you a hint, human." The shadow started to get smaller and soon I noticed the light coming through gaps in the shadow. I was surrounded by eight legs. I knew who it was immediately.

"How did you get here?"

"I think you already know," I said.

"You are very smart," he said. "You found a key."

"I did," I replied. I remembered that Janus told me to keep the form a secret.

At that moment, the pressure subsided from above me. The purple colors began to blend. He was no longer above me, but to my right. A spider. Not just any spider, Anansi the Spider. I had books about him throughout my childhood and on my bookshelf in my apartment. Anansi was the West African version of Loki or vice versa (Africa was probably first). Very powerful but also cunning, intelligent, a trickster, and ruthless. I remember the children's books my mom had about Anansi but those were always playful. They made Anansi more of a jester than the cunning trickster he was.

He stood taller than Janus and more intimidating. Unlike Janus, he did not try to shush me or reassure me that I had nothing to fear. He let me take everything in. I wanted to scream, but I didn't. Strangely enough, I remained silent. He was beautiful. He was black and purple with jewels decorating his eight legs. There were gold lines throughout his body like veins. Now the five eyes were scary, but they had flakes of gold in them as well.

"You are huge," I managed to say as my whole body quivered in fear and awe.

"That is why it was so dark. You may have noticed that I reduced my size," he relished. Huge to him seemed like a welcome compliment. I bet my fear was a compliment too.

"How are you able to move between the trees? You are as wide as they are." I didn't know how, but I was being incredibly logical even though I was scared. He quickly started to move, and I screamed unintentionally. He was fast, agile, and could reduce his size within seconds to move between the trees. He scurried up to a branch so high I could barely see. Then he lowered himself down like he was about to weave a web.

"I feel offended that you did not seek me out as the last human did," Anansi said. "That is most interesting."

"What happened to that person?"

"Humans still have a bit of magic, which is quite interesting." He was rotating on his web. I didn't like the way he was saying "interesting" either. He hummed as he spun around. Suddenly, his rotation stopped. I was looking at the back of a super large spider with a golden "yellow brick road" from the top of his head to the "butt."

"The human before you. I heard about him in Pangaea."

"Like actual Pangaea?" I asked. He turned around and all five eyes were staring at me. I wasn't dumb. I loved history and Pangaea existed long before 500 years ago. I took a few steps back because I wasn't sure if that look was studying me or saying "bitch, I'll eat you!" I wouldn't give him the chance to respond. I should ask another question. "How did you know about the key?"

He was silent for a few seconds. He dropped back onto the ground and reduced his size. He was still a big ass spider, but a little less intimidating. "If you listen to the rumors, there are several keys. I believe there is only one."

"Why do you think that?" I was interested in his theory. I let my guard down again. It was that easy. He didn't say anything, so I changed the subject. "How did you get here? How do you even exist?"

"Climb on." He lowered his legs for me to climb on. I hesitated for a moment. I wasn't sure where he would take me. I decided to climb on to him because I wasn't sure if anything bigger than him was waiting beyond the Wisteria trees. I made six attempts to climb on before finally succeeding. I did not need the five-eyed eye roll, but my upper body needed some work. Where was that "human magic" when I needed it?

"Human, we once lived on Earth, co-existing to a degree. Human beliefs were powerful and created us and our abilities." I tried to steady myself on a giant ass spider as Anansi told the story. "Of course, God was not pleased but it was the free will that kept humans creating. That belief was the strongest before Christ. After His death, we gods, goddesses, creatures, and objects still existed. God had to put us somewhere. Humans no longer believed. However, that did not mean we lost our power, but we could not stay upon the Earth."

"So, God put you here," I interrupted.

"Indeed. No one in and no one out."

"But I'm here and Janus said certain creatures and objects are always coming and going."

"Human magic still exists. Small things like unicorns and relics are less powerful than a 20-foot-tall god on Mt. Olympus or a 40-foot-tall deity inspiring the Mayans. Humans believe in certain things enough and they walk the Earth, but once that belief subsides, back to the front gates. A wonderful feature of God. He could not stop your free will, but He will have a plan for the consequences." Anansi had spelled out everything about the Mythos. "Each god has their own space. This is mine." My brain was going to explode with all the information.

"Where did you find this key?" Anansi asked. Keep the form a secret.

"I found it," I said, which wasn't a lie. "It was in this old chest."

"Most interesting, human," he said.

"Could you call me Elle, please? The way you say 'human' is off to me," I said.

"My apologies," he said. I knew he didn't mean it. I could feel it. I was looking around at the new area I was in. Anansi carried me in silence. At first, I did not want to break the silence, but I was curious about this area.

"Umm, Anansi," I whispered, "where are we?"

"My space," he said. Anansi stopped suddenly. I lost my balance and fell off. I stopped myself from hitting the ground by grabbing onto one of his legs. I didn't know I had such great reflexes and I never thought I would be dangling from a spider's leg, but there I was. I was about four stories above the ground. I reached with my left hand to hang on with both hands. This was hard because my upper body strength was atrocious. I hung on with all my strength. I refused to die now.

Anansi let me hang there for a while. It was as if he didn't notice me at all. I didn't say anything at first, but my grip was beginning to slip.

"Anansi," I yelled. He chuckled a bit, causing his whole body to vibrate, but lowered himself at the same time. By the time I couldn't hold on anymore, I wasn't too far from the ground. "Ahh!" I looked at my hand and it was cut. I grabbed the ends of my shirt to stop the bleeding.

"Remove your garment, human. Injuries do not last long here." He didn't seem very concerned that the hair on his body was sharp enough to cut my skin.

"My name is Elle," I snapped. I removed my shirt. I thought I imagined the cut because my hand was fine. Then I saw the bloodstain at the bottom of my shirt. Anansi, then, shrunk himself down to the size of a tarantula and crawled onto my shoulder. I was too preoccupied with my sudden healing to even notice him crawling up my arm.

"Are you ready human?" he asked. I jumped because even as a small spider his voice was bold and loud. I caught my breath.

"When did you get up there and why are you small?! My hand healed on its own!"

"Is this not better than my actual size?"

"I don't know what would be better in this situation. For all I know this is a dream." Even if I were dreaming, it would never feel that real.

I took a walk into the center of Anansi's space. I walked over to the first thing that caught my eye. The box was made entirely of stone. It was floating in midair in its own section. Each relic was within its own "window" to look at. The stone of the box looked like those nice white, smooth stones you find occasionally in large bodies of water. Like a large flat pearl, it had beautiful lines and swirls of black, gold, silver, green, and blue. I wanted to reach out and touch it, but a transparent wall kept me from doing that. When I touched the wall, it wiggled and hummed. So, the kid in me kept touching it. It was so cool and otherworldly. I only stopped because I could hear Anansi sigh. A spider sighed in my ear. I put that in the "never thought that would happen" pile.

"Is this…Pandora's box?" I asked Anansi. Even in this smaller form, Anansi was a beautiful spider. As a kid, I pictured a typical plain black spider. His amethyst hue mixed with the black of his body shined.

The gold lining was hypnotizing. His eight legs shined with gems like rubies and emeralds. No rough edge in sight. He glowed!

"You continue to surprise me, Elle." Oh, now he says my name and it sounded sarcastic. I couldn't win.

"I used my context clues and common sense. School was good for something, I guess. A random box in a room full of floating objects and it was the first thing that caught my attention. I was drawn to it. Who wouldn't assume it was Pandora's box?"

"That is the infamous box. I only received it days ago. It was easy."

"What do you mean?" I asked.

"I've been around gods and goddesses too long. They embraced our banishment here. I will never embrace it. The gods and goddesses are a boring sport for me. They never seem to change. That is why obtaining any of these objects has been easy for me."

I felt his anger at his current situation. I wondered how long someone could be disgruntled, because it has been over 2000 years. Could I stay that angry and frustrated for that long? Well, good thing I was mortal.

Anansi felt like I did. We were stuck in the same routine day in and day out. "The gods' personalities are set in stone. Predictable. I miss the unpredictability of humans. They fascinate me and anger me all at once," he said. I agreed in my mind but again the way he said humans, it felt like I shouldn't.

"Is the mountainous spider your true form? I remember in my childhood stories you could change forms. It's obvious that your ability to do so is true because you can change your size." I needed him to forget his anger towards humans quickly.

"I prefer the spider form. I can change, but this form is superior and stunning." I couldn't argue with that.

"Anansi," I said softly. "How do I get home?"

"You do not belong here. The Mythos should be expelling you soon."

"How soon is soon?" I didn't know how much time had passed

since I arrived. I didn't know how time worked here. Anansi did not answer me right away. He rode my shoulder as I found a place to sit.

"Why did you come here?"

"It was unintentional. I dug up some old stuff and came by an old key. I tried it on the chest and boom, onyx floor." I made up this story as I went.

"This was not your plan?" he asked.

"No, it wasn't. I just thought it was an old key to some box sitting around," I said. If I made the lie realistic, I could sell it.

"A random chance with a magic key. That is most interesting," Anansi said.

"I bet I'm supposed to be at work right now. How long have I been here?" I asked.

"In our time, nearly two days," he said.

"Oh shit, how long is it in my time?" I yelled.

"How would I know, human? I have been locked away in this prison for millennia."

"Oh shit, this is gonna be bad," I replied.

"Do not worry, Elle. You will be gone soon. I assure you our time is different than time on Earth. Do you feel like two days have passed?"

"No," I realized.

"Then sit," Anansi said. His voice was still powerful even in tarantula size.

"This visit wasn't intentional, Elle?" Anansi asked again. I told him "no" which technically wasn't a lie. Did I think riddles from a magical book would take me to another realm? Hell no! Did I know it was a magical book though? No. Do I believe I lost my damn mind? Yes! I either had to accept that something magical happened or realize I had lost my sanity. I chose to accept it.

I learned a lot about the Mythos from Anansi. He would ask me a question about Earth now and I asked him a question about anything. He has cosmic knowledge. I let my guard down. Again.

After what seemed like hours, I fell asleep against a big tree.

I woke up to one of Anansi's legs tapping me. "Oh geez," I flailed. It was a giant spider leg. No one would wake up normally to that.

"It is time to go, Elle," Anansi said. He was back to his giant size. Once I remembered where I was, I looked around and saw my legs were gone.

"What do I do?" I waved my arms trying to figure out what to do. I wasn't sure when it would happen or how, but I was super thankful it was happening. It didn't make the disappearing body less scary.

Within seconds, I couldn't see the lower half of my body. Anansi took my hand and whispered something, but I couldn't understand it or really hear him. Then I felt a sharp pain. As Anansi faded, I could see faded blue and white colors. Then a sharp pain on my left arm. The last thing I saw of the Mythos was Anansi's five eyes and a drop of blood from his fang.

Not Alone

I stood in the open doorway of the office I had just opened. I looked around at my surroundings and touched the door frame to make sure it was real. I went to the closest window and saw the parking lot was full. "Was it all a dream?" I whispered. "No, it felt too real." I touched my body just in case some random body part fell off. "Aahh!" My left arm was bleeding. I didn't realize that I scratched myself. I grabbed everything off the floor and rushed upstairs. There was a first aid kit there. I wasn't bleeding too bad, but I tried to keep it covered until I could clean myself up.

I wiped the cut clean and put a few big Band-Aids on it. I went back to my desk and remained seated for the rest of the day. I was hesitant to do anything. I felt unsure of where I was and what I was seeing. I was gone for about 20 minutes when I checked my phone. I took another 10 minutes in the bathroom. It was my last day at work, and I should just be quiet and still for the rest of the day.

It was 5:30 pm and I was free! I should have been the first one out the door, but I waited. I wanted a quiet, no traffic jam ride home. I looked forward to a stress-free weekend that Dr. Lynn ordered and some rest. I was free for the next 6 months.

The building, especially on a Friday, cleared out quickly. No one was working extra hours on right before the weekend started, no matter how much they "loved" their job. Even the cleaning crew was on the floor early. I grabbed my bag and headed back to the third floor. My maze was how I left it. The floor had the same layout. Nothing was different. I opened the door that took me to the Mythos but I saw nothing. I opened every single door on that floor and stood in the opening. I was never transported anywhere but into an empty office.

I saw nothing. I reached my hand out, but I didn't transport anywhere. "It wasn't real," I affirmed. I sighed in disappointment. I opened my book and saw my last answer but nothing else appeared on the pages. Only my handwriting was on the pages. I decided to leave the book here and unplug from everything for the first two weeks. I could always come back and get it. I put the book in a cabinet and locked it with the key left in the keyhole.

Oh, freedom! Welcome back!

My body was sore for the whole weekend. I ate and slept for those two days. I was always hungry. I didn't have the energy to do anything else. I ordered delivery because I didn't feel like cooking. The soreness in my body stuck around the whole weekend. On Monday, I start my two-week vacation. I couldn't afford two weeks visiting my mother, let alone go to the beach. It was a staycation. I booked a massage with a coupon I found. I had a few dates with Lucas and my friends. I wanted to have fun. I wasn't going to let a little soreness spoil my schedule. The weekend I would rest up and be normal by Monday.

My massage was on Wednesday. "I should make another one," I thought to myself. If the soreness wouldn't go away, I would go back sooner. I thought maybe a little exercise would help. It was a nice day and with the amount I've been eating, I could use a walk. My apartment had a greenway by it. I put on my work-out clothes and went for a walk. I had my music playing loud in my headphones. When no one was around, I pictured myself in a music video. I kept walking and dancing. I stopped at the tunnel to go under the highway. "I walked further than I thought," I said to myself. I didn't think I was gone that long.

I walked five miles within an hour when it used to take me 30 minutes to lightly jog one mile. I had to check my phone and smartwatch to make sure the time was right. Last week if I wanted to walk this far, I would just drive. Something was different about me. I was always hungry, always tired, and curious about things that I normally wouldn't care about. My senses were off. I hunted through my entire apartment looking for something. I don't remember what I was looking for. Everything was a little off.

I walked back home, baffled at my speed. My mind was racing and then confusion set in. I was happy to see the blue-gray door that led into my apartment. I needed a shower to relax because I didn't know how long I could keep my face scrunched up and my lips pressed thin. My brain was supposed to be on holiday. Instead, I was eating like two linebackers and walking exceptionally fast. I didn't need another mystery to solve. I didn't want one. I wanted to be stress and mystery free for a while.

"Human, relax your body."

I fumbled my keys. I was surprised at the voice I heard. I looked all around me and saw nothing. I knew that voice, but there was no way. It was all a dream.

"Why are you so tense?" I fumbled my keys again.

"Anansi?" My hands were trembling as I tried to open my door. I slowly opened the door to my apartment. I peeked in like it wasn't my house I was about to enter for the first time..

"Anansi, are you here?" I had no idea why I was whispering.

"I have been here since you returned but woke up only recently."

"What? How?!" He couldn't be anywhere in my apartment. No way I missed a 20-foot spider in my car or walking into my home. I would have felt his presence like before. Right? Was I dreaming again? I must have come home an hour or so ago and fell asleep on the couch. That was a more reasonable explanation than a god in my home. Was I losing my mind?

"You are as sane as some. I left the Mythos when you did." He answered. He was talking to me like this was a normal day. Why did he pop up now? I was "at" the Mythos on Friday. It was Tuesday.

"I thought you couldn't leave the Mythos. How did you get here?"

"A spell, human. I waited centuries to try it out. I missed my opportunity once. When you arrived, I could not resist," he replied.

"Is that what you said as I was leaving?" Everything replayed in my mind. I didn't know what he said but I guess that was on purpose. "Oh! The blood? Did you cut my arm?"

"I had to have an opening."

"An opening? What does that mean? Where are you?" I was looking around my apartment for a blinged out spider. I turned on all the lights and peeped around each corner, looking for him.

"I am up here, human," he said.

"The ceiling! Of course," I screamed. Idiot! I did not even think to look up. People were not meant to have their necks arched that long. My neck cracked immediately. I looked at every inch of my ceiling but saw nothing. Besides changing his size, was he able to be camouflaged, too?

"Ok, I give up! Up where?" I asked. I lowered my head and rubbed my strained neck muscles. Anansi sighed. I knew that sigh. I did it at work plenty of times. I knew I wasn't thinking with a full deck at that moment. There was a damn god talking to me from somewhere in my apartment. How rational would anyone be in that moment? It was all a dream a few minutes ago. Now, it was reality.

"I am in your mind, human. The spell worked. However, I am a god that is not able to walk on Earth anymore. The spell merges my body with yours. A vessel, I would say."

"Oh no! Oh no! It's happened." I grabbed my hair and paced back and forth. "I have officially lost my mind. I am going to be in a white padded room taking seven pills a day in no time. A vessel? That is shit you see on television or in movies." I had to get a grip and quickly.

"Human," he began.

"I told you to call me Elle!"

"Elle," he relented. "I am here, and I can prove it."

"How?" I snapped. I threw myself on the floor.

"Have you not noticed a difference within you?" he asked

I sat up and thought about it. I realized I was different. The appetite, the spikes in energy, the heightened senses, the need to sleep longer, and my ability to walk super-fast. "You caused all the hunger and stuff?"

"Yes. Your body is getting used to me and the power I have. You are not quite there yet, but you will be."

"Is my body going to explode if I can't withstand your power?" I watched enough movies and anime. The possibility of exploding was a side effect for being a vessel. Never saw my life being stranger than fiction, but hell, here I was. A god riding shotgun.

"You will need to train but so far you have been fine. I have stayed dormant to get used to you as well. You have the most interesting thoughts."

"Hey! Stay out of there." I was reeling for the moment. This wasn't real. Training? Will I explode? Was I imagining all these things? Anansi wasn't making any sense to me. I never agreed for him to be here. I started to shake and tilted my head. It worked when there was water in my ear; a god should come out, too. Again, I was not thinking rationally at all.

"Stop doing that," he said.

"Anansi, get out," I demanded.

"I cannot," he replied. "I am part of you now."

"I…I…" I started to cry. I was scared. "Why did you do this? Why are you here?"

"Please calm down, Elle. I am not meant to be locked away. I want to walk the Earth again."

"It's as simple as that, huh?" I asked. The tears wouldn't stop.

"Very simple," he replied. "Elle, can you tell me why you went to the Mythos?"

I paused. I didn't know that was where I was going. This was all the book's fault. Magic officially sucks.

"I don't know," I stuttered. "I didn't know I was opening a door to gods and goddesses of myths and legends."

"Humans are interesting and flawed creatures. They are not predictable like gods and goddesses. Humans created our personalities and there were only a few that will go against their programming. It is boring, Elle. My prison. My talents were wasted there. I saw an opportunity and I took it."

"You could have asked. I would have said 'no,' but still," I said.

"Why would you say no to being superhuman?" he asked.

"What do you mean superhuman?" This was all a work of fiction. A childhood dream to have powers. Super beings were myths.

"This is not fiction," he replied.

"Stop reading my mind," I snapped.

"I will do my best. This spell has never been used before. I would have stayed hidden a little while longer, but your body was strained today, and it affected me as well. I do not like that, Elle."

"Well, I would consider apologizing, but I did not know I was hosting someone else in my body. I feel violated." No matter how I felt, whether I was happy, sad, mad, high, drunk, or flirty, I found a way to be sarcastic. "Seriously, what the hell?"

"I still feel doubt within you," Anansi said. I growled at him through my teeth. "Pardon me, Elle. Do you doubt or mistrust yourself often? You are not imagining anything at the present time. This is real. Strange, but real. From what I can see, you do have an overactive imagination at times."

"You can really see everything." I was mad that he could read my mind. It felt like a violation. I essentially had no privacy. I didn't know what was happening. I... can't...breathe.

"Calm down! Breathe," Anansi instructed. My chest was tightening. The room was spinning, and the walls were closing in.

"Let's go outside, Elle."

I crawled towards my front door while gasping for air. I'd never had a panic attack before. I was unsure what a panic attack felt like. I hope it's not like this for people that do suffer from them on a regular basis.

I opened the door and stumbled away from the apartment building so I could avoid anyone who may try and help. Their "help" would get me to an institution quickly.

"Why were you panicking ma'am," they would ask.

"Oh, a 20-foot-tall god named Anansi lives in my body. Oh, and doctor, his true form is a spider with gold and gems decorating his body." Absolutely not.

My legs felt like jelly. I couldn't walk straight but I was able to reach a bench on the greenway behind the apartment. My breathing slowly returned to normal. It was a nice night out and the crisp air smelled sweet. I was surprised how clear the stars were in the sky. I only saw stars when I visited extended family in the country. The stars were bright in the sky, and I could see so many of them. I stared at them, trying to find different constellations like I did with popcorn ceilings. It was calming.

"Beautiful, isn't it?"

"Oh shit! Anansi!" I forgot he was there. So much for my calm, tranquil feeling. "It is beautiful. The sky is never that clear."

"And why not?" he asked. I wasn't sure if he was serious or not.

"Too much light now. Light pollution is what they call it. I bet the sky was beautiful when you were on Earth," I answered. It made me sad to think about what the Earth looked like when there weren't billions of people. Hell, thanks to colonizers, we barely have any information of what America was like when it was just the Native Americans.

"The stars were brighter. I could see them dance at times," he replied.

"Oh, I am so jealous. Dancing stars." I looked harder just to see if these stars would dance. They looked closer, but they didn't dance.

"Feel better? You feel warmer," Anansi assured.

"I do."

"Let's take a walk."

I hadn't fully accepted the thought that I had a god within me, but I wanted more time outside. A walk seemed like a good idea. I walked

144

away from the apartment complex and towards the main road. If anything, I could grab some food because I was getting hungry. I strolled along the greenway. I saw the occasional person walking their dog and someone jogging with their reflective gear. I would either stare up at the sky or down at my feet as I tried to accept what was happening. Real or not, acceptance would calm me down. Or so I thought.

Anansi was quiet. Hopefully, he would give me a minute. I also hoped he did not hear that inner thought.

"I am growing hungry," Anansi said.

"You seem to always be hungry," I replied. "There are a few places up the street. The way we walk now, we should get there quickly." I started thinking about the food places nearby and what I was craving.

"Try running," Anansi said. "We will get there faster."

"Ummm, these boobs do not run. Neither do my lungs," I laughed.

"Just try," he said. He seemed a bit humble. The normal arrogant tone of his voice was not there. I assumed it was hunger. I was nice, too, when I wanted someone to get me food. Lucas was notorious for bringing food for me as a surprise or as a pick me up. He knows me way too well. I needed him right now, but what would I say?

"Well," I relented. I did some random stretches, bounced on my toes for a few seconds and started running. I was fast; too fast. The wind was sharp against my skin and my eyes teared up. My vision was sharp as I moved around anyone that was on the street. It took a few minutes to get to the intersection with all the food places. Once I stopped, I was shocked. I was short of breath but not from the run. I was freaking out. I just ran over a mile, maybe two, within a few minutes. How is that possible? First, my walk was fast, now I run fast.

"Anansi, what the hell!" I was unaware of the people around me as I was panicking on the sidewalk. I needed to calm down immediately because someone was going to notice.

"That is something we can do now," he answered. The smugness returned quickly. I couldn't be as vocal as I wanted to be. I did not have the option of pretending to be talking through my headphones because I did not bring them.

"What the fuck," I said through my teeth.

"I am a part of you now. You will be surprised at what you can do now that I am here," Anansi cheered.

I knew it would be exciting for him, but it was like being strapped to a rocket. "Wait, is that why I can see the stars so clearly?"

"Yes, it is," he said. "I am still testing this new reality as well, human. I need you to be open to trying."

"Well, if you stop calling me human, then maybe."

"My apologies, Elle," he relented. He was being nice so I would do what he wanted. I let it rock because I was intrigued.

"That's going to take some time. I didn't even know you were here. I need more time with this, Anansi." I didn't even ask what he was hungry for. I grabbed damn near everything I wanted. A burger and fries from one place. A personal pizza from another and a half dozen cookies. "We are walking this home," I decided. I was so stressed; I ate the pizza on the way back.

I forgot my walk was faster, too. I got back to my apartment and all my food was still warm. I ate everything and chugged water. Anansi was quiet for the rest of the night. So was I. I didn't turn on the TV or text anyone. I laid in my bed and stared at the popcorn ceiling. "Superhuman, huh," I chuckled to myself.

I woke up the next day without remembering falling asleep. I had that type of sleep where there was no dream, no bathroom interruptions, and no noises heard. I was mad that I had to wake up. That didn't mean I wished I were dead. I wanted to sleep a little longer. My mind was heavy with thought and options. I wasn't sure if this was real yet. However, I hardly thought a mental breakdown would happen after going on leave. Anansi didn't speak all day. He gave me my space and I appreciated it. We may be sharing a body, but I was happy it wasn't too noticeable. I remained silent. I just kept thinking about my situation.

Besides eating like a football team, what else did I need to do? What would be the consequences if I didn't? If I accepted this, what was the value of having Anansi around? Too many questions swirled in my head. My life was changing, and the answers were not black and white anymore. Nor would they be easy to find.

"Fan-fucking-tastic," I thought. I sighed, decided, and planned.

Training

"Alright, Anansi, you there?" I woke up the next morning ready to get a full understanding of our situation.

"I am here," he replied.

"What will happen if I don't train?"

"I am unsure. Again, I have never used this spell. I am learning as we go along."

"Why use a spell you know nothing about?" I hated it when people applied for loans when they knew nothing about them and now Anansi was casting spells with unknown consequences.

"The Mythos is not where I am meant to be. I want to be on Earth. I deserve to be here."

"Yeah, yeah you said that." I sighed. "Okay, so that is an unknown unknown that I'd rather not find out about," I said. I decided last night that I did not want to deal with the consequences. It was either train or risk explosion. I took risks, but not this one.

"I will train." If I can avoid consequences, I will. "We need ground rules, and rules can be added as we learn more about this damn body-sharing you got me into." He was plotting something, too. I could feel it because I was doing the same.

"What are your rules?" Anansi asked.

"You can't read my mind. So, stay out."

"Understood," he agreed.

"Number two, if I start to think this is getting too dangerous, we stop." I had no idea what I was walking into, so I wanted to be able to stop at any time.

"Understood," he agreed again.

"Number three is transparency. If you discover something new about this spell and its effects, you gotta let me know." This was a serious one. I wanted to avoid any surprises. I wanted to have control.

"Understood," he agreed again. "I have my own rule to add for now, human."

"Ugh, it's Elle. Do I need to make that a rule too?" I snapped.

"Elle," he began, "you must trust in me. I know you will want to fight it, but the more you let me in, the more we can do."

"Like hell I will!" I didn't mean to shout that. We were both silent for a few minutes. "Can we take the trust thing day by day?"

"You will only delay greatness," he claimed.

"Maybe your greatness," I replied. "I know you have a scheme yourself, Anansi. Keep it secret for now but one day you must trust me, too. Until then trust comes little by little." We agreed to revisit the trust issues as they come up.

I knew more rules would come but for now that is all I could think of. Anansi only had one for now, "train everyday". After breakfast, Anansi nagged until I agreed to start training immediately. The first step was normal: strength and endurance. I changed clothes and went to the gym. I spent a full hour doing small things like running and weightlifting. I wasn't tired so I did another hour and increased my speed and weight limit. I thought it was a great start. Anansi thought I needed another two hours. It was easier, but that doesn't mean I had the "gym rat" mindset yet. Two hours was a good start.

I was starving once I stopped working out. I realized I would go broke eating out every day, especially the way I had to eat. I stopped in my apartment and grabbed all my grocery bags, headphones, keys, and went to the bulk store to stock up.

"Where are we?" Anansi sounded amazed once I walked in the store.

"We are at a giant version of a market. Everything here comes in larger portions. I am not going to keep buying food at restaurants. I will just need to meal prep for five people now."

"This is most interesting. Show me more," he asked.

I spent the next four hours shopping around the store. I never spent this much time grocery shopping. I would fill up a cart, pay, and then go back in. What made it enjoyable was Anansi's amazement. He tried to play it off, but I think this was one of those moments when humans entertained him. Having all that going on in my head while shopping was hilarious.

He asked about the cereal, where they slaughtered the animals, tampons, and the bakery. I knew it was wrong to laugh, but I couldn't help it. I answered Anansi's questions to my amusement, as I shopped. I always shopped with my headphones in. It was a great way to ignore someone asking for money or my phone number. I could ignore anything without feeling bad about it. Thanks to the headphones, I didn't look crazy around the other shoppers. They thought I was talking on the phone when I spoke with Anansi. I assumed I could talk to him without speaking but I also felt like he would be reading my mind. I stuck to speaking out loud.

My poor car was packed, and I had no idea if this was going to fit in my kitchen. I found it easier to get all the bags and boxes into the apartment with my new strength. Usually, this would have taken several trips, but I was done in two. By the time I got everything put away or shoved in random places, I was hungry. I food prepped, ate, took a shower, and collapsed on my bed. It was already a long day. I couldn't wait for my massage that afternoon.

Now, if I were doing these exercises for myself, I would take Sunday off. Not Anansi.

"Elle, you need to wake up." He was worse than an alarm clock. I couldn't hit snooze on his voice in my head. He was relentless until I got up, too. He was like that all week. My bonnet was halfway off my hair, my socks were all bunched up and crooked, and my pillows wedged between the headboard and the gap of my mattress. I didn't sleep pretty. I was exercising every day. This was not the staycation I was supposed to have. It was fucking work.

"Elle, get up."

"Uhhh."

"The sun has begun to rise," he began.

"So what? Let me sleep."

"We must train. Time to rise."

"It's so early though," I groaned. He kept insisting.

"Do I need to train every day?"

"Absolutely," Anansi asserted.

I was tricked. I hate this rule. Why did I agree to it? Before I could say anything, Anansi added a new rule. "Sunrise training and sunset training." I protested as much as I could but ultimately that was the compromise. My days went from maybe ten hours at most doing something I hated -- work -- to 13 hours of training. I get up, exercise, eat, and explain this new world to Anansi, eat, train some more, shower and then train again. Sleep was my only break. I started wearing headphones everywhere so it would look like I was on the phone. Anansi studied how I used the appliances, drove my car, and used the computer and phone. He was actually impressed by human innovation, if even briefly. His superiority complex always popped back up.

"Maybe Cronus should have hitched a ride with you so I could have more than 24 hours a day," I said. Anansi made a sound of disgust and didn't find my joke funny. Apparently, talking about The Mythos wasn't his favorite topic. Mentioning another god wasn't his cup of tea either. He wanted to talk about training. It was boring.

After showing him the entire Internet, I needed a break. Not with Anansi as your personal trainer. A break meant taking a run. Granted, that was the easiest to get used to. I liked being fast. I looked up the average time it takes an active runner to run a mile and picked up the pace. I ran five miles up the road and five miles back. I would never have been able to stand up after the first mile a few days ago. Now, I only started sweating at the last two miles back. I was impressed and excited to see what else I could do. My senses are sharper and strength was up. I hated the training but liked the change.

"That is why we train. You cannot be scared. We have limits to discover and break."

"Yeah, but doesn't this seem like something I should ease into?"

"We cannot 'ease' forever," he explained.

"You are more impatient than I am," I replied.

"Indeed," Anansi proudly confirmed.

What Anansi wasn't considering was the people around me. I couldn't run so fast that I lapped someone. That was too suspicious. I was only recently made aware magic still exists. If I found out, I knew the government knew magic still exists. I was putting myself in the crosshairs just so Anansi could show me how fast I could run. We needed more privacy for that.

After my run, I took a shower and an actual break from thinking. I ate throughout the day and decided to catch up on some reading, but even that was different. I read much faster. I finished one book that I started five months ago and started the second book in the series. I was halfway into the third book before it was time for my "sunset training." Anansi instructed me to go to the woods behind the apartments.

I was supposed to use my enhanced eyesight and hearing to run through the woods. That night I was going at a slow pace to learn about my enhanced senses. I was learning how to adjust my sight to the dark, and to hear and smell what was around me. The sense to avoid was touch right now. Touch was the last sense that should be used, according to Anansi's instructions.

"Find your way through the woods without touching anything," Anansi advised.

The wooded area near my apartment complex was small. It was basically the "wall" between my apartment complex and the next apartments. I went back and forth about 50 times that night. I had to change my path each time to avoid memorization. After the first few times, and about 100 small cuts and bruises that healed fast, I got the hang of it. The air was crisp, and it was like competing in an obstacle course. I was training my breathing and defense. The trees seemed to move little by little each time to increase the difficulty. I was having fun. Night training took up a lot of time, but it was my favorite. I decided to find a bigger wooded area to try after I memorized the whole layout of that small, wooded space.

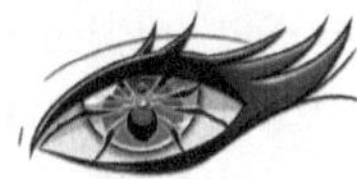

June

For a full month, I was doing the basics of basic training. In the morning, I trained my strength, endurance, and speed, and at night I put my senses to the test. Anansi tried to convince me to climb the trees near the apartment and jump off the complex buildings. He was growing tired of what I was doing, but I didn't want to draw attention. When I asked him why it was so important right now, he gave an answer that piqued my interest.

"Do you remember how my spider form moved? How light my steps were and the agility?"

"Yeah, I do. I was surprised something so massive could move that way," I replied.

"Well, think of you being that agile and stealthy."

"No way." I was shocked that I could get to that point. I was excited to get to the point.

"I have been finding out little by little that you will be able to perform some of my abilities with practice. I am not sure which ones or if you will be able to do it fully on your own, but we must push the limits more."

"Well, we can't do that here," I explained. This was why I needed isolation. He was trying to get me caught, I swear. Last thing I needed was unwanted attention and an unmarked black car pulling up to kidnap me. Government experiments and Black people don't mix.

Until I could find something, he was getting the basic training from me. I even joined a damn yoga studio. Avid yoga practitioners were weird as fuck, but "balance and flexibility are important, human." He nagged me more than my mom.

I told Dr. Lynn after the two weeks off I had that I needed another two weeks. "I wanted to spend more time with my family," I told her. She was a bit skeptical, but she gave me another two weeks. I avoided her the whole month.

I didn't know what excuse I could come up with next. Finding a magic book in her office was not a high priority topic for our sessions. I was worried I would slip up and tell her about a magical book and then she would order the 72-hour mandatory hold. "One thing at a time," I told myself. I had too many things to do. I threw a little fit, and cussed Anansi in my mind because I wasn't sure what he could do to my body. My leave was supposed to be easy. If anyone told me I would be working out every day, I would have shot them. I still might.

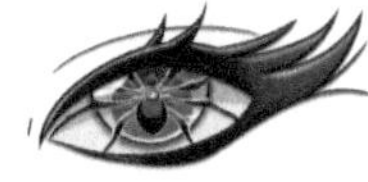

July

Since my summer began, I searched for the right location to move and worked on my budget when I had any down time. I couldn't take the nagging much longer. Whenever I found a place, the real estate agent would tell me, "Oh, I am sorry that is still on our website. That property has been sold." I was about to give up and renew my lease. I wanted to find enough space that had everything I needed. I needed isolation, open fields, and a healthy forest. All that against me, I should have stopped there. However,

154

Anansi's words kept replaying in my mind. "With me, human, you can change, become stronger. With me you can jump high, become light as a feather, land like a cat from tall buildings." So, I kept hunting. I wished he had an idea of how I would afford this.

The good thing about this search was that I had something to talk to Dr. Lynn about. I avoided the "did you journal" nagging as much as possible. She brought it up to see how quick I would pivot. I didn't appreciate the timer either. She added that shit to force me to talk about it. The timer would stay put until I talked about journaling. I only avoided the conversation because I felt the book may find its way into the conversation. It was supposed to be my journal. I wished Janus would have erased people's memories about that damn book. Nothing could be easy. Apparently, humans and gods liked to take the long way around.

I got lucky one night because I saw the "for sale" sign being put up. I had reached the back road from my run when I saw an older man hammering the post into the ground. I did not want to scare him, but this place was perfect. Secluded, down a small, paved road from the main road. Nothing else around, and a big, wooded area with a small open field. I didn't see any houses around.

His car's headlights were on to make sure he didn't hammer his hand by mistake. I tried to make some noise as I walked to him so that he noticed me. It didn't work. I cleared my throat again to get his attention. He turned around so quick that I took a leap back.

"Sorry dear, I didn't mean to startle you," he reassured. He was pretty good looking for his age. He looked a little older than 60, but judging by his reaction, he was quick on his feet.

"No, I am sorry," I began.

"Do you need some help?" the man asked.

"Well, I was interested in the sign you are posting."

"Oh yes, it is time to sell the field."

"Is it just the open field?"

"It's some of the wooded area, as well. About 15 acres of land and a very quiet area. You are the first person I've seen here in about a week."

"I'll take it!" I did not ask him anything else. This was exactly what I needed.

"Woah woah," he laughed. "I'm Mr. Otis. What's your name?"

"Oh, my name is Elle," I said. I reached out to shake his hand but static shock zapped us pretty good so we quickly snatched our hands away and laughed.

"Well Elle, what do you plan to do with the land?"

"Space is the biggest thing," I bullshitted my way through like a job interview, "after years in apartment after apartment, I want space and maybe get a dog. It feels right," I said. Mr. Otis gave me one of those skeptical nods.

We discussed the price and the exact property line. He agreed to take the sign down for two weeks to give me the opportunity to get my money in order. He was selling his property by himself. I knew I would have to do some research on this land and make sure he owned it. It could be a scam, but he seemed legit and answered all my questions. I felt right about this. We exchanged contact information. Mr. Otis seemed very nice.

"Why are you out so late?" I could ask him the same thing, but I minded my business.

"Burying a body," I laughed. He laughed, too. "I like a little isolation when I run. I found this road was a good spot. I noticed the open field before, but I didn't know it belonged to someone," I answered.

"You must have some dedication. Well, Elle, I will hear from you soon." He tucked the post under his arm with the hammer and stretched his hand out. I hesitated to shake his hand again. That shock I felt was a big one.

"Sorry. I've got dirt and sweat on my hands. I don't want to dirty yours." Being dirty was a good excuse to not shake hands. There were plenty of people couldn't care less about a dirty hand. Mr. Otis looked like he understood. He gave me a wink and went back to his car.

I cut my training short and ran back to my home.

"What do you think?" I asked.

"I am not sure what you mean by that question. It was a piece of land."

"I know. Is it enough space," I asked. "I think this may be the spot."

"Then how do we obtain this land? How shall we trick this Missstah Otisss?"

"Why did you say his name like that?"

"That is his name," he asserted.

"You said it weird, but we don't need to trick him. We need something that is much harder: money."

"Any idea in there, Anansi?" I asked. There was only one way I knew to buy the land from Mr. Otis -- a dumbass mortgage. I knew how they worked but I really didn't want to go through the process. I needed a faster way. "You got x-ray vision?"

"Even in my body, at 100% power, I do not," he said. We both let out a sigh of disappointment. I guess picking the right lottery scratch by chance was out of the question. Things couldn't be that easy. Ain't I the lucky one?

"Well, we gotta…wait, what do you mean 100% power? Are you not at 100% now?"

"Of course not. I must share a body. I will never be my full self. From what I have observed, I am currently at 10% and you are 90%. We balance at 100, you see."

"So right now we are 90% me and 10% you." This information should've been shared with me nearly two months ago.

"I wouldn't describe it as plainly as that, but yes," he said.

"Sorry, I forgot the fireworks." He was silent. He didn't fully get sarcasm yet. We were working on it. "What will happen if the balances change? Like 20% you or 15% me," I asked.

"An unknown until we try. We will need to add this to the training."

"I'm sorry I asked. More training? There aren't enough hours! I wanna see my friends," I pouted.

"Elle," Anansi said. I knew that tone.

"Alright, alright," I relented. "How do we train for that?"

Anansi agreed to give me the weekend off so that we could start "control balance" training and he could soak up all this information. I took him up on that deal immediately. I already made plans with the girls and Lucas for the weekend. I would have agreed either way because I hated to admit it, but I was curious. If this worked, I may get some cool power or some shit. Sounded cool to me. That didn't mean I wasn't terrified of going beyond the 90/10 baseline we have been in. The side effects of 90/10 control balance were extreme hunger and thirst. What if there were side effects to the rest?

"Ok, how do we train for this control balance?" I asked.

"It requires more trust," Anansi hinted.

"Well, that's not happening any time soon," I laughed.

"This is not a time to laugh," Anansi said sternly.

"I was only joking. Geez!"

"Mmmhmm."

"Can we figure out how to get this property first?" I had to figure out something. Mr. Otis wouldn't hold the sale for long.

I did my research and Mr. Otis was the deeded owner, he didn't owe back taxes, and he was over 80 years old. He looked fantastic! I needed that secret.

Short of robbing a bank, the only option was a damn mortgage. I rather trick Mr. Otis to be honest but I didn't know what Anansi meant by "trick" so mortgage it was. I loathe the process and shit that needed to be done but it was the only option. I used the bank that contracts with us to service all their accounts. I was the fastest mortgage and land purchaser according to my mortgage officer. I had negotiated a lower sales price. I was surprised that Mr. Otis accepted it. Most people wouldn't go that low.

I told my family once everything was finalized.

"I service all these accounts. I know the process like the back of my hand," I told them. The rate was good, the monthly payment was a little more than my rent, and fuck escrow. The 15 acres were mine. My mom was happy I was a landowner, and my friends took me out to celebrate. I could drink like a fish now and the weed never hit the same again, but I was happy to be out. Everyone's life was forming. I was happy when we could make time for each other.

"Are you going to build a house on the land?" Marie asked.

"I decided to get a tiny home. I'd rather have the space outside. Plus, it's just me," I answered.

"Not for long I hope," Elise said.

"I mean Lucas will be around, of course," I said.

"And…" Joy leaned in.

"And that's it," I said. Marriage and relationships were the very last thing on my mind right now.

I bought a tiny home to put on the field and I loved it. I had all this open space for training. I also bought a small storage shed to start storing things in. I may build a bigger house later. But if I did, I was going to rob a bank for that money. I decorated my home to fit me. It was colorful and even had a guest room. I saw it as an XL tiny home.

Lucas was a big help with my move, but he was worried. Lucas decided he wanted to come back on the weekend and bring his gun for shooting. He didn't like that I was out in the middle of nowhere by myself without protection. Plus, he wanted to utilize the space for a small gun range. I understood but came to realize it wasn't needed.

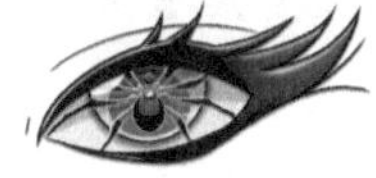

August

Training was easy up until now. With my new space, everything was about to change.

The open field was my track and the woods my obstacle course. My sight was clear as day at night. All my senses were improving -- although my sense of smell could take a back seat because dead animals, trash, and other gross smells were overwhelming. I felt extra sorry for dogs because people stink!

Training wasn't like when I was at the apartment. I could only do so much with people around. Now, I was in seclusion, and got excited to learn more. Anansi nagged nonstop in the apartment. There, I had an excuse. "Too many people could see," I said.

"Now we have no more excuses," Anansi gleamed.
The basics were down. It was time to build on it. The first thing was getting used to the control balance. The goal was to switch the balance quickly -- a seamless exchange that I controlled. Leave it up to Anansi and I probably wouldn't be myself. I had to move in and out of the control balance and climb some damn trees.

"You want me to climb?" I asked.

"Agility, Elle," Anansi explained. "Think of my spider form when we met. What did you notice?"

"How quiet you were. Your massive size would be noticed," I answered.

"Precisely," Anansi said. "Now, imagine that at your size. It will be easy. You will undetectable in the right situation."

"I like the sound of that," I replied. "So, how do we get there?"

I haven't climbed trees since I was a child. My upper body strength, before all this, was trash. Now I had a vertical leap better than any basketball player or Olympian. The first time I climbed, I did not go too far up because Anansi wouldn't let me climb back down. The only way he let me touch the ground was if I jumped. At a 90/10 control balance, I wasn't taking that chance. Height wasn't at the top of my list of fears, but it was still on the damn list. Apparently, through a control balance of 80/20 or 75/25 I should be able to be as agile as a spider in these trees. Jumping from tree to tree, branch to branch, becoming weightless on branches. Anansi had to be exaggerating. There was no way I could be as he was in spider form.

Once I got to a comfortable height, I sat on the branch and just enjoyed the view. It was only day one.

"Take a deep breath in, human," Anansi suggested.

"Who?"

"Elle," he said. "Take a deep breath in and let me in."

"Let you in," I repeated. I rolled back and dangled from my knees. I took my childhood abilities and flexibility for granted. I was upside down, looking at the ground. "If I do this, we gotta add another rule. Well clause A of another rule."

"This new rule is…?" Anansi asked.

"We always return to 90/10 control balance on my command," I said.

"Interesting," Anansi said.

"I don't like that 'interesting' you said," I mocked.

"I will agree to this rule if I may ask a question," Anansi said.

"…ok," I said.

"Where is the key," Anansi said. I heard the record scratch in my head. His voice was commanding. If Anansi was abiding by the rules, he was not in my thoughts.

"I don't know," I started. "Once I 'magicked' my way back to the office, I couldn't find it." Keep it hidden.

"Are you sure?" he asked.

"Yeah, I thought it was some old key. I shouldn't be surprised that a magical key can disappear so easily."

"I see," Anansi said. God, I hope he bought that excuse. If he was in my thoughts, he already knew the truth. We didn't fully trust each other but that was why we set rules.

"Let's try again," I said to quickly change the subject.
I took a few deep breaths. I felt a small jolt go through my body. My head throbbed like a bad migraine. I struggled a bit and lost my grip under my legs and fell. Good thing I didn't go too high. I could jump from this height as my normal self and be okay. I laid on my back still. The sky was turning orange, and I heard a few squirrels in the trees.

"That wasn't pleasant," I joked.

"I admit I found no favor in that as well," Anansi said. I silently mocked him and sat up.

"How much was that?" I asked.

"It was not much, I'm afraid. We managed 85/15 for a few seconds," Anansi answered.

"That's it?" I said. "A jolt of pain and a migraine for 85/15."

"We shall try again. Are you ready?" Anansi commanded.

"Hell nah, I ain't ready," I answered. "Give me a second to catch my breath." I knew I had to practice but I didn't want the pain. I wasn't climbing a damn tree this time.

"Alright, let's do it," I said. I took a few deep breaths again and focused. I could hear Anansi breathe as well. It was nice to know that Anansi's training rule applied to him, too.

85/15 didn't sound like a big difference but there was. I could see the wind and feel the tree I was leaning on begin to grow. It was surreal. I was living in a practical world with magic. The change to 85/15 was amazing. I didn't tell Anansi that. It would make that spider 60 feet tall.

Once the 85/15 was steady enough, I climbed the same tree as before. I stood on the same branch and jumped. I didn't land softly but I landed on my feet.

"We are going to get to the point that you won't make a sound from any height. Think light, Elle." Anansi laughed at me during my first few attempts. I took that personally and as a challenge. He could at least give me an "A" for effort. There was one of two things going on. Either I could really land like a cat or Anansi was living up to his trickster title. When we first moved out here, he told me he could sense precious gems beneath the ground. I spent a freaking week digging around. I didn't know why he lied but I was pissed off. He laughed. I forgot he was in isolation, too. I was the only person around to mess with, but he couldn't do too much without harming his vessel. He would be expelled back to the gate because he did not belong.

I trained all day and well into the night on trying to land properly and be "weightless." I failed every time. My legs hurt, I got tons of bruises and leaves up my ass. I broke my first bone in my arm. It took a week to heal. I had to make a second cast when I had to go to the doctor to "remove" it. Every day we went between 90/10 and 85/15 control balance.

Every day, I jumped from the same branch. I was angry. I couldn't seem to get it. The control balance wasn't easy. The hole in my wall can tell you how that is going. The split tree in the forest can also tell you a story. I punched the shit out of that one. This agility bullshit was frustrating. I would get to a stopping point and go into the house for a shower. My muscles needed to relax and wash off the dirt and failure.

"What am I doing wrong?" I asked.

"You are fighting me," Anansi answered.

"I don't mean to. I can get to 85/15 but that's not enough."

"No, it is not. You need to let me in more," Anansi advised.

I walked into the kitchen for my wine bottle and my super large wine glass. It was a housewarming gift from Elise and my sisters. I had the same gift from three different people. I named the glasses Monday, Wednesday, Friday. The weekdays were flying by fast. My leave would end before I knew it. I had to get this down.

I worked on the control balance training for the rest of the night. 85/15 wasn't enough. Anansi said 75/25 should be our goal. Tonight, I pushed to 80/20. I wanted to do this on my own. The first time, Anansi forced it. That was the one and only time I wanted to rely on him to do that. Going to 85/15 hurt the first time, but now it was easy. I had to push myself a little more. I sat in a comfortable yoga pose and started to breathe. In and out. In and out.

When I woke up in the morning, I decided to take a run. Not at any high speed, but just a normal warm-up to clear my head. It was a cool morning. Last night was another unsuccessful training. I needed to start again with a clear head. As I ran, I smelled the dew on the grass and focused on my breathing. I switched to an 85/15 control balance within a few seconds into my run. The sun was brighter, and I heard the animals running across the ground in the woods. I stayed focused and ran faster. Then I felt the same sharp pain as before. I was getting there, so I kept running. The pain went away more quickly.

"Anansi, are we at 80/20?" I asked.

"We are," he sounded a little strained. I guessed that a new control balance caused him discomfort each time, too.

"All right. Let's keep going," I decided.

In and out. In and out. Suddenly, I got a terrible headache. Even Anansi cried out. I stopped running immediately and collapsed on the back road. The heightened senses were making the headache worse. 75/25 had this amount of pain, I was scared to go any further. After a few minutes of pain, the headache went away. I tried to catch my breath as I got to my feet.

Woof. Woof.

I froze in place. A dog was close. I turned around to see where the barking was coming from. My sight was exceptional at 75/25 and I could see him hiding in the tall grass. It was a skinny pit bull. A massive black head and patchy black fur except for a white spot on his chest. He was growling at me. I kept my distance for a minute. He didn't run off when I focused on him. He kept growling and barking at me. It seemed like he was warning me or giving me an alert.

"Okay, okay," I said. I stuck my arm out to tell him to wait. He stood still, but kept barking. I relaxed a bit more and talked to the dog like a baby. "Hey little guy," I said softly. I was at my base of 90/10 instantly. Once I was "normal," he stopped barking at me. Smart dog.

For a starving animal, he was strangely happy. His tail wagged so I wasn't scared about his bark. He was a little hesitant at first. I didn't blame him. He must have been out here for a long time.

"Here boy," I whistled to him. "It's okay." My voice was several octaves higher than normal. I smiled hard to reassure him it was okay. He wouldn't move at first. I stood up and pretended to leave and that got him

164

to move. I tried to bend down to pet him, but he quickly backed away. So, I stopped trying to approach him and let him come to me. I walked back to my house and the dog was right on my heels. Poor guy must be hungry. I could tell he was super sweet, but not so trusting of humans. I couldn't blame him for that.

I walked into the house and got him a big bowl of water and food. He was staring through the doorway. It was funny and cute. He peeked around the corner looking at the place. He must have tried to make sure he was safe. He backed up again when I approached with some food and water, so I put it down on the ground and backed away. While he ate, I went into the woods to practice my jump. I gave the dog some space to eat and do dog things. I went into 85/15 and sat in a tree thinking. "Anansi, 75/25 is gonna take a minute," I said as I watched this floating cloud.

"Indeed, it will," he conceded. I jumped down again and still couldn't land right. "Anansi, I am calling it a day."

"I hate to admit it, but I need a rest as well," Anansi said. I was shocked and I wasn't going to say shit.
I walked out of the woods and back to my house. I didn't see the dog any-where. He finished the food and water, but I didn't see him. I could barely open my eyes to see much anyway. I assumed he ran off. I noticed I left my door open from earlier, so I walked right in and headed straight to my couch.

To my surprise, the dog was in my home. He chewed two of my pillows and peed on the floor near the bathroom. Hopefully, he hadn't had enough food in his system to poop in my house. I expected much more destruction from a stray dog, so I was happy it was an easy cleanup. What I wasn't happy about: cleaning up with this damn headache.

"Well, dude, that was a wonderful housewarming gift." He looked up at me with his big brown eyes and nudged me with his nose. "Oh! I can pet you now?" His massive head would intimidate anyone but all I saw was a big pushover. That pittie smile he had was part of the breed's charm. "I don't appreciate you chewing up my pillows, but I get it. Don't do that again." I said that like I was keeping him. He seemed to understand what I was saying, licked my cheek and then headed to lay down in the living room. I was right behind him. "Sweet dog. I bet your family really misses you. Don't lick me in my face again alright." I scratched the top of his head. I needed to give him a bath at some point.

I teared up a bit because I may not be able to keep the dog. He may be chipped and have a family looking for him. I could be selfish and never check but I wouldn't want someone to do that to me. I went and joined the dog in the living room. I turned on some of my favorite cartoons and we just relaxed. He was fast asleep before the second episode came on. I was right behind him. I didn't even remember falling asleep.

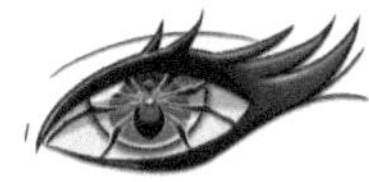

September

I finally landed like a cat. I jumped from a sturdy tree branch close to the ground first. I wanted to get a feel for what my landing should be like. It may have taken me a week or two, but I got the idea. I got the idea too slow for Anansi's liking, but what could he do? I climbed to higher branches and each time I had to jump and land without making a sound. Anansi said I should get to the point where the blades of grass wouldn't even notice I landed. Until then, I kept going to new heights and jumped. The next steps were to be so light that I could climb the dead trees with brittle branches without them breaking. I kept telling myself one step at a time.

The 75/25 worked out after all. I got a wicked headache nearly every time I gave Anansi 25%, but I got used to it. My training leveled up every time I achieved something new. I enjoyed it. Eventually, I had to put it to the test. I had to jump further, land gracefully from bigger heights, lift more, punch harder, and run even faster. I went in and out of certain control balances without even thinking about it. I relaxed and had fun becoming superhuman.

The dog stayed with me until I could get him to a vet. However,

I took my sweet time going. I liked having him around. He would run around with me sometimes and kept barking at me when my control balance was different than 90/10. I wanted a little more time with the dog before I had to return him.

I trained so much that I didn't have a chance to hang out with my family and friends. Everyone knew I was still alive, but I was far out, and everyone was going about life just like me. I sent a text to Lucas hoping he would come through soon. He texted me that he was on the way. "Not that soon," I laughed.

I wondered how the dog would be around another stranger. He already wasn't a fan of Anansi and vice versa. I gave them both the "be on your best behavior" pep talk. I cleaned up everything and cooked a chicken pot pie for dinner. I also made cupcakes. I told Lucas to bring the alcohol and weed. I died laughing when the dog and I both heard his car pull up. We both sat straight up. We were like twins. Our heightened senses matched.

I didn't fully understand why, but the minute I saw Lucas I burst into tears. He looked the same except for this giant beard. He held me as I cried. I missed him so much that all my emotions poured out. He hugged me tightly. I hope he felt the same but I was fine with him pretending. I didn't even notice that the dog was right behind me. He didn't bark. He looked confused.

"You got a dog," Lucas said. He kneeled and the dog approached him happily.

"Oh," I wiped my tears, "yeah, sorta. I found him in the woods. I should check if he is chipped at some point."

"But you are taking your sweet time," he interjected. God, I missed this man. "Not in the face, dog," he said.

"Let's get drunk!" I said. Lucas had other plans first. He took me down on the couch before we did anything else. He really missed me too.

The time could stop right there, and I would not complain.

It was after 3 am when I watched him drive away. He had to work in the morning and my house isn't really convenient. I knew he would be back, but I bawled my eyes out. I sat on the grass crying, but I wasn't alone. The dog cuddled up with me and calmed me down.

"Anansi, I am taking a week off. I miss my family and friends."

"Understood," he said. I expected a fight, but he let me take a break.

I would get right back to training afterwards.

The Wealthy Peasant

I started the week by taking the dog to the vet. I didn't want to grow further attached if he belonged to someone. He didn't. I chipped him that day at the vet. He was officially my dog. I celebrated by buying way too much at the pet store and picking out a name for him: Inu. After that, I called the family over throughout the week to visit and meet my new dog. He loved my mom more than me. It was so sudden. He was attached to her and her to him. I was just a servant to Inu while my mom was over. The week went by fast. Elise came over and updated me on Charlie and their life together. Marie thinks he will propose soon. My sisters think I should build a bigger house and Lucas came over with a damn arsenal. Lucas thought I should practice more. We hadn't been to the gun range in a while. The enhanced eyesight made shooting more fun. I was making impossible shots. It became a contest all day. I let him win two out of five. That's when I knew I wanted to train with weapons, too. I designated the shed as my weapons "safe."

I had a virtual meeting with Dr. Lynn. I kept it short, though. She wants me in the office at some point but virtual was all I could give. She was happy to see Inu.

"A pet could be just what you need," she said. "You will be returning to work in about two months, right?" she asked.

"Oh shit, I forgot all about that. I guess so," I replied.

"Take some time to get to know Inu. Do some weekend dog training exercises. It will give you something positive to focus on," she suggested.

"Inu, we have homework to do," I said. He gave me his cute pittie smile and went back to his toys. Inu's smart: we didn't have to train for long. He listened well and judged well, too. He loved running through the woods with me. We went in and out of the trees and even tried to catch a squirrel together. He was a good agility partner and Anansi detector.

I was outside practicing with the .9mm that Lucas gave me, and the gun jammed. After my last target practice with Lucas, I decided to train with more than guns. I even bought a bow and arrow. I bought more bullets, different guns, and accessories. The bow and arrow were a thrill buy. I pictured myself shooting arrows like elves in nearly anything fiction. I also found this interesting knives. I had to practice more with the knife and bow and arrow. I never planned to use any weapons. I was simply living out my fantasy world.

Inu was in a safe space while I was shooting. It was one of the commands we practiced. I shot up close, far away, and while constantly moving. The gun jamming was my sign to stop for the day and head in for the night. I locked up the shed that became my weapon storage and headed inside. Inu was squeaking away on his toy as he found his favorite spot in the house. I took a shower and made us something to eat. I had about two months left before I headed back to work. I needed to enjoy this break while I could.

Once I finished eating and got comfortable on the couch, I asked Anansi something strange. For the first time, I asked Anansi, "Can you tell me a story from when you lived on Earth?"

"Interesting," he began. "You never asked before."

"I know. I'm curious. What is a story that wasn't part of the fable and folklore?"

"I see. An unknown story," he hummed.

"I want a story no one knows."

"Let me see," he paused. "The story of this peasant I encountered may interest you."

Folu was a disgruntled child. He came from a family of farmers. They grew some of the crops for the village and for the chief's family. Every day was the same routine. Folu would help his father and mother bundle the crops and then Folu would take them into the market for sale. Folu and his family were peasants. They were on the fringes of the larger villages ruled by Chief Moda. There were four other families in Folu's village. All poor and with meager resources. Folu wanted to keep at least half of the crops so that his family could sell to others but retaliation from the chief's guards kept everyone honest.

Folu brought the harvest in every time while his parents stayed home. Folu had to pass by other villages on the way to the main village. He greeted the elders in those villages and took a few odd jobs on the way. The main village was filled with markets, healing huts, and music. Folu had to continue past the laughter to deliver to the chief's cooks. He wished to stop and join in the laughter, but he had obligations that could not be delayed. After he dropped off the crops, Folu would help clean the joining huts. The chief's and his wives' huts sat atop a hill. They formed a circle and in the center was their own courtyard for the royals to play in. Folu was tasked with cleaning around the outside. Any delay or distraction got Folu clubbed by the head servant.

Day in and day out -- that was Folu's life. When he reached age 14, he was subjected to hellish training. He grew strong and fast during the first two years. However, he always remained resentful. Some peasants felt this was a great honor and a way to help feed their families. They became part of the chief's warriors. They protected the villages and got the attention of the young women. Folu thought it was a trap. No peasant had returned from battling a nearby village the same. They were sent to fight for another man's greed for land and power. The spoils of war only went so far. The closer you ranked to the chief, the more you were rewarded. Peasants rarely made the proper ranks.

At the age of 17, Folu had had enough. He decided to run away and start new somewhere else. However, he did not go far. He quickly realized that no matter where he went or what village he went to, he would be a peasant. Folu collapsed on a fig tree and looked up at the stars. He was stuck. Folu wept, knowing that his past, present, and future were predetermined. He was to work the farm, serve the chief, be promised to another woman from his village, and farm again. He realized he was running and headed nowhere.

"I do not want this!" Folu screamed into an empty night. "I want more! There has to be more!" Folu began punching the tree until the blood from his knuckles dripped to the dirt.

"Poor human," I said.

What Folu was unaware of was that he was being observed. The fig tree was a great spot during the warm months. It gave sweet juice and healthy leaves for shade. The African sun is beautiful, bright, and brutal. Folu looked around, trying to find the source of the booming voice. The night stars did not help with visibility at far distances. Most tribes would attack at night because the element of surprise could change the course of any conflict.

"Who's there?" Folu picked himself up and raised a knife to protect himself.

"I'm up here," I said. I was the size of a regular spider, but my voice carried as if I were my natural size.

"Wha....what?" Folu was circling the tree looking for someone hidden in the branches. "Where are you? Show yourself," Folu demanded.

I am not one to take commands from others, especially a human. However, I lowered myself from my web to be at eye level with this human.

"I am right here," I said.

Folu stood still for a few seconds, rubbed his eyes, and froze. A talking spider is something new, but his reaction surprised me. Humans would usually run, trip, and then curse the gods for being so cruel. Humans were strange creatures to me. Folu did not run away. He did not speak. He remained still. I did not know how to respond. I spun around on my thread, thinking and looking for any other humans that may be around. I let the silence become louder until it was too loud for even me.

"Are you alone, human?" I asked.

Silence. I began to climb back up the tree when Folu spoke.

"Are you really talking to me, or have I finally gone mad?" he asked. "Have I lost all my senses?"

"I am talking to you, human," I reassured. Folu collapsed to his knees at the base of the tree and began to weep again. "Human, I assure you I am not an illusion. My name is Anansi."

"Anansi?" he asked.

"Yes, have you heard of me before?"

"No sir, I have not."

I must admit, I was not happy about that. Tales were told of me, yet this human had heard none of them. The human had the audacity to either ignore my works or news of my interaction with others never made it to his village. After I composed myself, I realized how this could be an advantage.

"Well, of course you haven't. Most would not talk about a spider in a tree. I am a god that enjoys the fruit on Earth. The spider is one of my forms. I have many."

"A god? Are you the god that ordains the royalty and power of Chief Mado?"

"I do not know of whom you speak, human," I replied. "Why do you cry?"

"I am tired of being just a poor farmer. I am tired of being a house servant. I am tired of fighting the war for others' greed. My life has been predetermined by the gods and it is not fair." Folu explained.

"You want more from this life, human," I said.

"I do, sir! You are a god; you have all that you need. I am a peasant of a small village. Ancestor after ancestor, my family stayed in that village. Some with pride that swells for helping the chiefs and some with defeat that they would soon be forgotten. I refuse to be either. My mother wants me to find a nice girl to settle with, my father wants me to continue to farm like his father before him. I want status, a hut of my own, and as many beautiful wives as I can satisfy."

Folu left nothing out. "Why have the gods only blessed the few?" He shouted to all the gods and stars what he wanted. Lucky for him, I wanted something, too. Folu was exactly what I needed. Anger and blind ambition were great motivators and a veil. When someone wanted something so bad, they would not see the ulterior motives of someone else. I could use Folu.

"Is this what you truly want, human?" I asked.

"It is," he replied.

"I can help you with that. I can help you obtain a possession that will change your life."

Folu wiped his eyes and began to smile.

"You can help me?" he asked.

"I can and I shall. I am a generous god. I do not like the idea of predetermination of any kind. Even us gods are hit with fate. Many of us do whatever it takes to change fate, and most will fail. I want to help you succeed."

Folu listened to a simple plan to obtain wealth. He worked in the chief's huts and knew where the chief's treasure was located. It was guarded every hour of the day and night. Folu had no idea what treasures lay beyond the doorway, but something in there would be worth more than his family would ever see. Folu would need to set a trap. A trap that would draw the attention to those within the chief's joining huts. The guards of the treasure would not move, but that was where I came in. My job was to bite the guards with poison in my fangs.

"It is not a fatal poison. It is just to give you enough time to grab as much as you can to change your circumstances," I reassured. "No one will get hurt," I added.

The best idea he could come up with was to start a fire on one side of the joining huts. It would have to be large enough to grab everyone's attention, even Chief Mado's. I wanted Folu to feel in control. I let him set the pace. Folu would be in and out without anyone noticing him. If he wanted to change his fate and fortune, this plan gave him that chance.

Folu returned to his village with me on his shoulder. His parents were happy to see him. They were concerned when he had not returned with a few of the other soldiers from training. He did his best to hide the cuts on his hands. His mother kept his food warm, but he could not eat a single bite. He excused himself from the hundred questions he would get from his parents because he wasn't eating. He washed the blood off his hands from the water pail outside and decided rest was the best thing for him. He twisted and turned all night. The next evening was going to change his life forever. He was not sure if it was excitement or dread that kept him awake. He knew he needed his rest. I told him all would work out and to get some sleep.

The sun rose to a new day, but the same daily tasks awaited Folu. He did not complain or grunt like he usually did, but he was smart enough to not seem overly content with the day. He gathered the crops, worked on the hill, and went to training until the moon tinted the tallest trees with a faint white light. Some of the soldiers brought in the night with drinks and women. Some retired back to their villages and their families. Folu headed up the hill. I stayed at the chief's house after Folu left for training.

The night was always the best cover to surprise the enemy. Folu learned that during training and the few battles he fought. He watched his footsteps carefully. A snap to a branch under the weight of the body could give away your position. He checked the guards first to see if they were taken down by the poison. They were on the floor, spears missing from their hands. Folu knew that he only had a few minutes to get to the other side of the hill and light the fire.

Folu ran as fast as he could to the other side of the hill. With two flint stones, he started the fire to the head servant's hut. He did not worry about her safety. According to Folu, that old, hateful woman would never die that easily. Folu knew she would make the biggest fuss. After the chief, his children, and wives, the head servant was the most feared. Folu set fire to the huts around the head servant and headed back towards the treasures.

Folu was correct. The old woman ordered everyone to her side of the joining huts. The wives and children were at risk, so everyone rushed to put out the fires. Folu then slipped into the treasure room and grabbed one of the shiniest items he could find. A golden cup, encrusted with valuable jewels. He knew this would be enough for his seed to have a better life. He concealed it as best he could under his clothes and started to exit the room.

"Human," I said as I blocked the exit. "I want to thank you for the distraction and leading me to such a treasure."

"No, it can't be." Folu stumbled back a little bit. "How are you human? You were a spider."

"I can be anything I choose. I am Anansi, a god." I replied.

"I held up my end of the plan. You should have known I would need a favor in return."

"I...," Folu was at a loss for words.

Folu was stunned. He had only been a tool. Used by someone else, like every other time. His envious desire was nothing compared to the desires of a god. I had transformed into a guard and pretended to be knocked out by the poison. I waited for Folu to start the fire.

"I will let you leave, but you'd better run fast." I stepped away from the passageway of the treasure hut to let Folu pass.

"I... what do...I," Folu stumbled towards the passageway but could not find the words to speak.

Folu walked past me and headed down the hill as the fires roared. He looked behind him to make sure I was not following. "I would hurry now," I winked. I let him get far away first.

"Thief! We have a thief! Folu is stealing the treasure!" I yelled. As I lay against the hut as if I were injured, I pointed the guards in the direction that Folu ran. I made sure my voice could be heard by all in the chief's joining huts and Folu. He ran faster as footsteps quickened behind him. As the guards chased Folu, the rest of the people atop the hill tried to put out the impressive fire Folu started. I gathered some valuable pieces of the treasure for myself and left without anyone noticing. I disappeared into the night.

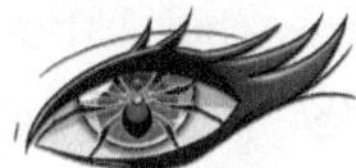

There was about a minute of silence.

"Is that it?" I asked.

"Yes, that is the end," he replied.

"Hold the hell on, Anansi," I interrupted. "What happened to Folu?"

"He ran back to his village. He had lost the guards, but it was only a matter of time before they made their way to his home. He obtained the wealth he so desired, but he could not go home. He couldn't even take the time to say goodbye. He was now marked as a thief. He would only be risking his parents' lives if he went anywhere near him. Folu had no choice but to keep running," Anansi explained.

"So, you wanted all the treasure for yourself. What could a god do with Earthly treasures?" I asked.

"I am more than a god; I am a trickster. Hanging out in fig trees can become boring when you are immortal," Anansi chuckled.

"So, you were bored and took advantage of someone wanting more for themselves. Why is the story called 'The Wealthy Peasants' then?"

"Were you not paying attention? A man, Folu, has been marked as a thief. They will search high and low for him. He got the best of Chief Mado and his men. Folu had in his possession the one thing that could change his fortune. However, he could never use it. Folu was on the run and hiding for the rest of his life. He lived by many names and as a peasant for the rest of his life," Anansi explained.

"All while possessing a golden cup that would make him wealthy,"

I concluded. "The Wealthy Peasant. Well, that sucks, and you are a major asshole."

"I do not know what that is. I am a god," Anansi replied. Well, he was an arrogant asshole then.

I yawned. Inu had already fallen asleep on my feet. "I know cuss words are ancient enough that you even know what an asshole is, seeing as you are one," I laughed. Now that I thought about it, tricksters in all mythology were selfish assholes. Anansi was no different. Most gods and goddesses in mythology were assholes. I had to keep reminding myself of that. However, now I wondered what his endgame was with me. The one thing Folu taught me is that everyone has their price. As I drifted off to sleep, I asked Anansi one last question. "What was so special about the golden cup? I bet it was one of many. He could have sold it."

"Not this cup," Anansi said. "This cup is known by many names. Stolen from person to person through centuries, race to race. You probably know it best as the Holy Grail."

"WHATTTTT????!!!" I popped up fast. I accidentally woke up Inu. I needed to learn more. So, Folu lost it at some point. "Tell me more," I demanded.

"Go to bed, human. We will have plenty of time."

Back To Work

October

The 75/25 control balance was second nature now. Anansi and I blended. I ran in and out of the trees, climbed and jumped gracefully, and my weapons became extensions of my arm. They reached where I could not. Inu was such a happy spot and I enjoyed training with him too. Inu and Anansi did not get along and it tickled me. If I go past the 90/10, Inu doesn't like it. Anansi isn't fond of Inu, either. They'll get over it.

Elise would come over and hang out. She was engaged now. She seemed happy and I was happy for her. A little fast for me but apparently something was in the water because everyone was getting engaged and in relationships. Even Lucas was getting into a relationship. Everyone's adult life was doing just that: "adulting".

The only one that seemed to be a little off was Anansi. I honestly thought all this happiness was making him feel sick. I didn't slack on my training, but I had no anger or frustration. I was in really good shape and could eat whatever I wanted. I was happy. Maybe this was the positive outlet that Dr. Lynn was trying to get me to do. "Of course she was right." I rolled my eyes and gave her credit. She is smarter than me.

As the days passed by, I tried not to think about the office. I liked my routine. I liked spending all day with Inu. I liked jumping through the trees and throwing knives. I was in a fantasy world. A regular "Isekai" training montage. I made time to spend with friends and family. I planned Elise's bachelorette party. My group chat was on a roll. Lucas was doing well and I can eat whatever I want and not gain wait.

I was in a good head space. My training was therapeutic. I updated Dr. Lynn on my progress but I never admitted to her she was right about finding a healthy hobby. I still didn't have regular sessions with her, but she would check in here or there. She thought I was ready to go back to work. I tried not to think about the day I had to return.

November

This break from the stupidity and mundane routine could not last forever. The holidays were coming up and it was an "all hands on deck" situation. I blinked and it was the Monday after my leave of absence was finished. I woke up annoyed. Six months flew by and now the rest of the year would drag on. I got up and did some early training. I let Inu out and put on my workout clothes. I took a few laps around the property and practiced my jumps from the highest tree I could find. I showered and dusted off the business casual clothes. I forgot to meal prep the night before so I would order something at work. I fed Inu and gave him another talk. I told him last night I wouldn't be at the house all day like before. I liked to think he understood what I meant. I cried leaving him all alone for the day.

I was greeted with telephones ringing off the hook. My co-workers were scurrying from cubicle to cubicle trying to find a quick answer. I got swarmed with questions as soon as I exited the elevator. Damn holidays. Once I answered as many questions as I could, I went back to my cubicle in the corner. Things may have stopped for me momentarily, but everyone else was busier than ever. The holidays were the worst. Coworkers and managers got sloppy; everyone tried to pin an issue to someone else. Those

180

issues were easily resolved but keeping everything on your desk was worse than giving it to someone else. The call center "forgot" how to do the simplest things. The customers were more needy and dumb. Customers were out overspending and wanted me to clean up their mess. My calls covered every problem the holidays brought. Insurance claims, financial strains, security breaches, and everything in between wound up on my desk.

Wes and I spent lunch together while he caught me up on everything. The gossip going around the office was the highlight of my day. More affairs had come to light, and a new project manager, whose name is Cherilus, finally got tired of Charla. He went straight to file a complaint. According to Wes, moving him to a different floor did not even help. She was beyond thirsty for a man, any man. With every new, somewhat good-looking Black man that entered the building, Charla made her presence known. If they happened to pay attention to someone else, Charla used her position to eliminate the competition.

"Has she learned nothing from the other dudes?" Wes laughed.

"I have never seen someone want a man that bad," I replied. I really hadn't, at least not in real time. Most of the time, I saw people pouring out their personal business for complete strangers to see on social media. Men responding to rejection with violence. Women, seeking love, putting themselves at the complete bottom for someone to step on. There was toxicity on both sides but instead of everyone realizing that humans are flawed, corruptive, destructive, and disruptive, they continued to rely on someone else for happiness. When that didn't happen, the minute someone let them down, the reaction was extreme.

"Cherilus better watch out," Wes said. "This is exactly how those fatal attractions start. You know the shows I'm talking about."

"Oh, you know I love those shows," I agreed.

Besides the gossip, my day was a normal Monday. It was like muscle memory. I didn't miss a beat. I did forget the last password I used, and we had a few new rules for the holidays. Other than that, I was back in my seventh circle of hell.

The phones never stopped during the holiday season. From October through February, it was nonstop. Most requests were simple enough and easy to deal with. I can handle a hit and run accident in my sleep, but the holidays gave me at least 20 per day. Someone was out shopping at the mall; the parking lots were packed. When they come out of the mall, hours later, there is "new" damage to the car. Most of those calls ended with a, "Sorry, can't help you." They never had the correct coverage.

There were disputes on charges, begging for loans, fear of scams and theft, hacking and, the worst, system crashes at work. When we had those crashes, whether it was our office or the companies we serviced, the panic filled the air. The one system that never crashed: the phones. We still had to answer the phones even though there was nothing we could do. The shit was annoying. Shut it all down!

I thought I could let those calls roll off my back, but hearing the misplaced anger 20-30 times a day caused frustration. It all comes back to due diligence, reading, and personal responsibility. Three things people had problems dealing with. I hoped the six months gave me the right tools to relax. That frustration returned fast and with a vengeance. I had to get my breathing under control because the frustration caused my control balance to change. I would get to 75/25 without knowing it if I wasn't careful.

"Humans really will never change," Anansi said that afternoon. I was mad at myself for getting back to this place. I was doing so well. October was nuts but I got through it. It was mid-November and Christmas shopping was mayhem. One department store had a security breach of the debit card information from shoppers; and then another one. We had to help with the data breaches and the debit cards. We literally contract with the department stores and banks. The phones ringing filled the air with too much noise. Everyone's voice is elevated to be louder than the person beside them because the caller said they couldn't hear the representative on the other end. My quiet corner was filled with sirs, ma'ams, pardons, apologies, and sighs. I even had foot traffic.

Between calls, I had instant messages asking for help and people coming to my desk when they couldn't find a manager to help. I was busy every day. I just got back and now I was answering people's questions. I haven't been here in six months for mental issues, and I was bombarded with questions. Complex questions, cool, but these stupid questions were another thing. "A member is on the line and asking why their overdraft did not pull." These were questions that the contact center should know. Why the hell were they calling up here. I could fight the entire 10th floor at this point. I'd been back for 10 fucking minutes.

The only upside was that my days went by fast.

Yessica called on some nonsense and wanted to know why she couldn't use her credit card. She had a $3000 limit and was over the limit by 10%. She knew why she couldn't use her card. She hoped playing dumb would help her. Wrong! She was part of a credit union we contract with, and they offered the basic-of-basic credit card. No rewards, no cash back; just funds to use. She used all her funds. Yessica did not believe me, though.

"There is no way I maxed out my card. I just made a payment," she argued. She was right. She made a payment of $50.

"Ma'am, you made a small payment, but you are still over the limit and the payment made was not the minimum payment due," I informed her.

"I still shouldn't be over the limit. I haven't bought anything," she claimed. Again, she was right. She hadn't bought anything. She took out nearly 10 different cash advances, then bought shit.

"Ma'am, you have several cash advances from your credit card to your personal account," I explained.

This was the dumbest conversation I'd had that day. How did she lose track of the money she deposited into her own account? The holiday season really got people high. They blacked out or overdosed on spending. When they came to, they were in debt and bought more gifts for themselves than others. Yessica was trying to magically make money appear. She tried to argue the money back into her account. No, Yessica, you weren't hacked. No, Yessica, you were not a victim of the data breach. No, Yessica, I did not file a dispute.

"Ma'am, are you currently looking at both your checking account statement and your credit card statement?" I had both pulled up and saw the exact date the transfers happened and the interest she was being charged.

"I can't believe I spent that much," she realized. I slammed my head on my desk -- not too hard, though. She wasn't the only customer that felt having a credit or debit card was access to unlimited funds. I can't make this shit up. That slimy tentacle was wrapping around my neck and slowly applying pressure. How are you even able to walk through a door?!

"Is there anything else I can help you with?" I asked. It was my code-switching phrase to say, "Get the hell off my phone."

"Is there a way to apply for a small personal loan?" Yessica asked.

I pounded my head into my desk again. She was serious, a damn personal loan. The nerve and audacity that some people have is astounding. I shouldn't be surprised. Yessica was past due on her credit card, over the limit, and now wanted a personal loan to put herself more in debt.

"You would like to apply for a personal loan?" I hope she heard the disbelief in my voice.

"I have rent and groceries I need. It's an emergency," she said.

It's funny how rent, utilities, and groceries need to be paid for all the time. The rent and utilities have the same due date each month. Everyone seems to hope all the joy and goodwill from the holidays would magically pay the bills. I wish I could be that optimistic. This is the season for miracles but that has never been one of them. I wanted to think she was just throwing out ideas to see what may stick. I did not take her question seriously. The one thing I can guarantee is a ton of mortgages will go into default by January. They always do.

"Hello? Are you still there?" she asked.

"Yes, ma'am," I replied. I did not even realize that I'd gone completely silent. My brain was not fully understanding why people were like this. By law, I could not deny her from making the loan application. I knew my answer, but I took all the information down. I barely asked her anything. I just copied and pasted her profile information into the application. I had to update her income based on what she stated it was. I was not going to question her because she was getting denied. She knew it and I knew it, but she took her shot.

"Alight, Ms. Santiago, I am going to put you on hold and have this reviewed for you. I should have an answer in a few minutes." I lied. I didn't need to have anything reviewed, but the last thing I needed was for Yessica to claim I was being biased.

"I will get an answer today," she asked.

"Yes, we can approve or deny within a few minutes," I explained. "I am going to put you on hold now."

I popped up to see how the pandemonium was going. Everyone was still running around, tripping over their own feet (I didn't mean to laugh), and waiting in line at different managers' cubicles, looking for an answer. I found my opening with Anderson and rushed to his desk. I did not realize I went a little too fast because I caused wind to kick up and blow papers on everyone's desks. I was at 15% without realizing it. I pretended not to notice and hoped everyone else would just think it was the AC. I heard the waves roaring.

"Hey, Anderson," I peeked into his cubicle.

"Yeah, Elle, what's up?" He never looked up from his computer.

"Can you deny this personal loan really quick?" I laid the application on his desk, and I sat in one of the chairs. I heard someone rush to Anderson's desk and realized I was already there. They waited outside the cubicle for their turn.

"Why do I need to deny this? You have authorization," he replied.

"This customer will definitely complain and ask for a review if I deny her," I explained.

"Alright, so what is going on?" Anderson asked.

"Long story short, she is dumb as hell. She maxed out her credit card and put it over the limit. If you let her tell it, she doesn't remember doing any of that. She did a cash advance to her checking account and just kept swiping her card. Now she needs money for the necessities," I growled. I didn't even notice that I did it until Anderson chuckled.

"So basically, she does not have the credit history to justify a personal loan," Anderson read through her credit report.

"Yessica has nothing to justify giving her this loan," I snarled. I was wasting my time on Yessica. I saw the files and dealt with people directly who mismanaged their money. Asking for a personal loan to cover basic needs was a spot I never wanted to be in. I didn't know why but Yessica's willful ignorance got under my skin. Her materialism jeopardized her livelihood and the worst part about it was that she wouldn't learn from this. We were going to deny her, but she could go somewhere else. Higher interest and predatory lending were right around the corner. Title loans, paid loans, high interest short-term loans, or this new option to make monthly payments available when you shop online. I assumed Yessica took that option as well. Where the fuck her money went was beyond me.

"Alright, I went ahead and denied it and put in some notes," Anderson said.

"Thank ya," I replied. I popped out of his office to a line of people waiting to ask him a question. I walked slowly back to my desk. I could hear the pings from the instant messenger. I had my own questions to answer once I got rid of Yessica.

"Okay, thank you so much for holding. I apologize for the wait. I had your application reviewed and unfortunately, we will not be able to approve you for the personal loan at this time." There was about 15 seconds of silence and then Yessica just let loose.

"You need to get me to a manager! You just kept me on hold for 15 minutes and denied this loan yourself. How am I supposed to pay my bills?"

I was silent. Self-awareness was at the bottom of the Mariana trench, eaten by the Kraken that dwelled there. The waves were rushing towards me.

"Interesting," Anansi whispered.

"Hello! Hello! I know you did not hang up on me!" Yessica shrieked.

"Ms. Santiago, I had a manager review the application. He denied it, not me. Would you like to speak with him? The current manager's wait time is 45 minutes." My tone was dry, and I spoke through my teeth. I was not trying to hide behind my corporate voice. I wanted to tell Yessica about herself by making her wait on hold for more time and having her hear a denial a second time. I hope she hears the word "deny" all the way to the president of the company.

"I do not want to be on hold that long," Yessica said.

"Unfortunately, it is the holidays and a busy time. Do you want me to transfer you?" I asked.

"Oh, now you are being rude to me."

I damn sure was, and I wasn't hiding it. "Do you wish to have your application reviewed by a manager?"

"Just transfer me and I will be making a compla…"

I already had the number queued up and did not wait another minute. I kept myself calm. I had tons of messages and emails to answer. I took myself out of the queue. Already! "Al-freaking ready" I thought. Then it hit me. My new "situation" aka Anansi could give me the high I had with Mr. Patel. Yessica needed a kick in the ass and the new me could get away with it.

In between emails, random pop-ups, and snack breaks, I learned about Yessica. I memorized her address, looked at her transactions, and stalked her social media. She was a vocal one on social media. That alone was reason enough to mess with her. No one cared about your relationship issues, Yessica. She was about to get all of these training from the past six months.

I kept my frustration at bay the rest of the day. Once I pulled up to my house, I let Inu out to explore while I changed. I did my usual warmups and then I gave Inu the command "safe space" and he ran up to one of his favorite spots. I threw knives from the ground and in the trees. I tried and hit the same spot from wherever I was. I emptied three 20-round clips while balancing on weak branches. I needed to get this frustration out. Jumping from tree to tree wasn't going to help. Inu was watching from a safe distance or chewing on his front paw. He had my nail-biting habit. Inu would bark when he heard the bullets hit anything metal. It was like he was counting out loud for me. That dog always had a way of calming me down. I didn't have to work out my frustrations for long. I calmed down and practiced being weightless for the rest of the night as a meditation.

Yessica gave me my first chance to be superhuman in a situation. I wasn't sure what I wanted to do to Yessica. I practiced my boxing against a tree while we, I, thought of a plan.

"What is the plan, Elle?" Anansi asked.

"Well, I don't know," I began. "She would be fantastic practice but I don't know what I should do with her."

"It appears you have done something like this before," he said.

"Yeah! Kinda. That was a spur of the moment and I could have easily gotten caught. With you around I can do more and get away with it. You got any ideas?"

"What did you do in the previous times?"

"Well, I beat the shit out of one of them, and with the other, I threatened her job and exposed her to her boss," I answered.

"I am not sure what you mean by the last part," he said.

"I told on her, basically," I replied. It sounded so childish when I put it like that.

"I see. Which one did you enjoy more?" he asked.

"How do you know if I enjoyed it?" I replied. I couldn't be that easy to read.

"You would not wish to try again if you did not enjoy it," Anansi pointed out. He wasn't wrong, but I hated it when he was right.

"Okay," I began, "I enjoyed it. I had a high unlike any other and I want to get that high back. Plus, you can relate to this, humans are dumb and want to be babied as adults…I can't take it."

My level of frustration was building, and the tree got the punishment. I swung with my right too hard and split another tree.

"Woah!" The tree began to split from the hole I made with my fist. "Oh tree! I'm so sorry," I said. I gave it a hug. I listened and could still feel the movement inside the tree. I needed to use a different punching bag.

"So, these are people who…"

"Dumb as hell! It is not everyone. I wouldn't have the time to kick everyone's ass. I experienced times where…," I sighed. "I feel a darkness consume me and I know that person deserved whatever I gave them. What is scary, especially with returning to work, is that it's not only the customers, but my coworkers, and the damn person who holds up the line." I could feel my frustration send fire through my veins and collect on my fingertips.

"Most interesting," Anansi began. "It sounds like you are ready to start chaos as a way of retribution."

"Chaos, hell I'll settle for giving someone a black eye and a slight inconvenience for some of the shit I deal with," I answered. I walked out of the woods and back to my home. Inu was right there waiting. Anansi sighed because I wasn't fully on board with his vision of "chaos." I returned to a 90/10 balance before I got too close to Inu. "Hey Bubba," I rubbed Inu's back and he followed me back into the house.

"Tell me why this is, human," Anansi asked. I didn't want to talk about it anymore. I'd rather think about this in the morning.

"Yessica was mad she didn't have enough money in her account to pay her bills. Based on her previous transactions, she paid for gifts and shit and forgot she had to keep a roof over her head."

"I understand. She squandered and then wanted someone else to fix it."

"Exactly!" I was surprised he understood that quickly.

"A person who wishes for the finer things but does not have the power or riches to do what their heart desires," he said.

"Well…that's a poetic way to say she is a label whore or terrible financial planner."

"Why don't we destroy the things she holds dear?" Anansi suggested. I sat up.

"Fuck her shit up," I said. That was perfect! We put the plan in motion that evening.

Work continued to be crazy and now my weekends were busy, too. I had to balance family and friend time for the holidays, do some Christmas shopping, and learn Yessica's patterns. Yessica has three children who are adorable but undisciplined. The way she complains about the fathers of these children, you would think she ran a tight ship. Nope. This was a situation I hated. I understood wanting to give her children the world, but stability and knowledge should be a part of that. She had three children and lacked financial and self-awareness. I didn't have high hopes for these kids.

However, Anansi says that human flaws were a sweet spot to exploit. He wasn't wrong.

Yessica lived in a two-bedroom apartment. It was in a large apartment complex with the typical playground, dog park, and pool. The leasing office was right in the center of the property. The buildings were older. The red brick had long turned brown, the weeds broke through the sidewalks, and the stairs were carpeted. That part, I did not understand. The stairs are outside and carpeted. That was gross. She lived on the second floor, so coming in through the window was going to be tricky. Good thing I knew how to climb.

The buildings had five stories and I had to get in at the second. I should climb up instead of down. The wooded area behind her building was a great cover. Yessica's apartment looks out over the woods on the left when I am facing the apartments. I had to learn the entire layout. I took Inu on walks near the apartment complex to look around. Inu made some friends at the dog park. However, one lady was tempting me to knock her ass out. She was so scared that Inu would attack her yappy Pomeranian. My dog minded his business and was running around and playing. Her damn dog, Lady, was the loud one. She was lucky my mind was working on Yessica. I should come for her next.

After a few days, I was ready to go in. Yessica valued the material things so much that she forgot she had living expensive. I decided to shatter that backward ass thinking of things first and a home for her kids second. I would try to avoid the children's things but I was going to destroy everything else in that house. Then Yessica had a real reason to ask for financial help and it would be an "NMP" moment. Not my problem!

I parked my car at an empty shopping center up the street. I needed to go in through the window. I climbed up the trees and jumped from branch to branch to her apartment. I would trash her apartment and then leave. Easy! Her kids are not home until around 9 pm because of her job. The apartment was going to be empty for a few hours. I bought my blue crossbody bag to hold my tools, a black hoodie, black shoes, a pair of gloves, and this cool knife I bought. Hopefully, the knife remained a last resort. It was about 6 pm when I got to the window.

I took off the screen on the window and used the flat end of one of my tools to push the lock on the window. I was immediately greeted with toys all over the floor. I came into the children's room. I carefully walked around the toys and entered the living room and saw the plastic Christmas tree to my right. It was in the corner by the patio door. The presents were tucked tightly under the tree and flowed onto the floor. The tree was too small to cover all the gifts. I felt it was too damn early, but that's just me. There was a nice 60-inch TV mounted on the wall with a few gaming consoles plugged into it. The master bedroom door was at the end of the hall.

Yessica's closet was filled with shoes and clothes. The clothes were on the floor, thrown on the bed and on hangers. She had more designer logos than the store that sells them. The bed was a mess, and the headboard wasn't even attached to anything. It became obvious where her money went. She had all this shit but no money for rent or to get a proper headboard.

I started with Yessica's room. I started ripping and cutting up her clothes. I doubted she would notice until she went about cleaning up. From the look of her room, that wouldn't be any time soon. I may leave the presents alone because the kids did not ask to be here. The knife I brought came in handy. I lifted the mattress and cut that shit up too.

"Elle!" Anansi was loud. "Focus!"

Shit! I let my frustration distract me. I wasn't using my hearing and sight. The door creaked open and Yessica and this random ass dude walked in the front door. I dipped into the closet and tried to blend in with the clothes. I adjusted my hearing to see what was going on. I was stuck. How the hell was I supposed to get out of here without being seen?

"Damn girl, you got a lot of stuff under that small ass tree," the guy said.

"Boy, shut up," Yessica laughed. "You know I got kids that want everything. Plus, you wanted something for Christmas too."

"Aww, I'm special," he teased.

"Come on! We don't have much time. The kids are still with my mom." I heard their footsteps on the carpet approaching the bedroom.

"Fuck," I whispered. I had a few minutes after they were finished doing whatever to get out of the house. I didn't want to hear what I thought was about to go down, though. "Please be as vanilla as possible," I thought.

She was giggling and kissing. He was grunting and kissing. I was about to throw up.

"Damn, move all these clothes," he said.

"Don't throw the clothes on the floor," Yessica said.

"Whatcha mean? You gots all yo clothes on the damn floor," he pointed out.

"Yeah, but these are clean, D," she explained. "Let me put them in the closet."

No, no, no, no, no. This can't be real. Girl, do this later. Let D give you those wonderful five minutes and then go get your damn kids.

"Man, hurry up," D shouted.

"All that bass in your voice needs to be fixed or you are leaving with a dry ass dick," Yessica snapped. I agreed with her on that. Dude, it's just sex, calm down. It was like time slowed down as Yessica gathered her clothes to put them in the closet. I raced to come up with a plan. I was hoping all these damn shoes and clothes would keep me hidden, but life is never that easy.

"Elle," Anansi began, "you need to think of something."

He was right, I had to think of something quick. I was in a panic.

"Shit, shit, shit," I whispered.

"Elle, calm down," Anansi answered. He was unbelievably calm. It must be nice. My face would be all over the news for a home invasion not a giant spider.

"How am I supposed to calm down? I need to hide my face," I answered.

I rummaged as quietly as possible through the closet to find a scarf or something to cover my face. I took this red silk shirt off the hanger, tied the sleeves around my head, and tied the bottom of the shirt around my neck.

"This will work," I reassured myself. I couldn't breathe. I pulled the shirt off and looked for something else. I was so panicked; I didn't even hear them arguing.

"Why don't you just go to that other bitch's house then," Yessica yelled. "All you need to do is hold on for a damn minute while I put the clothes up." Well, that escalated quickly.

"Man, I don't even know who you talkin bout," D replied. Oh, he knew.

The rest of Yessica's argument was muffled by the sound of my heartbeat in my ears. My breathing quickened and the walls of the closet seemed to close in on me. I was so thankful for the stupid ass argument they were having. I searched around the closet for something to cover my face when I started noticing her footsteps approaching the closet.

"Elle, there is no time. You need to calm down and let me take over," Anansi said.

"Take over," I stuttered. I did not have a plan, but I didn't want to know what Anansi meant. I didn't know what was about to happen or if I could come back. I was stuck between a rock and a hard place.

"Elle, you need to make a decision now!" Anansi was hiding something.

"Anansi, what are you not telling me? You know the rules."

"I think if we change our balance, one of my abilities can be used."

"Which one?"

"I don't know that yet," he said. That wasn't helpful.

I saw the doorknob turn, in slow motion.

"Fine, get me out of here," I whispered. I shut my eyes, not knowing what was about to happen. My head started to hurt, and my body tightened. I could pass out right now, but I remained standing. It felt like someone was trying to split my head right down the middle. I felt a warm sensation at the tips of my fingers and fell to one knee from the pain. It took all my current strength not to scream out. The closet would inhale and exhale along with me as I tried to catch my breath.

"Where are we on the balance?" I had to ask through my teeth because the pain was unbearable but I had to remain standing.

"50/50," he said. His voice sounded strained.

"What?!" Suddenly, I noticed there was smoke coming from my hands.

"Am I on fire?" I asked. I was eerily calm, but I think it was the pain.

"You are not. Remain calm, Elle. Just let it flow. Resisting will only make the pain worse." It sounded like Anansi was in pain as well. He sounded strained and I heard his breathing. In a matter of seconds, the closet filled with smoke. It was thick and oddly colorful. Within milliseconds, Anansi filled the entire room with smoke. It did not stop Yessica though. She still opened the door and was arguing with D.

They seemed oblivious to the smoke in the room. As soon as Yessica opened the door, I froze. She walked right up to me but didn't see me. She hung some clothes up and went to grab more. My feet moved before I knew it. I sped towards her. I grabbed Yessica by the neck, lifted her up and threw her into the wall. D was still arguing with her until he saw her fly into the wall. He jumped up from the bed. "What the fuck!" he yelled.

Through the smoke, I turned towards D before he could rush to Yessica. I didn't know where this extra strength came from, but I punched D in the stomach and sent him flying into the ceiling. It was like I was watching my body but unable to stop it. I was terrified and excited at the same time. I felt a new surge through my blood that was hot and soothing. Yessica was slumped over on the floor. I saw some blood coming from her head. D had blood coming from his mouth as he lay on the floor. They were both unconscious. I should be horrified at what was happening, but I was amazed at my speed, strength, and the fact that the room was filled with smoke from my fingers.

I knocked out two people! Why? They did not notice the smoke that came from my hands. Could they still see me? There was no blood on my hands, but there was still smoke coming from my hands.

"Anansi! What did you do?" I asked. "What did I do?'

"It's called halluz smoke," he answered. "I wasn't sure if I could do it at first. You can't change forms like I can. Surprisingly, you can perform some of my tricks."

"Halluz smoke?" I repeated. I stared at the two bodies on the floor. There was a big hole in the wall by the full-size bed. The ceiling was broken into pieces where D's body went. It caused a large crack to race from the bedroom door frame to the window. I still looked down at my hands. I know what just happened, but then I don't know what happened.

I went to make sure they were still alive. My right hand was shaking as I checked to make sure that Yessica and D were still breathing. I was happy they were alright, but I was craving more of a fight. I wanted them to get up. I wanted them to give me another reason. I was horrified at what I had done, but the power-up was an incredible feeling.

As I examined my hands a little more, I realized I never put on my gloves. "Shit! My fingerprints!" I found a hand towel hanging in the bathroom and started wiping everything down. I mean everything. I rushed to the kids' room where I entered. I reached into my bag and grabbed my gloves. I couldn't believe I lost focus. This was my first real test run and I botched it. Surprises like this cannot happen again. I needed to go about this better and eliminate the chances of getting caught. I doubted I would be lucky again. Mr. Patel took up all my luck, I bet. I did one final walk through. I heard D start to moan so I took that as a good sign -- and a sign that it was time to go. I opened the window to leave. The pain was getting worse and I felt like I would pass out.

I wanted to make sure the police would be scratching their heads. I never tried to balance on a narrow edge like the windowsill. "No time like the present," I whispered to myself. The window was dirty and there was a nail trying to force its way into the sole of my shoe. I swung my bag to the front and grabbed anything flat I could find to lock the window from the outside. Then, I put the screen back in place. It would fall the minute the window opened. Hopefully, if it were opened, the assumption would be the kids did it.

I am so happy it gets dark so early. My whole plan was a failure. I jumped into the woods but stumbled at the pain of landing. It was like my brain bounced as I landed. "Anansi, we need to get back to base, I can't go further like this," I said. I leaned against a tree.

"That is not an option. If you stay, you may be found." Anansi's voice was strained, too. Neither one of us was prepared for an equal balance.

"Well, do you have a plan? A fast plan?" I asked.

"Prepare yourself to run," he said.

"Okay…" I pushed myself off the tree and took a deep breath. I nearly fell to my knees. "Now what, Anansi?" I asked.

"Repeat after me: Mframa fa me."

"Mframa fa me," I repeated. I immediately started running, but this time was different. I ran faster than I ever have. The world blended into streaks of color. There was no sound except the wind. My vision was sharp, and I was able to avoid the cars, animals, and people in the way. They appeared frozen in time while I sped past them. It took me seconds to reach my car.

I stopped at my car, but the world didn't. My clear vision was now blurry. My car wasn't even visible. I started panicking because this was new.

"Anansi, base," I said. It was still blurry and my body was heavy. I leaned onto my side mirror to keep myself steady. "Are we still at 50/50," I asked. The pain was not going away.

"I am unsure, human. This is a new experience. It has caused me slight discomfort."

"Slight? This is the worst pain yet. I know you can feel it, too."

The world slowly came into focus. It was like the world had to catch up to me. I rubbed my eyes a little bit to try and force my vision clear. We never practiced 50/50 control balance. We never even got close to 60/40. Once I let Anansi in more, he went to a level neither of us was prepared for. Was power worth pain like this?

Everything in the world caught up to my sight. It was like taking off your eye mask after sleeping. My vision cleared up. I heard the cars on the road and the crickets on the ground. I went to open my car door and caught a glimpse of my reflection.

I screamed and tumbled back. I scratched up my car and broke a piece of the door handle as I fell back. My breathing became labored, and I crawled back from the reflection in my car and started touching my face.

"What the hell?!" I slowly stood up while pulling and tugging on my cheeks and eyelids. I went to look in the mirror. I screamed louder. "Ahhh! What...what's wrong with my eye? What is this?" I yelled. "Ouch!" I poked myself in the eye. Was this real?

"Calm down, human," Anansi sighed. I was freaking out so much that I did not even hear the human part.

"Anansi, what's happening to me?"

My eye wasn't an eye. No pupil, iris, or white part. My damned eye had a luminated spider in the center. There were flakes of gold, purple, and green, depending on how I turned my head. I rapidly blinked, but it didn't go anywhere.

"What is this? Anansi?!" He better not ignore me. I was trying to watch myself look left, right, up, down, and in circles. The eye moved just like my real eye. I even poked my eye again and felt it. "So, it's actually there," I realized.

"Are you quite done, Elle?" Anansi asked. He was always too fucking calm! Even in pain, he was calm. He knew what was happening and didn't tell me. That was against the rules.

"No! Look at my eye!" I couldn't believe it. I looked around to make sure no one was looking at me and freaking out about my eye. The pain was now an afterthought to the change on my face.

"It appears that when we are even in balance, one of your eyes changes. That is my eye you are seeing on your right and your eye is on the left."

"So will this always happen when we are in a control balance?" I asked. "I never saw it before." Granted, we were mostly outside training. I never saw a reflection until after we went back to 90/10.

"Not necessarily. This is us at complete 50/50. It shows that we are balanced. Any less of me and your eyes were normal, I assume. The eye may change colors, dilate, or turn just black when you control balance at certain lower percentages," he explained.

"We have to find out! I couldn't have anyone walk up to me and suddenly one of my eyes turn black or worse. They would think I was possessed by a demon. My mom will have me at an altar within seconds if she sees that." I just kept looking at my eye. I wondered if this has been happening since I got back to the office. The good thing about my back corner is that no one comes back there like that. Wes never said anything, and I barely look up from my computer, so I think this was the first time.

198

I closed both my eyes and focused on separating Anansi's mind and mine. I wanted to get back to our normal 90/10. I took a few breaths in and out, trying not to think about anything. The assault I just committed, my eye changing, and two new tricks with warp speed and smoke all needed to leave my mind. In and out. In and out. When I looked again, I was back to normal. I let out the biggest breath as if I had been holding it in for the past few minutes.

"Two minds sharing one body; it would be a surprise if there were not some consequences to it. The advantage is your enhanced senses and new abilities. The disadvantage is my eye will reflect a perfect balance of those two minds," Anansi said.

I drove home in silence, trying to process all my emotions. I was scared, intrigued, angry, unfulfilled, and excited about what happened. What really scared me was the enjoyment of using my strength and more power.

Once I got home, I let Inu out to play and go potty. I went to my bathroom to look in the mirror. I examined my actual face for a bit. I was nervous about the change. I haven't felt nervous at all since my training started. I took a deep breath and focused on the control balance. I heard Anansi let out his own sigh.

"Focus, Elle," I told myself, "and increase your senses." I decided to start there because it was familiar to me. My eyesight and hearing gave me the information I needed. What someone was talking about, when they were on the move, or whether they were excited, all had a sound.

I looked in the mirror and did not see any changes. I am at 85/15.

I went back to focusing. I kicked my senses up a notch to hear the animals on the forest floor and the trees. I could even hear the cars on the main road. I took another look in the mirror and saw no changes. This was the control balance that was great for my weapons training. At 80/20, I can slice someone's throat with a butter knife. I was the world's best sniper at this balance.

"That's not powerful enough," Anansi commented.

"Maybe you are just holding back on purpose so I do more," I replied. Anansi always wanted me to push more and to do more. He wanted to feel more powerful, like he was before, but he was limited. I was limited. I am human, as he liked to point out. He was in my body. He had to accept my choices. I barely had control of my life. Why would I give up the little I already had?

"Is that what you think? I encourage you to use me more. I would be pleased with more," he replied.

"Yeah, scratch that. I realized what I said. I need to do this on my own. Alright..." I made some type of grunt as I got off my couch. I held the mirror tight and headed for the front door. I looked around for my shoes and headed for the trees. I focused on 70/30, tucked the mirror in my pants and climbed up the tree to balance on one of the weakest branches. Once I was on the branch, I checked my face again. Nothing.

I let out a sigh of relief to have some idea of what was going on with my face. I could go to work with less on my mind. I needed to know when the change happened. We hadn't gone past 70/30. I got to the point where those control balances weren't painful to me or Anansi. How could I reach 50/50? Did I want to reach it? The pain was unbearable but that is what practice was for. I jumped from the branch and landed perfectly. I had more training to do.

I went back into the house, flopped on my couch, and fell asleep almost immediately. I went to sleep feeling high and that should have worried me, but it excited me.

"Anansi, what does "Mframa fa me" mean?"

"A loose translation is 'wind take me," he said.

"Wind take me," I repeated. "Why 'wind take me'?" I asked.

"The wind is a force that is. Even on a still, calm day the wind is around even when you can't see it."

"Mframa fa me," I repeated again. Anansi was right. Wind is around even when it is still. I became wind.

Test Subjects

My alarm woke both of us up because neither one of us was expecting it. I'm surprised Anansi didn't wake me up. I was supposed to be training before the sun came up. Was he just as wiped out as I felt?

I didn't remember plugging my phone into my charger or falling asleep. Inu gave a stretch and so did I. I shuffled to the door and opened it for him. He stretched a few more times and then walked casually out the door. "Not a care in the world, huh?" I said to him. He bounced his cute self out the door.

Whoever invented "casual Fridays" helped me so much. I was running late so I put on a pair of jeans and a plain black shirt. Easy. I picked up a colorful pair of tennis shoes and went to the kitchen. I chugged as much water as I could. I hadn't been this thirsty or hungry in a while. I guess my body still needed to adjust to Anansi in different stages.

Inu came back in and sat in the kitchen waiting for me. I put some water in his bowl and cooked up all the eggs I had left in the fridge. I searched for anything to add. I had some turkey deli slices, so I added that. I put some bread in the toaster and boom, breakfast. I gave Inu scrambled eggs and toast. Then I made myself a sandwich. I grabbed what I needed for the day and headed out the door.

As I was driving to work, all my questions came rushing in.

"Anansi," I began, "how does the halluz smoke work?"

"I usually use it to move around places undetected. Sometimes I hate changing forms, but a great spider cannot easily walk around unnoticed."

"So, shot in the dark here," I said sarcastically, "it causes hallucinations."

"That is correct," he replied. After all this time, he did not fully grasp sarcasm.

"Can people see it? The smoke?"

"No, they cannot. It is like the wind to them. It is invisible but flows freely in and out of the body."

"But it was so thick," I replied.

"I have yet to attempt this trick in your body. I may have gone overboard," he explained.

"So, it won't affect me, just the people around me."

"Correct," Anansi said.

"I don't like how you said that." Whenever he found something interesting, he wanted to test it out several times. That meant several bruises, cuts, body aches, and headaches for me.

I rushed in and out of traffic to make it to work on time. I may have driven on the emergency shoulder behind an ambulance. I merged in seamlessly, though. We were stopped on the highway for no reason anyway. I kept reminding myself to remain calm. "Don't let stupid get to you today. Stay in control," I repeated. The parking lot at work was packed. It was always packed but it seemed worse today. The little things annoyed me quicker than usual. I parked at the first spot I found and rushed into the building.

I went to my desk with so much on my mind. I wanted to pretend to work for the rest of the day. Which is nothing new from a "normal" day, but this time I really meant it. I did the bare minimum and at lunch, I went to the apartment complex across the street and laid on the grassy hill by the leasing office. The day wasn't too cold. It was a nice fall day and a good thing for the South. I could have a nice day even in November and December. What winter?

"I gotta add something new to my training again," I thought to myself. I let out a sigh and drifted off to sleep under the sun for the rest of my lunch break.

The migraine became intense almost immediately. I closed my eyes tightly, but it didn't help. The shade from the trees helped but the pain was unbearable. Light was my enemy, so I retreated to the shadows like a vampire. I collapsed against a large tree because the pain was unbearable. I was at 50/50. The headaches and sharp pains stopped a long time ago for the other control balances and they were a cake walk compared to this. I curled up in the fetal position and wrapped my arms around my knees. It didn't help. It caused my head to throb more. He would never admit it, but the change in control was hurting Anansi, too.

After a few minutes, the migraine went away. I didn't move from my spot. I had to catch my breath. I could hear Anansi doing the same.

"Why does this hurt you?" I asked through my teeth.

"I am within your body, Elle. I did not think going to a complete balance would have a negative effect on me as well. You practiced the other balances for so long that it is second nature. Your body and mind are not ready. We need to practice this more," he replied.

"This sucks." I tried to get to my feet. Unfortunately, the migraine made me dizzy, and my vision was blurry. I called for Inu so I could follow him back to the house. I could barely see. Inu was stumbling over himself, chasing squirrels. I heard his paws brushing against the floor of the woods. He stopped immediately and ran to me, but he wasn't his sweet self. He started barking at me and growling.

"Not now Inu. My head hurts," I told him. His barking was making my migraine worse. Inu just kept barking.

"He can sense me," Anansi said.

"No shit! He really doesn't like you," I laughed through pain. "Dogs can really sense otherworldly things."

I started digging my hands into the dirt and tree bark to steady myself as I tried to stand. The pain throbbed throughout my body. I had to get out of the 50/50 so I started breathing slowly. I had to calm myself down in tandem with Anansi to get out of 50/50. "Deep breaths, Elle," I chanted. In and out. Woof! In and out. Woof! Woof! In and out. The dizziness began to fade, and I was able to get steady on my feet. Inu went back to his sweet self and let me pet him. My vision was still blurry, so I let Inu lead the way back to the house. Going to 50/50 was scaring me, but what I could do in that balance excited me more. What was happening to me? Once I reached the front door, I was able to feel my way to the kitchen. I gave Inu a treat, got a dish rag, soaked it in cold water and flopped on the couch to cool myself down.

I watched the news to see what was developing. The news stations were having a field day with Yessica. Two people were attacked in a locked apartment. They were okay. I broke one of D's ribs and Yessica had a concussion, but overall, they were fine. The police were called by D when he woke up completely. According to the news, they thought he was a suspect at first. They ignored his injuries, thinking they were inflicted because of self-defense. However, that didn't stick. A locked apartment, two victims who were possibly high, and extensive property damage was all the police had or at least that's all they alluded to on the news networks.

People at work were talking about it, too. I stayed away from information on what I did for a while. Apparently, Yessica went to social media to tell the real story. The rumors and theories were all over people's newsfeeds. "They were high on a new drug," some said. "The police and news are exaggerating," others said. "That house was probably destroyed beforehand. There is no way one person caused that much damage and escaped unseen." Some people at work were convinced that something supernatural happened. They had no clue how correct they were. Some conspiracy theories were true, and this was one of those unbelievable things that needed an unbelievable explanation.

I listened to the funny theories and kept my head down. The news eventually went on to the next story. The gossip died down, but Yessica didn't. She still pleaded on social media for information. She wanted people to believe her and D (his full name was Derrick-Sean). I stalked their social media for a while. She had video of the hole in the wall and the ceiling. She complained that her landlord wouldn't return her security deposit. That part was kind of fucked up but icing on the cake for the damage I did. I did not fear a knock at my door. The comments were full of people claiming this was a hoax. Even the police, according to Yessica, accused her of making everything up. Even considering the real injuries, they thought she was covering up a domestic violence situation at the least. All this information added to my high. I might be fearful of what 50/50 could bring, but I was satisfied with my revenge.

I found myself on social media well into the night. That was a mistake. The internet was a mess. The theories that people came up with were wild. One person said they were abducted by aliens. The main theory in real life was that it was a domestic situation. But the most irritating thing was the spelling errors, grammar, and shorthand typing. It took me 10 minutes to realize that "asl" wasn't "age, sex, location" like when I grew up. That shit meant "as hell." If I saw that one more time, I was going to throw more people against a wall like Yessica. I wouldn't need the halluz smoke or to go 50/50 for that either. I had to stop my social media scrolling for the night. It distracted me long enough. I couldn't ignore the elephant in the room. I had to master 50/50 balance and test my new abilities: halluz smoke and warp speed.

Test Subject 1

I took Inu back to the dog park in Yessica's neighborhood and let him play around. It may be a bad idea to return to the scene of the crime, but I knew the perfect test subject. I could kill two birds with one stone. Inu could enjoy socialization with other dogs and I could test my new ability.

I was reading a book and listening to Inu. I knew my dog and with the control balance I could hear him from any spot. I would briefly look up from my book when I heard him yelp. A small dog nipped at him, but he would forget about the pain and continued to play. I could stay here all day because I needed the break. Inu needed the playtime. But on cue, she came to me.

She came up to me and cast a shadow over my book. I pretended not to notice her and kept reading. It was one of those moments when I knew someone was staring at me, but I ignored it. A few seconds went by, and I kept reading and listening to Inu, in case he needed me. Eventually, the lady cleared her throat and said, "Excuse me."

"Yes," I replied but never looked up.

"Is that black pit bull yours?" she asked. I kept reading.

"He is," I said. I kept my tone very neutral. I knew where this was going and that is what I counted on. I took my shades out of my bag to cover my eyes.

"Umm, he should be on a leash!" she demanded. She was that stupid.

"It's a dog park. Is your dog on a leash?"

"My dog isn't vicious," she replied.

I closed my book. "Neither is Inu. Is there anything else I can help you with?" I asked. I looked up. I wasn't too far into my control balance. I started to let go little by little. I wanted to ease into 50/50 because it still hurts going there.

"We would all feel safer if your dog was on a leash," she said. I noticed two other women behind her, Frick and Frack. They were not making eye contact. I guess she was the ringleader and they tagged along because it might benefit them later. I bet they ate a lot of spit from restaurants.

"I would feel safer if you minded your business," I replied. I kept a smile on my face and never raised my voice. I kept it very monotone. That seemed to infuriate her more.

"Your dog is dangerous," she said. Her voice was getting elevated and she had the nerve to put her hand on her hip.

"Oh really? Inu!" He immediately stopped playing and trotted over to me. He sat down by the bench and let me pet him on the head. He was a little out of breath. They looked on as I poured some water into a bowl. I looked up and they were still looking. "Can I help you?" I asked again.

"Are you going to put him on a leash?" she asked. Now she was tapping her foot. Since she was so intent on volunteering, I obliged.

"Inu, safe space," I said. He went off under a shady tree and laid down. Apparently, he was tired because I heard the snoring within seconds. I took deep breaths as I decreased and Anansi increased. I gave credit to the elevated emotions. I was in pain but I could take it. I must have practiced enough that the side effects were beginning to dull. I let the smoke flow from my hands. I was able to produce it faster than with Yessica. I concentrated on the direction of the smoke.

"Focus on where you want it to go," Anansi coached.

I remember that it was almost immediately for Yessica, but we were outside and Anansi was controlling the smoke. This was all me. I needed to learn to control it.

"Focus," he repeated. "Continue releasing the smoke. Consider the direction of the wind."

I needed them to inhale quite a bit for the hallucination to last. If I were constantly around, the hallucination could be endless, but I couldn't follow them around the park. I had to distract them for a bit so the smoke could work its magic.

"Does that look like a vicious dog?" I made sure to keep my voice steady but stern.

"He is on the vicious dog list, and he could snap at any time," she replied. Her neck roll was subpar. It would have been funny if I watched this on a video but when it happened to me, I was ready for assault charges. I applauded the people who resisted knocking a bitch out. Where I was at, fuck being restrained. At this moment, I was happy to use all my weapons.

"I can make him snap if you want. He is well trained, but he is also a pacifist. He doesn't like violence," I laughed. "Let me rephrase that, he doesn't like it when I get violent."

"Are you threatening us?" She did the one thing I hate most: her finger got too close to my face. Her "sidekick" was about to take out her phone to record when they paused. This hallucination was not going to be kind.

"Indeed, I am..." I trailed off because their bodies started to shake in fear. I debated what would be the hallucination. I was going to go to the extreme and do an alien invasion. Instead, I went with a hellhound. A giant, black beast with sharp fangs and red eyes. That's the picture they had about my sweet Inu. The ladies screamed and ran around the dog park. People were looking on in horror and some of the dogs thought it was a game. They saw a hellhound chase them down and bite at their flesh. I tried not to giggle as one of them fell in shit. For two minutes, they clawed at the grass, tore at their clothes and ran around. A few people recorded the antics on their phone, and I think someone called the police.

After two minutes, they snapped out of their hallucinations. They were dirty and on the ground crying loudly. They looked around and noticed the hellhound had disappeared. They inspected themselves. They were not torn to shreds or bleeding. A few people went up to them to help them up and asked if they were alright. I stayed on my bench and Inu was still fast asleep under the tree. I guess I should have run to help them, but nah. I studied their behavior to see what they remembered. Yessica and D were unconscious. I couldn't study them, but I could watch these three.

They started asking if anyone saw what they saw. They even pointed at me and asked if I saw the hellhound. I played stupid and gave a small summary of what happened right before.

"They just started freaking out," I said calmly. I wanted to fall down on the bench from the pain but I remained standing. Inu was still fast asleep. "Without one fucking care in the world," I whispered to myself. I laughed but I knew I needed to focus on bringing myself down to 90/10.

Within seconds, I heard the sirens. The police were close by and, unfortunately, I couldn't leave. It would be too suspicious. I joined the crowd and pretended to be concerned. As the two police cars pulled into the parking lot, the "dog-patrol" was sitting at the gate getting fanned by another person. I focused on my breathing to bring the control balance down.

"Anansi," I strained.

"Yes," he sounded strained as well.

"How far can this shit travel," I asked.

"In this form, I am unsure. Use the flow of the wind to direct the smoke. It floats on gentle waves." The time to be poetic was not right now.

"Okay," I said. I remembered floating in the middle of the sea on gentle waves. I let the smoke do the same with the direction of the wind.

Next time I'll go to a Black-owned dog park. Is there such a thing as a Black-owned dog park? I needed it. Some dog parents are weird as fuck.

"Ma'am, are you okay?" The first officer was a tall, bald, white guy. He had a beer belly that he led with when he walked. I could outrun him even before I had Anansi strapped to my back. The next officer was a shorter Hispanic woman. The first cop towered over her. She might be able to catch someone in a chase but that damn utility belt cops wore would slow her down. She started questioning the people at the park while the first officer talked to the ladies. I wanted to call them worse, but I think I had done enough.

"She was talking with that woman over there before she started freaking out," someone said.

I knew they were pointing at me, so I got ready. I knew I was back to my 90/10 but I kept my eyes slightly closed just in case.

"Inu, come!" He woke up quickly and walked over to me. I put his leash on him and waited.

"Ma'am, can I speak with you for a minute?" the female officer asked me. There was some chatter coming through the radio as she approached the bench.

"Sure," I said politely.

"Can you tell me what happened? The witness is stating that you had a few words with the ladies over by the gate," she said.

"Well, umm...."

"Officer Martín."

"Well, Officer Martín, my dog Inu was playing and running around the park when those three approached me. They said that my dog was vicious and needed to be on a leash while in the park."

"But this is a dog park," she said.

"Exactly. I said the same to her. My dog wasn't hostile to anyone or their pets. He got nipped a few times by that white Pomeranian and just kept playing. I told her I wasn't putting my dog on a leash."

"Then what happened?" she asked.

"They were worried he was vicious, so I told him to distance himself." I could tell she was confused so I explained, "Oh, it's one of his commands called 'safe space.' He went over and found a shady spot."

"Smart dog," she nodded to Inu.

"The weirdest thing happened right afterwards. They froze mid-sentence. I didn't know what was going on."

"Did they say anything?" Officer Martín asked. She pulled out this little notepad. I was watching a crime drama in real life, sort of.

"No, they just started screaming and then ran away," I replied. As I was talking to Officer Martín, the halluz smoke was moving towards the three woman. Right on queue, the hellhound returned. The three women started to run again but I wasn't paying close attention. Officer Martín's partner, Officer Byrd inhaled a bit, too. That officer jumped at the illusion at the same time as the three women, but he stopped. He didn't inhale enough. The cop I was talking to ran over immediately. Both officers tried to catch the women and calm them down. The other witnesses at the park moved closer to me for some reason. I looked over at Inu and he was barking but not at the women; at me. I was in 50/50 and he wasn't happy.

"There is a beast!" she yelled.

"Ma'am, please calm down," the officer yelled. Officer Martín was fast but the utility belt restrained her full speed. The big guy stopped running. He tried to grab whoever got within arm's reach. After another two minutes, they stopped screaming and running. The two officers called for back-up and medical assistance.

"Something is wrong with them," Officer Martín said. The ladies were shaking and constantly looking around.

The officers were unsure what to do. Three women claimed they saw a large black beast with red eyes, while everyone else in the park saw nothing. The women claimed their clothes and skin were being ripped to shreds but the only thing on them were scratch marks. Many of the people in the park gathered around to hear the story as well. The head scratches and shoulder shrugs in disbelief were a bit funny. Everyone tilted their head like a confused dog.

"Everyone, please clear the park," the big guy said. I could hear the sirens. They let us go but most people stayed to watch. I, pleased with my work, called Inu over and left the park. I even forgot about the pain.

Inu slept like a fat baby on the ride home and I was dealing with a migraine. Lucky for me, the police didn't ask for any ID or personal information. I bet in the end, the officers and the others in the dog park thought the women were pill popping housewives that had some bad reaction to their Xanax or whatever.

Let's call this test a success.

Test Subject 2

I should have become a recluse to avoid the decision I made. I decided to keep pushing the limits. After the dog park test, I kept practicing during training. I had finally tested 50/50 enough that the migraines and most of the pain stopped. I taught Inu a new command: "hold your nose." I had him do it after getting to a safe space. Then I would let the halluz smoke out. I learned from Inu that it could work on animals, and I wasn't about to hurt my baby.

The holiday season was in full effect. Work was crazier and I tried my best to stay home. I hated the crowds but, unfortunately, I had some business to take care of, so I needed to go out and endure the weekend traffic. I took Inu to doggy day camp so he could play with other dogs. I gave the squirrels a much-needed break from the nips at their tails. And there wasn't some entitled housewife trying to police a neighborhood; an old ass neighborhood.

After I dropped Inu off for the day, I debated hard about hitting the mall during the Christmas season. I felt the irritation slide up my spine. It stiffened my neck and made me grind my teeth. I dreaded the thought of having to walk into this crowded mall with more stupid people. I dealt with enough of that shit at work. I needed a plan to make this as fast as possible. I made a list, only took cash to limit my spending and only focused on one section of the mall. As I headed to the mall, I reminded myself to watch my emotions. Hopefully, I can get in and out.

The parking lots were full; giant trucks squeezed into the compact spots. Apparently, everyone went blind because they refused to look while driving or walking. I was irritated before I even found a parking spot. That was the first domino. The feelings I felt at work affected me more and more outside of work. I did not know what made me think shopping in person, during the holidays, would be a good thing. I went to a few stores I call "home markets." They have the most random things for home décor and needs. I always find a gem or two or 16 in these stores. Half of those items were ocean and lavender scented candles. The other half would make good, personalized Christmas gifts.

I was proud of myself. I kept calm through some long lines and dumb people who stopped as they were walking through the mall. I sad-

212

dled my frustrations at people not paying attention to the lines moving. I tried to ignore the pedestrians that walked with their heads down, looking at their phones. I took deep breaths when some random lady tried to skip the lines because all she was doing was making a return. I tried disregarding the desire to whoop unsupervised, loud children. "Where are your damn parents?" I yelled at one. He cried and ran away. I felt good about that one.

There were a plethora of things getting on my nerves, but it was a couple waiting for my parking spot that broke me. One of my pet peeves was people who demand faster movement from others but then they take their sweet time once they get it. Customers did that shit all the time. I tried, unsuccessfully, to keep my grievances to myself. The couple had the audacity to be impatient with me. My body had to squeeze in the little space between my car and the van parked over the damn line. "How is that even possible? They just got out and thought, "Oy, that'll work," I figured.

The man behind the wheel honked the horn and snapped me out of my frustration with the terrible parking. I stopped and looked at them. He was giving hand gestures for me to speed up. I shook my head and slowed down on purpose. I turned sideways to shuffle to my driver side door. They honked again and laid on it.

"Oh, oh, oh, this bitch," I laughed. My laugh was manic at this point.

I laughed as a reflex to something stressful. "I was gonna go home but someone begged me to fuck up his day. I shall oblige them," I mocked. I focused on a 50/50 balance immediately to push this damn van into the parking spot correctly, but it was a crowded, CCTV area. I got my door slightly opened. Only a bundle of printer paper would be able to fit through. Then I heard them honk again. I threw my bags into my car and walked back. I put my hood up and I approached the car casually. If I was being filmed, I wanted to seem as calm as possible. I was fuming but they wouldn't be able to tell. When they saw me come back out, walking towards their car, their faces turned pale. They never thought someone would approach them. Up until this day, this couple was probably never punished for their behavior. No one ever corrected them. This may be presumptuous, but they were probably spoiled privileged kids. But not today. Driving a damn minivan. They got some nerve.

"Anansi, you got any ideas?" I asked.

"Let us talk for a while with these humans," he said.

I walked up to the driver side window. It was a small, gray minivan, and I knew they would probably park as crazy as the person beside me. The van had some pink sorority plates on the front and a pink steering wheel cover. My eyes couldn't roll back far enough. The driver was a 40ish-year-old Asian man and the wife was this petite Asian lady. They were talking to each other. Arguing, from what I heard as I approached them. His hand gripped the steering wheel tight, and I could see the sweat starting to drip from his forehead. I knocked on the window. They tried to talk through the glass. He was talking to my chest and wouldn't look me in my eye.

"You need to get away from my car," he screamed.

I knocked on the window again.

"Move away from my car," she screamed.

I knocked a little harder. Maybe it was a little too hard because I cracked the window.

"You see how busy this parking lot is. You need to get away from my car before I call the police," he said through the crack of her window.

Without lowering my head, I said, "There will be no need. We will be gone before they get here." I let the halluz smoke out.

"You need to leave," the woman said. Then she had the nerve to honk the horn again. She was in the passenger seat but her audacity filled the car. The smoke started to seep through the crack in the window and fill up their car.

"You still honking that horn," I calmly said. I bent down to look her directly in the face. I did not try to hide the way my face looked. The smoke had filled up the car.

"Sir, the parking lot is full," I said. "It is best to go to the overflow parking lot and take the shuttle. It is free," I reassured.

The hallucination I put them in wasn't a detailed one. They saw me as a parking attendant. They drove off towards the overflow lot. I let them get a few minutes ahead. I didn't want to appear to be following them. The overflow parking lot wasn't real. They stopped doing that shit years ago. Too many break-ins and hit-and-runs. I'm glad that shit stopped before I started working because I can only imagine the file volume.

There used to be an overflow lot. When it was there, the overflow lot didn't have CCTV. The mall found it was cheaper to stop the over-flow option than to put in more security measures. Plus, online shopping shrunk the number of people shopping but not by much. I couldn't follow close behind, but I needed to see how long the halluz smoke would last. The parking lot was about 10 minutes up the road. I could see the smoke was still in the car. It was decreasing in volume but very slowly. I guess the cold weather helped because they kept the windows up. Enclosed spaces meant the smoke would stay longer.

"Do you have a plan, Elle?" Anansi asked. He had been so quiet today that I forgot he was there.

"I am making it up as I go along. How long do you think I have?"

"Eh, possibly a few more minutes, then they will return from their hallucination," he replied.

"They should be at the parking lot by then." I paused. "Good."

I stopped following them and went a few streets behind the park-ing lot. I grabbed the gloves that I had bought for my mom. This was the perfect time to test warp speed, too. I had only run around the acres of my property in warp speed. I was testing two abilities in one. "Mframa fa me," I whispered. I ran at top speed, and I beat them to the parking lot. The warp speed did not have the side effects of pain. But the blurry vision when I stopped sucked. I put the glove on my left hand and started forming smoke with my right. I made a mental note that the halluz smoke can last for ten minutes for two people in an enclosed space. They parked the car, and I heard them talk. They were slowly realizing they were in a different location. I ran up to the car, opened the door, and filled the car with more smoke. I concentrated on keeping the smoke flowing as I thought of what to do next.

I should have used my left hand for the halluz smoke and put the glove on the right hand. My left hand made me clumsy. They sat still in the hallucination of watching a movie while I looked around. I checked their IDs, stole the cash they had for the hell of it, and memorized two credit card numbers as well. As I robbed them, I got a very weird idea, but it could work. I had them both imagine the other was trying to attack them. Fight or flight situation but they wouldn't be able to flee. I would be able to get a few licks in myself. Well mostly me. I needed these two to hit each other so when the police were called, it looked confusing. I realized how messed up this situation was. At the same time, I felt my power surge back up. The woman attacked first. She was quick and scratched his face. Then he punched her, but neither one stopped. I would hit him then pull-on her hair and clothes. I didn't let him hit her too much, but she needed some bruises.

Then something happened to me. I started hitting them both. Again, and again and again and again until the woman let out a scream. I stopped.

"Elle, I am surprised," Anansi said.

"Surprised how?" I was staring at the man, knocked out on the floor. He was bleeding a lot. I took the ripped shirt to stop some of the bleeding. I checked his pulse twice to make sure he was still breathing.

"I did not think you had it in you," Anansi replied.

"I am blaming this on you. You didn't stop me," I snapped. "I thought the smoke couldn't affect me."

"It doesn't," Anansi snapped back. "Why did you stop?"

"Her screams seemed to snap me out of it," I replied.

"I see," Anansi said.

I hated it when he said things in that tone. I knew that spider brain was ticking away. He knew something. Any down time, I tried to outthink

Anansi. I always interpret "I see" or "interesting" as "I am smarter than you are, human." I would think about that later. I looked back at the couple. My hands shook. I wanted to hit them more, hit them harder. I unleashed some buried frustration on them that I didn't know I had. This was all their fault. Right?

"Mframa fa me," I recited. I got to my car within seconds. As the world was catching up, I removed my gloves. For the first time, I saw debris floating through the air. The world was quickly speeding back up, so I needed to get ready to drive away. I looked around at the debris and saw a plastic bag. "Perfect," I clapped. I grabbed the bag and put all my stuff in it. I was worried there may be some of the man's blood on it. I did not want to risk having it anywhere in my car or a camera seeing that.

Inu was as happy as ever leaving his doggy daycare. I had them bring him out to me because I was tired. I didn't hear his nails clacking through the parking lot, so his grooming went well. He doesn't mind the bath part, but I have the hardest times clipping his nails. He didn't obey any commands when it came to his grooming. Everything else was easy but apparently even a dog has non-negotiables. He had a new toy in his mouth. I told them to let him pick out a toy if he was a good boy with his grooming. Unfortunately, this one had fluff in it. When I picked out a toy, I made sure it didn't have stuffing. I was tired of cleaning that up or seeing it in his poop because he thought it was edible. His pittie smile and that cute little bounce in his walk made me feel a little better. Looks like I was going to clean up more fluff.

We drove home in silence. He played with his new toy in the back seat while I ate three large fries by myself. I got Inu a cheeseburger for when we got home. In the silence, I noticed that I was choosing violence as a punishment for my targets. That wasn't even the worst part. I enjoyed it. 50/50 was a difficult emotion for me. It excited me and scared me all at once. What would happen when 50/50 became second nature like the other lower balances? I made a deep mental note about this feeling. I realized later how I ignored my instincts and common sense. My pet peeves annoyed me more than trying to maintain my sanity, and the bad influence Anansi was.

I was so happy to be home. I let Inu out and headed towards my tiny house. I walked around to the back to throw away the gloves and clothes into my big trash can. Then I changed my mind. "I need to burn this shit," I realized. I stripped down to my socks and drawers and I walked into the house. Inu was munching away at his new toy and I searched for a lighter or matches. I found one of my candle lighters, grabbed a snack cake, and walked to the backyard to burn everything. When I was sure everything was ash, I went to take a shower. I washed my hair and body. I didn't want the hot water to run cold but I was lost in thought. "I need to order a fire pit."

Did I want to know what else I was capable of? I made an appointment with Dr. Lynn for next week. I had avoided her long enough and I missed talking to her a bit.

Next Target

I practiced halluz smoke every day in the woods. I knew there was more I could do, but I took it slow. At 50/50 control balance, I had one crazy eye, smoke that caused hallucinations, and crazy speed. Even if I wanted to push the limits more, I didn't have much time after work. Shit, I would like to sleep or have an evening off to eat cookies and pizza and do hood shit with my friends. The holidays were busy, moving fast, and breaking the bank.

I had plenty of other moments to test the "halluz". It was useful for the people who decided to stop right in the middle of the walkway in a busy mall. Or for people who decided that the "customer is always right" was a universal code to live by. I appreciated the employees who maintained a calm demeanor. I bet you they cried in the car. A lot of people could see hellhounds, aliens, and bugs. I wanted to try something so extreme, but I decided to keep it to things I was familiar with. Thank God for my active imagination. I realized there would be some collateral damage. My targets may not be the only ones affected. I had to make sure the halluz went in a specific direction or an enclosed space.

I practiced it in the office a little bit. It was usually for minor things, like picking the empty stall beside me when there were four stalls open. Leave a buffer door. I made whoever that was see their teeth fall out. I timed it with the flush, so they would see everything in the mirror too. Small things. I started to see the fun in my abilities. At times, I felt drunk with power and most of the time I felt mischievous.

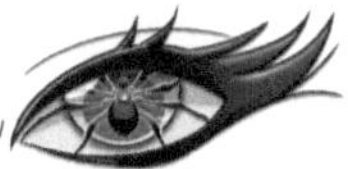

The phones and system failures in the office kept us busy. It was a good thing we had some gossip to give everyone a break from holiday madness. I used Wes as a source of information, but I heard the whispers of everyone else. Charla and Cherilus were about to go into their hearing for sexual harassment and even the rented-out suites of other businesses knew what was happening. It was the best thing ever! I enjoyed every minute. Charla has been getting away with way too much. I couldn't wait to hear the details.

"Cherilus had enough," Wes laughed. "The tea is that she got his number by using someone else's phone. He told her no and she went the long way around to get his number."

"Who does that?!" Seriously, I wanted to know. At Charla's big ol' age, she shouldn't be that desperate. It's just a rumor but I decided I had to tune into that hearing when it starts.

Between phone calls and emails, my coworkers gathered to vent, get water, and gossip. I stayed at my desk. Usually, I would escape to the third floor, but my sanctuary was off limits. I remembered Janus's warning constantly while I was in the office. That's why I was only doing virtual visits. I avoided any spaces that the book was in.

I just got back from break when Sara Sheriff typed her way into my mind. Miss "know-it-all." She thought the rules didn't apply to her. She was a "regular" and as such that means privileges beyond her job title. This wasn't an awards program, Sara; you don't get fucking rewards for regular use. At this point, she was trying to work less or avoid calling her customers to ask for information. I received her request at random. I remembered her from her previous request and my answer to her was always the same.

No.

Sara wanted access to one of her co-worker's files. No matter how many times she was told, there was always someone that gave in and gave this woman access to shit she wasn't supposed to have. This time she landed on my phone line. I was not going to argue with her.

"Sara, I am sorry, but you are not allowed to access that information. You will have to call their client and get the information," I said. I refused to argue with her. She was too afraid to call a client and say, "Hey, could you resend this document?" Instead, she was bold, rude, and in her "frequent flyer" privilege bag when she talked to us. She wasn't getting my help. If something came back, my name and keystrokes would not be anywhere near her shit.

Of course, she ranted and raved about giving her a hard time. I did not budge. She needed to put on her big girl panties and call the client. I put a high priority note in her file about her continuously calling to violate privacy guidelines. She sighed big, huffed and puffed, but the answer was still no. She wouldn't let up. She didn't ask to speak to Anderson because he was on the "no" train, too. Then that feeling came. I could hear the waves rushing towards me. Sara was used to getting what she wanted because someone would rather buckle than stand up to her.

"Sara, is there something I can help you with besides that?" She wasn't getting any code switching from me anymore. I heard a click on the other line and went back to my search. I think she is begging for karma at this point. I looked to see if any notes were put in our call logs about her. I would be able to see which employee was the last to talk to her. Most of the notes were like mine. She called, we told her no, she got mad and asked to speak with a manager. Even the managers made notes like everyone else. "So, who keeps helping her?" I whispered to myself. Then I started to hack into the system a little bit. I needed to see who was ruining the day for the rest of us. I realized that a few of the notes by my co-workers had the same manager but that manager never made a note. The logs and keystroke showed this manager going into certain files.

"Gotcha, bitch!"

The manager was Kevin. Freaking Kevin! I should have known. He was a manager who bent the rules all the time and if you were his type, he would break the damn rules. We all avoid having to go to Kevin for anything. Kevin was a Black man in his late 40s. He is about six-feet-tall with some gray in his beard and fresh waves with a bald spot in the middle. He has been here for a while, but you could never tell. I knew more than him about this damn job but he is a manager. He was nice the first few interactions but his whole demeanor was off to me. I kept my distance. Kevin was like the male version of Charla. Bopping around the office, never minding his own business, and thirsty for attention. There were rumors that Kevin and Charla used to sleep around.

His "charm" worked on someone because he was married, but you could never tell. Any girl -- brown, white, purple, alien -- would turn his head. It was like he never had vagina before. He used what he could to flirt. Why did he keep giving Sara access? Maybe he didn't want to hear her argue but everyone else was on the same page. Why not him? They both were what I needed – more target practice.

I won't be surprised like I was with Yessica. I had to watch these two for a little while before letting out my frustrations. I hated the system, but I hated those who felt they were an exception more. If I follow guidelines and regulations, I expect everyone to be held to the same standard regardless of position. Your title doesn't give you a "do whatever the fuck you want" pass.

"Human, you seem excited." I flinched. I forgot Anansi was around again.

"You can really read my mind," I answered back.

"That is against the rules. I can feel your energy and make my conclusion from there. I need your permission to have access to your thoughts directly, remember," Anansi assured.

"I can deal without the cocky tone. Stop calling me human, damn!" I went to the company directory to get info on Sara's office. She doesn't work for our company. My office had a contract with her company to help. There wasn't a solid plan yet. I needed to follow Kevin and Sara. The revenge to satisfy my frustration, that would be determined later. The preliminary plan was to find Kevin's car so I knew what to follow. I needed to run to Sara's office to figure out what car she drove, too.

I took a quick 15-minute break and went to Sara's office. This was a perfect time to use my warp speed. I hadn't tried this distance before. The furthest I ran was three miles. Once I stopped, I threw up everything but the air in my body. I wanted to avoid the 'exorcism' this time. Sara's office was five miles up the road. I didn't have much time. I ran to my car and drove up the road for about five minutes. I was within three miles and then I could use my warp speed. I had the profile photo from work to know what she looked like. Sara was a petite brunette. Her picture screamed sorority life. I could see her in her office. I kept my distance from the building as I watched her. I did not have much time; I just needed to get a good look at her.

She was bopping around her office. I felt annoyed immediately. I tried to see if she had anything around her that would give me a hint to which car was hers. I noticed that she had a "Delta Epsilon" lanyard attached to her keys. I looked around the parking lot and found this green sedan with the sorority custom license plate. "Perfect," I said. I wrote down the car's plate   and description, went back into warp speed, and got back to the office before the break was up.

Work finished up as usual, but Kevin wasn't usual. This man leaves the office at least 45 minutes before his shift is over. All the time. I had no idea how he got away with it. He came in late and left early and didn't do shit while in the office. I walked around the building to see where he was. It was nearly the end of the day, so everyone was moving around. I wanted to make sure I watched Kevin close, but not obviously close. I logged out of everything and packed myself up. The good thing about having the last cubicle is that no one comes back here because of the dead end. It worked to my advantage because this wasn't the first time I dipped out a little early.

I walked the damn building three times, but no Kevin. I finally went to where his team was located and asked someone where he was. Apparently, Kevin was on vacation for two weeks. Damn, I had to log back in.

"Who is this Kevin?" Anansi asked.

"Someone that needs his ass whooped," I replied.

"I do not know what you mean," Anansi said. "Is that English?"

I giggled because he was beyond old. I know he can speak English, but slang was new to him.

"Sorry," I laughed. "Kevin is a manager here who needs to be punished, I suppose." I guess punishment was the best word for it. "The issue is, I need some information on him, but he's gone."

"You intend to punish this man. What has he done?"

"He thinks the rules do not apply to him. To make things worse, he has other people thinking they are exceptions to the rules too."

"But don't you…" Anansi began. I knew exactly where he was going. He had some nerve. He was the damn god of rule breaking.

"Before you even start, they are making it hard to do our jobs. Granted, I hate this job, but I won't make my time here harder. I also don't want to make others' jobs harder," I interrupted. I pulled up Sara's and Kevin's social media to learn more about them as I waited for 5:30 to show on the clock. I had no excuse now to cancel with Dr. Lynn. The virtual meeting would go as planned.

So much had changed within a short period of time. I had to make a few small lies believable to her. She was a "myth buster" when I tried to lie to her. It was like she had known me forever.

Once I got home, I let Inu out and set up my computer for my session. I checked in at the front desk and waited in this virtual waiting room. I felt a rush of nervousness as I waited to be invited into the session. My leg kept bouncing and my palms were sweaty. I wasn't sure what would unfold in the appointment and I didn't want to think about it.

"Elle, I am connecting you with Dr. Lynn" the front desk said.

"Anansi, take a back seat. I mean way in the back, please," I asked.

"I am unsure of what you are requesting," he replied.

"Rest for a bit. This is kinda private," I said.

"Understood," he said.

I saw two screens pop up and Dr. Lynn and I didn't miss a beat.

"It has been a while. Elle. How have you been?" Dr. Lynn started.

I went to my spot on the couch and got settled. "It's been good. Back at work, working out. You know -- the basic stuff," I answered.

"You have been back for a bit. How does it feel?"

"It's hell like usual," I laughed.

"Are the new habits helping with that? The working out and your sweet fur baby?"

"Yeah, I guess."

"So why is work 'hell'?" she asked.

"It's the holiday season. It's crazy for any job."

"Well, this is true," she laughed. "We talked a bit during your leave. Virtual conversations, which I did not fully agree with." She peeked at me from the top of her glasses.

"I know. I was doing a lot during the six months. I bought land and an XL tiny home. I got a dog who understands me --way more than most humans."

"You were really productive during your break. I wished you would have kept your appointments during those milestones."

"Yea…about that," I trailed off.

"Do you remember how setting those goals and reaching those milestones felt in the moment?" Dr. Lynn asked.

These milestones would be amazing to others. Except Inu, my job spoiled those milestones. I didn't have stars in my eyes about owning land or getting my first home because I knew those milestones were overrated. "I mean it was easier for me than others. My mortgage officer didn't have to do much. Mr. Otis, the guy I bought the land from, made things easy too."

"Well, that sounds like an endorsement for the benefits of your job. Do you see that?"

"I'll give the job credit when needed. Doesn't make my workday any better though."

"Have you felt overwhelmed since you returned to work?" she asked.

"Of course, but it's only the overwhelming stupidity that didn't stop while I was gone. I just have better ways to deal with it." Technically, this was true, but it wasn't some stupid breathing exercise or writing in a journal. It was magic and chaos that soothed my mind. The punching helped, too.

"I want you to use your dog and exercise as a way to manage your stress."

"I hear you, mom," I said sarcastically.

"Dogs can be a wonderful support and mood stabilizers." She has told me this before. She wasn't wrong.

"He is way smarter than the people I come across." I found this the perfect time to stop the interrogation and give Dr. Lynn a story to take up the rest of our time. I told her about the dog park incident and the "pill popping" housewives that went crazy. Dr. Lynn was fascinated by the story. She laughed and asked what the cops did. Before I knew it, the hour was up.

"Elle, you need to come to the office once a week," Dr. Lynn said. "Just because you had a good break does not mean you should stop doing the work."

"I hear ya, 'Mom,'" I laughed. She may be right, but I wasn't comfortable. Everything that annoyed me before my leave still annoyed me. I didn't have to talk about it or journal about it anymore. I ended my meeting with Dr. Lynn, unsure if I would return anytime soon.

I had a great session with Dr. Lynn, but I didn't forget about Sara or Kevin. I took out my frustration with those two idiots during target practice with the 9mm. I flew through the air, tree limb by tree limb, shooting at the target.

I stumbled when I wasn't focused. I got scratched by tree branches

I could easily avoid. I made mistakes that shouldn't be made. "Oh shit!" I slammed to the ground. I slowly lifted myself up. I felt a sharp pain in my right wrist. The gun was still in my grasp but my wrist was broken.

"Elle, you were not focused," Anansi said.

"I know that," I snapped. I held my wrist in place. The break would heal fast. I wouldn't be able to use the hand for the rest of the night. "Inu," I called. I heard him run towards me. I liked having him around me when I injured myself. He was like an extension of myself. He licked my face, against my wishes and waited for me to get up. I grabbed the gun with my left hand and walked slowly with Inu out of the woods.

"I need to settle down," I told myself. I turned on some soothing music, usually classical, sat in the middle of the floor, and took some deep breaths. "Lord, what is going on?" I whispered.

After a few minutes, my mind settled. I grabbed a cookie and tried to focus again. "I need to figure out what to do with Sara and Kevin," I whispered to myself. I saw nothing but black as I closed my eyes. The light usually gives me the shape of what I saw last before I closed my eyes, however, this time, I saw black. I could use halluz smoke, but when would be the best time? For some reason, that thought seemed too dull. I was getting worried at how quickly I considered violent options. I kept shaking my head, trying to get those thoughts out of my mind. Then it hit me. Think like the trickster I shared a body with. The "wealthy peasant" plan was beginning to form.

The rest of the night I asked Anansi different questions. He gave me insight into his thought process. I was exhausted by the end.

"What can we offer them, Elle?" Anansi asked.

"I'm not sure yet," I replied. "I need to follow them to find out. Damn, I hope this doesn't take long." I feared a surprise like I had with Yessica. I wanted to make sure no one could sneak up on me. Anansi and I went back and forth with ideas. In the end, I fell asleep with Inu on the couch.

Kevin was trying to catch the elevator. He was back from vacation. I had ducked in the elevator, headphones blasting K-pop. I didn't hear him yell to hold the door. Easy mistake, it happens. Not according to Kevin, however. He decided that whole day that the "little girl" that did not hold the elevator was rude, inconsiderate, and did it on purpose. I didn't. He also pointed out to one fellow manager, Wes overheard, that this was the reason people think Black girls had an attitude. If I had a button, that one was it. What he said may have been exaggerated, sure. Did I fucking care? Hell nah. He was already on the list. I was chilling for the last two weeks. I even ignored Sara. Now, I was about to be super petty. Sorry, Sara, you almost got away with it.

I decided to follow him right after work. This morning gave me all the motivation I needed. All I knew about Kevin was that he didn't do shit during the day. It's amazing how one of the last people to get into the office was always the first to leave. To be honest, the clock says 5:30 and I'm out in a flash. Following Kevin would have me leaving around 4:30 pm. He had the audacity of a tricky god. I had to figure out how to explain to Anderson I needed to dip out early.

All day, I increased my senses levels. My cubicle was the last one on the left. Kevin's team was on the right side of the building. I had to memorize Kevin's footsteps, breathing pattern, heart rate, and smell. Kevin's left foot pronated, so he did not pick his feet up much while walking. His heart rate remained constant even when he was walking at a faster pace or trying to flirt. I assumed he worked out. His cologne was strong. I did not need to do too much to recognize it. It was a citrus smell mixed with a little mahogany. His wife bought that no doubt. It was the kind of smell women would like their man to have. That assumption was totally based off my own experience. What the hell did I know about what scents people like in the opposite sex.

Kevin had one distinct habit that made it easy for me to pinpoint his location. He constantly ate breath mints. He shook the aluminum tin, leaned his head back and let a few pieces drop into his mouth. No matter if he was talking to someone or not, he kept popping breath mints.

He was headed to the elevator. It was a little before 5:00 when he called the elevator -- a little later than usual. I was a bit surprised. I sent Anderson an email that I was leaving early to get to an appointment. I needed to buy Anderson a fruit basket or something. That guy was so understanding.

I grabbed my bookbag and went to the stairs. I could make it down the stairs in a flash but there were cameras, so I just needed to go at a brisk pace. I adjusted my hearing so I could hear the elevator. Kevin reached the ground floor, and I was on the first. I did not want him to notice me at all. Once I heard the automatic door close, I left the stairwell. I used the smokers' back door to get to my car. The managers have the best spots. Kevin would get to his car quickly. Once I was out of camera view, I sped to my car. Kevin tossed his bag into the passenger seat of a funky little sports car. He looked like he was driving from the back seat. That car was that small compared to Kevin's size.

He made a left out of the parking lot towards the main road. I followed. He passed the exit for the highway. It looked like we would be taking the main roads. There was traffic on the highway and the main road but they were two different types of traffic. Traffic with traffic lights annoyed me more. Although, how I get to a dead stop on the highway in traffic defies physics. This was going to take forever; I could feel it. Kevin's choice of travel added to my frustration. Let me "wealthy peasant" you and make that shit convenient, please. He blasted his radio and texted while driving. I had to keep my distance. I really couldn't care less about the boys' group chat. They exchanged twerk videos and memes. What caught my interest was a message from "agent." The text feed was minimal.

"Thurs meeting as usual. 8:00 pm. We have 2 go ova paperwork."

That was all the messages said repeatedly. Either Kevin sent the text, or he received it, but the text always said the same thing. Kevin gave a thumbs up emoji, and nothing further was said.. I wondered what I would find on Thursday. After about 45 minutes going through the street, Kevin pulled up to this cookie-cutter neighborhood. House on top of house, uniform mailboxes, and two-car garages. There was a big sign out front, "Model home open M-F 8am to 5pm. Starting at lower 750s". That was too much to pay for a home where I could breathe on my neighbor from my kitchen window. What I dreaded was a neighborhood watch and a nosey HOA.

"Slow. Kids at play" signs were located at the entrance of the neighborhood. I was not above hitting kids when they just jumped out in the middle of the street, unsupervised, in my mind. I would probably stop but some days I wanted to keep rolling. I stayed parked at the entrance as Kevin approached his home. It looks like he was one of the first families to buy in this development because his house wasn't off any adjacent roads. He was the tenth house down on the right. There was an adorable little girl playing in the yard while this brown toy poodle barked around her. I wouldn't hit her with my car. She was precious. The little girl ran in tiny circles laughing as this small dog barked and chased her. There was a woman in her early twenties, watering the plants near the front door. She was sun-kissed brown with long black hair. She was thin, tall, and in shape. She was a very pretty girl. She was too young. I prayed that wasn't the wife.

Once Kevin pulled in the driveway, the little girl ran up to the car, "Daddy's home! Daddy's home!" He parked the car, scooped her up, and twirled her around. It was cute.

"Hey, Gabby! Thanks for watching Ira for us today," he said. I let out a sigh of relief that Gabby was just the babysitter.

"Oh, no problem. I enjoy it," Gabby replied. She waved at them as she walked down the street. I did not see another car in the driveway or parked on the side of the street. "Oh, so she lives down the street. Gotcha," I said to myself.

"Are you talking to me?" Anansi asked.

"No, thinking out loud," I replied. "It's nice to see some neighbors being neighborly."

There was only one person missing: the wife. It was nightfall by the time the second car approached the driveway. It was a black midsize SUV with a "baby on board" sticker. Although the little girl was at least five or six years old, that sticker remained. It was probably super hard to get it off the window.

"This must be the wife," I said. Then silence. Light skin, with a few freckles on her cheeks. Her curly hair dyed honey brown, large earrings, with a floral dress that complimented her curves. Her stilettos hit the pavement with a statement and the large purse was firmly placed in the bend of her arm. She must have had a long day at work because she still had on her sunglasses.

"Anansi, this time I was talking to you."

"How was I to know this?" he answered. That answer and the accent made me laugh. I fell out. I laughed way too long at him. All he kept saying was "eh eh" and that made me laugh harder.

Before she entered the house, I heard Ira say, "Momma's home!" She has some sharp hearing. They seemed like such a sweet family. Most people would hate to put a damper on that. Fuck that! Fuck compassion! I was a zero for empathy. My job for the past few years has killed my empathy levels. His adorable daughter and wife were innocent, but Kevin could kick rocks with open toed shoes on.

I moved my car to the area of the neighborhood still under construction and ran to the back of the house. I looked for my best vantage point to spy. There weren't any houses behind Kevin's and the houses in front weren't plausible. I went to the house on the right side of Kevin's to see from the side window. I could only see the living room and part of the kitchen. They changed clothes and got dinner ready to end the day. I had to be in their backyard to see directly in the kitchen. The blinds were slightly open on the window in the kitchen, but I couldn't risk it. I relied on my hearing.

"How was your day, baby?" Kevin asked.

"Stressful. We have a new client who is impossible to please. I have no clue how he wants to decorate this office building," she replied.

Kevin chuckles, "He keeps changing his mind."

"Exactly," she replied, relieved that her husband knew what she meant.

"I hope your day was less eventful," she suggested.

"Same old, same old. We are supposed to roll out internet work orders starting next week so maybe something difficult will come across my desk," he said.

I was ready to take a bat to his car right then, but I kept listening. "Same old, same old," he said. This man did nothing and knew nothing. If they were rolling out new internet work orders, that was just another thing Kevin would not be helpful with.

"No interesting office gossip? I love hearing about that." She leaned in so he wouldn't speak too loud around Ira. It may be something she was too young to hear. I leaned in too, but that was reflex; I could hear fine.

Kevin filled his wife in about the human resource complaint against Charla. "She has not left that man alone since he started working there. He was hoping that giving her the cold shoulder would stop the advances, but nope. She was always popping up at his desk unannounced and trying to include him in manager outings when his job wasn't even dealing with our customers. This man wanted to be left alone. Charla wasn't getting it. Granted, I have a feeling this wouldn't be the first complaint that woman has gotten," Kevin whispered. I wanted Kevin to say more, but he stopped there.

Kevin's wife laughed and laughed. The thirst was real. Within 45 minutes they were at the table eating dinner. They had a typical evening, made for television. I didn't need to stay long. I needed to get home to let Inu out.

I went through my normal morning routine at work, waiting for Kevin to arrive. He finally strolled in around 9:30. Late as usual but what made me angry is that he didn't go straight to his desk or notify his supervisor. He did his rounds for the day. I was so focused on learning Kevin's movements that I barely remember anything else that happened at work. I kept going in and out of control balancing all day.

"Have you found his desire yet?" Anansi asked.

"Not even close," I sighed. There was this tiny glitch in my "wealthy peasant" plan for Sara and Kevin. I had to fucking talk to them. I only gave Kevin the polite "hello" or "excuse me" if I crossed his path. It wasn't only small talk either. I had to have one of those oversharing drunk moments with Kevin and Sara. "Anansi, this idea is getting more and more complicated."

"It is not the most convenient of plans," Anansi admitted. "This will take some time."

"Ugghh!" I broke into Yessica's apartment and was surprised. If I wanted to avoid that happening again, I really had to watch Kevin's and Sara's habits. The thought of my time wasted on two idiots had me punching the air. I would weigh the pros and cons on my floor but I had to avoid the third floor.

"Anansi, I need another plan," I groaned. This was my opportunity to let this go and focus on something else.

"Your lack of patience baffles me," he said.

"Is that a compliment?" I asked.

"It most certainly is not complimentary. I have been locked away for centuries."

"Yeah, and the minute you got your chance, you escaped. I bet you would have escaped right after being locked up if you could."

"Eh, eh...I cannot argue against you," he conceded.

"Ha," I mocked.

I studied Kevin in between calls. I memorized his smell, the sound he made when walking, and his heartbeat. The phones were busy, the follow-ups were ineffective, and the damn food truck was late today. I was looking forward to that. Food truck Thursdays are the best. No doubt it was Davidson's idea. He was obsessed with a good food truck. Every company virtual meeting, he started off with a new food truck discovery. The man had good taste for an old white guy.

I worked the bare minimum today.

"Hey, Elle?"

I barely heard my name because I was so focused on hearing Kevin. Anderson snuck up on me in my cubicle. I popped out my headphones and laughed at him scaring me. It usually lightened the mood if I were about to get in trouble for having my headphones in.

"Hey, Anderson, I didn't even hear you call me," I answered.

"No, it's fine. I forgot to send out the reminder. We have a team meeting. You can go to the big conference room after you wrap up your last file." He was a bit flustered that he forgot to send out the memo. He usually doesn't forget but it's a madhouse here. I wrapped up my last file and walked to the room.

My team had about ten employees. I liked my team. Sandy was the team mom, Asia was the super smart one, Ronnie was somehow still employed, and the others made me laugh. I wasn't the newbie anymore; that was Taylor. She was a nice girl, but I am afraid she drank the company Kool-Aid immediately. She would find out soon enough, but that didn't mean she wasn't a happy drone for now.

I went to the conference room quickly so I could get a seat in the back. I hoped the seat in the back meant little interaction. Five minutes went by before anyone showed up. I was able to thumb through my phone, played a level on this stupid word game Elise had me download, and sipped some water in peace. Eventually, I would have to deal with making small talk until everyone was in the room. One by one, or in small groups, the room began to fill up. Soon, I realized it wasn't just my team but Sarya's team as well. My manager, Anderson, was the last to arrive.

"Sorry I'm late, gang. I hope you weren't waiting too long," he said. Anderson was a skinny white guy with black, thick-rimmed glasses. He was a good manager and backed us up when needed. His khakis were always a little too short; his ankle showed whether he was sitting or standing.

234

I assumed that outside of work he was a hippie. Soon after he arrived, in walked Dara.

Dara was eccentric to say the least. Dara was a skinny, petite, white lady that came fresh out of the "looking glass." She dressed like she was due for dinner with the Red Queen. However, the black dress I wore to work was "inappropriate" according to her and Charla. She bippitty-bopped to the empty chair in the corner, like she was overlooking the entire meeting. I wasn't sure what was going on but if Dara was here, it would be interesting.

"So, gang," Anderson began, "we called this meeting between these teams because we are implementing a new procedure." Everyone started to look around and I started to drift off to Neptune. "We are now accepting internet work orders. Our claims, IT services, and financial services can now be received online from our customers."

"So," Ronnie interrupted, "the customers can now submit requests and such online instead of calling?"

"Correct," Sarya replied. The rabble started around the conference room.

"Sarya's team and mine," Anderson continued. "We will be the teams that will be handling the online requests first. We are the guinea pigs."

"Does this mean no phones?" That caught my attention. That moment of joy was quickly extinguished.

"Only while on the internet work orders," Sarya replied. "Eventually every team will have their internet work weeks, but we are the first."

The meeting went on with us talking about the who, what, when, where, why, and how of internet work orders. We were also getting the internet work orders from colleagues who were face-to-face with customers or needed IT help. They went over the new system to retrieve the orders. We got procedure guides and would be doing classroom training for the rest of the week and next week. I was happy about that because training was like a mini vacation for me. I never really paid attention. I was a hands-on learner. I did better when thrown into the fire. I learned quickly but that was not a good thing in the office. I learned quickly that the better I was at my job, the more responsibility they gave me without extra pay. I gave this job my "C-" work. They wouldn't ask me to do anything extra.

That meeting took up the rest of the day. Some employees were super excited to do something new, while others were skeptical of the new system rollout. New systems always came with new problems and that slowed everyone down. I was happy about the two-week break from our actual job and no phones. It was what I needed. As we all left the conference room for the day, everyone was muttering to each other about our new job description. We wore too many hats at this job. I'd rather each team focus on one task instead of everyone doing everything.

They dismissed us and we went back to our desks for the last hour of work. I took the scenic route because this was the time that Kevin leaves. Something was different. He was at his desk. Not packed up or packing up. He looked like he was doing work.

"He is up to something," I whispered.

"Why do you assume so?" Anansi replied.

"This is not his pattern. He is a creature of habit. Everybody notices and they don't have enhanced vision." I walked over to Wes's desk.

"Hey, Wes," I whispered. He jumped. "Oh gosh, I'm sorry," I laughed.

"Sneaking up on me, gurl," he laughed.

"Quick question. Why is Kevin still here?"

"He always leaves late on Thursdays. I don't know why, that nigga don't do anything," he whispered. We both laughed in agreement.

"I keep forgetting, I can't see all the way over here."

"Why are you over here anyway?"

"Oh, we were just in the conference room. I'm taking the long way around because I don't wanna deal," I sighed. "Let me go back before they come looking." We fist pound and I head back.

So, Kevin leaves late on Thursdays. While everyone packed up and left, Kevin stayed at his desk. I pretended to pack up too. By 6, the whole floor was empty except for a few employees. The cleaning crew was going around doing their job. They always seemed surprised when they saw someone in the office. It was like the late workers disrupted their routine. I was looking out the window when I saw Davidson leave, but Kevin didn't. That was impossible. "Why is he still here?" I wondered. I went to 80/20 and that's when I noticed his heart rate increased. Maybe this was my opportunity. I knew Kevin didn't want to lose his job. I needed to find a way to guarantee he could keep his job, but bind him. How? I got up to peek at his desk, because I couldn't see through a damn wall, to see what he was doing. He was packing up. I ran quietly back to my desk, grabbed my stuff, and hit the elevator.

The elevator was quick, so I was able to get ahead of Kevin and make it to my car. I did not want him to know I was watching him, and I did not want it to appear on camera that I was following him. It was about 7:30 pm before he got to his car. He was no longer looking somber and defeated. He was energetic and rushing to his car. Whatever Kevin had planned lifted his spirit quickly. He looked at his phone one last time and then cranked his car up. I adjusted my mirrors and got ready to follow.

I could hear the radio on the old school R&B station. Kevin threw his tie into the back seat and floored it out of the parking lot. How the hell is he so happy? He is one minute past 8:30 am from losing his job. The way he was moving and shaking in the car, I knew something was up. As we drove, Kevin made a new turn. He wasn't headed home. We were headed downtown. I was about two cars behind him at a red light when I saw that he was texting someone. The name said "wifey."

Hey babe, I have my managers meeting and team builder tonight. Just reminding you I will be home late, but I will bring back food if there are any leftovers like last time.

I know damn well that was a lie. If there was a manager's meeting, it was always in the middle of the day at the most inconvenient time. It usually left the senior employees overwhelmed with questions and the emails backed up. A manager's meeting was never considerate of the other employees or the clients. And somehow the meetings were scheduled on the busiest day of the week. They were in that meeting nearly all day.

"Where the hell are you going?" I thought.

Kevin kept driving and jamming to the radio. He took peeks at his group chat at the red lights. The amount of twerk videos these guys sent screamed addiction. Now, some of them were impressive. My ass didn't move like that. However, the more I looked at the clips, the weirder the videos became. But I was not a guy, and they probably didn't feel that way. Anansi's viewpoint was hilarious. I pictured him like a confused dog the first time he noticed it.

"What is the point of all these vid-e-os?" Anansi asked. I laughed.

"Well, I really don't know how to answer that for you. Attention, money, and arousal are the only reasons off the top of my head," I replied.

"Humans are strange things. After all that evolution, self-control never manifested," he realized. I couldn't argue with that. That was why the "wealthy peasant" plan was going to work. But it was Anansi's turned up nose and sighs coming from him every time that made me laugh.

I followed Kevin to the downtown area of the city. Even without traffic, it takes about 40 minutes to get here from the south side of the office. The night was bringing the lights from the buildings. The foot traffic was picking up at the restaurants and bars. I didn't expect Kevin to come downtown. Maybe it was a dinner with a business associate. Downtown traffic was making it harder to follow Kevin. Quickly, Kevin pulled his car into a parking garage for Hotel Sauna. It was one of the nicest hotels in the city. I came here once for a friend's bridal shower. I never wanted to leave.

"Kevin, whatcha doing here?" I said. I took the first parking spot I found. It was easier to follow on foot. I put on my green hoodie from the back seat and headed towards the hotel lobby. I didn't want to be seen in the lobby. I ran across the street that the lobby looked towards.

The hotel lobby was nicely decorated. The pearl marble flooring was clean. The gold accents on the chairs and check-in desk made the guests feel rich. The chairs were oversized and comfortable. There were places to charge your phones or tablets but no magazines or newspapers. The ambiance of a water fountain in the lobby and soft music caused relaxation in even the angriest guest. The up lighting to keep the gold color moving towards the ceiling set the mood. I could smell the mud facials in the spa at the end of the lobby on the right and heard the clink of wine glasses at the restaurant to the left. The Hotel Sauna had two restaurants. The main lobby bistro and the skyline experience on the top floor. The elevators were glass so the guests could see the lobby as they went up. If you were scared of heights, there were other elevators that were in the back.

I waited for a few minutes, but Kevin didn't enter the lobby. Did he already go to a room or the restaurant? I had to check the parking garage. I tightened my hood with the strings and ran to the back towards the parking garage. I heard the RnB music on the third level of the garage. I found him! He was still in his car, listening to music. He sprayed himself with more cologne because his smell was powerful. I bet a normal person could smell it. He laid that shit on thick.

For 45 minutes, I listened to this tone-deaf man sing along to his radio. He laughed at random moments, too. I assumed it was the group chat or videos online that he looked at as he waited. Who the hell was coming? I was sitting against the concrete wall on the ground level and Kevin was on the third floor. I hated not being able to see but I wasn't risking being seen right now. Not until I knew what was going on.

Suddenly, the music stopped, and Kevin stopped singing.

"Hey, girl," he said. I heard a door close. "Don't you look sexy with those heels on." She started giggling. I looked around to see if anyone was around. I didn't see anyone, and it was much darker now. I climbed the walls of the parking garage. There were cars going in and out, but I didn't pay any mind. "Who is this?" I whispered. Once I got to the third floor, I peeked over the ledge. I saw a petite blond woman approaching him. That was not his wife or a managers' meeting.

"Freaking Sara!" I saw her. "What the hell is…she…" I paused. No fucking way!

"Hey!!" Sara bopped around and leaped into Kevin's arms.

"No fucking way," I whispered. My hand started to feel on fire again. I tried to bring my emotions down, but I was mad!

Sara had transformed into a schoolgirl. She kissed him and they headed to the door to the main lobby. He tapped her flat ass a few times and followed right behind her. I jumped down and ran back across the street to see the lobby better. Kevin and Sara approached the reception desk. That wasn't necessary when you were using the spa or going to restaurants. They were getting a room.

The front desk clerk handed her the room keys and pointed towards the room elevators. I wondered when all this started. Sara works for a different company we contract with. Did all this start from one phone call to the office? Did they meet elsewhere and then found out their jobs were intertwined? I was confused and mad. Kevin went behind everyone's back for someone he was sleeping with. He was compromising his family. He compromised my sanity. He left his team to struggle. I headed straight towards the lobby. My feet moved by themselves. I didn't watch for traffic or anything. The light was setting behind me and the darkness would consume me.

"Elle," Anansi said sternly. I stopped instantly. "You will be seen if you go inside," he pointed out. He was right. I couldn't follow them like this. I started to look at my surroundings. The hotel was the tallest building on the block. The building to the right was too short. I had to get to the roof of the building to the left to see some of the hotel rooms. I watched Kevin and Sara hug and kiss each other until it stopped on the 12th floor.

"One, two, three, four," I counted. The roof of the building was on the 15th floor of the hotel. I would have to look down to see the 12th floor. I ran back across the street to climb the fire escape. I climbed faster than I ever had. I didn't use the stairs of the fire escape because it would take too long.

"Interesting," Anansi said.

"Yeah, it's a damn soap opera," I replied.

"That is not what I meant," Anansi said. "Men have always been the weaker of the two. They are driven by more personal desires than communal ones. This man is a typical weak human. You are the interesting one."

"What are you talking about?" I asked. I am trying to focus on my breathing and channeling this anger. Two people made others miserable. I didn't know who I was mad at more. The entitled dickhead or the lazy dickhead. What made it worse was they were having an affair. I don't know why, but it is just getting under my skin.

"Stop!" Anansi yelled.

"Shit, I nearly missed a step. What the hell are you yelling for?" I was right at the 9th level on the fire escape when Anansi stopped me.

"Look at yourself, Elle." Anansi sounded serious. His authoritative voice only came out when I was failing during training or wasn't listening.

"Like introspectively. I know I shouldn't care about this, but I do."

"No! In the reflection," he replied.

I tried to find a reflective surface. I looked for a window. There was no light inside when I saw myself. "Ahh!" I couldn't believe it. Not only my eye but my hair changed. My blue curly bun was now lavender and long, really long. I have thin, fine-textured, shoulder-length hair. I tried nearly every trick to get my hair to thicken up and grow. All I had to do now was get angry enough. When I put my hand up to touch my hair, I noticed my hands were on fire. I screamed and patted my hands on my body and brick wall to put the fire out. I didn't go out but it didn't burn either.

"Someone would have heard that," Anansi said calmly.

"How the hell is this possible?"

"You continue to amaze me, human. You can use fire!"

"I can use what? My hands are on fire!"

No matter what I did my hands were still on fire. "I gotta calm down," I realized.

"And you need to leave. Someone heard that scream," Anansi pointed out.

I looked around and realized I had to jump down. I stood on the edge, took a deep breath, and just walked off. I focused on the ground, and I did not want to hurt myself. I was landing on concrete.

"Focus, Elle," Anansi whispered. "Focus on how you want the landing to feel and stay there."

"Like a cat on carpet, like a cat on carpet," I kept telling myself.

The ground was coming fast. "A cat on the carpet." I landed. The ground wasn't soft, but it was damn sure softer than concrete. The wind from my landing blew upwards and even lifted my shirt. I did it. I could land softly on concrete now. Part of me felt like the concrete landing scared me enough to focus. I was used to my forest; I did not fear getting seriously hurt there. My cuts from the weapons training healed fast and I was too cautious to suffer any broken bones at the beginning. I feared real injury this time.

I peeked around the corners and the streets were still busy. Everyone was in their own world. They ignored anything around in hopes of not drawing attention to myself. I could see the protection in that, and I could also see the advantages of someone trying to rob. I didn't have time to dwell on that now. "Mframa fa me!"

As the world around me was returning to normal, I took deep breaths. Breathe in and out. In and out. In and out. I saw the fire die from my hands. I kept taking deep breaths and saw my hair and eye go back to normal. I took a few more breaths and checked again. Everything was back to normal.

"This is amazing, human," Anansi said. I listened to Anansi as I inspected my face, hair, and hands. There weren't any burns on my hands and besides actually seeing the fire, the heat was bearable. I felt the fire, but it didn't burn like it should. I was okay. My fear and disbelief blended with my excitement and curiosity. I could do more. "Anansi," I began, "what was the control balance?"

"I estimate we were at 30/70," he replied.

"Seriously!" I inspected my hands and hair one more time.

"It is only an estimate, but you continue to surprise me. Fire is an immensely powerful tool. I am surprised that your body can withstand it. Your resolve is spectacular."

"How the hell did we get there? Shit!" I realized.

"Your emotions, I assume. We forced the 50/50 control balance. Your body naturally…umm pardon…your body naturally reached these levels. How are you feeling?" Anansi's words were slowing down.

"I am feeling everything. I was angry, curious, determined. I had to see everything these two were doing." I saw more than enough and didn't need to watch the rest. I needed, and wanted, to go home. My body felt heavy and my strength was depleted as I pulled off and sluggishly headed home. Literally, I had people honking their horns because I was going too slow.

"Anansi, my body feels heavy," I said.

"I feel it too, Elle," Anansi sighed. He sounded tired, too. I drove slowly all the way home.

I woke up right beside Inu's bed. He was asleep on his back and kicking me in the back of the head. I didn't want to know if it was my drool or Inu's on the floor. I looked at the clock and saw the time was 7 am. I jumped up, rushing to get ready. I scared Inu awake. I opened the door for Inu and threw on some clothes. I filled up Inu's food and water and rushed out the door.

I pulled up to the office just in time. My body felt sore, so I was slow that morning. I was on my fourth refill of water and sixth bag of chips by 9:15. The vending machine was my breakfast. I wasn't surprised that I saw Kevin's cheating ass stroll into work like he wasn't nearly an hour late. I let it go for the day. I was tired. Anansi was tired. It was the last day at the office before Christmas and the New Year. Our training for the new procedure would begin after the holidays.

I worked quietly as the hours ticked away. Anansi didn't talk at all.

I clicked away at nothing. I replayed the events of last night in my head. I remembered feeling hot, but I thought that was because I was angry. I was on fire. I was fast on the fire escape and landed on concrete right the first time. What scared me about all of it was the control balance of 30/70. I accepted the even split, sorta, but this time Anansi was more in control. I did that naturally. He didn't force it, so he said. Did I want to explore this more? I kept asking myself if I was ready to go further.

I didn't know exactly where to start with this new trick. Getting to the 30/70 control balance wasn't easy. The more I lost myself the worse the pain got. The side effect was "stone." My body became heavy, and it was hard to move. The longer I was in 30/70, the heavier my body got. I collapsed for 20 minutes once. That was the longest I was immobile on the ground. Inu came and laid with me because I couldn't move. He saved me from a few squirrels.

Besides the "stone" side effect, I loved using fire. I could control the intensity, temperature, and smoke. The fire was amazing. The fire could burn blue, red, white, and orange. It was beautiful. Anansi did not have a name for this trick. Calling it fire wasn't fun, so I called it "hellblaze." The fire didn't affect my body but was dangerous even when it was gone. I touched the trunk of a tree to steady myself once. I burned through some of the bark. It took a few seconds after setting back to 90/10 before my hands were completely cool. Good thing I calmed down before touching my car the first time. I hoped the "stone" would go away, but my headaches really haven't, so this was going to take some time. I had to master 30/70. Fire and lavender hair is fine, but the stone side effect I needed to combat. Practice usually helped.

I enjoyed seeing my parents and laughing with my sisters at my parents' expense during Christmas. Those resting bitch faces they have for each other had us on the floor laughing. Inu was enjoying the extra love and attention from Grandma, and I was enjoying the food I didn't have to cook. My dad gave mom a hard time too. He did that on purpose to join in on my sisters and I laughing at them. He wanted to tell the joke but not be the subject of the joke. As we got older, our parents became more entertaining than scary. After my family left, I had a week before New Year's Eve to practice hellblaze.

I decided to host New Year's Eve. I bought all the alcohol, wings, and taco kits from the store. I ordered cupcakes because I didn't feel like baking. I set up the firepit with Lucas. We did our best because it wasn't quite done yet. I didn't know how we all were gonna fit in my tiny home but we can make it work. Elise brought her fiancé, and it was like a domino effect.

Everyone was getting into serious relationships and getting engaged and all this love was making me sick. Seriously, I saw Elise kiss Charlie once and I threw up. I was nauseous from training but that visual didn't help. It was a couples-filled NYE party. Lucas was my date since he wasn't in a relationship anymore. He came through at the last minute because we had to convince his friends to pick someone, anyone, to "boo up" for the night. They wanted options, I wanted to avoid the blind date Joy tried to set up. Marie laughed at the idea, loudly and in my face. She was no help, but I loved cracking jokes with her.

I resisted the urge to use my "smoke" smoke. I wasn't going to make my friends guinea pigs but the random people they brought were fair game. Right? I wanted to use it to play some tricks on people. All the drinks pouring, they would be considered drunk. "I'll leave them alone," I decided about an hour before everyone was set to arrive. I should enjoy the evening. After the holidays, Kevin and Sara would to be dealt with. I shouldn't let my anger with them consumer up my vacation. My "wealthy peasant" plan wasn't forming like I wanted it to because Kevin had more to lose than Sara from my perspective. I hadn't had the chance to follow Sara before finding out about the affair.

"I am making this too complicated," I realized.

"What are you thinking?" Anansi asked.

"The wealthy peasant plan is out. It will be much easier to expose them to everyone," I answered. That was when the new plan began to form.

Kevin's and Sara's affair was going to be laid out in front of the ones that could cause the most damage. Davidson, Kevin's wife, and whoever I dig up for Sara would see what those two have been up to.

Inu's smile welcomed me back into the house. He was enjoying the extra love.

"That dog is a problem," Anansi scoffed.

"You're a problem. I am stuck with you. Inu is a problem I welcome," I smiled and skipped away. "Let's get drunk!"

The night was filled with booze, music, and arguments over every single game we played. Uno and spades were the most hostile and the most fun. I used to want days like this all the time. But my friends are going through their adult stages in life. Could we go back to days like this? I knew we couldn't stay this way forever. Plus, I didn't want to stop. I didn't want this high to go away.

The Punishment

My carefree vacation from work came and went. We were all back in the office on January 3. I should have taken the whole week off, but seniority gets the good days first. I prayed like hell I didn't get to that many years on this damn job. This Monday was exactly like the others. The phones weren't too bad because people are still traveling and getting settled. It was a matter of time until the tax calls began. Another busy season right after Christmas. The good thing was that I would be in training for most of January. It wasn't my problem.

The rest of the week at work I was stuck in the conference room learning about the new system and our job procedures. I did all I could to stay awake and focus. It was easy to avoid thinking about my blackouts if I paid attention to the training. I enjoyed the break from the phones because the Lord knows I needed it. However, the training wasn't much better. Now I had to listen to the stupid people I worked with. There was no escape. Our managers wanted us to baby the customers and now baby our other coworkers. That was the last thing I wanted to be trained in. Get someone else to do it.

Ruby was a sweet girl. She was on Dara's team. They must cover for her because she did not know much. She was in the training class right before mine, so she should not be just now finding out how to use the search bar on a folder. Ma'am, where have you been the past three decades at least? You should know how to do that simple task. It was the last question she asked that took the cake.

"How do we ensure that everyone on the email gets the reply?" I literally smacked my head on the table. I got some laughs, was scolded by Anderson, and got a wicked headache. I hope she felt embarrassed because how did she still have a job? How did she get through the day?

By 5 pm, I was at my limit. My frustration level was through the roof. I needed this weekend to get here faster. I was going to do absolutely nothing. With training, I hoped to relax a bit. Instead, I got tweedle dee and tweedle dumb asking basic questions that they should know the answers to. I took the scenic route to eavesdrop on Kevin, but he was already gone. Apparently, I wasn't the only one looking for him. A few people on his team were complaining about it. They were not shy about voicing their frustration either.

"This is getting ridiculous," one guy said. I swear, I wouldn't know these people existed on this floor.

"I already sent an email to Davidson," someone else said. I continued to eavesdrop on their conversation. It was about time someone said something. Next time Kevin came into the office late, he would have the best email waiting for him. I passed Wes's desk and gossiped a bit.

The new year hit the ground running. I should take note.

January 4 will go down in work week history for the 14th floor. Everyone settled into the normal morning routine. But guess who wasn't at their desk yet? I didn't know if Davidson got to his email yet. Davidson was in the office way before anyone and usually one of the last to leave. Anderson reminded me a lot of Davidson. Cool, calm, knowledgeable, fair, and understanding. Kevin clearly took advantage of that. Retrospectively, I did the same with Anderson sometimes. The difference, I knew what the fuck I was doing.

It was 9:08 am when the office went completely silent.

"Kevin, before you get settled," Davidson began, "can I speak with you?" He had a nice tone, but I knew he wasn't asking a question. Davidson, like everyone, had his limits. At this point, being constantly late was disrespectful and Davidson was going to let it be known this year. I needed to apologize to Anderson and buy him a car for the number of times he has covered my ass.

I did not need my god-like hearing because it felt like the floor had paused. It was like everyone had a god on their back and were able to hear through walls. The phones were put on mute, the keystrokes were quieter, and suddenly everyone had to go to the bathroom. Second cups of coffee needed to be filled immediately and the hallway printers were the only ones that were working. Even Kevin's team huddled up at their corner cubicle. I knew they were fed up. I adjusted my sight and saw smiles and a few people whispering, "It's about damn time." A shitty manager ruined the day every time.

Kevin was in Davidson's office for a good hour. The floor was quiet even when the congregating stopped. I knew Kevin's team had a bunch of instant messages from everyone around the building. I kept my hearing focused on what was going on in the office.

"Kevin, I have been more than understanding when you have an emergency. However, those excuses are just that. You come in any time you feel and leave while your team is still hard at work. My other managers are overworked, picking up your slack. At times, you even need help from an employee. They seem to know more than you. You are to be a resource for your team, not a burden on the entire office." Whoever snitched on him, good job.

Nicely put, Davidson. I applauded him for being very straightforward. Davidson was not one of those older white guys stuck in the old ways of the company. He may be a little slow on the technology, but he knew what he was talking about. I have sometimes cut out the middleman and gone straight to him for an answer. Not so much now. but when I started. It was nice to know his door was always open. Davidson constantly learned and called out bullshit from the higher-ups on the top floors when it happened. He was an advocate, but I did not want to cross him. If I did my job and did it right, Davidson was easy. Be a "Kevin," and he would exert his authority.

"Davidson, I am so sorry. I have no excuse for this. I was already running late and then an accident added to the traffic. I just...there is no excuse," Kevin stumbled.

"It hasn't gone unnoticed about your tardiness. Complaints have been made well before now. I can't cover for you any more." Davidson trailed off.

Was Kevin about to be fired?

"Sir," Kevin pleaded.

"Consider this your first and second warning. You are currently on probation. If you are late again without proper notice, or leave early again without proper notice, you will be terminated. Is that understood?"

Kevin didn't respond.

"To make it clear, proper notice means the two weeks we expect from all employees. Emergencies come up, but you have abused that privilege. I have noticed that as well. Your pay will be adjusted to account for the stolen time. I haven't told my boss about that yet. So, consider this super probation."

He didn't respond. I have super senses now, but I can't see through walls. Was Kevin nodding his head in understanding?

"Wait, Anansi?"

"Yes, Elle," he sighed.

"First, the tone sir. Secondly, can I see through walls?" I was a little overeager to hear the answer to this question.

"Pardon," Anansi said. I waited a few seconds.

"Can we see through walls?" Maybe it would be a control balance issue that I needed to overcome.

"No," Anansi replied.

I totally missed the end of Davidson's conversation with Kevin but the slow, somber pace he had all day was a clue. He barely left his desk the whole day. Maybe he would do some damn work. The day went on as normal. I did everything that was asked of me and then some. I kept my eyes and ears on Kevin, but he only left his desk for water and the bathroom. I heard his random sighs, but there were different moments where his heart rate increased and then suddenly went back to normal. It happened randomly throughout the day.

For the first time ever, I was so busy I didn't even notice when 5:00 rolled around. Usually, my days would drag on. I thought it was 3pm when it was only 9:30am. The atmosphere was different because all day people were gossiping about Kevin. Charla even went to his desk for a minute. She was going to get some information if it was the last thing she did today. He couldn't be that stupid to let the walking HR complaint have any information. A good drama made the time go by faster.

Wes popped up at my desk to exchange information. His information was sort of right, but I knew the whole truth. I sprinkled in some information, but I did not let on that I knew everything. Well, almost everything, except for at the end. I was too busy trying to figure out if I could see through walls.

The office cleared out like normal. At 5:30pm, everyone was packed up. A few people were making small talk with Kevin's team as they walked to the elevator and stairs. When something interesting happened in the office, it made the air feel light. Everyone was more relaxed. Crazy customers and other clients did not have the same effect. Once that call was over, the gossip started right back up. I found myself talking to someone on the other side of the floor like we were old friends. Everyone was fishing for more information. Whether that information was right or wrong, didn't matter. Hell, the wrong information was more fun. Did Kevin cuss Davidson out? No. Did Davidson accuse Kevin of stealing? Technically yes but stealing time and getting money for it. Were items thrown? Could be. Making the story interesting was what helped this day go by a little faster.

I went home and trained. That was my schedule every day per Anansi's "suggestion". I took it as a command. A rule is a rule. Stone was the hardest side effect to get past. I dragged myself out of the woods for days by my hands. My hair reverted to its normal color quickly, but my body didn't get the memo.

Every morning before work and every evening after work, I was in the woods getting used to all the control balances. I can deal with the headaches and migraines, but the other side effects had to go. I decided I wasn't going to execute any plan until I conquered "stone." Anansi was determined, too. He hated this side effect more than me.

"Your human body and DNA is complex and complicated," he said.

"Well, it wasn't my design, sir," I replied.

"It has been a few weeks, Elle," he groaned.

I leaned against the burned tree while my control balance went back to 90/10. That rule no longer applied. The higher the control balance in Anansi's favor, the harder it was going back to my new "normal" state. It was instant at first. Now, I let in more magic and the price was less of myself or my "humanness." That should have been my queue to stop, but like Dr. Lynn, I looked at myself as a guinea pig. There was something more here and this was just the beginning. I jumped down this rabbit hole and I hadn't hit the bottom yet. "Shit, I need to set an appointment with Dr. Lynn." I made a mental note. I could blame the holidays for my absence.

"This one is tough, Anansi," I sighed.

"Most uncomfortable," Anansi agreed. I used the tree to get myself up on my feet. I heard Inu running around chasing squirrels.

"Let's try one more time. It's getting late."

It took until mid-February for me to dull down "stone." I felt heavy but it was now like I ate too much food. I wasn't frozen or clawing with my hands to move. The good thing was getting back to 50/50 was much easi-er. That was now my base. 90/10 was now called "rest" after Anansi and I amended that rule.

For the rest of February, I kept training. Kevin was on his best be-havior since he had his talk with Davidson. He still didn't know shit, but at least he was at his desk. Our training classes ended, and we were all back at our desks. My team and Dara's team were still off phones. We were focused on the new internet orders. I was a wiz at it. Even Anderson would double check with me. I could have tolerated this job much sooner if this was all I had to do. But of course, when did work make my life easier or less stress-ful. Eventually, everyone would have to do internet orders and talk on the phone.

I had a lot of free time during the day because these internet orders were a new option, so there wasn't much at first. How other people were struggling to finish was astonishing to me. I missed my free time at the 3rd floor, but I was avoiding that place like the plague. Anansi hadn't asked about the key after the last time, but I still followed Janus's warning to keep it hidden.

My free time at work was another type of training. I enhanced my senses to keep tabs on Kevin and during lunch, I went to Sara and memo-rized her movements.

"Anansi, this sucks," I said.

"What do you mean?" he asked.

"I wanna see through walls," I pouted.

"We have been over this, Elle. I do not have that ability in my full form but I found that something does…suck, as you say." I laughed every time he used slang.

"What sucks?" I asked.

"Your human form cannot shapeshift. God was very detailed with the human form."

"My hair changes though," I pointed out.

"That is a mystery to me as well. Quite interesting," he said.

"Great, just great. Even you don't know why that happened."
On the last two Thursdays of February, I made sure to be in place at the hotel to watch Kevin and Sara. I took sunglasses, a hoodie, and a wig I stole from my sister to remain unseen. I could have executed my plan sooner, but I gave a little grace. It was like watching a soap opera in real-life. I enjoyed the show a bit more.

I learned that they asked for a room on the 10th floor or higher. Probably because they would be harder to see. I noticed on the last Thursday in February, they liked to keep the blinds open. They didn't want to be seen but wanted to increase the chances of being seen by keeping the curtains open. Sexual thrills made people stupid and careless. It frustrated me but I used it to my advantage. I took pictures when they entered the hotel but that wasn't enough for me. Next week is the beginning of March and the grace period would be over.

The Thursday

Kevin pulled into the garage first. He was blasting the same music as last time. He parked his car and waited for Sara. Sara's office was further away so she was always last to arrive. I was on the top level of the parking garage looking down at the entrance. I followed them the two   Thursdays before this one to learn more about Sara's sounds. I learned her heartbeat, how she walked, and her habit of cracking her fingers with her fingertips as she walked. I assumed it was a nervous tick.

He applied more cologne as he waited. The smell still burned my nose. It was too strong, but it was a smart move. His cologne overpowered Sara's perfume. He never smelled like another woman. He wasn't going to be able to explain tonight to his wife. Not one story he could think of would sound right. I ran to the lobby for their check in.

They were hand in hand as they strolled into the lobby. It was around 7 pm. The front desk recognized Sara right away. A regular at this hotel got special treatment. Not a discount but at least some perks. "Welcome back, Miss Morrison! We have room number 1212 ready for you."

Perfect. I watched them head to the elevators, then set my plan into motion.

The building next door was nearly as tall as the hotel. The hotel designers wanted to make sure it wasn't in the shadow of another building. I would have to get to the roof to see inside Kevin's room. I went across the street to watch them take the glass elevator to their floor.

Ding.

From what I remember and room location signs, 1201 through 1205 faced the front, 1206-1210 faced the next block, and then 1210-1215 faced me. This is a big ass hotel. The rooms on this floor are suites so the rooms are huge.

Ding.

"How much longer?" Anansi asked. The doors of the elevator opened and I saw Kevin and Sara walk out onto the 12th floor. I knew where I needed to go. But when I needed to go was the tricky part. Once they entered the room, their clothes were coming off before the lock engaged.

I dipped into the alley. I made sure the alley was dark enough and then I jumped up the fire escape and made my way to the roof. I stood on the edge of the roof to see my full surroundings. The intense honking I heard from behind me told me that the busy street filled with bars and restaurants was that way. People were moving out of parallel spots and pedestrians were getting in the way. Everyone in the cars was annoyed at this point. So, that means to my right is the main road in and out of downtown. The rooms to my right will be facing the other buildings on the busy strip and the rooms on the hallway behind will have a view of the streetlights.

"Elle, this looks nothing like when you are having sex."

"Anansi, I really do not want to talk about this with you," I replied. It's bad enough he was there. I tried not to think about it before, during, or afterwards. "Wait, what's different?"

"Your human seems more relaxed. He is not trying to impress you like this human is."

"I don't know if I should take that as a compliment or be grossed out that you watch," I replied.

Anansi was right, though. Lucas and I had history. We've been having sex on and off since high school. We still had fun, but he wasn't trying to impress me anymore. To be honest, I liked our normal, awkward sex. I liked the fact that I could laugh in bed, and he didn't think I'm laughing at him. Sara couldn't laugh. Even if she was getting what she needed, she faked it. I liked how comfortable we were with each other. I did not need the flash anymore. I'm tired of finding cute outfits or sucking in my stomach. I was too tired to show off. Sometimes I was not on my "A" game, and I knew Lucas wasn't giving his "A" game every time. I wasn't going to admit to Anansi he was right.

"You are watching them, are you not?" he asked.

"Oh, shut up," I said as I watched. Anansi laughed.

I watched them for a good minute. My phone zoom can only do so much. The pictures came out grainy. They were still in foreplay mode as I took more grainy videos and pictures.

"Alright, I got time," I camped out on the roof. How he got away with explaining to his wife that the manager meeting always ended when the bar closed, amazed me. Not this time. This time he would be staying overnight. I wanted to believe his wife already knew but didn't have the evidence. She was gonna get it now. All part of the plan. Between "rounds", I was going to sneak in and get their phones for more evidence. I think the video was enough evidence for the wife, but I was leaving no doubt for her. Plus, my zoom sucks. No matter how much was spent on a cell phone, a real professional camera was needed for a good long-distance shot.

Kevin and Sara were not just going to be exposed to a spouse. Someone was getting fired! I was going to expose everything I could. This may seem like a bit much. Maybe I was going too far for something as small as inconvenience at work. Oh, well! Day in and day out, I had to deal with people from all over the world. People who stopped reading, comprehending, using critical thinking, and troubleshooting. People buy an expensive ass phone but apparently their phone was the only one without a calculator app. Kevin made everyone's job harder. It was like a group project, which I hated with passion. He was the weakest link. The one everyone else had to make up for. Pull your own damn weight.

In doing whatever he pleased, he encouraged an entitled woman. A damn Karen. And fucking her on top of all of it. My anger was building up and I had to be careful. I couldn't make a mistake on this one. I took my gloves off and started playing with hellblaze as my anger and excitement became my "stance." I threw a small ball of fire from one finger to the other as I waited until they fell asleep.

I looked up and saw them fast asleep. "Now, that is careless," I whispered.

"What do you mean?"

"This ninja is getting too comfortable. It's risky falling asleep in a hotel with your mistress but luck is on my side tonight."

It was about 10:45 pm. I stood on the edge, took a deep breath, and walked to the opposite edge of the roof. I tightened my crossbody bag and put my gloves on. The leap from this roof to the hotel was a big one. I practiced but this could fail. The hotel was taller than the building I was standing on. The good thing was the buildings were close together. I took a few deep breaths, remembered why I was here, and took off running. I was able to grab the edge of the roof.

"Oh, shit!" I dangled there for a little bit and caught my breath. I pulled myself up and climbed one more level to the rooftop of the restaurant. I wouldn't have been able to clear that jump. I planned to exit from the roof, too. There were fewer cameras going to the roof than going to the guest floors. The skyline restaurant was right beneath me. I heard the laughter, frantic kitchen orders, and clinking of glasses. It was freezing up here and the wind was strong tonight. I didn't have the cover of the buildings to soften the wind. I looked over downtown and enjoyed the view for a few seconds. I see why this restaurant was so popular. On a clear night, the view was relaxing and beautiful.

I walked to the roof's door to the stairway. "Oh shit!" I realized I didn't bring one tool to open the room door. I had my bag, but the tools were for picking locks -- regular locks. These damn fob doors could fuck up my whole plan.

"You did not consider this," Anansi pointed out.

"No one asked you," I snipped. "But nah, I completely forgot about the lock."

I had to think quickly. I hadn't had to rely on it much, but it was a good time to test it. "We are gonna use brute strength on this one. Fa me," I said. I ran at warp speed to the hotel room door. The second I stopped; I focused on pushing the door open before the world caught back up. I gave one push and the door opened. I slid into the room and then checked to see if I caused any damage.

"Okay, the lock was broken except the hide-away lock on the in-side. Good, it can be on one of their tabs," I whispered.

"Next time, plan better," Anansi said.

"Lecture me later," I said.

There, safe inside the room, I let the world catch up. Soon, I heard the snoring, and the room was clear. The jackets, the dress, and the shoes were kicked off and tossed everywhere. I avoided stepping on anything. It was a damn maze to get to their phones. One was thrown on the couch and the other one was on the dresser. I headed for the one on the couch first. I looked at my phone and saw that it was 10:50. I took off one of my gloves and started to fill the room with halluz in case one of them woke up randomly.

I pulled out my phone and a cord to link my phone with theirs. Once I cracked the passcodes, I went through everything. I copied all the text messages, emails, photos, videos, and GPS searches. It would take about five minutes for both phones. Kevin's phone was first. Apparent-ly, Sara was not the only woman he was flirting with, but the other ones weren't going as far as meeting for sex -- yet. The group chat was funny, misogynistic, bro-mance, and thought-provoking all at once. I did not know how that shit was possible, but there it was. I let the information spill into my phone and waited.

The halluz filled the room and some escaped under the door. I explored the suite as I waited for the phones. I kept the halluz going as I walked around. The bathroom was nice and the robes were super soft. If I had the space in my bag, I would take one with me. I saw the green light indicating the transfer was complete and I moved over to Sara's phone.

As I walked over to the phone on top of the dresser, I looked at Kevin and Sara. They were still fast asleep. Kevin was cuddled up with her without a care in the world. Anger came over me and I jumped on the bed and stared at them. They didn't move. I knew how to land like a cat. I fought the urge to knock them the fuck out. "I should," I whispered as I got closer to them.

"Elle," Anansi said.

"Maybe some other time," I retreated. I went back to the plan. I took everything off Sara's phone, too. "Well, well..." I started looking through Sara's phone. Kevin wasn't the only man for Sara, either. She was having sex, though. Kevin, please tell me you used a condom. As the information was flowing, I looked on the floor for a condom, a wrapper, a piece of foil, something. But I saw nothing. "Mutha..." I nearly yelled. That was all I needed. I looked in the closet and found a spare pillow and sheets. I ripped the pillowcase up to hide my face except my eyes. I waited until most of the halluz had disappeared.

I jumped on the foot of the bed, sat down, and crossed my legs as they woke up.

"Well, good evening," I said. They jumped back and scrambled out to the bed. They were both naked, so it was kind of funny.

"What the fuck! How did you get in here?" Kevin yelled. I rolled my eyes because he had some nerve. He didn't even protect Sara.

"It looks like the front desk gave me the same room as yours," I laughed. Sara was on the edge nearly sitting on the nightstand, crying.

"Who are you?" Kevin yelled.

"I would appreciate it if you didn't yell," I taunted. "You'd better hope the guests assume you have your TV on too loud. Take a seat." I patted the bed right by me. Sara remained balled up and Kevin stood there with his dick swinging. "You don't wanna sit down," I shrugged. I flipped off the bed and walked towards my phone.

"I was going to let you two sleep but I changed my mind. But don't worry, I won't be here long." I walked over to Sara first.

"Hey! Stay away from her!"

"If you were really worried about her, you would be standing over here. So, you're just trash, period," I taunted.

"What are you talking about?" he said. He tried to catch his breath. I saw him tiptoe to the door. Sara had her face in her knees. She didn't want to look up. "You ain't slick. I can get to that door faster than you." I stood right over Sara. She never lifted her head. Kevin's heart rate was elevated. He wanted to run to the door, but fear kept him frozen. Good.

"I only have a few moments before I get all the information I need. Sara," I said. Her head popped up because I knew her name.

"How do you know?" she cried.

"Your name? Don't worry about it. You shouldn't worry about it either, Kevin." The night only let some light in, but I could see that his eyes got big. "Yes, I know your name, too. Now, Sara, I have a quick question. Did you use a condom tonight? Do me a favor, don't lie to me." She shook her head no. "Do you ever use condoms?" She shook her head no again. I couldn't contain it. I grabbed her by the neck and lifted her up. "You should have lied to me," I growled. I held her there for a few seconds and then dropped her on the bed when she passed out. Then my focus went to Kevin.

"No, please, I have a family," he had the nerve to say.

"Oh really," I walked over to him. "You weren't thinking about this 'family' of yours, laying up with her. At this moment, I started letting the room fill with halluz again. I gave Kevin the best left hook and I wasn't as strong in my left hand. I caught him before he fell to the ground. I put him back into the bed as well. I tucked them underneath the covers as if nothing happened.

"Why did you decide this?" Anansi asked.

"An email isn't enough," I replied. "No condom is reckless behavior and they really deserved worse."

The green light came on indicating Sara's phone was finished so I headed out. I made another last-minute change to the plan and warped to the parking garage. Why not add salt to the wound? I got what I needed but I wanted to do something more.

I found Sara's car first. I went to a 30/70 control balance and went into warp speed. I melted the tires that were furthest from sight. I melted them down to the rims and had the rims melt into the concrete. I sealed her car in the parking garage. I wanted to set the cars on fire, but this was more subtle, less attention. Kevin's car was next. I had to search for that stupid sports car.

I found his car on the 4th floor. After melting Kevin's car to the ground, I headed to the edge of the parking garage and was about to step off. Instead, I went through the entire parking garage and melted down random tires in warp speed. I laughed the entire time. A little mischief was good for my mental health. I couldn't tell Dr. Lynn that.

"This was fun," I thought. "Should really make that appointment at some point with her before she comes looking for me." I jumped off the edge of the parking garage into the alley. I waited for the world to catch back up. I peeked around the corners and the streets were still busy. I looked at my watch and it said 11:07. Everyone was in their own world. I looked to the sidewalk, put up my hoodie, took off the pillowcase and walked to my car. I was pleased with my work. Not a thought or worry on my mind.

"You continue to surprise me, human," Anansi said.

"Humans are surprising," I replied. I didn't feel degraded this time when Anansi said that. I felt proud of exceeding his expectations. I understood his opinions about humans. We left two humans knocked out with all the audacity in the world.

I was starving the minute I arrived at my car. I stopped at a drive-thru and got enough for a party of 15. Inu made up three people and I could eat for the rest. I blew through a lot of energy in a short period of time. My body felt heavier as I drove home and drove slower than usual. I finished all four sodas by the time I rolled up to my driveway. I was still thirsty and tired.

Inu was barking loudly. He was mad I was late, but I brought treats so he would forgive me. I struggled to open the door with everything I had in my hand. I finally got it opened and Inu flew out the door. He almost knocked me over. I wasn't steady or particularly strong at this point. A good gust of wind could knock me over. I left the door open and went straight to eating.

Once Inu came back in, I had his burgers unwrapped for him.

Friday, Saturday, and Sunday, I put everything together with what I found on Kevin's and Sara's phones. Davidson would receive an anonymous email with the work violations. Kevin's wife, whose name is Sundae, would receive an email with all his text messages, photos, and videos. Sara's manager would receive her email about her work violations which weren't "you are fired" worthy, but her friend Hyleigh would set Sara straight. The spelling of her name made me want to punch her parents. Hyleigh was my dark horse because Sara liked unavailable men, including Hyleigh's new husband. What was worse, Sara was in the damn wedding party. Hyleigh needed to learn that a sorority friend did not always equal a true friend. She was one of 12 bridesmaids. Ain't no way they were all "close" and the group chats showed that. Oh, let me add in Brenda, I realized. I had to send the chat to Brenda because everyone thought that girl was a trainwreck. Of course, I cc'd Kevin and Sara.

The send was scheduled for 7:30 am Monday.

I could not wait until Monday morning! I watched the news through the weekend, and they said nothing about an assault. But the melted tires in the parking garage had everyone scratching their heads. Social media buzzed about the melted tires at the most expensive hotel in the city. Nothing on camera and no clear motive. Well, except vandalism.

The Aftermath

I woke up bright and early on Monday morning. I did not want to miss any of this. I had my clothes laid out the night before as if it was the first day of school. I wanted to hear everything. I was giddy to see my handiwork. Anansi was oddly quiet, but I considered that a plus. He didn't nag me this morning about training. I gave Inu some extra love before I left for the day. This damn dog had a better life than I did. The bum, so cute. I giggled to myself and headed to work. I was ready for everything that was coming.

The drive to work was just as difficult as usual, but I did not care. The buzz around the office would be worth it. I was on a happy cloud. I felt this high after getting my revenge. I wasn't absolutely sure that Kevin would even show up to work but he definitely wasn't going to tell his wife the truth about why he was at Hotel Sauna.

Everyone was pulling into the parking lot and getting ready to start the day when I arrived. The wait for the elevator was annoying, but I waited. I usually took the stairs to avoid the human traffic jam that early in the morning. I was in an easy-going mood. I could tolerate the crowded elevator. People were discussing their weekend, but I didn't care. Someone was coughing way too much for my comfort. If they got me sick, I wouldn't be responsible for my actions, especially now. I walked to my corner and went into my control balance to hear everything. I listened to Davidson first. He was always in by now, headed to some meeting. I knew he saw the email.

I heard him in his office. He was printing something and speaking with someone.

"I think this is the best option. We cannot have this continue," he said. "Yes, send me the paperwork and I will get it completed by the end of the day." Davidson shuffled around for a little bit and then left his office – more than likely going to a morning meeting like always. I listened for Kevin, and he was at his desk, but his heart rate was through the roof. "So, he did come to work today. Interesting," I said.

"You seem happy," Anansi said.

"I didn't think he would show up." Kevin's blood was racing through his veins, indicating a shortness of breath. And he was smacking his dry mouth. It was a symphony to my ears. That was the sound I wanted to hear.

He saw the email. I got up to talk to someone, anyone, near Kevin's desk. No one was available. I pretended to use the printer to scan something, a blank piece of paper, while I peeked at Kevin. He was sweating right through that suit. It was black and I could see the sweat pouring through. His eyes were rapidly moving back and forth. Hopefully, he realized that he was stuck. He couldn't leave his job. He couldn't call his wife because he may confess when he may not have to. And he shouldn't call Sara because that was admitting something was going on. Granted with all the shit I found, the "it wasn't me" defense damn sure wouldn't work. He was stuck at his desk, waiting to see if Sundae called.

Sundae surpassed my expectations. Ol' girl pulled up. It was just after 9:30 am and everyone was settling down when I heard the wheels of a car screech to a halt. I looked out the window before anyone noticed. That well put-together look she had was gone. She was ready for war. She left that car in the middle of the road and entered the building. I sent a quick message to Wes about the "angry" person entering the building.

This situation was exactly why we got those emails about tailgating. They didn't want us to hold the door open for someone behind us. It was southern politeness to hold the door for someone. It was like muscle memory. They wanted that politeness to be left in the parking lot. Plus, the door closes slow as hell. There was no way to shut the door quickly behind you in someone's face. I had to actively pull or push the door closed while someone tired to keep the door open. It was a funny situation when I pictured it.

Sundae strolled right into the office as if she worked here. Her feet stomped firmly across the carpet. I heard her come around the corner with an elevated heart rate. She was asking random people where Kevin Johnson sat. She was getting louder every time she asked someone. People were silent at her question, or she was pointed in the direction to go without any specifics. The phone conversations with our customers slowly stopped or mysteriously disconnected as people popped up from their cubicles. It was like a giant game of whack-a-mole. I stood up and followed the crowd gathering around the cubicles.

Sundae did not care. That woman was on a mission and Kevin recognized that angry voice once he heard it. He ran out from his desk and interceded Sundae.

"Baby, please not here," he pleaded.

"Oh yes, the fuck here. Where is she!"

"Please, can we go outside and talk? I will explain everything," he pleaded. He was using his weight to try and nudge her to the elevators. It didn't work. I made my way to Wes's desk, and he had me on the floor laughing. That man was holding his teacup close to him while he watched. It was the funniest shit I ever saw because the cup was empty. Sundae crossed up Kevin and started ranting and raving around the office looking for Sara. Lucky for Sara, she worked somewhere else, but that doesn't mean we don't have a Sarah or two located in the building.

"So that's your manager's meeting, Kevin?! Where is she?" I was proud of the floor that they never pointed out any Sarah. They watched the show or sat back down to avoid Sundae's wrath. He pleaded with her to go outside, and it finally worked. They headed to the elevators and like a wave, everyone ran to the windows. They wouldn't be able to hear much. It would be muffled. The people in the front pressed their hands and faces against the glass to see below. I heard them clearly, even in the elevator. It was a bunch of intelligible crying and "let me explain." He never explained. Every time he started, Sundae interrupted and cussed him out.

The phones were ringing off the hook, but no one cared. The managers were watching this mess unfold, too.

"You got me fucked up, Kevin," Sundae yelled. "I do everything for you, EVERYTHING!! And you do this to me. With some white girl? Are you serious!"

"She doesn't mean anything to me. It just happened," he replied. "Please, baby, I'm sorry."

"Get the hell out of my house, Kevin! Your shit will be outside by the time you get home. Get out of my house!"

"No, baby, think about Ira."

"You didn't think about Ira! Fuck you!"

Sundae jumped in her car and sped off. Kevin ran back into the building, and everyone scrambled back to their desks and pretended like nothing ever happened. The whispers continued as Kevin ran to his desk to get all his things to follow his wife home. No one said anything. The phones continued to ring but everyone stayed silent. Kevin was frantic and cursing under his breath as he collected his things. He packed a box because he knew he wasn't coming back.

No one approached him. The only person who didn't seem to understand the gravity of the situation was Charla. She was either oblivious or didn't give a fuck about Kevin's situation. The audacity. She wanted the scoop and to also be mad at Kevin for picking Sara over her. Charla would have been a willing side chick, but she was ignored.

"Kevin, what the hell is going on?" she asked as he was gathering his things.

"Not now, Charla, I gotta get home."

"But if you leave, Davidson might fire you," Charla pointed out. This gave Kevin a quick pause but then he kept going.

"I wasn't coming back anyway," Kevin decided. "I need to go."

Charla followed him to the elevators and even rode them down just to ask Kevin questions. She wanted to know which Sara(h) it was, too. The inspiring sleuths already went to the Sarahs in the office to ask them. But who would admit that at a time like this? Charla got zero answers from Kevin. He screamed at Charla to "fuck off" when he got off the elevator. Kevin approached a different car than his sports car. I laughed because his car was probably still stuck in the parking garage of the hotel. Kevin reversed recklessly and the tires screeched as he left the parking lot.

The office was on fire with gossip the rest of the day. Davidson was briefed by the managers on what happened. Everyone walked by his office slowly to try and hear anything. Wes and I kept messaging back and forth and my group chat with my friends and family was busy with trying to get all the details from me. It was a fun day at work, but the show wasn't over. The high kept giving and Anansi was quiet. This day was everything.

The gossip, jokes, and social media stalking filled the air in between phone calls. I heard so many conversations that I reduced my control balance to tune out all the noise. One of Kevin's team members figured out the actual Sara and the ball started rolling. I looked around Sara's social media, and low and behold, her emails were read, too. I knew my email to her manager may not put her job in jeopardy, but Hyleigh could. She had the same pull-up mentality that Sundae had. I appreciate that. The difference is that social media exposure was added to this confrontation.

In part one of the video, I saw Sara rush out of her office to Hyleigh who was waiting near her car in the parking lot. The difference between Sara and Kevin was that Sara stood ten toes down in her dirt. "Interesting," I thought to myself, sounding a lot like Anansi.

"Well, it was obvious, Hyls. You were just too stupid to see it. He didn't just sleep with me," she said.

I saw that on Sara's phone, too. Hyleigh got all the dirt on her so called "friends." Her man was a cheater, her friends weren't loyal, and Hyleigh had some tough decisions to make. I realized that Sara and Kevin had so many lives in their hands. My punishment forced their hand, and those lives became collateral damage.

"You are a snake, Sara, and a slut." Without a second thought, Hyleigh pounced. It was stupid for her to film the assault but great entertainment for me. Hell, for everyone in the office. The link to the video was going around the office, too. I forwarded the videos to my group chats as the plot I created thickened. The whole day was nothing but entertainment.

I rode this high for about a month. I trained, but I was lazy. I hung out with friends more. I felt so distant from everyone for nearly a year after meeting Anansi. Lucas dropped by whenever. Elise's wedding was soon and the bachelorette party planning was nearly done. I had a few other wedding invites and baby announcements from family and friends. I even started to see Dr. Lynn once a week in her office. I was high, seeing colors in the wind, chasing a dragon, nodding off. All the side effects of a drug I experienced, and it made me calm.

At work, Kevin was fired, and Sara lost her job, too. Not because of my email to her manager. It was my email to Hyleigh that was posted online. I didn't know that one of the men Sara talked to was the boyfriend of her coworker. That was a happy coincidence. Hyleigh posted everything, including her fights with her other friends. That friend group was disbanding live on social media. Sundae went dark on social media. I never returned to Kevin's house.

Everything seemed to be on the upswing for me. The phones weren't even a thought. I walked in a field of buttercup flowers, tasted the best chocolate, and loved a little more. For the first time in a long time, work wasn't a worry.

The office barely had a chance to cool down from Kevin's drama when the hearing started for Charla. Charla suddenly had a ton of best friends at work. Everyone was salivating at the details she would undoubtedly tell them. That woman couldn't hold water. This hearing could go on for months. I caught a peek at the secretaries' calendars. Honestly, I hacked in. The hearing was blocked off for the rest of the month. They couldn't plan further than three weeks at a time. There must be a lot of evidence to get through. Neither party was barred from working, but they were put on separate floors.

The first day of the hearing was boring. The hearing was on the top floor of the office, in the largest boardroom in the building. You had to have clearance to go up there. No one had it on this floor, not even Davidson. The first day of the hearing was the lawyers stating their cases. There were three main attorneys. One for Charla, one for Cherilus, and the other for the company. Cherilus was suing them, as well. I didn't know opening arguments took that damn long. The episodes of some of my favorite police series had the opening statements done in five minutes. I guess that was only television magic. These lawyers talked for hours, giving an outline of their case. I hoped the next couple of weeks would be more interesting.

The rumors of the hearing got crazier by the day. The executives, lawyers, and assistants taking notes kept their mouths shut. The litigants, however, had loose lips, yapping gums, and foul tongues. I expected this from Charla, but Cherilus was as talkative as she was. I guess if he was comfortable around someone, he wouldn't shut up. His favorite phrase when he told a story was "long story short" then he continued for another 30 minutes. He was long winded and annoying. They deserved each other.

One of the first rules of office life was not to get comfortable with people. Anyone could throw you under the bus when their money was at stake. I had great work friends, but they only knew things that couldn't be used against me. Wes didn't know the trick I used to avoid answering the phones. The way the rumors and gossip swept through the office, I kept my business to myself.

I had enjoyed every piece of the rumors and gossip for the past month. It was keeping my high from the Kevin and Sara incident going. I knew the facts, but the stories everyone came up with were far more interesting. It was amazing how gossip was like a game of telephone. The more people the information passed through, the more it changed. This building housed different companies and there were plenty of people that heard the gossip about our office. Some people said, "I don't want any part of this," but that didn't mean they shut off their hearing. Hell, even the visitors to the office were getting a piece of the gossip.

Charla told whoever would listen, which was damn near anyone, that Cherilus was so full of himself. "He thinks everyone wants him. He took my kindness and willingness to help as a pickup line," Charla said. "I was just being a welcoming manager, you know." What made me laugh was the reaction I pictured most people having. Everyone knew that Charla was a desperate woman. She was being more than just helpful. I bet they said, "oh yea," "sure sure," "oh I hear you," "that's crazy," and the cliché, "whaaaaattt" when talking to her.

I wondered if anyone's eyes glassed over as they tuned her out. Unless she was talking about the harassment hearing, no one gave a shit. My eyes did that when I was part of a conversation I had no interest in. Wes was lucky enough to be her confidant for some of these venting sessions. He didn't keep this juicy information to himself. Wes soon found out that Charla was inconsistent. She would tell him one thing and then say something else to someone else. She had a hard time keeping up with her lies and people were catching on. I shouldn't get enjoyment from watching her scramble and trip up. Chaos was forming and I saw why Anansi enjoyed it.

Charla was a difficult, annoying, self-righteous, unhelpful person. She was quick to get someone in trouble but remained unchecked for her lack of knowledge and barely doing her supervisory duties. Hopefully, this hearing was just what my floor needed. Kevin was gone and Charla better be next.

It was a random day when my ears picked up some of the best information. Information I couldn't share at work. I knew I needed to call

Elise the minute I got to my car when the day was over. Charla was hit with a right hook in the hearing. Cherilus claimed that she was texting him daily. Cherilus explained during the hearing that he never gave Charla his phone number. I heard she used another co-worker as a long way around to get his number but I wanted to hear more.

"How did she get it?" I whispered. I even leaned in, like that would make the hearing louder. His lawyer asked him the same question.

"I was not sure at first," Cherilus stated.

"Did you come to find out how she obtained your phone number?"

"I found out that she threatened…"

"Without proof you cannot claim that sir," Charla's lawyer interrupted.

"Mr. Willis, please answer the question without any assumption or conclusion at this time." The attorney cleared his voice.

"I was told by another coworker that Charla got my number from them."

"Please note, that coworker will be a witness later in the proceedings. Mr. Willis, what happened when Charla obtained your number?"
I continued to type as I heard more about Cherilus' claims. She would send pictures, recipes, ideas for trips they could take, and short videos from social media that were NSFW.

"Did she ever discuss work in the texts that you received?" his lawyer asked.

"Only to speak ill of another employee or to spread gossip," Cherilus answered.

"Please give examples," I whispered. On cue, the lawyer asked the same question. Unfortunately for me, Cherilus picked Kevin as an example. I knew that shit already. I wanted the print-outs the lawyers had. Hopefully, they were diligent enough to get phone records from the cellular companies. Those messages could not be erased. I wondered if Kevin was the witness or if there were more people.

I tried to appear busy at work while listening to the hearing and the gossip. I was so nosey, I did not notice that Anderson was at my desk.

"Oh shit!" I jumped once I noticed Anderson. He laughed. "How long were you standing there?"

"Not too long," he laughed. "Sorry I scared you."

"I was lost in space. Sorry," I replied. "What's up?"

"We need you to train a few teams on the internet work orders. You are a whiz at them, and I think you will do great."

"Who is we?"

See, this is what happens when I showed off a little bit. I get asked to do extra work with no extra pay.

"Will it get me off the phones?" I had to find some perk. If they were trying to give me nothing in return, then forget it. I was ready for a good negotiation.

"Oh yeah, you will be training each team for two weeks. It will be on a virtual basis for some and in a classroom for others." He seemed a little excited about this.

"Throw in some overtime and I'm there," I said.

"Hahaha, that's funny," Anderson laughed. I laughed back too, but I was serious. I would fudge my paychecks if that wasn't too obvious.

"When will this start?"

"It will be in the next few weeks. I will know for sure during our managers meeting next Wednesday," Anderson assured.

I said, "Okay." As he turned to go back to his desk, I shouted, "Ask if there is a new job title with this, too." He gave me the thumbs up and then disappeared behind his cubicle wall.

Drama at work made the day go by faster. The end of the day came fast. I packed up everything and headed to my car. Elise's number was dialed. All I needed to do was press the call button. Elise and I laughed and laughed as I drove home. She couldn't believe what happened at my office. I gave her the facts sandwiched between the rumors. It gave a little drama to the story. I should have studied theater in school for the drama and theatrics I needed in everyday life.

"What are you doing this weekend?" I asked as I pulled up my private road.

"I am supposed to spend some time with Charlie," she answered.

"Oh, gonna be all romantic, I see," I teased.

"You should be doing the same," she teased back.

"I absolutely will be cuddled up this weekend," I said. I let a few seconds of silence fill the call. "With Inu," I added. We both laughed.

"Well, I'm home. I will text you later," I said.

"Alright, love ya," she said.

"Love you, too."

I hung up the phone and opened my front door to let Inu out. He stopped waiting for me to give him some love and ran straight outside. He jumped up and down in the grass and then marked every tree twice. I went to change into my workout clothes and train outside. I trained everything multiple times at night. Everything was becoming second nature.

This whole drama at work was our real-life soap opera. If I wasn't talking to Elise about work, I told Lucas and my family and Dr. Lynn. She said I needed to work on not finding joy in these situations. I didn't listen. It was about time stupidity was met with consequences bigger than correction. Especially to the ones who refused to learn from it. I made sure the consequences were bigger and now I was walking on cloud 9.

Plus, I received texts from my friends and family asking for some more gossip. Does that mean we all have this small section in our brains that takes pleasure in seeing a train wreck? Metaphorically and literally speaking? The more I went through life, the more I noticed that humans are just functioning psychopaths. Why else would reality television be a thing? It was scripted now, but the scripts still have the audience watching crazy situations. The viewing audience loved it and kept tuning in. People tried to rationalize it. They may say, "This can't be actual real life." But truth is stranger than fiction and I read some wild fiction. Nothing compares to the story of someone's life. Making that shit up caused brain damage.

Anansi had been eerily quiet lately. He randomly asked me about certain words as the gossip floated around. I nearly spit out my water when he asked what "buss it open" meant. I never laughed so hard. His accent made it even worse. Anansi was the only other person that had all the facts. I felt Anansi was itching to cause more chaos and mischief but I wasn't anymore. I felt I was finally filled up after Kevin and Sara.

Fang

The memo subject line said, "Disciplinary Hearing." I read the subject line three times. That couldn't be right. The body of the paragraph only stated that there was a complaint and that there was a meeting scheduled for the next day at 10 am. My anger boiled way over. I left the building fast as I covered my face. I knew my right eye was full spider and my hair was changing colors. I didn't need anyone to see that.

Once I got to my car, I nearly flipped it over. I was doing okay. I wasn't bothering anyone. Hell, everyone was bothering me about this stupid hearing. I should report everyone else. Who reported me? Hellblaze was coming out of my fingers before I knew it. I had control until my emotions got the best of me.

"Elle!" Anansi called.

"What?!" I yelled back.

"The raging anger is new," he replied. As he was talking, my hands seemed to be moving on their own. I was inspecting them and patting myself down. "This is a very new feeling," Anansi said.

"Are you doing this?"

"It appears so."

"How?"

"This is interesting," Anansi answered. He wouldn't give more than that. Instead, I was watching myself. Those were my hands, but I couldn't feel them. Those were my legs walking, but I didn't feel the concrete and pebbles under my flats. I could not feel the sun or the wind. I was just walking around the parking lot, but it felt like I was watching it happen. I was in a dark space in my mind, unable to move my feet. The waves were coming, but this time seemed different. I tried to move, to run from what was coming but I was stuck.

Then suddenly the feeling came back.

"No!" Anansi yelled.

My fear of what was happening outweighed the anger that brought me outside. I looked into someone's car and saw my eye slowly going back to normal.

"What is happening?" I asked.

"I am not sure, human," Anansi answered. I knew he was lying. He knew what happened. I lost control and Anansi was in control of my body. No matter how high the percentage goes, I was always in control of my body, but not this time.

"No! Tell me what is happening?" I yelled.

"Someone may have heard that," he answered.

I played it cool, but I told myself to control my rage. That was how I ended up here, yelling in a parking lot. I stayed outside for a little bit. I found my favorite clear, grassy spot to soak in the sun. I was gone for over two hours. Now I had a reason for the meeting tomorrow. Let's talk about something I actually did. I knew this meeting was utter nonsense, but I couldn't wait to find out who complained.

I went home and refused to do anything. Anansi was ignoring me, so I took a shower and cuddled up with Inu. We put on a cartoon and fell asleep on the floor. I woke up at random times of the night to eat. Inu joined me and stayed close by. He might have sensed something was wrong. When Anansi egged me on, Inu told me to chill the fuck out. I did not get a good night's sleep, but he did. I had this uneasy feeling that I couldn't shake.

I woke up in a petty mood. I took my time getting ready for work. I made a big breakfast and stopped and ran a few errands before pulling up at 9:30. I was giving them a reason for a disciplinary hearing. Work was still buzzing with gossip, but I was in a tunnel. My meeting was at 10:00 and until then, I did nothing. I was really being petty at this point.

Each minute ticked by slower than the next. I tapped my chewed fingernails on my desk as I waited for the meeting. I should have gone to Anderson to see if he knew about it, but he wasn't on the email thread. It was just my name and Davidson's. I was worried that this feeling was me being nervous or scared. But there was nothing for me to be scared or nervous about. I tried to calm the anger that was building up. I lost control of my body yesterday and I wanted to keep that from happening again. I felt like lava was running through my veins. It was like hellblaze, but I could feel it all over -- not just in my hands.

"I need the time to hurry up," I whispered to myself. I leaned into my computer, trying to think of something I did. Could it be a customer complaint? It couldn't be a coworker, or a manager. I limited my interactions with damn near everyone at work. My leg was shaking, and I needed to get up and move. I walked to the breakroom. I walked outside to my grass hill. I couldn't sit still. I went back into the building and without thinking went to the empty third floor. I opened the door from the stairs and realized the third floor wasn't empty anymore. There was a whole crew working on the floor. My maze was gone, the carpet was new, there was a smell of fresh paint, and the exposed wires were tucked away. The cabinets were all stacked to one side. "Fuck!" I yelled and shouted into my arms.

"What is this?" Anansi asked.

"I don't have time for this shit," I replied and went back to the stairwell.

"Why did you stop there, Elle?" he asked.

"It used to be an empty floor. That's all," I said.

Breathe in and out. In and out. In and out. I walked the stairs slowly from the 3rd floor to the 14th. I was wasting time until my meeting and needed to think. I had to get back to the third floor, but I couldn't think of how. Anansi may not listen to my thoughts, but he saw everything I saw. And I was still raging about the damn hearing so that my thoughts were thrown into chaos. A full damn circle. My high couldn't just stay. I took a deep breath and walked to Davidson's office.

I knocked on the door. I knew I was at 70/30 control balance. I needed to get down to my "rest" of 90/10 but I was still mad. I took another deep breath and knocked on the door.

"Come in," Davidson answered.

I slowly opened the door and got the shock of a lifetime. Charla's dumb face was staring up at me as I went to sit in the empty chair across from Davidson. I could feel the heat starting at my fingertips, but I knew I needed to remain calm. Charla should be upstairs getting fired, not in here.

"Elle, thanks for coming," Davidson began. "Charla has brought to my attention that you may be in violation of our employee conduct guidelines."

"What exactly does that mean?" I asked. I kept my eyes on Davidson because he was only responding to a manager's concern. He was doing his job, and I was less angry with him. The heat now reached my wrist, but focusing on Davidson helped steady my breathing.

"Well," Davidson began, "Charla, would you like to explain?"

That was a smart move for Davidson. He didn't want to summarize nor take any of the blame because he stayed in his office most days. My cubicle was in the back corner. No one at his level had any reason to go back there or interact with me.

"Well, Elle," Charla began, "some have noticed that you are on several different unauthorized websites instead of helping our customers. Your numbers are much lower than others on your team."

"Are you serious?" My job title and duties changed because I was a trainer now. I didn't have the same quotas as everyone else.

"Elle, who is this person?" I had no time for Anansi to pop up right now. I ignored him and waited for Charla to answer my question.

"Well, yes. Your numbers are quite low."

"If that is an issue, shouldn't Anderson be in this seat and not you?" I replied.

"All the managers look at the numbers," Charla scoffed. At this point, Davidson leaned in closer. His brows damn near met in the middle because he was confused now. "Why didn't Anderson say anything?" he probably thought. The heat now was in my chest and back. The one thing that was funny in all this is the heat sensation in my nipples. I was now looking down. I was at 60/40.

"Well, did you discuss all this with Anderson before calling this meeting?" I wanted Charla to feel as righteous as possible so I could knock her ass down.

"Again, any manager can address these issues. You should not be surfing the internet on sites not appropriate or needed for work." Charla was so sure she was right. The fact that she didn't know my job changed and did not look it up was expected. She was a busy body, who never had all the facts, couldn't keep her mouth shut, and had the weirdest chip on her shoulder.

"Davidson, sorry to put you in the middle of this, can you pull up my job title please?" I asked.

"Umm...sure, yes," Davidson replied. My request surprised him.

"You are a senior specialist," Charla answered. That was a mistake. I nearly grabbed Charla.

"It says you are an employee IT training specialist," Davidson said.

"What do you mean?" she replied.

"It means you did not look up what my job is now. My numbers will be low because I am a trainer right now. You should have talked to Anderson or looked me up before complaining."

Davidson leaned back in his chair. The sudden realization that Charla wasted his time was clear on his face. Charla stuttered for a bit. Then the heat started to burn my spine and rushed throughout my body.

"Elle?" Anansi seemed excited and concerned at the same time. I did not realize that smoke was coming out of my hands. I quickly looked down to hide the change in my eye. I was at 50/50 and I knew this was going to get worse.

"Oh, well, I did not know that," Charla retreated. "But there are some other concerns about your engagement with your coworkers, tardiness, and dress code violations."

"So, you are just trying to save face at this point," I replied. "You are really stupid, and I hate stupidity," I whispered. Charla's voice changed but not her self-righteous arrogance.

"What did you say to me?" Charla asked. "What is wrong with your…" I realized I looked up and put my head back down but it was too late. She saw it. I looked up. I didn't care that the halluz hadn't had time to go into full effect. Davidson was sitting back in his chair a little and then leaned forward. Did he notice my eye change? I produced more halluz directed towards Davidson. The halluz filled the room and started flowing into the air vents. I put Davidson into a regular workday illusion. To him, the meeting was over and Charla and I left. Hopefully, he would be exposed enough to believe he was never in a meeting. I had no time to consult with Anansi. My anger made me forget Davidson was in the room eventually too. I turned away from Charla and I walked over to the window overlooking the adjacent road by the building.

"Don't you have a hearing to go to?" I asked. "You are wasting my time and Davidson's time. You are in trouble and don't want to go down by yourself. I have never interacted with you. I don't care enough about you to share oxygen. What is your problem?"

What was Charla's problem? I wasn't the only one she picked on in the office. I guess she assumed I was going to roll over since I don't say much. Wrong! Not this time, Charla!

"I do not appreciate you speaking to me this way," she replied.

"I don't have time for this. I was in a fabulous mood until one pitiful human decided to place themselves in my way," I said. I didn't sound like myself. I saw my hair change to lavender. I practiced long enough to control the fire.

"Davidson," Charla interrupted, "I made no mistake. She is still in violation of our guidelines." Silence. "Umm, Davidson, do you hear me?" she asked.

He did not react when Charla spoke. He typed away on his computer. She looked up and noticed my hair had changed.

"How…your hair," she stuttered.

"Davidson can't hear you. You were foolish, Charla." I turned to look at her. As my anger rose, so did the control balance.

"You, you are a demon," she shook. "I knew something was wrong with you," she jumped up to the door, but she wasn't faster than me. I jumped on Charla. She screamed as I sank my teeth into her right arm. I had this instinct to bite her. She fell to the floor, and I stood over her, breathing heavily.

"Amazing," Anansi said.

"What just happened?" I jumped back.

"You can use my fangs," he replied.

"What the fuck, Anansi?"

"You can use my fangs. I am really surprised. How do you feel?"

"Forget how I feel! What is this?" My anger ceased as soon as I bit into Charla.

"So, remember my story about Folu. I can trick anyone but sometimes I don't have the time. Once bitten, the infected becomes empty. I can tell them to do anything, and they will."

"You use this shit for convenience," I yell. I walked over to look at Charla. Her eyes were glassed over. They looked foggy. Her arm was bleeding, but she just stayed on the floor. She was blank, empty. Davidson was still in the illusion but the smoke had stopped. The illusion won't last much longer. The office was shifting. They must have heard the commotion going on outside of the office.

"Shit! They heard her scream."

I had to think fast. I had to get out of the office without it being suspicious. I paced back and forth in the office as more and more people began to gather. I looked at my reflection and saw the fangs had retreated, but Charla was still a fucking zombie on the floor. Davidson was focused on his computer and my eye was in full spider mode.

"I gotta clear everyone out of here," I said.

It was like a light bulb went off. I used hellblaze to set fire to the wires on the computer and the outlets. Davidson snapped out of his delusion due to the fire and rushed to the door.

"Fire!"

Perfect! The crowd that heard the scream ran from the fire.

"Where is the fire extinguisher?" Davidson yelled.

"Down the hall," someone yelled back.

I couldn't let that happen. I increased the flames and had the fire leave the office and enter the hallway. I made it as intense as possible and stayed out of sight of the cameras near the stairs and elevator. Charla didn't move. I had to pat out the small embers that started to singe her clothes and hair. I knew she wore synthetic wigs.

I needed to leave the room. The panic had reached the entire floor because the fire was spreading. But Charla wasn't moving.

"What the hell am I supposed to do with her?" I asked Anansi.

"She is blank, Elle, give her a command."

I peeked out into the hallway. The alarms were sounding, and the elevators and stairway were getting crowded. A few people tried to use the fire extinguishers, but my fire was stronger than that. I created more fire to travel much further and burn hotter. I needed to create an opportunity to get my stuff and get out. I was looking for a way around the crowd to get to my desk. I used the outlets in Davidson's office to increase the heat. I had to fight through the crowd to get to my desk. I was the only idiot moving away from the exit.

As I went to leave, I hesitated. How could I get through this crowd I just created? I looked around to think. "Shit, Charla." She was still on the floor, oblivious to what was happening. I had no time for this. "Shit my hair!" I could hide the eye in this commotion but not my lavender hair. I was wearing a cami under my blouse so I took it off and wrapped my hair up. I would use brute strength to get through the crowd.

"Charla," I paused. I looked at the stampede of people trying to get out of the building. "Charla, get out of the building quickly." That was all I had. I should let her burn, but that's what the hearing upstairs would do for me. Plus, there were too many witnesses around. After I gave Charla the command, I focused on getting back to my desk. Once I got my things, I could escape into the crowd to get out of the building. The crowd would give me enough time to calm down to 90/10.

The hallway filled with smoke, but I could see clearly and breathe normally. Everyone else was coughing and bumping into anything and everything as they tried to see through the smoke. It was great cover for me. I looked behind me to see if Charla moved and she calmly walked out of the room and followed me.

"Anansi, why is she following me?"

"She is following your command," he replied. I knew I passed a stairway on the way back to my desk, so maybe she was heading that way. I hooked a left towards my cubicle, setting a few more outlets on fire. I realized that I was finally doing the one thing I longed to do to this office.

"I wanna burn this building down to the ground," I used to say and wished I could. Now, I was burning it all down. The feeling of excitement, fear, panic, joy, and anger made a perfect tornado. I thought I was getting a good grip on my emotions, but there are some things that are so absurd, stupid, or illogical that my brain cannot comprehend. So much so, that I unwillingly give Anansi a 10/90 control balance. I willingly learned 30/70. I never intended to go any further. Fang was too scary for me to try that shit again willingly.

I reached my desk and grabbed my bag, phone, and keys. Then I heard glass shatter. People began to scream louder. I thought the fire made the windows burst. I ignored the screams and headed for the stairs. I wanted everybody to make it out of the building with the least number of injuries. The floor was almost clear, but the stairwell was crowded. The entire building was evacuated. The smell of sweat, smoke, and panic filled the stairway.

Once I made it outside, I was able to go slip into 90/10, and watched the building burn. It was smart to target the outlets. Everyone was moving to a safe distance to watch as the building filled with smoke. Everyone was coughing and dirty as they exited the building. The first fire truck had pulled into the parking lot and the firemen sprang into action. They moved so fast. I was in awe of it all. I saw someone rush to one of the firemen and point to the side of the building. Something was happening, so I headed over there, too. I heard more screams as I got closer to the crowd.

There was a small crowd gathered in a circle. I heard cries, prayers, gasps, and dry heaving. I noticed that Wes was towards the back of the crowd, so I went straight up to him.

"Hey," I tapped his shoulder, "what is going on?"

"It's Charla." Wes looked like he had been crying. He had ashes on his face and the smell of smoke was all around us.

"What about Charla?" I felt my heartbeat increase. I told her to get out of the building. What did she do?

"She jumped out of the window," Wes said.

The whole world spun. Everyone blended into colors as I shoved my way through the crowd. I did not hear Wes call for me. I did not see the firefighter making his way through the crowd too. I pushed the closest people away and there she was. Her body was bent and broken from a fall from the 14th floor onto the concrete. There was blood coming out of her head and ears. She had glass sticking out of her face and body. I looked up and noticed the broken window that still had smoke coming out of it.

The world began to spin again. I was pushed out of the way as the firefighter was trying to block off the area. I stumbled back in a daze. "Why did she jump out of the window?" I asked.

"You told her to leave the building," Anansi said.

"That wasn't what I meant!" My brain was all over the place. "What the fuck does 'fang' do Anansi," I yelled. I didn't care who heard, the chaos surrounding me was a great cover.

"The venom that is injected through the bite makes it easier to control someone. However, reasoning isn't a part of it. It's the one design flaw." Anansi chuckled.

"It's not funny! She's dead," I said.

I wanted to get in my car, but I couldn't leave. "She jumped out of the damn window. I wanted her to just leave with the crowd. What the fuck! How am I supposed to explain this? How is Davidson going to explain this? Shit, where is Davidson?" I looked around and saw him in the parking lot. His clothes were messed up and he had that white stuff from the fire extinguisher all over him.

The crowd got larger around Charla's body until more windows burst because of the flames. Everyone ran away from the building to avoid the shattered glass. I barely moved as people bumped into me as they fled from the burning building. I stared as each floor went up in flames including the third floor. My anger was so overwhelmingly powerful that I forgot one important thing. I watched the building burn and along with it, the key that changed my life.

"So, the key is in that building. Most interesting," Anansi thought.

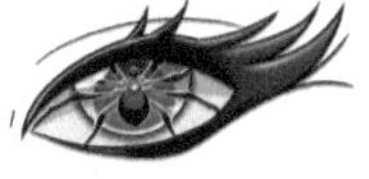

Part 2 coming soon...

Acknowledgments

First and foremost, I want to acknowledge God! This book and the many stories to follow would be a passing thought without Him. There would never be pen to paper. He answered a prayer I forgot years ago and set fire to my purpose. Never forget your dream and always dream big!

To my loving, supportive Mom who always reminded me that I have been writing since I was a child. She never stopped me or my siblings from trying something at least once. Of course, she always knew the one that would stick. She is amazing, smart and weird. I am her twin. To my loving, supportive Dad who always wants his daughters to have the world and see the world. He always meets my doubt with enthusiasm, even when he doesn't know it.

To my ride or dies; my best friends; my sisters! I can never thank them enough for always being there. We encourage each other, we make fun of each other and we protect each other. When I was unsure of an answer, they were my sounding board. If I doubted my writing or myself, they lifted me back up. Their encouragement and support helped me bring Elle to life. To my beautiful nieces: This book is for you! The future stories I write are for you! They are young black girl nerds who love school, writing, drawing, reading, anime and dancing. I can't wait to see where they go!

To my best friends: Thank you, thank you, thank you for letting me be crazy. When I had writer's block, they let me call and ramble until I figured it out. They had great input rewrite after rewrite.

When I considered complacency and giving up, they wouldn't let me. Thank you for the inspiration of Elle's support system and safe space. Their influence, vibes, craziness and love will be expressed in every story. I couldn't make it through college or adult life without them.

To my publisher, editor, agent and friend Danielle and Books & Things Publishing: Thank you for giving me this opportunity. Through the no's and lack of response, you saw my book with potential. When I thought my ideas were too obscure or weird, you saw the shine and helped me polish it. When I doubted myself, you helped me write through it. Thank you for being a cheerleader for my first novel. Here is to more stories together!